*Silent Kills*

"A dark and atmospheric thriller that takes an unflinching look at the primal urges—and disturbing fears—we all share. Sharp, distinct detail and an unnerving plot."
**—Steven James**

"A startlingly suspenseful novel—an unforgettable and deep portrait of the mind of a killer. Don't miss this extraordinary page-turner—Lawrence is a first-rate story teller."
**—Cody Mcfadyen**

"A sophisticated thriller with robust, fascinating characters . . . an intense psychological ride . . . a great story."
**—J. T. Ellison**

*Silent Victim*

"C. E. Lawrence's writing is so compulsively readable, you won't just tear through the pages, you'll scream through them."
**—Chris Grabenstein**

**More Praise for *Silent Victim***

"Lawrence pushes plot and character boundaries to put an entirely new twist on the whole concept of the serial killer. . . . Lawrence provides surprises and bumps in the night and day, even while assembling a cast of characters who are by turns odd, quirky and memorable. I simply cannot wait for her next book. . . . Lawrence's ability to create flawed and memorable characters and to take a familiar plot in unexpected directions has me hooked."

—**Bookreporter.com**

"This vivid, chilling serial-killer thriller will have readers jumping at every sound. Although serial killer thrillers glut the market, C. E. Lawrence's flawed champion makes for a strong tale."

—**Harriet Klausner**

"*Silent Victim* is a very good, complex thriller . . . and a very interesting look into the mind of an insane person."

—***Tracy Reader Dad Book Reviews***

***Silent Screams***

"Criminally compelling, *Silent Screams* nails you to your seat with a fascinating NYPD profiler who's hurled into the case of his lifetime. This journey into violence and the soul is unforgettable."

—**Gayle Lynds**

"Pulse-racing, compelling, first rate. Lawrence knows how to build and hold suspense with the best of them . . . a wild ride down a dark road."
—**John Lutz**

"C. E. Lawrence has achieved a rare level of authenticity, not only in character development but also in the realistic use of behavioral science. If you want to read a serial-killer thriller that's solidly based on frightening reality, this is the one."
—**Louis B Schlesinger**, Ph.D.,
Professor of Forensic Psychology,
John Jay College of Criminal Justice

"C. E. Lawrence delivers finely honed suspense, with unique twists, and accurately captures the logic and intuition of a profiler under pressure."
—**Katherine Ramsland**

"*Silent Screams* is a wickedly brilliant, carefully wrought thriller where the roles of hunter and hunted are skillfully blurred. . . . An escalating torrent of murder you won't soon forget."
—**Gregg McCrary**

"*Silent Screams* beckons C. E. Lawrence to become a repeat offender in the thriller genre."
—**Marina Stajić**, Ph.D., DABFT, President of American Board of Forensic Toxicology

"A dark, intriguing thriller . . . Lawrence assembles a quirky group of detectives and experts, all strong characters who can support future books in the series."
—***Publishers Weekly***

ALSO BY C. E. LAWRENCE

*Silent Screams*

*Silent Victim*

*Silent Kills*

# SILENT SLAUGHTER

C. E. LAWRENCE

PINNACLE BOOKS
Kensington Publishing Corp.
www.kensingtonbooks.com

PINNACLE BOOKS are published by

Kensington Publishing Corp.
119 West 40th Street
New York, NY 10018

Copyright © 2012 C. E. Lawrence

All rights reserved. No part of this book may be reproduced in any form or by any means without the prior written consent of the publisher, excepting brief quotes used in reviews.

If you purchased this book without a cover, you should be aware that this book is stolen property. It was reported as "unsold and destroyed" to the publisher, and neither the author nor the publisher has received any payment for this "stripped book."

All Kensington titles, imprints, and distributed lines are available at special quantity discounts for bulk purchases for sales promotions, premiums, fund-raising, educational, or institutional use. Special book excerpts or customized printings can also be created to fit specific needs. For details, write or phone the office of the Kensington special sales manager: Kensington Publishing Corp., 119 West 40th Street, New York, NY 10018, attn: Special Sales Department; phone 1-800-221-2647.

This book is a work of fiction. Names, characters, businesses, organizations, places, events, and incidents either are the product of the author's imagination or are used fictitiously. Any resemblance to actual persons, living or dead, events, or locales is entirely coincidental.

PINNACLE BOOKS and the Pinnacle logo are Reg. U.S. Pat. & TM Off.

ISBN-13: 978-0-7860-2563-3
ISBN-10: 0-7860-2563-8

First printing: August 2012

10 9 8 7 6 5 4 3 2 1

Printed in the United States of America

*For Aunt Julie and Uncle Dave Siegel,*
*who will always be in my heart*

Mathematics, rightly viewed, possesses not only truth,
but supreme beauty—a beauty cold and austere,
like that of sculpture.

—BERTRAND RUSSELL

# Prologue

Edmund watched the young couple stroll arm in arm up First Avenue, slinging each leg forward in perfect symmetry: left, right, left, right. The girl was tall, blond, slim, the boy a few inches shorter, serious and scholarly looking in his wire-rimmed glasses and Eastern European dissident haircut. His left hand was draped at an oblique angle over the handlebars of a bicycle, which he wheeled along effortlessly without disturbing the smooth rhythm of their stride. They had such an ease about them that Edmund couldn't help staring. It was the grace of youth, of hope, of people who had only known a world in which they felt utterly and completely at home.

Their insouciance was arrogant, their happiness an insult. He decided then and there to take the girl. He increased his pace until he was just a few steps behind them.

*Golden Girl . . . she won't know what hit her.*

# CHAPTER ONE

Lee Campbell drove his fist into the unyielding leather of the punching bag and felt the satisfying jolt travel up his right arm. Sucking in a lungful of air, he thrust again at the bag, delivering a vicious uppercut with his left hand. He followed with a solid round-house and a quick jab: left, right, left, right. *Jab, jab—left, right.* As he punched harder and harder, he felt the sweat tickle his forehead, until it ran in rivulets down the sides of his face and neck. *Jab, jab—left, right, left, right, left.* He worked to a steady rhythm, comforted by the regularity of the blows. With every punch, he could feel his body loosen, anxiety melting each time he made contact.

Behind him, the grunts of weight lifters and the clang of metal weights reverberated and echoed off the rafters, amplified by the building's high ceilings. He paused for breath, wiping his face with the terry-cloth towel around his neck. It was late afternoon on a Monday, and there were three other men in the exercise room. Lee was the only white guy today; the rest were African American. The air was thick with sweat and testosterone. Lee mopped his brow as he watched a powerful-looking black man with massive shoulders load up a bench press bar with so many weights that the steel rod bowed under their combined gravity.

Lee liked it here. The Asser Levy Recreation Center was one of a dozen or so public rec centers run by the Parks Department. Membership was only seventy-five bucks a year, and it had everything: a serious weight room, exercise classes, outdoor and indoor pools, basketball and handball courts. There was even a Ping-Pong table.

He returned to his workout, pounding the bag until his knuckles stung and his muscles twitched with fatigue. Finally spent, Lee pulled off his boxing gloves and headed for the water fountain, incurring a raised eyebrow from the massive weight lifter and perhaps the hint of an approving nod. There was an unwritten code of behavior among men at gyms: only the briefest of eye contact, and smiling was rare. Most information was conveyed through nods and grunted one-syllable exchanges, maybe because anything more might be interpreted as a come-on.

The weight lifter's nod was not a flirtation; it was an acknowledgment of solidarity. Lee returned the nod, taking care not to smile, and headed past the lobby's stone urns to drink from the elegant fountain decorated with frolicking dolphins. The water was crisp and clear, and he drank deeply; then, slinging the towel over his shoulder, he headed for the shower.

Half an hour later he emerged, tired but relaxed, into the majestic lobby. Sunlight filtered lazily through the high windows as his footsteps echoed on the marble floors. Perched alone on a windy block of East Twenty-third Street just off the FDR Drive, the Asser Levy Center had been built nearly a hundred years earlier as a bathhouse. Unlike the drab institutional buildings of present-day New York, it was a magnificent neo-Romanesque structure with vaulted ceilings, balconies, and skylights. There were other city gyms closer to him, but he liked this one best. Old buildings gave him a sense of being connected to the past. He pushed open the heavy door and walked past the heavy stone columns, down the steps onto Twenty-third Street.

Behind him loomed the twin high-rises of Kips Bay; directly to the south were the lower brick buildings of Peter Cooper Village, already festooned with colorful Christmas decorations. Two blocks to the east, the icy waters of the East River flowed sluggishly south into New York Harbor. He loped across the four lanes of Twenty-third Street into the grounds of Peter Cooper, past an apartment with a first-floor window almost entirely obscured by blinking green and red lights. A cardboard reindeer beamed out at him from amid the bulbs, its oversized nose cranberry red. "Rudolph the Red-Nosed Reindeer." Dozens of Christmas pop songs were composed every year—why had that one in particular caught on? A story about the redemption of an outcast—*too bad that in real life such redemptions were rare*, he thought.

An arctic blast of wind from the river swooped between the buildings and pushed against his knees, slicing through the denim of his jeans. He pulled his jacket collar up to shield his neck and shoved his raw hands into his pockets, wishing he'd remembered to wear gloves. Lee had taken up boxing at the suggestion of his friend Chuck Morton, and as he wove his way through the secluded courtyards of Peter Cooper Village, he thought he had never received better advice. There was nothing like whaling away at a punching bag—or an opponent—to calm the nerves.

As he was about to cross into Stuyvesant Town at Twentieth Street, he realized he was ravenous. He turned west toward First Avenue, heading for his favorite bagel joint, Ess-a-Bagel. Just as he reached the avenue, his cell phone rang. He dug it out of his pocket, holding it close to his ear to compensate for the roar of traffic. This stretch of First Avenue had earned the nickname Bedpan Alley (a pun on Tin Pan Alley) because of the number of hospitals lining the street, and the traffic was constant and relentless.

"Campbell here," he said, cupping his other hand over his ear.

"Hiya, Doc." It was Detective Leonard Butts, formerly of the Bronx, recently reassigned to a Manhattan precinct.

"Hi. How's life in the big city?"

"Yeah, very funny."

Lee liked to tease his friend about his new post, though both of them knew that his old Bronx beat was far rougher than the relatively posh Thirteenth Precinct, where he was now stationed. His new beat included the neighborhoods of Gramercy, Chelsea, and the Peter Cooper Village/Stuyvesant Town complex.

Butts cleared his throat. "Listen, I got somethin' I'd like to run by you, if you got the time."

"Where are you?"

"Can you come to the station house?"

"I'm right around the corner. I'll just grab a bagel and meet you there."

"Ess-a-Bagel or David's?"

"Ess-a-Bagel."

Butts sighed wistfully. "What kind are you getting?"

"Whole wheat, everything."

Lee could tell that Butts was struggling with his conscience.

"Can you, uh, get me one too?"

"Sure. Same thing?"

"With a schmear—thanks."

Lee smiled as he shoved the phone back into his pocket. Food was his friend's greatest weakness. He had never known anyone who loved to eat so much. At his wife's insistence, the portly detective had recently gone on a diet. He'd succeeding in dropping ten pounds, but it was a constant battle, and he complained bitterly about it.

The woman behind the counter at Ess-a-Bagel was built like a linebacker, tall and broad of shoulder, with shoulder-length, brassy blond hair. After giving his order, Lee realized he was short on cash. He pulled a credit card from his wallet and waved it at her.

"You take plastic?"

She snatched it from him. "I take everything except children and husbands. I have enough of one and no need for the other." Her accent was an unlikely combination of England's West Country and Queens. Her heavy blue eye shadow was pure Maybelline, circa 1963.

She gazed defiantly at him, her large eyes doleful under a massive layer of frosted Azure Sky. He laughed dutifully and saw her face soften as she thrust a brown paper bag of bagels at him, still warm from the oven. Saliva spurted into his mouth as he clutched the bag in one hand, signing the receipt with the other.

"Thanks," he said. "Take it easy."

"Honey, I take it any way I can get it," she said, flicking a few stray poppy seeds from her apron. "Have a nice day," she added, displaying a set of prominent teeth that might look good on a Kentucky Derby front-runner.

"You too," he replied, and he made his escape into the frosty December air.

In this town, everyone was an armchair philosopher or a closet wit; wisecracking was a way of life, and everybody had an opinion. There were more characters in New York than there were potholes. Still, he thought as he pulled his collar up against the wind, that was one of the many reasons he loved this town.

# Chapter Two

When Lee arrived at the station house, he found Butts pacing in the lobby. The detective took the bag Lee proffered him, pulled out his bagel, and bit off a chunk.

"What do I owe you?" he grunted through a mouthful of bagel and cream cheese.

"Nothing," Lee said, looking away, his appetite shriveling before the smudges of cream cheese clinging to the detective's thick lips.

Detective Leonard Butts was one of the homeliest men he had ever seen. Short and pudgy, everything about him was round. He had a thick body, fat sausage fingers, and a plump, fleshy face. Even his head was unusually spherical, like a basketball, with a wispy thatch of sandy hair that never seemed to lie flat, no matter how much he combed it. His eyes were small and close-set, dwarfed by a bulbous nose and continuously inflamed complexion. Boils erupted like sunspots on his oily skin, perhaps encouraged by his atrocious eating habits. In spite of his wife's newly imposed regimen of diet and exercise, the stubby detective strayed easily and often.

He chewed on the bagel, a blissful expression on his face. "Man, this is good."

"So, what do you have for me?" Lee asked.

"Follow me, Doc," Butts said, leading him through the lobby to a small office at the end of a short corridor. "My new digs," he said, closing the door behind them. Three desks sat spaced evenly apart in the cramped room. Two were tidy and orderly; the other was a mess. Butts sat down at the third desk.

"Nice," Lee said. "Your own office?"

"Naw, I share it with two other guys, but still, it's better than the Bronx." Butts shuffled through some papers with one hand, the other still clutching the half-eaten bagel. "Have a seat," he said, clearing off another pile of papers from a beat-up captain's chair next to his desk.

"Thanks," Lee said. He sat down and looked around. A frugal afternoon sun crept listlessly through the single window, filling the room with pale gray light. "Who's this?" he asked, pointing to a photograph of a young woman tacked to a large bulletin board on the wall.

"Lisa Adler," Butts said. "Her mother reported her missing two days ago."

"That's what you wanted to talk to me about?"

"Not really." Butts took another bite of bagel and scratched his head. "Although I suppose there could be a connection. Ah!" he cried triumphantly, plucking a sheath of plastic from the clutter on his desk. He thrust it at Lee. "Have a look at this."

Inside the plastic sleeve was a letter. Neatly typed, in Times New Roman font, it could have come from any number of mass-produced laser printers. He read the letter without removing it from the plastic.

> Dear Detective Butts,
>
> I just thought I'd say hello because you'll be seeing a lot more of me. Or, rather, hearing a lot more. I very much doubt you'll ever see me. Still, you never know—anything's possible. I hear you work with that hotshot profiler. Good luck to both of you ever catching me.
>
> The game's afoot!
>
> Yours,
> The Professor

There was no signature or handwriting of any kind on the letter.

"You've dusted it for prints?" Lee asked.

"Completely clean. The envelope he used is on the other side."

Lee turned over the plastic sleeve and studied the envelope. The letter was addressed to Detective Butts, Thirteenth Precinct, Manhattan, printed in the same font as the letter. There was no sign of handwriting anywhere on the envelope.

"Probably a waste of time to do DNA testing," Lee remarked. "He avoided using his handwriting. I doubt he'd be stupid enough to lick the envelope."

"That's what I was thinkin'," Butts agreed. "Plus, there's been no crime to link it to yet, and the labs are backed up as it is. What does it mean, Doc? Do we have to worry about this guy?"

"I'm afraid we do."

The department got hundreds of crank letters every year, most of them irritating but harmless. Lee's experience told him that this one was different. The writer was clearly literate and intelligent. Worst of all, Lee was quite certain, he was very dangerous.

"What do we do now?" Butts asked.

"You're not going to like my answer."

"Try me."

"We wait."

As he spoke, the weak afternoon sun lost its struggle with the advancing darkness and slipped behind a dense cloud cover, leaving the room in the gloom of early-winter twilight.

# Chapter Three

Edmund gazed lovingly at the girl on the bed. She had stopped struggling now and gazed up at him with terror in her eyes. Small-animal sounds came from her throat, like the whimpering of a rabbit. The black duct tape over her mouth made it impossible for her to make any serious noise. He took in the sight of her, reveling in every detail: the fair skin with its faint dusting of freckles, the nails with their chipped polish, in need of a manicure.

*Too bad,* he thought. She had had her last manicure. Lust surged through his body at the thought of the complete power he had over her.

Most of all he liked to watch their eyes. The moment when their fear turned to pure animal terror was delicious—it never failed to send a shiver of pleasure down his spine. There was an instant when they all realized they were going to die, and watching the hope drain from their faces was thrilling, an intoxicating nectar. And the more he drank, the more he craved.

He had it all planned out—the who, what, where, and when, right down to the last detail. The key to success was organization.

He glanced at the wall clock. It was exactly six, the big and little hands forming a perfect 180-degree angle, a straight line . . . the shortest distance between two points. The sight of it sent warm little shivers down his spine. *Six o'clock, and all's well.* Time to get to work.

# Chapter Four

Lee left Butts with instructions to inform him of any updates and headed back to his apartment through the descending December dusk. He decided to walk the mile or so home, turning south on Second Avenue. The storefronts sported festive holiday decorations, the nodding Santas and grinning elves in stark contrast to the grim thoughts running through his head. As he walked, he pondered the nature of the letter writer and didn't like his conclusions. *Intelligent, mature, organized. And cruel.* The man's coldness practically leaped off the page.

Of course, there was no telling what his crimes were or would be, but this was no ordinary jealous husband or bitter ex-employee about to go on a rampage. This man would be more difficult to catch than the average criminal because, more likely than not, he would not know any of his victims. He was in complete control, and he was enjoying himself.

In short, Lee concluded, he was very likely a sociopath.

Similar thoughts crowded his mind as he passed the cozy, misted windows of the Stage Restaurant, a tiny Polish hole-in-the-wall serving fabulous homemade soups, pierogis, and the best turkey burger in the East Village. Next door to the Orpheum Theater, it served a constant stream of actors and audience members, both locals and tourists. The customers perched on the stools lining the counter were not thinking of roaming sociopaths as they hunched over bowls of steaming cabbage soup.

That was his job. As the only full-time NYPD profiler, Lee was technically a "civilian adviser"—but he was called in on the hardest cases, the ones resistant to forensics and ordinary detective work.

He turned west at the corner of Second Avenue and Seventh Street, where for many years the Kiev was a popular place for late-night revelers as well as the neighborhood's elderly Eastern European residents. The Kiev was gone now, replaced by a trendy Korean restaurant, the kind of place where sleek young Asian waiters looked as bored as the well-heeled clientele.

The venerable Veselka still remained, though it had lost some of its downtown charm in a renovation a few years ago. He preferred it in the old days, when he would squeeze past the hodgepodge of tables scattered at odd angles in the crowded front room to get to his favorite table in the tiny back room, underneath a narrow winding staircase leading up to a tiny, cluttered office.

Dusty ferns and spindly spider plants festered in moldy pots on the windowsill, as they had for decades, watching over endless cups of coffee served to aspiring actors and anarchists, scholars and scoundrels. That was the Veselka he loved—dirty and rumpled as an old coat. The new one, with its forest green trim and tidy paint job, was indistinguishable from Starbucks. New

York was constantly reinventing itself, and it could break your heart. But he was hungry, so he stopped in for a bowl of soup.

By the time he reached his building, it was nearly seven. As soon as he'd turned the lock in his apartment, the phone rang. He saw on the caller ID that it was his mother. She hated cell phones and only called him on the landline. He suspected one reason for this was a decline in her hearing, but she would never admit that. Fiona Campbell was a classic example of Scottish stoicism. Never complain, never grovel, and never admit to weakness of any kind. She was a virtuoso of denial, gifted in the art of deflection—so successful, in fact, that she had delegated most of her darker emotions to her children. And now that Lee's sister was gone, the role of "surrogate empath" fell to him.

He picked up on the third ring.

"Hi, Mom."

"Hello, dear." She sounded annoyed. He knew Fiona didn't like caller ID, and he enjoyed irking her.

"Good timing—I just walked in the door. Are you calling about this weekend?"

"I just wanted to know if you were still planning on coming."

Lee rarely cancelled plans on his mother, yet she always called to double-check. Her determination to avoid disappointment no doubt stemmed from his father's abrupt departure years before. Lee suspected she had never fully recovered from the shock, instead devoting her life to keeping other people at bay. Vulnerability did not come naturally to Fiona Campbell, and after his father left, she had constructed her firewalls carefully.

"I'm still coming, Mom," he said.

"Good. Kylie is counting on you."

*"Kylie is counting on you." Good one, Mom—projecting your needs on to your grandchild. For God's sake, don't admit you want to see me.*

Kylie was his sister's only child. Since Laura's mysterious disappearance six years ago, Fiona had shared the care of her granddaughter with Kylie's father, who also lived in New Jersey's Delaware Valley. Lee saw his niece as often as possible, and he was planning to drive out for her school Christmas concert over the weekend.

His cell phone buzzed in his jacket pocket. He dug it out—it was Butts.

"Sorry, Mom, I gotta go," he said. "I have another call. See you this weekend."

"All right," she said stiffly, and hung up. He sighed—her ruffled feathers might need some smoothing when he saw her.

He picked up the cell phone. "I'm here," he said. "What's up?"

"They found the girl," Butts said. "Lisa Adler."

"Where?"

"In the back of Shinbone Alley, off Bond Street. It's him, Lee. It's the guy who wrote to me."

"How do you know?"

"He left a note. I'm on my way to the scene now."

Lee glanced at his watch. "I'll be there in fifteen minutes. Call Krieger, and tell her to meet us there."

Elena Krieger, forensic linguistics specialist, was the most glamorous cop Lee had ever met. She was also the most difficult to work with. But her skill was needed now—and even Butts, who couldn't stand her, must realize that.

The detective was silent.

"Call her," Lee said. "We need her."

"All right." Butts didn't sound happy about it.

"See you there."

"Right."

He hung up and threw on his coat, pausing to pull his curtains closed as night settled over the East Village. The sound of Christmas carols floated out from the Ukrainian church across the street: "I Heard the Bells on Christmas Day." He recognized John Calkin's setting of Longfellow's words.

*Then pealed the bells more loud and deep:*
*"God is not dead, nor doth He sleep;*
*The wrong shall fail, the right prevail*
*With peace on earth, good will to men."*

As he turned out the lights in his apartment and closed the door behind him, he could only hope that Longfellow was right.

# CHAPTER FIVE

New York City had an excess of many things—buildings, people, noise, poverty and glamour—but it was severely lacking in alleyways. More modest East Coast cities, such as Philadelphia and Baltimore, boasted far more, and Boston was fairly bursting with them. Real estate in New York had always been a numbers racket, and through the years buildings had been crammed next to one another like cupcakes stuffed into an undersized bakery box. One casualty of the city's unbridled real estate frenzy was its alleys.

Shinbone Alley was one of the few remaining of its kind. Nestled between Lafayette and Broadway on a block of Bond Street still sporting its original cobblestones, the alley was separated from the street by a tall metal gate that now stood open, bordered by yellow crime scene tape.

Lee Campbell nodded at the pair of uniformed cops guarding the entrance and ducked under the tape. He walked toward the group of people huddled at the far end of the alley, his steps echoing in the narrow canyon formed by the buildings on either side. Floodlights mounted on metal poles gave the scene an eerie resemblance to a movie set.

In the apartments above them, a few windows had been opened, and several people leaned out to watch the proceedings. Even in New York, where you could see just about anything, people were curious. Lee couldn't blame them—it wasn't every day you saw a body dumped on a city street like this. In recent years Bond Street had been transformed from its funky East Village roots of crumbling storefronts and underground theaters to a gleaming showcase of upscale boutiques, galleries and chain croissant shops. Aging hippies, low-rent artists and folk singers had been replaced by well-heeled young Asians, NYU students and Euro-hipsters.

Lee had liked it better in the old days.

Crime scene technicians were everywhere—photographing the body, dusting for prints, carefully inspecting the sidewalks for trace evidence.

Butts looked up as Lee approached and shook his head. "I'll say this. He's an arrogant son of a bitch, to dump a body in a place like this. Anyone could have seen him."

"You have the cause of death yet?"

"Looks like ligature strangulation. Petechial hemorrhaging, bruises around the neck—the whole nine yards."

"Who found her?"

"The building super's son," Butts said. "Snuck out to the alley for a smoke, found her there." He glanced at a slim Latino youth huddled on the stoop of the western building's entrance. The boy sucked heavily on a cigarette, his eyes haunted and vacant. A short, dark-haired woman had thrown a protective arm around his shoulders—probably his mother.

"Did he see anything else?"

"Naw. Kid's in total shock. His parents didn't even know he smoked."

*They do now,* Lee thought, studying the boy and his mother. He didn't look older than about fourteen, and his mom stared at them defiantly, as if challenging them to arrest her son. Lee glanced up at the onlookers in the windows above them. "You interview any of them yet?"

"Detective Chen is on it. He's got a sergeant with him—even so, could take a while."

"You mean Jimmy Chen?"

"Yeah, why?" Butts said. "You know him?"

"I went to John Jay with him. We used to hang out together. Last time I saw him, he was working Chinatown."

"He was transferred to the Sixth Precinct after 9/11. They were hit pretty hard and had a shortage of experienced cops."

"I guess I haven't seen him since before then."

What he didn't say was that he hadn't seen much of anyone during those dark days. He didn't like to dwell on it.

"Technically this is Sixth Precinct territory," Butts said, "but since the first note was sent to me, I'm the primary on this one."

"Lucky you," Lee said, looking down at the body.

The girl was young—very young, from the look of it. Tall and thin, with golden blond hair, she had a sweet, round face. She lay on her back, hands folded over her stomach as if she were sleeping. The pinky finger of her left hand had been neatly severed. There was no blood, which could mean one of two things: The cutting could have been done somewhere else, and the killer cleaned her up before leaving her here. The other possibility was that the amputation was post-mortem. Lee hoped it was the second explanation.

A note was fastened to the front of her down jacket with a safety pin. He remembered seeing his sister's bus number pinned to her blouse in just such a manner on her first day of school. He shook off the memory and focused on the girl in front of him.

"This is the note?" he asked Butts.

"Yeah."

"Have you read it?"

"As much as I could without moving it. It's the same guy, Lee. Calls himself The Professor. Arrogant prick," he muttered, turning to one of the crime scene techs, a black-haired young woman with a serious face and a pronounced widow's peak. "You done here? Can I remove this?"

The young woman nodded and handed Butts two pairs of latex gloves. He put one on and handed the other to Lee. He bent down and carefully extracted the note, taking care not to rip the paper.

Just then Lee heard the assertive click of heels on cobblestones behind them. He turned to see Elena Krieger approaching.

"Well, here I am," she said, striding across the uneven paving stones with the arrogant confidence of a runway model. "What have you got for me?"

*Nice to see you too,* Lee thought, shaking his head at her typically abrupt entrance. Still, he thought, there was no doubt about it—Detective Elena Krieger was a knockout. She was dressed in a clingy gray cashmere sweater over tight black pants and knee-length leather boots, topped off by a white fake fur jacket and silk scarf. The outfit was sexy, but it didn't really matter what she wore; she was the kind of woman who would turn heads even if she was dressed in a burlap sack. Her thick auburn hair was stacked on top of her head, exposing her downy neck and small, close-set ears. She wore no makeup except a slash of bright red lipstick on her full lips.

Detective Leonard Butts was unmoved by her charms and thrust the note at her.

"We got this," he said. "What do you make of it?"

She slipped on a pair of latex gloves and took it, eyeing him coolly. The two detectives disliked each other intensely, their enmity tempered by a grudging professional respect. She held the note up to the light and squinted.

"No chance of fingerprints, I suppose?"

"Too early to tell," Butts said. "But it doesn't look good so far."

Lee looked over her shoulder at the note. It was typed, just like the first one.

Dear Detective Butts and Friends,

Well, we meet again. Not actually, of course—we'll save that pleasure for later. It's always nice to have something to look forward to, don't you think? How do you like my work? I'm rather proud of it myself.

So now you have a little puzzle on your hands. Isn't One the loneliest number? The Shinbone's

connected to the knee bone . . . for now, anyway.
Maybe the next time I'll be going all to pieces.

Bye for now,
The Professor

Lee turned to see Butts pacing behind them, chewing on a toothpick.

"Well?" the pudgy detective said. "What do you make of it?"

Krieger ignored the question. "You have the other note?"

"Back at the precinct. What can you tell me about this one?"

"He took his time writing it. It's possible he wrote it before he killed her, or even before he abducted her. The whole thing was carefully planned—he even knew exactly where he was going to leave the body."

Butts frowned. "How do you know?"

"*Shinbone* is capitalized—it's clearly a reference to the alley as well as the body part. He knew exactly what he was doing—he made a plan and followed through with it."

"Which means he's highly organized," Lee added. "And intelligent."

"Very," Krieger agreed. "I'd guess he's well educated. He even has a sense of humor—his use of language is sophisticated and filled with jokes."

"Very funny," Butts muttered.

"He's definitely enjoying himself," Krieger remarked. "This is a game to him, and he feels totally in control."

"Yeah?" said Butts. "Then he's in for a real surprise."

# Chapter Six

"Any sign of the missing finger?" Krieger asked from the backseat as they drove back to the station house in Butts's oversized Chevy.

"Nope. It's probably his trophy," Butts remarked as he swung into a parking space that looked way too small for the big sedan. Lee winced, waiting for the scraping of metal on metal, but to his surprise, the car fit.

Interviews with the neighbors had yielded little useful information. Several people reported hearing what sounded like a trash pickup in the alley but thought nothing of it. New Yorkers were used to sanitation trucks coming and going at all hours of the day and night, so it wasn't surprising that no one had gone to a window to look out until later.

Jimmy Chen had stayed behind with a couple of sergeants to finish up the interviews before joining them at the precinct. Lee was looking forward to seeing his old friend—they had been inseparable during their graduate student days at John Jay. They had met a few times after graduation, but careers and the concerns of daily life had a way of interfering. And then there was Lee's struggle with clinical depression, which he didn't really like to share with anyone.

Butts led the way to his office, which Krieger entered with the air of a prisoner being led onto death row. She observed the clutter on his desk with a disdainful wrinkle of her perfectly straight nose and perched on the edge of a chair in a corner.

"Are there any similar cases you know of?" asked Krieger.

"Nope," said Butts. "I already checked on that. There's nothin'."

"Well," said Lee, "in that case—"

"Wait," said Butts. "Before you do your thing, Doc, mind if I take a crack?"

Lee smiled. When they'd first met, the detective was disdainful of what he called the "mumbo jumbo" of profiling. But since then they had worked quite a few cases together. Butts had come to see the value of analyzing the psychological aspects of a crime, rather than relying entirely on forensic evidence.

"Go ahead," he said. "Have at it."

"One thing's clear," Butts began. "This guy is damn smart."

"I already *told* you that," Krieger muttered.

"You were talkin' about the note he left," Butts replied. "But I mean the manner of the crime itself."

"Go on," said Lee.

"This perp leaves his vic in an alley in an upscale neighborhood, where he could easily be seen—"

"Under the cover of darkness," Krieger remarked languidly.

"Yeah, but why not wait until the middle of the night, when most people are asleep? He could, but he doesn't. So he's daring, and he's smart."

"And arrogant," Lee said. "Don't forget that."

"Yeah, right," Butts said, scribbling on the white-board against the far wall.

- *Risky MO*
- *Intelligent*
- *Arrogant, daring*

"How am I doin' so far?" he asked Lee.

"You're doing great. I don't see what you need me for."

The detective turned back to the board. "What else?"

"He probably owns a vehicle," said Lee.

"Which he used to transport the body?" Krieger said.

"Right," said Lee.

Butts wrote it on the board.

"Don't forget organized," Lee said. "He's highly organized."

"Right," Butts said. "He took a low-risk vic—a nice girl, from a good family, not a street hooker." He turned and wrote on the board.

- *Low-risk victim*
- *Organized*

"And he took the time to type out the note," Krieger remarked.

Butts frowned. "You think he did that before or after he killed her?"

"Hard to say," Lee replied. "Either way, he's a cool customer. And given the ritualistic aspect of the crime and staging of the body, it looks like we have a repeat offender on our hands."

"That's just great," said Butts.

"Well?" Krieger demanded. "When are you going to give me the other note?"

"Oh, right," Butts said, fishing out a photocopy from the pile of papers on his desk. "Here it is."

Krieger snatched it from him with the eagerness of a child with a Christmas present. After scanning it briefly, she said, "I can tell you something else about him."

"What's that?" Butts asked, obviously intrigued but trying to hide it.

"There's a good chance he's English. Or at the very least, he was educated in a British school."

The detective's face expressed astonishment mingled with disbelief. "How do you get that?"

"It's the syntax of his sentences. 'I very much doubt you'll ever see me.' Americans don't talk like that—'I very much doubt.' That's British—upper class, I'd say. Probably public school educated."

"What else?" Butts asked.

"It's subtler, but this phrase also struck me: 'Still, you never know.' "

"What about it?" Butts said.

"I get it," said Lee. "Another typically British locution."

"Right. By itself, it's not much. But taken together with the other phrase and the reference to Conan Doyle and Sherlock Holmes, I think we have something."

"What reference was that?" asked Butts.

"Why, Detective, I'm surprised at you," Krieger said, obviously relishing the chance to admonish him. "In the first letter he said, 'The game's afoot.' "

"Oh, that," said Butts, his already florid complexion reddening. "Yeah—of course."

"I'm impressed," Lee said. "Well done, Detective Krieger."

Krieger shrugged, but the corners of her mouth twitched upward. She was a woman who worked hard not to show her feelings, which he found ironic, since she was clearly a hotbed of roiling emotion and passion.

"How sure are you about the British thing?" Butts asked, fishing around in his desk drawer.

"About seventy percent," Krieger replied.

"Or he could just want us to *think* he's English," Lee said. "What else can you tell us about him from his writing?"

"Some of it is obvious," Krieger answered. "You are correct with regard to intelligence and organization."

"What about this reference to One being 'the loneliest number'?" said Butts. "Is he tryin' to tell us he's lonely?"

"I don't think so," said Lee. "He's too in control. He sees himself as superior to us. He's not likely to be baring his soul."

"It is interesting, though," Krieger agreed. "What exactly *is* he referring to—the girl herself?"

"So maybe it's a threat to take more victims?" Butts suggested, pulling a half-eaten sandwich from his desk drawer. An expression of disgust crossed Krieger's face. "What?" Butts said. "This is dinner. Actually, it's left over from lunch. You want some?"

Krieger wrinkled her nose. “No, *thank* you.”

“You sure? It’s turkey—not half-bad,” he said, taking a bite. “Never used to like turkey, but the wife insists I eat healthier.”

“It could be a reference to the song lyric,” Lee said. “ ‘One is the loneliest number.’ ”

“Hmm,” Butts said, chewing thoughtfully. “Who recorded that?”

“Three Dog Night, I think,” said Lee.

They both looked at Krieger. “Anything there, linguistically speaking?” said Butts.

She frowned. “I’m afraid I don’t share your knowledge of American pop tunes.”

“It’s not a ‘pop tune,’ ” Butts said. “It’s classic rock.”

Krieger shrugged. “Whatever.”

“Look,” Butts said. “We gotta wait for the results on forensics from the lab, and it’s already after ten o’clock. So why don’t we meet here tomorrow morning around nine?”

“Okay,” said Lee. “But first, add one more thing to your list on the board.”

“What’s that?”

“Sense of humor.”

“Yeah,” Butts said, frowning. “This guy’s a laugh riot. But you know what they say. He who laughs last—”

“Right,” Lee agreed. But even as he spoke, he could hear the sound of the UNSUB’s laughter, mocking them. He was having fun—and the fun was only just beginning.

The game was afoot.

# CHAPTER SEVEN

Edmund stood at the kitchen table, peeling an apple. He stroked its glistening red skin carefully with the knife, applying just enough pressure to separate it from the firm white flesh underneath. He took a deep breath and smiled to himself, thinking about what pleasures lay ahead of him. He sliced the apple cleanly into four quarters and bit into one.

Murder burned like fire in his belly. Apart from mathematics and Bach, it was all he thought about, all he desired—to kill, again and again, in a never-ending orgasm of bloodlust and death. There was something dark and rotting at his core; he knew that, had known it since childhood. He felt contempt for the people he saw enjoying their little lives, or pretending to. He always suspected there was a pretense with the really "happy" ones. How could you enjoy this lousy existence, so full of pain and loss and sickness and disappointment? The sodden, sullen center of his being resisted the pull of commonplace pleasures; he found true satisfaction only in the taking of pleasure from others.

He sank his teeth deeply into the apple chunk, chewing thoughtfully. The fruit was just an appetizer; it was almost time for lunch. *Lunch.* He liked the crisp sound of the word, the final consonants crunchy, like bones snapping between teeth. *Lunch.* Delicious and nutritious, carnivorous . . .

He put down the apple and laid the tools of his trade out lovingly on the kitchen table: the long, serrated hunting knife with the inlaid mother-of-pearl handle, the roll of duct tape, coil of rope, blindfold and, of course, the handcuffs. He had selected each item with care: the rope had to be white and new and of good quality, the duct tape had to be black, and the blindfold was always pure silk. He liked the touch of elegance. He usually used black or purple and hand-washed it carefully after each victim.

The handcuffs were trickier. He preferred British models, his favorite being the old fashioned "Darby" handcuffs he had found in an antiques store a few blocks north of Gramercy Park. Dating from the early fifties, they were sturdy and harder to pick than some of the more modern ones. He was also pleased that his purchase would leave no trail for law enforcement to follow. Who would think to trace a pair of handcuffs to an obscure antiques store on Lexington Avenue?

He smiled and caressed the smooth, cold metal, imagining it wrapped around the tender wrists of a youthful victim, the harsh steel cutting into the smooth young flesh. He shuddered with pleasure at the thought. *Monster.* The word made him smile. Down deep, he believed all men had these fantasies, if only they would admit it to themselves. He looked forward to the rush of adrenaline as he stalked each victim, carefully planning each attack as though it was a military campaign, complete with maps and diagrams.

He believed that every man secretly wished to enjoy the pleasures he had cultivated so carefully—if only they were as clever as he was, as brave and resourceful. It wasn't virtue that kept other men from indulging in the chase and capture; no, it was their cowardice, their fear of being caught, their lack of imagination and daring. This he believed as surely as he knew that within the next phase of the moon, he would step out in search of more prey. He took another bite of apple and shivered with the pleasure of anticipation.

# CHAPTER EIGHT

"Hey, Angus—long time, no see!"

Lee Campbell knew that voice could only belong to one person—Jimmy Chen. He turned to see his old friend striding into the Thirteenth Precinct as if he owned the place, his shiny black hair bouncing, wearing the same lopsided grin Lee had first seen in their student days at John Jay. The two men embraced, awkwardly—a precinct house was no place for emotional bonding. But it had been a long time, and Lee realized how much he had missed Jimmy.

"So, Angus, how's that hot mother of yours?"

Lee smiled. Jimmy Chen had a sly sense of humor. Even at John Jay, where gallows humor was common, he had raised some eyebrows. A lot of the other Chinese cops had a serious, studious attitude, but Jimmy referred to himself as "your atypical Asian dude." He was unusually tall, well over six feet. Jimmy's family came from north of the Yangtze River, where the people were taller. His grandfather had been a leader in one of the notorious *tongs*, the organized gangs operating in Chinatown.

He had started calling Lee "Angus" when he got a whiff of his Scottish ancestry, and he'd had Fiona Campbell eating out of his hand within minutes of meeting her. He'd flirted outrageously, then sent her flowers the next day. She had never stopped asking Lee about "that nice Chinese friend of yours." He didn't have the heart to tell her Jimmy was a compulsive flirt—or that he also happened to be gay.

"My mother is just fine, thank you," Lee said.

"I'll say she is," said Jimmy with a wink and a slap on the back. "Give her my best, will you?"

"Always."

"So what have you been up to?" Jimmy asked as they walked to Butts's office in the back of the station house. "You doing okay?"

There weren't many people in Lee's life who knew the intimate details of his sister's disappearance and his subsequent nervous breakdown. Jimmy Chen was one of them.

"I'm doing okay, thanks. You?"

"What is it your mom's boyfriend says? 'Can't complain—even if I did, no one would listen.' "

"Yep—you got him, all right."

"What's his name—Stan?"

"Yeah, Stan."

They reached the office, and Lee reached out to knock, then glanced at his watch. It was five minutes after nine. Hildegarde Elena von Krieger was notoriously punctual, and if she was alone with Detective Leonard Butts for any length of time, he figured, it wasn't going to be pretty.

He was right.

When he and Jimmy entered the office, he could tell from Krieger's body language that it wasn't going well. She sat, arms crossed over her Wagnerian bosom, staring coldly in front of her. Crime scene photos were spread out on Butts's desk. The pudgy detective clutched a cinnamon roll in one hand and a newspaper in the other. He tossed the paper onto the desk.

Lee looked at the headline screaming out with the combination of alarm and relish typical of the city's tabloids.

***Alleyway Strangler's Young Victim***

GRUESOME DISCOVERY—HORRIFIED NEIGHBORS FIND GIRL'S BODY

Butts flung the paper into the recycling bin. "More trash from the garbage mill." Detective Leonard Butts did not like the media.

Elena Krieger uncrossed her arms. "They are just doing their job, same as we are."

Butts snorted. "And they're providing *such* an important service to the community."

Krieger rolled her eyes. "Why don't you just get over yourself?" She turned to Jimmy and extended a hand. "Hello. I'm Elena Krieger."

"Jimmy Chen," he said, shaking her hand. "Pleased to meet you."

"Okay," Butts said. "Now that we got the introductions over with, let's cut to the chase."

"I was wondering if you think there are previous victims we haven't discovered yet," asked Krieger.

"That's a good question," Lee answered. "He seemed awfully in control of the crime scene, and his careful posing of the body indicated that his fantasy has been in place for quite a while."

Jimmy leafed through the crime scene photos. "Man, this is some twisted stuff." He held up a shot of Lisa's left hand. "Why did he take that finger, do you think?"

Lee studied it. "I think it's an important aspect of his signature, but it's early to draw any definite conclusions."

Butts ran a hand through his thinning wisps of sandy hair. "But what does it *mean*?"

"One obvious interpretation would be that it represents castration anxiety," said Lee.

"How so?" asked Butts.

"That he sees women as potential threats to his masculinity, so he cuts off their appendages before they can remove his."

Krieger cocked her head to one side. "He cut off her pinky finger. He must have a teensy-weensy penis."

Jimmy stifled a laugh, and Butts glared at him.

"It's not a direct correlation," said Lee. "And it could signify a dozen other things."

"Do they know if it was postmortem or antemortem?" Jimmy asked.

"We're waitin' on the ME's office for that," said Butts.

The phone rang, and he snatched it up.

"Butts here." He listened, his face grim. "Okay, I'll be right over." He hung up and turned to the others. "That was the ME's office. I'm goin' over to look at the body."

"What is it?" asked Lee.

"They didn't say, just that I'd wanna have a look."

"I'm coming with you," said Lee. "Jimmy, you in?"

"I've got to type up all those interviews," his friend said, avoiding eye contact. "I think I'll wait for the photos, if you don't mind."

Lee nodded. Jimmy wasn't exaggerating about the paperwork—never ending and exhausting, it was the bane of a cop's existence. But Lee knew something about his old friend: Jimmy Chen hated being around dead people. An odd trait in a detective, perhaps, but everyone had their weakness, he thought as he watched Butts stuff the last remnant of his day-old turkey sandwich into his mouth before throwing on his coat.

He turned away before Elena Krieger had a chance to roll her eyes in disgust.

# CHAPTER NINE

The office of the Medical Examiner of the City of New York was a short cab ride up First Avenue. Within minutes they disembarked in front of the square, featureless building that housed the city's morgue and evidence processing and toxicology labs. It might just the be the ugliest building in Manhattan, Lee thought as they swung open the stainless-steel and glass doors and stepped into the dowdy lobby with its scuffed plastic chairs and anemic ferns in the window. It was a perfect example of the drabness of governmental bureaucracy—there was little care or thought put into the design of the building and even less into its upkeep. A sickly Christmas tree scantily decorated with dusty ornaments perched in its lopsided metal base, listing drunkenly to one side.

The drowsy clerk behind the front desk sent them down a dingy hallway to the morgue, where a couple of lab technicians stood over the body of Lisa Adler. Draped with a crisp white sheet, she didn't look asleep—she looked dead. Her flesh was waxy under the harsh fluorescent lights, the deep purple bruises around her neck vivid against the pallor of her skin. No wonder Jimmy

Chen hated this, Lee thought with a shiver. The older of the technicians, a stocky, middle-aged white man with a neatly trimmed beard, gave a nod to the younger one, a thin young Latina Lee had seen before.

With one clean movement, as though unmaking a bed, she pulled back the sheet. Lee heard Butts gasp before he was aware of his own sharp intake of air.

"Jesus," the detective murmured.

The girl's body had been pierced multiple times.—Precise and round, the tiny stab wounds appeared to have been made with something the shape and size of an ice pick or barbeque skewer. After his initial shock wore off, Lee could see that the wounds formed a distinctive, swirling pattern.

"Ante- or postmortem?" Butts asked the older man.

"It's impossible to say for certain. Her killer cleaned up any blood before dressing her and leaving her at the crime scene."

"He did this while she was alive," said Lee.

They all turned to look at him.

"It's classic piquerism," he said.

"What's that?" asked Butts.

"It's a form of sexual perversion where you stab, prick or cut another person, usually multiple times."

"How do you know it was while she was alive?"

"Because he's a sadistic bastard. He needs to see her suffer."

The young Latina turned away, and the older man shook his head.

"I can't yet come to any definite conclusion based on the forensics."

"Okay, thanks," Butts said. "You'll let us know about any prints, DNA, trace evidence that turns up?"

"We'll let you know the minute we have anything." He handed the detective a manila envelope. "Here are some photos."

"Thanks," said Butts.

They took a cab back to the station house, where they found Krieger and Jimmy waiting for them. Jimmy was typing up interview reports on his laptop, and Krieger was studying the two messages from the killer, jotting down notes in her neat, cramped handwriting.

"What did you find?" asked Jimmy.

In response, Butts pulled out the photographs and tacked them to the bulletin board against the wall.

"Christ," said Jimmy, staring at them. Krieger looked through them, stone-faced, without saying anything.

"They can't tell us whether the injuries were ante- or postmortem," Butts remarked. "The perp cleaned her up too good before leaving her in the alley. Doc here says the bastard did it while she was alive."

Krieger folded her arms, her face still impassive. "Why do you say that?"

"It's based on the type of offender I believe him to be—a power-excitation killer. He gets off on inflicting pain and humiliation on his victims."

"Are you certain?"

"Not a hundred percent. But there are indicators—"

"Yes, this is piquerism," Krieger finally agreed, studying the photos. "What's the point unless you're using it as a form of torture?"

Butts shot a glance at her. "How did you know what that was?"

Krieger shrugged. "It's from the French word meaning *to prick*, and it's a type of sexual perversion—"

"Yeah, yeah," Butts interrupted. "Doc already explained all that."

"What about prints, DNA, trace?" Jimmy asked.

Butts shook his head. "Nothing so far."

Lee stared out the window at the bleak winter sky, which matched the mood of everyone in the room.

"Okay," Butts said, shaking off the gloom settling over them. "Who wants to interview the family? They live in Westchester. Both parents are doctors. The girl was a student at Yeshiva University."

"I'll go," Jimmy said. "I've always wanted to see how the other half lives."

"I'll go with him," said Lee.

Butts gave Krieger an evil smile. "Looks like you and me will have a cozy little time together holding down the fort."

Krieger returned a steely smile. "I look forward to it, Detective."

# Chapter Ten

The Adlers lived in Waccabuc, a well-heeled neighborhood near the upscale town of Katonah, a few miles from the Connecticut border.

"Get a load of this, Angus," Jimmy said as they drove past rambling white clapboard houses snuggled against the rolling hillsides of Upper Westchester. The homes were elegant, roomy and expensive-looking, sitting on gently sloping lawns bordered by rows of majestic oak trees.

Jimmy nodded toward a three-story Cape Cod–style mansion festooned with tiny white fairy lights. "There's some major money here."

"Yeah," Lee said, wondering which of the tasteful nineteenth-century houses were home to Wall Street swindlers, drug kingpins and real estate developers who financed cheap, ugly high-rises so they could live in sequestered Old World luxury.

"Wonder how much of this money is legit?" Jimmy said as they passed a golf course bordered by looming maple trees.

"I was just thinking the same thing," Lee said.

Jimmy smiled. "We always did think alike, you and me. I mean, considering you're a Round Eyes."

*Round Eyes* was the derogatory term some Chinese people used to describe Caucasians.

"Hey, watch it," Lee replied. "You don't want me to tell my mother that you're prejudiced, do you?"

"Don't threaten me," said Jimmy. "Or I won't invite you over to dinner."

"Your dad is an amazing cook."

Jimmy's father used to run a restaurant in Chinatown that was very popular with the locals. He'd sold it to a cousin some years ago but continued to give advice to the kitchen staff, often immigrants who spoke only Mandarin Chinese.

"I know, and my mom didn't even marry my dad because of his cooking."

"Okay, I'll bite," said Lee. "Why did she marry him?"

"Because of his enormous—"

"Oh, here we go," Lee groaned.

"I'm just *saying*," Jimmy said, keeping his eyes on the road.

"I can't believe I actually missed you. What was I thinking?"

"Oh, Angus, stop being such a dour Scot. Leave that to your mom."

Lee smiled. Jimmy always cheered him up. Since his bout with depression, a lot of people treated him with kid gloves, but not Jimmy. He was the same pain in the ass he had always been, always looking for trouble and very often finding it.

"Seriously, how have you been?" Jimmy asked, not taking his eyes from the road.

"Can't complain, because if I did—"

"No one would listen. No, I mean it—how have you been?"

Lee looked out the window as the car zipped past a meadow bordered by a low stone wall. "Good days and bad days."

Jimmy nodded. He had the good taste not to pry too much, to back off when it was called for. "Any news about your sister?"

"No. It's a cold case by now."

"Hey, cold cases get solved all the time."

"Not when there's no evidence—and no body."

"Seriously, no evidence at all?"

"They had some leads early on that went nowhere. It's like she just dropped off the face of the earth."

Jimmy shook his head. "Man, that's rough. I know if anything happened to my little brother, I'd freak."

"How is Barry?"

"He's doing pretty good. Thanks for asking."

Jimmy's younger brother, Barry, was severely autistic and lived at home with his parents. He was something of a savant with numbers and had memorized pi to a thousand decimal places. It was people he had trouble with—the simplest social exchange could leave him baffled and perplexed. He idolized Jimmy, who was fiercely protective of him.

"Here it is," said Jimmy, turning down a tree-lined lane. "Old Post Road. Jeez, think these people are rich enough?"

The Adlers' house fit in well with the neighborhood, and so did the Adlers, Lee noted as he and Jimmy were ushered into their home. Tasteful, well-spoken, understated—and rich. At least they had worked for their money, Lee thought, since they were both physicians. Dr. Eli Adler was short, Jewish and energetic, and Dr. Rachel Adler was willowy, blond and reserved. It was obvious Lisa had gotten her looks from her mother.

Jimmy and Lee were led into a living room with a Steinway concert grand and a Persian rug the size of the Croton Reservoir. The whole place dripped with taste and money, from the elegant Japanese silk screens to the Tiffany lamps and inlaid card table. Complimenting the couple on their aesthetic sense after they had just lost their only daughter seemed inappropriate, so Lee took a seat on the olive green sofa next to Jimmy, who whipped out a notebook and rested it on his knee, pen poised.

"I suppose you'd like to know if we have any idea who'd want to hurt our daughter," Mrs. Adler said, folding her elegant hands on her lap. She wore a simple blue silk blouse over straight black pants, her ash blond hair pulled back in a tight bun. "Well, we don't. Everyone loved Lisa."

"No, ma'am," said Jimmy. "Actually, we'd just like to hear you say anything that comes to mind."

Dr. Eli Adler frowned and twisted the thick gold wedding ring on his left hand. He wore a black turtleneck over gray slacks and creamy brown leather loafers. "Anything?"

"Anything at all. It doesn't even have to relate to your daughter."

Mrs. Adler gave a little cough, as if the detective had just committed a faux pas she was too polite to point out. "Isn't that a little—*vague*, Detective?"

"It's the way I work. You've undergone a terrible shock, and your brains are already having trouble processing what's happened. So rather than ask you to focus on specific questions, I like to start out by letting you say whatever's on your mind."

"I'll tell you what's on my mind," her husband said. "I'd like to get into a dark alley with the animal that did this to our Lisa. Just five minutes—that's all I ask. I swear, I wouldn't care what happened to me, as long as I—"

His wife laid a hand on his arm. "Eli, I don't think that's the kind of thing the detective is talking about."

"Actually, that's exactly the kind of thing I'm talking about," Jimmy said. He turned to Mrs. Adler. "What about you?"

"I—I can't really . . ." She looked down at her hands, and a single sob shook her body. No tears fell, though, and when she looked up again, her face was contorted with grief and fury. "I—want—to—*rip*—*his*—*face*—*off*." The words shot from her mouth like bullets. Lee could see that her rage was even deeper than her husband's. Mr. Adler looked at her with astonishment, as if he had not known her to be capable of such feelings.

"Okay," said Jimmy. "I understand that you're both angry."

"No, Detective, I don't think you do understand," Mrs. Adler continued. " 'Angry' doesn't cut it, not by a long shot. I think what my husband and I are saying is that we'd like to *kill* someone—specifically, the man who . . . did this to Lisa."

"How do you know it's a man?" Lee asked.

She looked at him with pity mixed with contempt. "Oh, *really*. I don't even watch those crime shows on TV, but even I know that this kind of crime points to a sexually motivated predator. Stop me if you've heard this one."

"Okay," said Jimmy. "So, any ideas?"

She looked at her husband, who shook his head. "Lisa's boyfriend, Carl, is the nicest kid on the planet. He's devastated. We know his parents—his father was the rabbi at our son's bar mitzvah."

"So it wasn't her boyfriend," Jimmy said. "Anyone else hanging around her? Any suspicious e-mails, phone calls, text messages?"

"Your forensics people have her cell phone. So far we haven't had a single call from anyone who wasn't a friend or fellow student."

"She was at Yeshiva University?"

Mrs. Adler nodded. "On Lexington Avenue. She loved it—used to eat in the Korean restaurants all the time."

Lee nodded. Part of Murray Hill had become known as Little Korea, with a high concentration of Korean restaurants, students and tourists.

"What was she studying?"

"Psychology," her father said with a bitter laugh. "Ironic, huh? Guess all that book learning wasn't enough to protect her from a psychopath."

"No one's safe from people like that," Lee said. "It wasn't her fault."

"Sure," Dr. Adler said. "As a parent, you know that. It's just that you never think it will happen to your . . ." He resumed twisting his wedding ring.

Lee looked at Jimmy, wondering if he noticed. "Did she ever seem . . . secretive about anything?" he asked.

The Adlers shook their heads in unison. "Never.

Lisa didn't have secrets from us," Mrs. Adler said. "We were very close. Almost like sisters."

"Please don't take offense at this, but did your daughter indulge in any . . . risky behavior? Drugs, casual sex, that kind of thing?"

Mrs. Adler's patrician face tightened, but her husband laid a hand on her shoulder. "Rachel, they *have* to ask these questions." He turned to Jimmy. "Lisa was a quiet girl. Her idea of a big night out was to go to a revival cinema with her boyfriend and sneak in homemade popcorn. That's about as wild as she ever got."

"What about her friends? Did you get a chance to meet them?"

"Lisa was very close to her roommate," said Mrs. Adler. "Have you talked to her yet?"

"Not yet. Do you happen to know how to reach her?"

"I think I have her cell phone number, if you'll give me a minute," she said, getting up from the couch. She left the room in the direction of the kitchen, and when she was out of earshot, Eli Adler leaned toward Jimmy and spoke in a low voice.

"She seems to be handling this well, Detective, but she's not—trust me. Lisa was all we had." He paused to collect himself and continued to twist his wedding ring as he spoke. "There's a few things about Lisa that my wife didn't know about. For instance, she—uh, she liked to pose for art students at Pratt sometimes. Life drawing, you know?"

"Nude modeling?" said Jimmy.

"Shh! Keep your voice down, please," Eli Adler said with a nervous glance in the direction of the kitchen. "I don't want to upset Rachel any more than necessary. Yes, sometimes the classes called for nudity. But it was all very professional, you know—I mean, they were art students, right?"

"Just the same, I'm glad you told me," said Jimmy. "It's worth checking out."

"My wife doesn't need to know about it, though, right?"

"Not if you don't want her to. Unless it turns out to be relevant to solving—uh, the crime."

"Thanks," said Dr. Adler as his wife returned to the room carrying a small green address book.

"Here it is," she said. "Her roommate's name is Carrie Lieberman, and here's her cell number."

"Thanks," said Jimmy, writing it down.

After a few more routine questions, they finished the interview. The Adlers continued to be polite and helpful, though Lee had the mounting sense that Mrs. Adler longed for the interview to be over. That wasn't unusual for grieving parents—what was interesting was that Mr. Adler seemed eager to talk with them and sorry when they got up to leave.

Back in the car, they waited until they were halfway down Old Post Road before Jimmy said, "Interesting—he wanted to talk, she didn't."

"Exactly what I was thinking," said Lee. "The question is, why? She seems afraid of something."

"As my grandfather would say, 'Mankind fears an evil man, but heaven does not.' "

"The same grandfather who ran the *tong* in Chinatown?"

Jimmy shrugged. "He was a complicated man."

"Even heaven might be afraid of the guy we're looking for."

"Then we'd better catch him fast," said Jimmy.

*Amen*, Lee thought as he gazed out the window at the elegant landscape of Upper Westchester decked out in tasteful holiday decorations. *Amen.*

# Chapter Eleven

Back in Manhattan, Jimmy dropped Lee off in front of his building before continuing down to Chinatown to see his parents. Jimmy was a dutiful son—he stopped by at least once a week to see if there was anything he could do to help out. On the other hand, his parents still didn't know he was gay. *Family*, Lee thought as he ascended the steps of his brownstone. Secrets were inevitable, he supposed; the question was whether they would backfire in the end.

A light snow had begun to fall as he stood on his front stoop and fished his keys out of his pocket. He was about to go in when the faint sound of singing floated across the street. It was coming from the Ukrainian church on the south side of Seventh Street. He crossed the street and walked up the stone steps of the church. The heavy wooden door gave way when he pushed, and he tiptoed inside. A choir of about thirty people was singing Christmas music, perhaps getting ready for an upcoming concert. They were launching into something by Benjamin Britten when he took a seat in the last pew.

As he sat listening to the ethereal voices floating high into the arches of the vaulted stone ceiling, a contemplative mood settled over him, as it so often did when he listened to music. *What strange creatures we are,* he thought, *capable of the best and worst Nature has to offer.* At home in the ballad and the battlefield, a race of choirboys and murderers.

He looked around the church. Poinsettias with crisp red bows adorned the altar, and boughs of holly had been fastened to the entrance to each pew. Lee had always loved the trappings of Christmas—the decorations, the lights, the rituals and aromas. Gingerbread baking, candles glowing softly in a stone chapel, the sound of carols drifting in from the street. He found a richness and sense of the sacred in the long, dark nights of winter lacking in languid, promiscuous summer days. When the earth was dead, and Nature had pulled up her tents and crept away into the deep of night, he felt the center of existence all around him—there, in the very death of things, was a sense of the Infinite.

He remembered a Christmas evening many years before—and the discovery of a secret that revealed exactly what it was his mother blamed his father for.

Late one night, when he was home from Princeton for the Christmas break, he and Laura were left alone in the house in Stockton, New Jersey—his mother was at a party in the neighboring town of Pennington. They had just put up the tree and were rooting around in the closet where Fiona kept the Christmas ornaments. They had been drinking eggnog liberally spiked with rum, and Laura was humming Christmas carols as she pulled out boxes of ornaments wrapped in crumpled bits of tissue paper that were faded and brittle with age. Fiona never could stand to throw away anything that might be useful, including old tissue paper, so the ornaments were carefully wrapped in the same ragged, yellowed bits of paper year after year.

Laura was in the middle of a verse of "Hark! The Herald Angels Sing" when she leaned forward and pulled out a green leather scrapbook.

"Hey, look at this," she said to Lee, who was perched on a stepladder trying to fix the star on top of the tree so that it was pointing toward the ceiling instead of toward the first-floor broom closet.

"What is it?" he asked, trying to balance on one knee on the stepladder so he could adjust the star without getting stabbed by its pointed silver spikes shooting out in all directions. His mother always had a star at the top of the Christmas tree. It was one of those unquestioned traditions, like plum pudding and roast beef on Christmas day.

"Ouch!" he said as a pine needle pierced his sleeve. His mother always favored the sharp, short-needled trees, disdaining the ones with long, soft needles as "not real pine trees."

"Come down here and look at this," his sister said, pulling up a chair to study the scrapbook in front of the fire blazing merrily in the hearth.

There, placed in the middle of the scrapbook between the pictures of him and his sister as children—playing with cousins, opening Christmas presents and dressing their cat in baby clothes—was an envelope filled with love letters. They were from a woman named Chloe, and they were written to Lee and Laura's father. With trembling hands, they read the first one.

*Dearest Duncan,*
*How long it has been since I've seen you! The days crawl on unbearably, until I think I will go mad. When can you come see me, my love? Hurry, hurry to be by my side—I will count the days!*

*Your only love,*
*Chloe*

For the next hour, Lee and Laura sat on the floor next to the half-decorated Christmas tree and read the letters, one by one. Some were short, like the first one; others were longer, filled with happy accounts of events and places and people—skating at Rockefeller Center, boating in Central Park, dinners at cozy restaurants. Chloe, whoever she was, lived in the city, and their father had been seeing her for some time, over at least a two-year period, according to the dates on the letters.

Finally, their necks stiff from bending over the pages, they returned each one to the envelope and slipped it back inside the scrapbook. They sat there without saying anything, until finally Lee spoke.

"So that's what happened."

They both agreed not to mention it to his mother—it was a secret she had been keeping for a reason. Maybe she didn't want their pity, maybe she didn't want to relive that horrible time, maybe she was ashamed. It was even possible she was trying to protect their memories of their father. Whatever the reason, they agreed it was her right to keep her counsel, no matter how they felt about it.

Lee was jolted back into the present by the sound of

chairs scraping across the stone floor. The choir had finished its rehearsal, and the singers were moving chairs back into place before leaving. Before anyone could come to the rear of the church and ask him what he was doing there, he rose from the pew and crept out into the night. The snow was falling heavily now—several inches were already on the ground, and the Weather Channel was predicting more, a good old-fashioned winter snowstorm.

*Good,* he thought as he snapped his front-door lock into place and stomped the wet from his shoes. Maybe it would slow down the killer they were pursuing.

As he shook the snow from his coat and pulled off one shoe, the phone rang. Thinking it might be Detective Butts, he snatched up the receiver.

"Hello?" he said, standing awkwardly on one leg while he tried to remove his other shoe.

"Hi."

It was Kathy Azarian. He took a deep breath and sank into the red leather chair by the window.

"Hi," he said, keeping his voice steady, uninflected.

"I, uh, just wanted to call and see how you're doing."

"Fine. And you?"

"I'm okay." There was a pause and then a deep sigh. "Oh, God," she said, "can we just—"

"What, Kathy? Just what?"

"Can I see you?"

"Why? Do you have something to say?"

"I just want to see you, for Christ's sake. Is that a crime?"

"In some states it might be."

She laughed, a short burst of misery. "I'm glad you still have your sense of humor."

Her unhappiness gave him unexpected buoyancy. He sang softly, " 'No, no, they can't take that away from me—' "

"Now you're just milking it."

"May I remind you, I'm the injured party here?"

"You make it sound like a goddamn lawsuit," she snapped.

"Just calling it like I see it."

"So now you're an umpire?"

"Look, if you want to talk, we'll talk. But if you want to argue—"

"I'm on my way into New York. Can we meet tonight?"

It was the last thing he wanted. Their breakup, if that's what it was, had been confusing and painful, and he didn't really want to dive back into that dark pool just yet. She had met someone else, or so she said—so why come to him now?

"Okay," he said. "Where do you want to meet?"

"Battery Park City, if you don't mind."

"Okay."

"I'll call you again when my train gets in, and we'll set it up."

"Right," he said, and he hung up.

He sat in the red leather armchair and looked out at the cold, still night sky, void of twinkling stars, their pale light eaten up by the voracious wattage of the city. Things had started so well with Kathy. They spent that first summer hurling themselves into the humid air, driven by hunger and romance, to dark, cozy corners in their favorite hangouts. There was the Life Café, with its Goth waitresses slouching between tables, all purple eye shadow, pale skin and green hair, sleek in tights and black skirts, serving strong coffee and heaping burritos, or the Royal India, steaming platters of papadam and vindaloo that set their tongues on fire and their eyes streaming. And of course McSorley's—dirty, loud and boisterous, where the waiters were ex-cops and the clientele future felons.

But it all went wrong somehow, as these things sometimes did, and now she was reaching out to him again—but why? He put on his coat to begin the long trudge down to Battery Park, where the Hudson River emptied out into the roiling currents and channels of New York Harbor.

Perhaps, he thought as he slung on his coat, he was not the only one abroad on this cold winter night.

# Chapter Twelve

They agreed to meet at a little seafood joint overlooking the Hudson River in Battery Park City, where Kathy would be staying at a friend's place. The snow was falling heavily when he arrived ten minutes early—big fat flakes tumbling from the night sky. She was already there, tucked away in a dark corner, underneath a white life preserver with the name of the restaurant stenciled on it in bold black letters. An empty wineglass sat on the table in front of her.

"My train was ahead of schedule," she said apologetically when he slid into the seat opposite her.

The place was quiet—Tuesday evening was a good time to avoid crowds in New York restaurants. A young couple sat at the bar, their hands resting casually on each other's knees. A grizzled man in a parka perched on a stool at the end, watching the evening news on the bar's TV.

They were the only other patrons. A few of the kitchen staff sat at an empty table, resting their feet. They were young and stocky with caramel skin and straight black hair—probably Mexicans or Guatemalans. Lee had often thought that every restaurant in New York would shut down if Immigration suddenly decided to ask for papers for every kitchen worker in the city. Kitchens in Chinatown were filled with illegal Chinese immigrants, and a steady stream of workers from Central America kept hungry New Yorkers fed. They were hardworking, smart and efficient—they took the jobs no one else wanted and excelled at them.

A slim young waiter with slicked-back hair slinked up to them and took their drink orders. Lee asked for a Scotch, and Kathy ordered another glass of Cabernet.

"Looks like you're already one step ahead of me," he remarked as the waiter removed her empty glass.

She avoided meeting his eyes. "I kind of needed it."

"I would have done the same thing."

Looking at her, he finally felt that the connection between them was broken. It was as if he was seeing her for the first time—but not in a nostalgic, romantic way. A veil had been lifted from his eyes, and all that was familiar and dear about her had vanished. His view of her was suddenly coldly objective. The person sitting across from him was small and dark, with a sallow complexion very different from his own. All that was foreign and exotic about her, all that had excited him, struck him now as odd and off-putting: the preternatural whiteness of her teeth, her dark eyes with their long black lashes.

Even the wayward curl in the middle of her forehead failed to stir feelings of desire. Instead, he found himself wondering if she arranged it that way on purpose, knowing how fetching it was. The thought of something so charming being intentional crushed its allure for him. If the curl was planned, then it was no longer so enticing.

He mentioned none of this. Instead, he said, "You want something to eat?"

She lowered her head, the rogue curl flopping lower on her forehead. *Was that on purpose? Did she know what he was thinking?*

"No, thanks," she said, not looking at him.

He took a swallow of Scotch and felt the welcome burn in the back of his throat. "I'm thinking of getting a cat."

She looked up. "What?"

"My therapist thinks it will be good for me."

She frowned, deepening the dimple in her chin. "Men don't have cats."

"Isn't that a sexist attitude?"

"Why not a dog?"

"Too high-maintenance. A cat is easier."

She gave a little smile. "What will your therapist come up with next?"

"She's someone I can rely on."

"And I'm not—is that what you're saying?"

"I wasn't trying to make a point. But it's important to have someone you can trust."

"Look, I know I'm not really there for you right now, and I'm sorry about that."

"So," he said, lurching into the conversation they had both been avoiding for weeks, "do you think you have a future with him?" He wasn't going to say the name, though it was written in neon in his brain: *Peter. Peter, Peter, Pumpkin Eater . . .*

Her lips tightened, and she clasped her hands so tightly, the color left her fingers.

"I don't *know*."

"Is it something you want to explore?"

She raised her gaze to meet his. He had never seen her face look so dark, so troubled.

"I wish you wouldn't be so goddamn *agreeable* about this. You should be angry at me."

"What makes you think I'm not?"

"Then why are you behaving so damn *decently*?"

"What do you mean?"

"You're just making it more difficult."

He felt the anger bubbling up in his throat and fought it back down.

"I'm sorry if I'm spoiling your getaway plan. We can just call it quits right now, if that's what you want."

"I know I've been impossible lately. It's just that I don't know when . . ." She stared out the window at the moody gray waters of the Hudson. A hardy little band of mallards made their way upriver, paddling strenuously as they struggled against the current, the harbor lights glistening on their shiny green feathers.

"You don't know when I'm going to shake off my depression and anxiety and behave normally."

"I don't blame you—"

"But it's hard to live with."

"And not being able to talk about certain things—"

"Like my father."

"Yeah."

"Look, I'm glad your father is a swell guy you have a good relationship with. But it doesn't work that way with everyone."

"I *know* that, Lee; it's just—"

He wrapped his fingers around the tumbler of Scotch and gazed into the tawny liquid. "*Do* you know, really?"

"I don't want to lie to you and pretend everything is fine. . . ."

"You know what?" he said. This conversation was exhausting, and he had had enough. "I think we both need some time off to think about this, and I've got other things going on."

She looked a little stunned by his tone of voice. He hadn't meant for it to come out so angrily.

"Okay."

"Fine," he said, getting up to leave. He dropped two twenties onto the table. "I'll be seeing you around."

"Lee—wait."

He turned back to her.

"What?"

"I—I still care about you, you know."

"Let me know when you have it worked out. And good luck with the pumpkin eater."

He pulled up his coat collar and walked away without looking back. He left the restaurant and headed down the steps to the river, the snow stinging his face. He could hear the water lapping up against the moorings, and the creak of the ropes as the boats strained against them. The seagulls circled and cried high in the sky above him, their harsh voices floating out over the waves, only to vanish into the thin, wintry air.

# Chapter Thirteen

He decided to walk home and struck out across the icy tundra of Battery Park. The storm had sculpted a thick layer of frozen snow and ice over the benches and fence posts. It reminded him of the white frosting his mother used to spread over angel food cake, his father's favorite. He shook off the memory—he hated thinking about his father.

Walking north toward the Winter Garden, Lee was surprised that he didn't feel overwhelming sadness. Emptiness, yes, but it wasn't entirely unpleasant. Part of him longed to wash his hands of everything he had known—to make a break and sail away into an unknown future. He had read of people who left their lives behind and invented new identities, and had always wondered what that would be like. Of course, most of them were con artists in search of another mark, but there was something enticing about walking away from responsibilities and expectations and the exhausting rituals of human interaction. Then it occurred to him: that was exactly what his father had done—at great cost to the people he'd left behind.

Such thoughts like could be a precursor to a major

depressive episode, so he tried to steer his mind elsewhere. He couldn't afford illness right now; there was too much riding on his ability to help solve the Alleyway Strangler case. But everyone and everything in his life felt like a burden. He loved his mother and his niece—and Kathy, he supposed—but he felt hemmed in and longed for some air.

He found solace walking alone through the city on nights like this, when few people ventured out onto the icy streets. He loved wandering the nearly empty blocks of one of the world's most populous cities. New York became his own private park, a landscape both charming and gritty but always interesting.

At the front entrance to the Winter Garden, an elderly couple in matching red parkas picked their way carefully across a patch of ice. The man held the woman's elbow protectively, steadying her. He wondered if he and Kathy would ever be that couple, or if it was finished between them forever.

He turned east on Vesey Street. With each step he felt lighter. What was wrong with him? He cared about Kathy—loved her, even—and yet he was relieved. *She* had made the decision, not him, and that lightened his burden. He felt guilty that he didn't feel worse, as he waited for the light at West Street.

The traffic wasn't as thick as usual, but a steady stream of cars crept along the four lanes of highway. Chunks of ice and snow rattled beneath their tires, picked up and then spit out a few yards later. The city's snowplows couldn't keep up, even though sanitation workers had pulled double shifts to work through the night. He always thought it would be kind of fun to be on snow patrol during a storm—but then, Lee supposed most jobs looked better from the outside.

People at parties were sometimes impressed with what he did for a living, but they didn't realize it came with a grinding sense of responsibility and pressure to solve a case. He was often called in as a last resort, when ordinary crime-solving techniques failed. There was little glamour in police work. Mountains of paperwork, sore feet, and long hours, but not much glamour.

He headed north through Tribeca, once an area of dilapidated warehouses and deserted factories, now one of the swankiest neighborhoods in Manhattan. Sturdy redbrick Beaux Arts buildings presided over boutiques, upscale restaurants and specialty food palaces like the Gourmet Garage. The rents here rivaled those of the penthouse suites of the Upper East Side. Glancing at the menu of a pricey Italian joint, he was glad he lived in the East Village, where the NYU student population kept the prices down.

He felt his cell phone vibrate in his jacket pocket. He dug it out and saw that it was Chuck Morton calling. He flipped it open.

"Hiya, Chuck."

"Hi." His friend didn't sound good at all. His voice was flat, dead.

"What's the matter?"

"Mind if I stay with you for a few days?"

That was Chuck, always getting right to the point.

"Is everything okay?"

"I'd rather not go into it right now."

"Sure," he said, stepping over a snowdrift. "When did you want to come?"

"Can I come tonight?"

"Okay. Where are you?"

"I'm at the Port Authority."

"Wow. I'm headed home now—can you give me about thirty minutes?"

"Thanks. I owe you one."

"No problem—see you soon."

He slipped the phone back into his pocket and continued to trudge east through snowbanks and ice. He welcomed the extreme weather; somehow it put the emotional pain on hold, took his focus off it.

The bleakness of the landscape was a comfort as he plowed his way from one river toward the other. At times like this he was reminded that Manhattan was an island—and not a very big one. The borough was so rich and fascinating that it was easy to forget it was less than thirty-four square miles.

But now his mind was on the imminent arrival of his old college roommate and best friend. Susan Beaumont Morton was trouble; he had known it almost from the day he'd met her in college and certainly by the time Chuck married her. She was a piranha in pink, a carnivore in Chanel, a velociraptor in Versace. Her expensive taste in clothing and jewelry was matched only by her voracious appetite for adulation. It wasn't men she liked—it was the attention they gave her. Once she had a man's devotion, she quickly tired of him.

Lee had done her the indignity of tiring of her first, and she'd never forgiven him for it. It hadn't taken him long to see that beneath the Southern manners and fluttering eyelashes lurked the hungry soul of a predator. She'd quickly moved on to his roommate, Chuck, who was so stunned by her beauty and charm that he toppled hard and fast—and never got up.

Until now, at any rate. Marriage and kids in the suburbs was a far cry from privately staffed eating clubs, rugby parties, and classes in the hallowed ivy halls of Princeton. Maybe the bloom was off the rose, and Chuck had finally seen past her act. But what had made him snap? Lee would soon find out.

Ahead of him, a plow rumbled up the Bowery, throwing a thick sheet of snow onto the curb, its engine whirring and howling like a wild beast as it continued relentlessly northward. Susan was like the plow—inexorable, unstoppable. Or maybe she was more like the storm itself, a force of Nature.

On the sidewalk, a couple of small boys dug into the drift made by the plow and hurled snowballs at each other, laughing and tumbling into the soft mounds of snow. Children knew how to enjoy the cold weather. He had an impulse to grab a fistful of snow and fling it at someone—anyone. But the urge passed, and he continued home. Chuck would be waiting for him.

# CHAPTER FOURTEEN

Lee had been in his apartment for about ten minutes when there was a knock on the front door. He opened it to see Chuck Morton standing there, suitcase in hand, a hangdog expression on his face. Stiff spokes of blond hair protruded from the blue stocking cap on his head; his cheeks were flushed, and he sported a day-old beard growth.

"Your neighbor let me in downstairs," he said. "It's just for a few days, I promise."

"Don't worry about it," Lee replied, opening the door wider. "Come on in."

Chuck stepped inside and looked around. "I can't believe it's been so long since I was here."

"Life has a way of intervening." He decided not to add a comment about Chuck's being married with kids. "Come on, I'll show you to your room."

He took Chuck to the study on the other side of the living room.

"This is your bed," he said, pointing to the pullout sofa. "It's pretty comfortable, actually. And you even have a closet. Sorry it's not very big."

"No, this is great, really. I could have stayed with friends in Jersey, but they're all married, and—well, I'm trying to keep it low-key right now. I'll try not to be in your way."

"We managed to get along in college with a lot less space."

"We were just kids then."

"How do young people do it?"

"I guess they don't need as much privacy."

"You hungry?" Lee asked.

"I could use a drink."

"Scotch?"

"Red or black?" said Chuck.

"Black. Unless you want a single malt."

"That would be a waste—I'm drinking for the effect, not the taste."

"Black it is, then. Ice?"

"Sure, thanks."

He poured Chuck a double shot of Johnnie Walker and made an orange juice for himself. They sat in the living room, Chuck on the sofa and Lee in the leather armchair opposite.

"I like the piano there next to the window," Chuck said. "You still play?"

"Yeah. It keeps me sane—relatively speaking."

Chuck gave a nervous laugh. "Yeah, right."

"So you want to talk about it?"

Chuck took a swallow of Scotch. "Not really. But I guess I have to, right?"

"Something happen?"

He clenched his fist. "Of all the goddamn people—a goddamn dentist."

"Dentist?"

"Yip Whitely. What kind of a goddamn name is that, 'Yip'? Sounds like a fucking dog."

Lee waited. He had a good idea of where this was going but wasn't about to jump in.

"I'd been hearing stray remarks, you know, but I'd been hearing rumors about Susan ever since we got together at Princeton. You know how people could be about her."

"Yeah, I know." What he didn't say was that those rumors weren't always false.

"So I ignored it, and then I happen to see her cell phone bill one day. She does all the paperwork, the bills, that kind of thing, but it was just kind of lying around, so I happened to glance at it, you know?"

"Right." Maybe it was more than that—maybe he'd dug it out because he was suspicious, but if so, Lee had to grant him that little white lie, to protect his pride.

"So I see this phone number, a lot, and I ask her who it is, and she says it's her friend Julie. Something about it didn't sit right, so I called the number, and a man answered. I hung up and did a reverse directory search, and it was Yip Whitely—her goddamn dentist." He ran a hand through his short blond hair. "I mean, Christ, I'm a cop—does she really think she can keep secrets from me?"

"You're not just a cop—hell, you're a damn commander." Chuck Morton was Captain of the Major Case Squad in the Bronx, a position he had worked like a dog to get—and hold on to.

Chuck looked shell-shocked. He had the kind of vacant stare Lee had seen on crime victims. Marital infidelity wasn't an easy thing for the two of them to talk about. They might be best friends, but they were still men, more comfortable wielding a hammer than talking about their feelings.

But, not for the first time, Chuck Morton was full of surprises. Gulping down the last of his drink, he set the tumbler on the coffee table and leaned forward.

"You used to be a therapist. What do you think I should do?"

Lee gave a nervous laugh. "Hell, *that's* not a loaded question, is it?"

It was even more loaded than his friend knew. Chuck was only aware of some of the history between Lee and his wife. Of course he knew that the two of them had dated at Princeton. But there were other things he had managed to ignore—Susan's flirtations with Lee over the years, her rapacious need for the attention of other men, her unpopularity among women.

People were fooled by her blond beauty and Southern charm, but it was a mask. She could flatter her way into any situation, and usually by the time people wised up to her, the damage was done.

Lee did what any other coward would do under the circumstances—he stalled for time. He pointed to Chuck's empty glass.

"You look like you could use a refill."

"Thanks."

In the kitchen, Lee poured his friend a generous shot. He grabbed some ice from the freezer, plunked a few cubes into Chuck's glass, and went back to the living room. He realized he couldn't stall forever, but he couldn't help hoping the phone would ring.

He handed Chuck his drink and eased himself back into the armchair. Cold weather aggravated an old rugby injury in his right knee.

"Leg bothering you?" said Chuck.

"It's not too bad." *Safe territory, sports injuries*. He decided to stall some more. "How's your shoulder?"

"It's okay." Chuck did his best to smile and almost pulled it off. "It was worth it, scoring that try against Yale." A *try* was the term in rugby for scoring, like a goal in soccer.

"Only try of the whole season scored by a fullback," Lee said.

"Yeah."

"You were a damn good fullback."

"That's nice, coming from the team captain."

"And now you're a captain, and I'm just a team player."

"I wouldn't put it that way."

"Mind if I ask you something?"

"Shoot."

"Does she know where you are?"

"I had to tell her. The kids, you know. Hope she doesn't bug you with phone calls."

"Don't worry about it," he said, but he was thinking, *I hope so too.*

Lee knew that Susan, entrenched in the lifestyle of a police captain's wife, wasn't going to give up easily. The question was, how hard was Chuck prepared to fight to break away?

"So what do you think I should do?" Chuck said again.

"I can't tell you what to do, but you can stay here as long as you need to."

"Thanks," Chuck said, giving another painful smile.

The smile slid away, and he took a shallow, ragged breath. A strangling sound came from his throat and turned into deep, heaving sobs.

Lee watched with empathy and embarrassment as his best friend cried like a baby. A third emotion bubbled up inside him: anger. The woman who had caused so much pain wasn't worth the price of one piece of expensive jewelry on her elegantly manicured hands.

"Christ, Lee, tell me *something*," Chuck said. "Tell me I'm an idiot to be with her."

"You know that's not for me to say."

"I know, I know. I just—I can't seem to stop loving her, even when I think she's no good. Am I just a damn fool?"

"You wouldn't be the first one."

Chuck leaned forward, elbows on his knees, his hands tightly clasped. Lee noticed he was still wearing his gold wedding ring.

"Has she come to you?" Chuck asked quietly.

"I haven't spoken to her in quite a while."

"So she hasn't called you?"

"No."

"You'd tell me if she told you anything, wouldn't you?"

"I don't see why she'd come to me."

That wasn't entirely true. Susan Morton enjoyed flirting with him, just to see if she could get a rise out of him. She did that with every man she met, but especially with Lee. She didn't like rejection, and he had rejected her. Even though it was years ago, it still rankled her, and she was punishing him for it.

He looked out at the snowflakes flinging themselves against the windowpanes. It was going to be a long night.

# Chapter Fifteen

"Man, you look awful," Jimmy Chen said.

"Thanks," Lee replied, rubbing his right temple. However tired he was this morning, he figured Chuck must be feeling worse—he would be fighting a hangover along with lack of sleep. But he was already dressed and gone by the time Lee woke up around seven.

"You sure you're up to this, Angus?" Jimmy asked. "I can handle it on my own, you know."

"I'm fine. Let's just get on with it."

"Feeling touchy this morning, are we?" Jimmy said as they swung onto Fourteenth Street off Seventh Avenue.

"Put a sock in it," Lee replied.

They entered the creamy Beaux Arts building housing the Manhattan campus of Pratt Institute. The interviews with Lisa Adler's roommate and boyfriend hadn't turned up much, so they had lined up interviews with members of the art class Lisa had posed for. It didn't seem like a very promising lead, but in an investigation like this, thoroughness was everything. As

Butts liked to say, "You never know what vermin are hiding out underneath the woodpile."

There didn't seem to be any vermin hiding under this particular woodpile—just a handful of frightened-looking design students huddled around the grand staircase leading up to the art gallery.

No one seemed to know Lisa very well; the only one who even knew her name was the graduate student who had hired her, a handsome young Iranian named Amin Rasmani. He was the last one they talked to, as the others wandered off in the direction of various classes. Lee had observed before that art students often had a dreamy look, as if only part of them was physically present at any given time. Laura had had that look sometimes, and he wondered if it had made her vulnerable to whatever creep snatched her away.

"So how did you meet Lisa?" Jimmy asked, peering intently at Amin. Lee wondered if he was trying to intimidate the kid, but Amin Rasmani had too much poise to fall for that. His accent was the King's English, with only a hint of his Middle Eastern origins; his manner was aristocratic and refined.

"She wandered in one day while a life drawing class was going on," Rasmani said. "I saw her out in the hallway. When I asked her if she was looking for someone, she said a peculiar thing."

"Yeah?" Jimmy asked. "What was that?"

"She said, 'I'll know it when I find him.' "

Jimmy gave a short laugh. "Sounds like a come-on to me. I'll bet a lot of chicks go for you, huh?"

Rasmani looked insulted by this remark. "Detective, I have a fiancée in Iran."

Jimmy wasn't about to be put off the scent. "I'm just sayin', I'll bet you're a chick magnet, with those big dark eyes and all." He shot a glance at Lee, though Lee had no idea what response he expected. Whatever game Jimmy was playing, it wasn't going well. Rasmani's body language indicated that he was about to clam up, so Lee decided to intervene.

"Your English is perfect," he said. "Have you been in this country long?"

The question seemed to relax him. "Not long. I read philosophy at Cambridge and spent half my childhood in England. My mother is British," he added, with a glance at Jimmy.

Lee's intuition was right—the kid came from money and privilege all the way. He would have had that in common with Lisa Adler. He wondered what else they might have in common.

"Did you socialize with Lisa at all after class?" Lee asked.

"Not really," Rasmani said too quickly. His eyes darted to the side, and in that moment Lee knew he was hiding something.

They couldn't get him to admit anything, though, and finally let him go, after Jimmy gave him a business card and the usual "call-me-if-you-think-of-anything" spiel.

"He did her," Jimmy said as they emerged into the afternoon bustle of West Fourteenth Street. "He's trying to hide it from us, but that guy totally *did* her."

"You have such a charming way of expressing yourself," said Lee. "Did anyone ever tell you that?"

"Only me dear old mum," Jimmy replied in an atrocious attempt at a Cockney accent. "She's not nearly as hot as your mom, though," he added, poking Lee in the shoulder.

"Don't you ever let up?" said Lee as they hailed a cab back to the precinct.

"Not 'ardly, mate," said Jimmy, taking another stab at the Cockney routine.

"You sound like a drunken Benny Hill," Lee remarked as they climbed into the cab.

Jimmy grinned. "Oh, *snap*. You got me, bruthuh, right where it hurts—my ability to mimic the Round Eyes. Jimmy stick to cooking pork flied lice," he added in an exaggerated Chinese accent.

The cab driver, a Sikh in a white turban, shot a glance at them in the rearview mirror. Lee poked his friend and put a finger to his lips. Jimmy got the hint and shut up for the rest of the journey.

# Chapter Sixteen

Jimmy and Lee reported in at the precinct house to tell Butts what they had learned. He listened, chewing on a Slim Jim. When they were done, he tossed the remainder of the beef jerky into the trash, stood up and stretched.

"Okay, talk to you tomorrow. Wife's waitin' at home—I think it's meat loaf tonight."

"Right," said Jimmy. "By the way, I like the Columbo routine."

Butts frowned, merging the pockmarks on his forehead. "What?"

"The whole rumpled thing, the turkey sandwich in the pocket, the absentminded routine—it's very good. I thought maybe you copied it off *Columbo*."

"What do you mean?"

"You mean, it's not an act?"

Lee tried to catch Jimmy's eye and failed.

Butts stopped putting on his coat, and his eyes narrowed. "Look, Chen, you're a pal of Doc's, and so I guess you're okay. But do I need to remind you who's in charge of this investigation?"

"No, I just thought—"

"Well, don't, okay? It's not working out too well for you right now."

Jimmy flushed and turned away. "Jeez. I didn't mean anything by it."

"Never mind," Lee said. "We should let the man get home to his meat loaf. I'm sure he'll be in a better mood tomorrow," he added with a meaningful glance at Butts, who just grunted.

Lee and Jimmy headed down Third Avenue together, wading through the puddles of slush gathered in the intersections. Snow didn't stay pretty in New York very long, and a warm front had turned the streets into a slushy mess.

"I didn't know—really," Jimmy said as they walked downtown in the gathering twilight. "I thought he was putting on an act."

"Don't worry about it," said Lee. "He's a little odd."

"A *little* odd?" Jimmy laughed. "He's a goddamn cartoon character!"

"You know," Lee said, "we all have our . . . idiosyncrasies."

Jimmy stepped over a pile of slush. "I don't like where you're going with this, Angus."

"I'm just saying . . ."

"Listen, I gotta stay with my little brother tonight. My parents are going to my aunt's in Boston."

"Boston?" said Lee with mock astonishment. "There are Chinese people in *Boston*?"

"You velly funny, Round Eyes," Jimmy said.

"How are they getting there?"

"They're taking the Fung Wah bus," Jimmy said, sidestepping a beggar with a greasy beard and wild cocaine eyes. "Twenty bucks round-trip."

The man wore a Santa hat; Lee imagined him crashing someone's Christmas party. The panhandler started to approach them but thought better of it and turned away, muttering to himself, "Twenty bucks round-trip to *hell*. What a bargain—buy 'em while they last."

He tottered up First Avenue, steadying himself on parking meters and lampposts. No one looked directly at him; other pedestrians strode briskly past him, averting their eyes like good New Yorkers. You could always tell out-of-towners by the way they dealt with panhandlers—too much eye contact. That's all the encouragement most of them needed to launch into their spiel. Lee watched the man thread his way through the rush hour throng of pedestrians crowding the avenue, wondering what his story was and how he'd gotten to that point in his life.

"I've heard about these Chinatown buses—so they really are that cheap?" Lee asked Jimmy.

"Yep. Of course, you take your life into your hands with some of the drivers, but Chinese people love to gamble, so that's part of the fun."

"Thank God you're above racial stereotypes."

"Cultural, my man, not racial—there's a difference. Are you telling me you white Anglo-Saxon Protestants aren't repressed? When's the last time you went dancing?"

"Actually, I like to dance."

"When's the last time you *went*?"

"Okay, you win—I'm repressed, all right?"

"And my old man likes to gamble. So what? It's part of our culture," Jimmy said, turning to look at a young man in tight jeans with windswept blond hair. He preferred dating Caucasian men, whom he called "humpies."

"Hey, I've never met your brother," said Lee. "You want some company?"

"Sure, if you got nothing better to do. What about that girl of yours?"

"That's on the rocks."

"That's a shame. She sounded nice."

"How did you know about her?"

Jimmy winked at him. "I get around, Angus. My Chinese name means *The Shadow*."

"Really?"

"Actually, it means *peaceful clarity*." Jimmy laughed. "Doesn't really sound like me, does it?"

"*Peaceful* doesn't exactly fit you."

"That's what I'm saying," he agreed as they passed Great Jones Street, home to a beautiful old firehouse. A couple of firefighters lingered outside Engine 33, Ladder 9, leaning against the brick building, suspenders dangling from their black rubber trousers.

In post-9/11 New York, firemen had become what movie stars were to the rest of the country. In this town, every waiter was an actor and every restaurant hostess a model, and most people took the presence of celebrities casually. Film stars were routinely glimpsed on the Seventy-ninth Street crosstown bus, viewed using the stair machine at the gym or seen shopping at Zabar's; they were even likely to turn up at a Wednesday night AA meeting in a local church basement. It was a point of honor for any true New Yorker to regard these people as part of the scenery, hardly worth a second glance. Oh, they felt the reflected glory, all right—down deep, New Yorkers believed they were living in the center of the universe.

But after September 11, firefighters were more than celebrities: they were gods. The city embraced its fallen heroes and their comrades with a fervor uncommon even in a city of extremes. There was an air of ragged desperation around the edges of this fervor, but then, in the months following the attack, everyone had been a little overwrought.

Jimmy smiled at the firemen, and one of them gave a friendly wave—a handsome devil with thick black hair and eyebrows. No wonder Kathy was so taken with New York firefighters. But then, every woman Lee had ever known said the same thing: firemen were dreamy. Judging by the look on Jimmy's face, he agreed.

"Hey, I could go for pizza," his friend said, eyeing a storefront with a large pepperoni pie in the window.

"What about your lactose intolerance?"

Jimmy held up a bottle of Lactaid. "Meet the Chinaman's best friend, my man. Come on—I'm buying."

Lee had always felt that Jimmy's restless energy was hiding something—a darkness of the soul, perhaps, or a secret sorrow—but his friend never exposed that side of himself. He always radiated the buoyancy of a game-show host or a tour guide, and Lee had to admit, sometimes it was easier just to go along for the ride. Like the Fung Wah bus, though, it felt a little crazy, as if things could spin out of control at any minute.

He took a breath of frosty air and followed Jimmy inside. It occurred to him that maybe he, too, liked to gamble. But like a lot of gamblers, he realized he might not know it was time to pull out until it was too late.

# CHAPTER SEVENTEEN

Jimmy's parents lived above the restaurant his father once owned, the Happy Good Luck Palace, on Pell Street. The smell of Peking duck and Sichuan pepper sauce floated up the creaky stairwell as they ascended the narrow steps to the second floor. The Chens' apartment took up the entire floor, which was probably not more than twelve hundred square feet. The rooms were small but tidy, the windowsills laden with many different varieties of plants.

"My mom's into growing her own herbal remedies," Jimmy said as they passed clay pots of exotic vegetation. "It's a habit she brought over from China."

"You'll be in good hands if you burn yourself," Lee remarked, glancing at a robust-looking aloe vera plant.

"Yeah, right," his friend said, leading them to the back of the apartment to Barry's bedroom. Jimmy knocked on the flimsy wooden door, waited for a response and, getting none, knocked again. When he was again met with silence, he opened the door and went in.

The lighting in the room was minimal; the two small windows facing north were covered with thin white cotton curtains. Lee could see in the dim light that the room, though small, was uncluttered and almost obsessively orderly.

"Barry doesn't like bright light," Jimmy said. "It makes him anxious."

His brother sat in front of a flat-screen computer monitor, studying math problems. In the green light from the computer screen Lee could make out Barry's features, though the thick glasses he wore obscured his eyes. Though not as handsome as his brother, Barry Chen had the same long face and aquiline nose. He had the frank, open expression of a child, though he looked to be in his thirties.

"Hi, Barry," said Jimmy. His brother responded by rocking back and forth in his chair and waving both hands in the air. It was hard to tell if the wave was a greeting or a signal to leave.

"Nice computer," said Lee.

"Nice computer," Barry echoed, his expression unchanging. His voice was flat and nasal, curiously uninflected. He continued to rock back and forth, staring at the screen.

"He does that sometimes," Jimmy told Lee. "Especially when he first meets people. Don't take it personally."

"Don't take it personally," Barry said, still looking at the computer.

"No problem," said Lee.

"No problems except math problems," said Barry. "In *fact*, math problems are the best."

"Is that what you're doing, math problems?" Lee asked.

"Doing math problems," Barry replied, typing.

"Jimmy says you're very good at math."

"Jimmy says," echoed Barry in his nasal voice. "Jimmy says this, Jimmy says that."

"Hey, Barry, tell Lee what your name is short for."

"Barrington. Barry, short for Barrington," he said.

"Wow," said Lee. "Nice name."

"Isn't that a kick?" said Jimmy. "My parents wanted to give their kids hyper-British names, so they chose Barrington."

"Barry, short for Barrington," said Barry, rocking.

Jimmy shook his head. "That kills me—Chinese parents trying to fit in, so they choose the most Anglo-sounding name they can think of, one of those hyper-British names like Winston or Nigel or something. Who names their kid Barrington, for Christ's sake?"

"Barrington, short for Barry," said Barry.

"You've got it backward," Jimmy said. "It's the other way around."

"Asymmetry," said Barry. "In *fact*, I prefer symmetry."

"You mean, like in math?" asked Lee.

"In math, in *fact*, in life, and everywhere."

"He likes numbers," said Jimmy.

"In fact," Barry said, "numbers have a relationship to each other. No two numbers are alike."

"We know, Barry," Jimmy said gently.

"In fact, if you line up prime numbers on a grid, you can get—"

Jimmy put a hand on his shoulder. "Barry, my friend can't stay very long, okay?"

His brother looked at him with the same blank expression. "How long is he staying?"

"I don't know exactly," said Jimmy, "But not long."

"*Exactly* how long?" Barry said, rocking. "How long?"

"Five minutes and twenty-three seconds," Jimmy blurted out.

That seemed to calm Barry. He turned back to his computer screen and typed the numbers, while reciting them under his breath. "Five-minutes-and-twenty-three-seconds . . . twenty-three is a prime number, of course, and the number five is common in Nature." He typed some more, peering at his screen.

"He loves the Internet," Jimmy whispered to Lee.

Barry stared at the computer, reading. "The starfish has five legs, we have five fingers on each hand, and many flowers have groupings of five petals. Five is the basis of the geometrical shape of pentagrams—"

"That's all very interesting, Barry," Jimmy said, "but my friend has to get going."

"In five minutes and twenty-three seconds," Barry said, waving his fingers in the air. He peered at the clock at the bottom of his computer screen. "It has now been exactly one minute and forty-eight seconds."

"He loves clocks too—anything to do with numbers," Jimmy said.

"That's great," said Lee. "You're very good with numbers, Barry."

"*Very* good," said Barry. "In fact, I am *very* good with numbers."

"Nice meeting you," said Lee. "I have to go."

"Nice meeting you," Barry said, imitating his inflection precisely. "You have to go."

They left Barry typing away at his computer, hunched over the screen in the dim light.

Back in the living room, Jimmy threw himself onto the couch. "I didn't mean you have to leave. It's just that sometimes it can be hard ending a conversation with Barry."

"That's okay—I really should get going. I have a boxing lesson tomorrow early."

"You've taken up boxing?" Jimmy said, kicking off his shoes.

"Yeah."

"Very cool. Maybe you'll get to use it against this UNSUB, huh? I'd like to take a few swings at him myself."

"Yeah, right," Lee said, but they both knew that finding the killer was going to be the real challenge. "Well, see you tomorrow."

"See you then."

He went back down the rickety staircase, inhaling the intoxicating aromas coming from half a dozen restaurants. The odor of lemongrass and ginger from the Vietnamese restaurant next door combined with the vinegary smell of hot-and-sour soup, garlic sauce and fried fish at the Happy Good Luck Palace. He stopped in and ordered some House Special Lo Mien and Chef's Special Fish in Hunan Sauce.

Walking uptown carrying his bag of steaming Chinese food, he couldn't help wishing he could pick up an order of Happy Good Luck along with the noodles.

The moment he entered his apartment, the phone rang. He dropped the bag of food onto the coffee table and picked up the receiver without looking at the caller ID. When he heard the flat, metallic voice on the other end of the line, his heart pulsated rapidly in his throat.

"Why, hello. I hope you haven't forgotten about me. I certainly haven't forgotten about you."

"What do you want?" Lee said, fumbling to turn on the tape recorder attached to the phone.

"Just checking in to see if that red dress had turned up yet."

"I thought you knew more than I did about all that."

"I never said that."

"My mistake. I thought you knew everything."

He wanted to keep the conversation going to get as much as he could on tape, but he knew the caller would hang up before the call could be traced. Anything he said was giving the man what he wanted.

"I think you're just trying to keep me talking," the caller said. "I'm hanging up now."

The line went dead. Lee stood with the receiver in his hand, then pressed the Stop button on the recorder. Knees trembling, he sank down onto the couch. Steam seeped from the bag of Chinese food on the coffee table in front of him, but he had lost his appetite.

# Chapter Eighteen

Lee stopped by the precinct the next morning after his boxing lesson, to see if there were any developments in the case. There weren't—the lab had determined there was no sign of sexual assault, and so far no helpful DNA had shown up.

"You okay, Doc?" Butts said. "You look a little rough."

"He called again last night."

"That jerk who claims to know something about your sister's disappearance?"

"Yeah."

"How long has it been since you talked to anyone who worked on your sister's case?" Butts asked, sniffing at a white bakery bag.

"It must be about three years now."

"You might try finding the guys who worked the case," Butts suggested. "Look 'em up, see what they have to say. Tell 'em about the phone calls. Anyways, couldn't hurt, right?"

"The primary on the case was a Detective Brian O'Reilly."

"O'Reilly?" Butts said, digging a doughnut out of

the bag. "Think I heard of him. Came from a line of cops. His dad was a captain back in the day."

"That's him."

"Rumor was, he used to drink heavily."

"Still does, far as I know."

Butts shook his head. "Bad habit to get into. Can't let the job get to you like that." He bit off a chunk of doughnut and chewed thoughtfully. "I think he retired about a year ago. Lives in the Bronx somewhere. Moved in to look after his mom or something like that."

Butts turned out to be right. According to his personnel file, Detective Brian O'Reilly had left the force two years ago, taken an early pension and moved back to Woodlawn, where he'd grown up. Lee tracked down his phone number, which was unlisted, and called to ask if he could pay a visit. The detective was guarded over the phone, but Lee persuaded him it wouldn't be a long visit, and he finally agreed. With the weather continuing to break, the air warm and foggy, Lee took the long subway ride to the borough that took its name from a seventeenth-century Scandinavian farmer, Jonas Bronck.

Brian O'Reilly lived in a five-story brownstone just off Katonah Avenue in Woodlawn, a predominantly Irish neighborhood in the North Bronx. Unlike the South Bronx, this part of the borough was almost entirely white, mostly lower middle class. His street was just around the corner from the Emerald Isle Bakery and Murphy's Pub. When Lee rang the buzzer, O'Reilly appeared at the door almost immediately, as though he had been watching through the lace curtains in the front room.

"Come on in, then," he said, after glancing both ways up and down the street. What he might be looking for Lee had no idea—maybe years of being a cop had left him with an instinct for surveillance.

Brian Seamus Timothy O'Reilly's thick body sagged with years of defeat. In the years since Lee had seen him, he seemed to have aged decades. His skin had the ruddy sheen of a heavy drinker, and his square Irish face wore a permanently stunned expression, as if he had never gotten over the things he had seen in his years as a cop. Even his voice was sad. His tone was soft, every sentence descending in volume and pitch, as if sliding down a slope of hopelessness. If he wore his philosophy of life emblazoned on a T-shirt, Lee thought, the front would read, WHY BOTHER? The message on the back would be, IT'S NO USE ANYWAY.

He shuffled down the front hall into the kitchen, flicking on the fluorescent light over the sink.

"Have a seat," he told Lee, indicating a cane-backed chair at a white enamel table. Surprisingly, the house appeared to be in good repair, not in the derelict condition Lee would have expected in the home of a drunk. The curtains on the windows were cheerful and freshly washed, and the floor had been recently swept. He concluded that someone was looking after O'Reilly—a son, perhaps, or a daughter.

"Want a drink?" O'Reilly asked, reaching for a bottle of Jameson on the counter.

The last thing Lee wanted right now was a drink. But if he was to get anything at all out of the man, perhaps the best strategy was to play the role of drinking buddy. Then maybe he could slip his questions in without spooking the retired detective.

"Sure," he said. "Why not?"

O'Reilly grabbed a couple of tumblers with one hefty hand and poured them both generous double shots. He slung his doughy body into one of the cane chairs and plunked the glasses down on the table. He slid one of the tumblers toward Lee, then knocked back his drink in one gulp. Wiping his mouth with his sleeve, he leaned back and closed his eyes.

"That's better," he said. "Now, what can I do for you? Has there been a break in your sister's case?"

"I'm afraid not," Lee said, sipping his own drink. This was harder than he'd thought it would be. He could feel the pain of the man across from him. It was palpable, like the scorching blast from a furnace.

O'Reilly squinted at him through bloodshot eyes. "You know, I just about killed myself on that case."

"I remember."

"I put in eighteen-hour days. Couldn't sleep, stopped eating."

"I know, I just—"

O'Reilly leaned forward, his elbows on the table. His meaty forearms were blotched, the skin mottled dark red.

"You ever get a case that gets under your skin?" O'Reilly said. "That just won't let go, no matter how hard you try to convince yourself you've done all you can?" He got up and lurched over to the counter, grabbed the bottle of whiskey and filled his glass.

Lee stood up. "Look, I don't want to . . . maybe it's better if I leave—"

"Sit down," his host commanded. "Now that you're here, we're gonna talk about it, so we are." He poured himself more whiskey but left it on the table. Resting his fingers on the lip of the tumbler, he stared down at the tawny liquid as if it held the answers to the questions that tormented him.

"So," he said, "you want to know if there's anything I can tell you about your sister's disappearance."

"But first I want to see if you can help me with something."

The detective straightened up in his chair. "What's that?"

Lee told him about the mysterious caller, omitting no detail. O'Reilly listened carefully and appeared to sober up as Lee talked. The detective's long-honed investigative instincts seemed to be taking over—his expression became sharper, more focused.

"You got a recording of this asshole?" he asked when Lee had finished.

"As a matter of fact, I do." He pulled the tape recorder out of his jacket pocket, placed it on the table, and pressed the Play button. The familiar metallic voice snaked out of the machine, its flat quality emphasized by the recorder's tinny speaker.

"Why, hello. I hope you haven't forgotten about me. I certainly haven't forgotten about you." Then the brief, loathsome chuckle, which made Lee dig his fingernails into his palms.

O'Reilly listened intently, hunched over the table, his body motionless. When it finished, he said, "Play it again."

Lee rewound the tape and pressed the Play button, and again the reptilian voice filled the room. He couldn't help noticing the involuntary clenching of his fists, the rage churning in his stomach.

"Okay," the detective said when it was over.

"You have any idea who this might be?"

O'Reilly leaned back in his chair and crossed his arms, his expression unreadable. "Don't get excited," he said, "but I might know something that could help. But first, how about another round?"

This time, Lee didn't hesitate. "Oh, yeah," he said. "Make mine a double."

O'Reilly smiled for the first time since he had arrived. "That's more like it. We'll make a goddamn cop outta you yet."

# CHAPTER NINETEEN

Edmund sat at his desk preparing his notes for the next day's class. He loved writing his lectures—if only he didn't have to actually deal with students. People were so messy, so unpredictable. He sought refuge in numbers and the music of Bach, both of which were pure and beautiful, instead of complicated and ugly, like life.

He stared out the office window at the stark landscape of the campus in winter. The buildings lay silent, their sharp right angles in muted tones of white and gray. Winter was his favorite season. He enjoyed its purity; it was, he thought, the season most like mathematics. If only people could be like numbers—malleable, distant, perfect. He understood that language intuitively. But people were different—always behaving in illogical ways, driven by passions and desires and *needs*. Numbers needed nothing—they just *were*. They had always been there and always would be, long after human civilizations had annihilated one another with their petty greed and unruly passions.

Edmund smoothed the paper on his immaculate, orderly desk and sighed with pleasure. The sight of columns of figures had always had a calming effect on him. Black on white, squiggles of ink that held the secrets of the universe. Mathematicians had an understanding of the world no one else possessed; he knew that, and it made him feel superior.

As he studied his lecture notes, his hand crept unconsciously to the long, thin scar that snaked from his forehead to his chin, his fingers tracing the raised line of skin. When people were rude enough to ask about it, he told a different story each time. He once told one drunken young graduate student at a faculty cocktail party that it was a dueling scar he'd received defending the honor of the Duchess of Schleswig-Holstein. He had no idea whether Schleswig-Holstein had a duchess or not, but it sounded like the kind of place one might engage in a duel. The graduate student was getting his doctorate in psychology, so Edmund figured he wasn't very bright. Sure enough, the idiot bought the story entirely—Edmund overheard him repeating later it to a group of people at the party.

Another time he told an old lady in line behind him at the grocery store that he was a Croatian who had been tortured by a guard in a Serbian concentration camp. That shut the old biddy up quickly enough; she avoided eye contact with him after that. He didn't plan his stories; they just came out when people intruded on what he considered to be a private matter. For him, lying was as natural as breathing. He lied not because he had to but because he could. It gave him power over other people. Besides math and Bach, that was the only thing that made life worth living.

As to how he really got his scar—well, that was a scene he had buried deep in the underside of his brain.

It was so many years ago, and yet it could burst into consciousness at any moment—a look, a sound, an angle of the light. Or a smell . . . how he remembered that smell! Couldn't forget it, even if he tried. And he had tried. God, how he had tried. The odor of his own burning flesh . . . even now it sickened him, made his stomach heave and push at his esophagus as though it wanted to jump out of his body. And his father had laughed at him for vomiting that day—mocked and belittled Edmund, in his Devon accent, thick as clotted cream. *You're lucky I didn't cut your little pecker off! You disgusting little bugger! If I ever catch you doing that again, you'd better watch out!*

His fingers traced the raised edges of the scar. He did watch out after that—his father never did catch him doing that thing again. Oh, he did it plenty of times, but never when his old man was around. His father was stupid; Edmund had nothing but contempt for him. His mother was the brains in the family—he had inherited her mind, her gift for logic, her work ethic. He'd adored her and would have done anything for her. So when she left his father for another man, abandoning him and his sister, he never forgave her. He hardened his heart, chipping away at his love for her until there was nothing left, like a sculpture that had been whittled away to nothing.

His sister accepted their mother's invitations to visit, but not Edmund. He knew his father was a nobody, a lout and a bully, but he was damned if he was going to see his mother in the arms of another man. It was around that time he started exposing himself to the girls in school. First the younger girls and then the ones in his class—until finally a teacher caught him in the act. And then it was off to boarding school, which he rather enjoyed—at least it got him away from his father.

But his urge to do dark things persisted. It grew over time, like an evil vine, until it threatened to choke all that was light and good about him. He set fire to his roommate's bed over an argument, bullied the younger children and tied firecrackers to the tails of cats. He stole whatever he could get away with and lied whenever possible, just because he could.

But then he discovered mathematics, and his world changed. Here was something he was good at—really good at, "scary good," as his sister said. He was graduated a year early, finessing his S levels. Accepted by King's College at Cambridge at the age of seventeen, he had his doctorate by the time he was twenty-three. Everyone called him a genius. A "success story," an example of what hard work and talent combined could do. He had "turned his life around."

But the darkness inside him remained, and his fantasies continued to grow. Always a part of him, they began to take on a life of their own. The higher he rose in academic circles, the more they demanded attention. They wouldn't let him alone. Putting an ocean between him and his homeland hadn't changed a thing.

As much as he lived for mathematics, he could feel the dark urges in his soul pulling him down into their undertow. *Psychopath.* That's what those idiot psychologists called him. But they were the lowest rung on the food chain. The social sciences were for idiots—he only had respect for real science. And behind science—and music, his beloved Bach—lay mathematics.

Edmund looked at his watch, the hands at a perfect 180-degree angle. It was six o'clock. He looked out the window at the pallid waning moon, low in the darkening sky. A smiled played at the corner of his mouth as he thought about the careful preparations he had made. It was time to go hunting again.

# Chapter Twenty

Brian O'Reilly was the only person Lee had ever met who seemed to get more focused the more he drank. He was already several rounds ahead of Lee, but his voice was sharp and clear, his hands steady.

"I can't say for sure, but that voice sounds familiar," the retired detective said after listening to the recording for a third time.

"Who does it sound like?" Lee said, trying to hide his eagerness. His host was clearly an "old school" cop—haunted by his failures, coping with them by drinking heavily while maintaining his brusque, Irish-machismo attitude.

"There was this other detective briefly assigned to the case," O'Reilly said. "He was weird. He gave me the creeps, so I asked that he be transferred. I didn't wanna work with him—come to think of it, no one in the squad house did."

"What was his name?"

O'Reilly pursed his lips, rubbed his forehead and stared at the ceiling. Then he shook his head. "I'm tryin' to remember. It wasn't an Irish name, or Italian . . . it was a name I'd never heard before, I'm pretty sure. Let me think about it some more."

"So you think the caller might be him?"

"He had a voice like that. Flat, you know—cold. Soulless, like there's nobody he ever cared about or who ever cared about him."

"Any idea what happened to him?"

"He left the force shortly after, I think. May have been some kind of fracas—I don't remember. I had other things to think about."

"Would he still be in the personnel files?"

"I don't see why not. If it is him, it would explain how he knew about the red dress. That detail was never released to the public, and, far as I know, the press never got hold of it either."

He swallowed the last of his whiskey, and all the sharpness seemed to leave his body. He looked old and tired, the skin on his face puckered and pasty in the pale afternoon light. "You know," he said softly, "we must have interviewed a hundred people, but we never developed a decent suspect. Couldn't even come up with enough evidence for a grand jury."

"I know," Lee said. "It's not your fault."

"It's like she just vanished—*whoosh.* Here one minute, gone the next. What is it those nutty Christians call it? The Rapture. It's like that—like she was air-lifted to heaven."

*The Rapture. Yeah, right.* Laura wasn't dead—kidnapped, assaulted and killed by some psychopath—but had somehow zoomed straight up to heaven without suffering the pangs of death and dying. Trouble was, Lee didn't believe in God, and he didn't believe in miracles.

He sometimes wished he could, especially when he saw the comfort people took from their beliefs, but it wasn't an option for him.

"The file on your sister is still in Records, if you want to go through it," O'Reilly said.

"Thanks—maybe I will." He stood up. It was time to leave this sad man in his clean, well-appointed kitchen, with his bottle of Jameson for company. "Thanks," he said again. "For the whiskey and the talk."

"I didn't do anything," O'Reilly said. "But I'll ask around and see if anyone else remembers that cop's name."

"Thanks."

He emerged from O'Reilly's into the chilly evening air, the sun sliding behind a line of cloud cover. A couple of kids raced by on bikes, legs pumping, hair flying in the wind. The girl had pale hair the color of winter wheat, and the boy had a forest of flame-colored curls. He watched them careen around the corner onto Katonah Avenue, laughing and shouting, just as he and Laura had so many years ago. But that was a different state, bordered by a different river, and it felt like another life by now.

He headed toward the subway, suspended in a strange mixture of hope and dread—hope that at last the mysterious caller would be identified, and dread that he might be. Lee wasn't sure of his own reaction. He wasn't at all certain that murder was out of the question. He didn't trust anyone right now—least of all himself. He pulled up his collar and ducked into the subway, to be swallowed up by its vast system of tunnels like Orpheus descending into the underworld.

# Chapter Twenty-one

When he emerged from the subway, there was a message on his cell phone from Lucille Geffers, chairman of the philosophy department at John Jay College of Criminal Justice. He knew there was a vacancy in the psychology department, and Lucille was on the search committee. After a meeting with Butts and Krieger, he took the train to the Upper West Side to meet with her.

Lucille Geffers lived in the Ansonia Hotel, an ornate Beaux Arts structure one block north of the intersection of Broadway and Amsterdam at Seventy-second Street. Lee loved the playful attention to detail in the elaborate stone carving, the wrought-iron balconies, the looming mansard roof, its copper coating green with age. The building was as fussy and overdecorated as a wedding cake, and he thought it was perfect.

The nattily dressed doorman informed him Lucille's apartment was on the third floor, so instead of taking the elevator, Lee walked up the ornate winding staircase, the marble steps worn concave from decades of opera singers and musicians treading upon them. He knew about a few of the more famous tenants, like Arturo Toscanini and Enrico Caruso.

He found Lucille listening to a late Beethoven quartet, the one with the Grand Fugue in the first movement. Her Irish setter, Rex, was by her side, wagging his feathery tail gently.

"Come in, please," Lucille said. She wore a blue cable-knit turtleneck, jeans and moccasins. The look suited her. So did the apartment. It had the quiet, understated charm of someone who had grown up amid privilege, education and taste. A built-in bookshelf occupied one entire wall of the spacious foyer, the carpets were old and expensive, and the French Impressionist paintings didn't look like prints.

"Thanks for dropping by on such short notice."

"No problem. Hi, Rex," he said, stroking the dog's silky fur. Rex responded by shoving his cold nose into Lee's crotch.

"Rex, stop it!" she said, tugging on his collar.

"Nice place you have here."

"Thanks. My father was an opera singer—sang in the Met chorus for years—and I managed to get on the lease before he died. Oh, I don't like the way that came out," she said, wincing. "It sounds kind of cold."

"Don't worry—I knew what you meant."

In New York, real estate was everything. A rent-controlled apartment in a good neighborhood was the equivalent of winning the lottery—people would lie, cheat and steal (and in some cases, murder) for one. Otherwise you were subject to the steadily mounting cost of housing. In Manhattan, rents only went in one direction: up.

"So you grew up in this building?" Lee asked.

"Yeah, pretty much."

"Is it true Caruso lived here?"

"Yep. They say he chose it because of the thick walls. I was just making tea. Would you like some?"

"Sure, thanks."

She poured them each a mug of strong black tea and showed him to the living room. Rex padded after them, his toenails clicking softly on the hardwood floor. They sat for a moment sipping their tea while listening to the majestic opening of Beethoven's Grand Fugue.

"God," Lucille said. "Can you imagine being able to write something like that?"

"Must be amazing, being a conduit for something that glorious."

"A 'conduit'? What do you mean?"

"When I hear something this profound, it feels like Beethoven is tapping into something universal. If I were religious, I'd say it's a piece of the Divine."

Lucille stroked Rex's head, running her hand over the silky fur. The dog looked up at her adoringly. "So you think Beethoven was 'channeling' his greatest music?"

"Well, if you put it like that, it sounds silly. I'm not expressing it well."

"Okay," Lucille said. "I'll admit, I didn't just ask you here for tea. I have an ulterior motive."

Perhaps in response to the surprised look on his face, she added quickly, "Not *that*—it's professional. I mean, you're a good-looking man, but you're not my type. Not enough X chromosomes."

"Oh," he said, and then, "*Oh.*"

"I probably shouldn't even be telling you this, though I suppose it's no secret that I'm a Friend of Ellen."

"Got it."

"I don't know if the kids at John Jay spend any time talking about their moldy old professors," she went on, "but I'm pretty sure most of them have me figured out. Which actually leads me to what I wanted to talk to you about."

She sat across from him on the divan and put her mug on the coffee table. "As you may know, there's an opening at the school in the psychology department."

"Right."

"Tom Mariella was going to ask you himself, but his father died suddenly, so he asked me to feel you out on it."

*His father died suddenly.* Lee didn't even know if his own father was alive or dead. There were too many open chapters in his family, too many unresolved chords.

"Ask me what?" he said.

"If you'd like to be an adjunct lecturer at the school. It would mean giving a couple of talks each semester—you could pick the topics yourself, more or less, as long as Tom agrees with them." She saw his hesitation and said, "Maybe the timing isn't good right now."

"No, it's not that." He couldn't tell her that the news about Tom's father had sent him spinning into a wild series of conjectures about his own father, long ago departed—though not necessarily from this world. He looked at Lucille, sitting across from him, perched on the edge of the sofa, the ever-faithful Rex pressing his body against her shins. "Can I think about it?"

"Of course—take all the time you need. I'll tell Tom

we talked about it, and when he gets back into town, he may give you a call."

"Thanks. I appreciate your interest."

"Good. And now," she said, rising from the couch, "if you'll excuse me, I've got a hot date with a stripper. *Kidding*," she said in response to his surprised expression. "Not about the date but the stripper part. God, you're an easy mark." She laughed. "Oh, one more thing, before I forget. We just had a cancellation for our guest-lecturer series. Very well-respected FBI profiler—you probably know of him—was going to come, but there's an illness in his family. So rather than cancel, we'd like to plug someone in. Can you do it?"

"What was he going to talk about?"

"Wait a second—I have the schedule right here," she said, studying a pamphlet on her desk. " 'The sadistic sexual offender.' "

"When is it?"

"Thursday morning. Are you free?"

"I could do it. Is it open to the public?"

"Yes."

"Then I should warn you, there's a very good chance that the UNSUB in the Alleyway Strangler case will attend."

"We can have some undercover officers in the audience."

"Not a bad idea, though I doubt if he'll announce himself. And you can't really arrest someone for attending a lecture. Still, it can't hurt."

"What are the chances he'll come, do you think?"

"I'd say they're pretty good."

She shivered. "It's a creepy feeling, isn't it?"

"What?"

"To think you'll be in the same room with a murderer, and that he'll know who you are, but you won't know him."

"Yeah. Real creepy."

But even then he was thinking, *What if I do recognize him? What do I do?*

He didn't say it out loud, because as yet the question had no answer.

# Chapter Twenty-two

Detective Leonard Butts liked his life in Nutley, New Jersey. He liked his plump little wife, Muriel, their son, Joey, and their cozy little house just down the road from the headquarters of the drug manufacturing giant Hoffmann-La Roche. People in Nutley called it The House That Valium Built. The drug's inventor, Leo Sternbach, was a tenacious researcher who had persevered against the directives of his bosses, creating one of the most profitable drugs in the world, earning the Swiss company billions of dollars. Butts liked to use the story as proof of Jewish ingenuity. Butts was only half Jewish on his father's side, but he identified strongly with his Polish/Jewish ancestry.

He drove down Kingsland Street, past the company's vast research and manufacturing plant, its smokestacks belching out God only knew what toxic by-products, and turned right onto Terrace Avenue. He wasn't that crazy about living near Roche, but the houses close to the plant were cheaper—theirs had been a real bargain when they bought it. It was the last one on the left before the road dead-ended into Princeton Street—a nice, leafy corner lot with a decent-sized lawn. He and

Muriel had agreed they didn't want anything too roomy—he wasn't big on property upkeep, preferring to spend his weekends barbequing with friends or attending his son's baseball and soccer games. Neither he nor Muriel were sporty types, so it had been a surprise when they produced a natural athlete like Joey. Butts was proud of his son but rarely talked about him, for fear of becoming one of those boring parents obsessed with their children's accomplishments.

As he entered the house through the kitchen door, he heard the *Jeopardy!* theme song coming from the den. He hung up his coat and tiptoed downstairs to the renovated basement that served as their TV room and den, where he found Muriel stretched out in the black leatherette recliner, watching the show.

He and Joey had strict instructions not to disturb her during this daily ritual. They were not to speak to her, make comments or, worst of all, give answers to the questions. Muriel alone was allowed to play along, muttering responses under her breath—often long before Alex Trebek had finished giving the clue, and usually correctly.

Butts sat quietly on the sofa until the first commercial break. His wife picked up the remote, muted the television and smiled at him.

"Hello, Buttons." It was a nickname she had used since their second week of dating, when he had picked her up wearing a jacket missing two buttons.

"Hi," he said, getting up to give her a kiss.

"How was your day? Catch any murderers?"

Butts smiled indulgently. It wasn't that his wife took his work lightly—she was supportive and proud of what he did. But Muriel had a sly way about her, an offhand manner of dismissing important things like life-threatening diseases or disasters. He supposed some people might find it annoying, but he found it comforting. It defused his anxiety about the importance of succeeding in his job and gave him space to breathe and relax a little. It was easy to get eaten up by the job. He had seen it happen to other guys on the force, but what was the point of doing this kind of work if you were going to let it destroy your life? He had decided a long time ago that that was a price he wasn't willing to pay. Some might call him callous, but he didn't care. He liked to joke that he might be part Jewish, but he was no masochist.

He kicked off his shoes and lay back on the couch. "I'll tell you all about my day when your show is over. How's it going?"

"I'm rooting for the librarian. She's good with literature and history, but she has a weakness in geography."

"How're you doing?"

"Not bad. I cleaned up in Odds 'N' Ends but was stumped in Pop Tunes of the Nineties."

"I don't know why you don't audition for that show."

She waved aside his comment dismissively. "I'd never make it."

"You're better than most of the contestants."

"Here in my living room, sure. But I'd wilt under the pressure."

"That's a load of bull. I don't see you wilting under nothing."

She laughed. "Always the supportive husband, Buttons, aren't you? Oh, the show's coming back on," she said. Picking up the remote, she pointed it at the TV just as Alex Trebek came back on-screen, smiling from ear to ear of his big Canadian head.

"And now it's time for Double Jeopardy," he said, without losing that superior smile of his. Butts despised Alex Trebek.

*Double Jeopardy.* Butts thought that just about described his life right now. Each time another day went by without apprehending the man they sought, another girl was in jeopardy.

He looked at his wife. She was no beauty, but he loved her bright, intelligent eyes, upturned nose and rosy cheeks. Like him, she was short and pudgy, but she had a *way* about her, always had. It stirred something inside him and grabbed his heart the same way looking at the oak tree in the corner of the garden in the early-morning light did. His attraction to her went deeper than sex. Over the years they had grown together like two vines intertwined; the only way to separate them would be to cut away parts of them. He loved his son, but he couldn't imagine life without Muriel.

One of the categories on Double Jeopardy was Mathematics. The librarian went right for it, starting with the first clue.

"This American physicist and mathematician, known for his diagrams, received the Nobel Prize in 1965 along with two others for his work in quantum electrodynamics," said Alex.

"Who was Richard Feynman?" Muriel barked. She was right—and she proceeded to get every answer in the column right, along with the librarian, who ran through the entire category, putting herself squarely in the lead.

"Good," Muriel said when the next station break came. "I think my librarian friend might pull it off after all." She muted the show again and turned to her husband. "So how did it go today?" They had long ago fallen into the habit of talking about trivial things as though they mattered and important things as though they didn't.

"No real leads. This guy is smart, and he doesn't leave clues behind, unless he wants us to find them."

It was against policy to talk about an ongoing investigation with anyone outside the force, even family members, but everyone he knew had broken that rule at one time or another. He avoided talking about things in front of Joey, but it was hard to leave your work behind each day. Everyone in the NYPD knew that, and no one talked about it. It was understood.

"That's too bad," she said.

"Where's Joey?"

"Soccer practice. He'll be back in time for dinner."

Then the show came back on, and she returned to watching it.

Butts got up and wandered into the kitchen. He reached for the icebox door and saw the note dangling from a refrigerator magnet in the form of a carrot.

*ASK YOURSELF: DO I REALLY NEED THIS RIGHT NOW?*
*OR IS IT JUST HABIT??*
*REMEMBER, HABITS CAN BE BROKEN!!*
*REPLACE BAD HABITS WITH HEALTHY ONES!!!*

He let go of the door handle and turned away. Muriel was trying to reform him and lose some weight herself in the process. *Healthy habits* . . . The man he was chasing had already formed some very nasty habits indeed, which would be much harder to break than overeating. No amount of notes on refrigerator doors would change his actions at this point; they would only become more ingrained over time.

He picked up an apple from a bowl of fruit on the kitchen table and took a bite. It wasn't the same as a doughnut, but he chewed dutifully and swallowed, determined to control his own impulses. Somehow, he felt that might bring him one step closer to catching a man whose impulses had already spun dangerously out of control.

# CHAPTER TWENTY-THREE

Edmund looked out over the sea of smooth young faces. So innocent, so trusting, so . . . *unformed.* Empty vessels to be filled with knowledge and experience—and, in some cases, terror. He opened his folder of lecture notes and cleared his throat. The room instantly quieted down. He had that effect on people. Maybe it was his stature and air of quiet authority, or maybe it was the jagged scar on his face. He could cover some of it with a longer hairstyle, but he deliberately wore his hair short to catch people's reactions when they saw him.

He enjoyed cataloguing the variety of responses. There was disgust, pity, revulsion, indifference and—most interesting of all—desire. He found it fascinating to watch the women who, when confronted with his deformity, displayed signs of arousal. Their eyes would widen as their lips grew plumper, and all the muscles in their face would soften. Those were the ones he spared; they already had some of the same darkness in their souls that he did. They knew something of his struggle, his pain, his eternal, gnawing loneliness, and they were attracted by it.

No, it was the others he went after—the ones who were so naïve and stupid that they knew nothing of how the world worked. They knew only softness and ease, the luxury of being young and pretty and desirable and privileged. Those were the ones who needed to be taught a lesson—that life hurts and that other people can't be trusted. He had learned that at a tender age, and now he had to pass it on.

He gripped the lectern with both hands and leaned on it.

"Mathematics is an exacting science, and it can be a stern master," he said. "But once its secrets are revealed to you, you will enter a world of surpassing beauty. You will discover that it is as much an art as a science, a discipline of the imagination as well as of the logical mind. Mathematics has spirit, as surely as music or painting or sculpture. It is perhaps more austere but nonetheless beautiful."

He looked at a girl in the front row. She was lovely, with alabaster skin and black hair, like Snow White. She looked up at him with such trust in her blue eyes—pathetic, really. Someone would have to remove that trust and replace it with terror. He smiled down at her, and she returned his smile.

She was perfect.

# CHAPTER TWENTY-FOUR

Brian O'Reilly poured himself another drink and watched through the kitchen window as the last of the gray winter light faded from the sky. He took a swallow and felt the whiskey slide down his throat, harsh and burning. He was having a bad day. First there was the visit from the dead girl's brother—that's how he thought of Laura, as the dead girl. It galled him that they hadn't even found her body, let alone her killer—she'd disappeared as if plucked right off the earth by the giant, unforgiving hand of God. In spite of his Catholic background, he never had much time for religion. Oh, he believed, all right—he just thought God was an evil bastard. The Campbell case was simply a prime example of God's many transgressions. No one knew this better than Brian O'Reilly—his years on the force had given him enough insight into the evils of God and man to last a lifetime.

And the Campbell case came as close as any to making him want to pull his hair out. A missing girl was always upsetting, but there was something else about this case, something that galled him to the bone and filled his stomach with acid. Maybe it was the complete lack of viable suspects; usually with missing-persons cases there were a couple of creeps hanging around that he could sink his teeth into during the interview process. It might not solve the case, but it made him feel better, like he was doing *something* toward solving the case.

He took another swallow of Jameson and leaned his elbows on the Formica table. Nothing irked him more than feeling impotent. Cops in general didn't do well with feelings of helplessness, and Brian Seamus Timothy O'Reilly was no exception. He had always been hotheaded; that's what his Irish grandmother had called him, God rest her soul. And now the dead girl's brother shows up and starts digging around, bringing up loathsome feelings of helplessness, the ones he'd joined the force to avoid. It nauseated him and made him feel hollow right in the center of his gut, as if someone had carved his stomach out of his body.

The phone rang, and he snatched up the receiver. Probably his sister calling to see if he was sober. He wished she would just leave him alone—the guilt of letting her down only made things worse. He was about to hang up without answering when he heard the voice on the other end of the line—a man's voice, flat and cold and insinuating. His hand shaking, he held the phone to his ear.

"Well, well," the voice said. "Trying to resurrect the dead again?"

It was the same voice on the recording Lee Campbell had played for him—he was sure of it.

He clutched the receiver to steady his hand and tried to focus his thoughts.

"Who is this?"

"That would be telling."

"What do you want?"

"To know what it feels like to have the biggest case of your life go unsolved."

"You'd better watch it, mister—there are laws against this kind of thing."

"Against what—having a friendly chat? I don't think so. Have a nice day, Detective."

The line went dead. O'Reilly stood looking at the phone in his hand, then hurled it against the wall, smashing it to pieces.

# CHAPTER TWENTY-FIVE

Fiona asked Lee to drive out early on Friday for the weekend, before Kylie got home from school. She said there was something she wanted to talk about but refused to elaborate. After a morning meeting with Butts and the rest of their team, he picked up a rental car in the Village and was on the road by one, after stopping by Myers of Keswick for some Cornish pasties. Fiona had recently discovered the British import shop in the West Village owned by a colorful Englishman by the name of Peter Myers. She said his meat pies reminded her of her childhood in Scotland.

Rush hour hadn't started yet, so traffic was light, and he reached Stockton a little after two thirty. The small town was quaint at any time of year, but it seemed tailor-made for the Christmas holidays. Every store on the main street was outlined in white fairy lights, and the lampposts were festooned with large red bows. The tall blue spruce next to Errico's Market was decorated with old-fashioned Christmas bulbs glistening in the damp air. The sky was a dull gray—an opaque shade that local forecasters on the radio said was a sure sign of another snowstorm.

Lee thought about that Christmas so long ago when he and Laura had discovered their mother's secret sorrow buried amid tissue wrapping paper. There was another, perhaps even more painful secret he had come across more recently, one that affected him even more deeply now that Laura was gone. He had almost had a little brother—the child stillborn to his grieving mother when he and Laura were very young. She had wrapped that secret up along with her other unspoken sorrows, buried it deeply within her heart, and if Lee hadn't stumbled across the birth certificate last year, he might never have known about it. Though he had died in his mother's womb, the boy was given a name: Adrian. Lee tried saying the words, the syllables heavy with sadness: *Adrian Campbell.* His little brother—almost. The date of his birth coincided with the time his father was involved with Chloe, so he could only imagine how his mother must have suffered. It pained him that she had never spoken to him of any of this—not for his sake but because he knew that grief borne in solitude could be unbearable.

He turned on to the country lane leading to his mother's house. The sky looked foreboding as he turned into the familiar driveway. He pulled up next to the overgrown holly bush, its bright red berries scattered like droplets of blood on the shiny green leaves. *High-velocity blood spatter . . . indication of blunt-force trauma.* There was no blunt-force trauma on the Alleyway Strangler's victims, and no blood. The whole thing was too damn tidy, he thought as he walked up the flagstone path to the house. This killer was in control—or thought he was. There was always a chance he'd slip up—but when? They couldn't afford to wait until he made a mistake; they had to catch him at his own game.

Lee found his mother in the tiny kitchen in the back of the house. She had cornered a bowl of cucumbers and was dissecting them on the counter.

"Hello, dear," she said, giving him her usual peck on the cheek. He couldn't remember Fiona ever giving him a bear hug—not even when his sister disappeared. Fiona Campbell was a handsome woman, tall and slim with dark eyebrows and iron gray hair spattered with black. Lee could remember when it was long and as black as a raven, but now she wore it in a brisk, no-nonsense bob, cut close around her long face with its high cheekbones and strong jaw. She wore a long white chef's apron over a crisp blue and white striped shirt and black slacks. Even in low heels, she was just an inch shy of six feet tall.

"Are you hungry?" she asked. Food was the currency of love in his family—it was so much easier than emotion.

"Not really," he replied, inhaling the room's familiar scent of eucalyptus, apples and polished wood.

"I'm almost done here," she said as her knife sliced cleanly through the pale green flesh. "I'm making cucumber salad for Stan."

"He's coming over?"

"He's going to have dinner with us before the concert."

"Great."

Stan Paloggia lived next door and was in love with Fiona. He followed her around like a one-man posse, being helpful in any way he could, whether it was by offering gardening advice or making plumbing repairs.

"What about George?"

George Callahan was Kylie's father—a big, bluff and cheerful man of endless good cheer and high spirits but limited intellect. He couldn't have been more different from Duncan Campbell—which, Lee suspected, was why Laura had chosen him.

"George is with his mother in Pennsylvania this weekend," Fiona said. "She's not well."

"Too bad he's missing the concert."

"He's a good son," she said, still chopping cucumbers. Lee decided to let go of any accusation lurking behind the remark. He watched as the blade of the knife rapped sharply against the tile countertop. *Rat-a-tat.* His mother leaned over the counter, her mouth pursed, concentrated on her task, as if it was an important scientific experiment. Her thick salt-and-pepper hair bobbed as she worked. *Rat-a-tat-tat-tat.*

"Can I ask you something?" he said.

"Of course," she said, but her tone was clear. *Go ahead, but don't expect me to like it.*

He took a deep breath. "Why didn't you tell us about the death of our brother?"

He had to hand it to her. The question must have been completely unexpected, but she didn't stop slicing the cucumbers. Her knife continued its relentless motion, and she didn't so much as glance at him.

"You were *children,* for God's sake!" she muttered between clenched teeth.

"So we didn't have a right to know?"

*Swoosh, slap.* She pressed so hard on the knife, he could hear the blade scoring the wood of the cutting board. Then she dropped the knife onto the counter and turned to him.

"He died in the womb, Lee—*my* womb. Can you imagine what that was like?"

"I think I can, actually."

She hugged herself, wrapping her long arms around her body.

"I *wanted* to tell you, but the time never seemed right. It's hardly the kind of thing you open a conversation with."

"It's exactly the kind of thing you open a conversation with, Mom."

She picked up the knife again, but there was nothing left to slice. The cucumbers lay dismembered, their shredded flesh strewn all over the cutting board.

"Tell me something," she said, getting a bag of carrots out of the refrigerator. "How can you possibly know what to say to a child when you've never had any?" She began whacking away at the carrots, the knife hitting the wooden cutting board with a solid *thwack.*

*Touché*. A skillful playing of the trump card of the fruitful over the childless. He'd seen it before, and it always worked. The unassailable assertion of superior knowledge born of experience, with its subtle implication of moral supremacy. Once again, he had to hand it to her. She would have made a hell of a trial attorney. He didn't have the energy to punch through her defenses.

Suddenly she stopped what she was doing. The knife fell from her hand and clattered to the counter. She turned to face him, the fear in her blue eyes alarming.

"She's cutting herself, Lee." Her voice was low, desperate. "Kylie is *cutting herself.*"

*"What?"*

"George doesn't know what to do about it. He's at his wit's end."

"God, Mom," Lee said. "When did this start?"

"George told me the school guidance counselor called him yesterday, and he went in to talk to them."

"Have either of you talked with Kylie about it?"

"No. They said not to mention it until she talks with the counselor."

"What are we supposed to do—just ignore it?"

"I don't *know*," she said, anguish in her voice. He hadn't seen her so upset since Laura disappeared. "Apparently it's something young people do when they're feeling out of control and distressed."

"I'll talk to her," he said. "And don't worry," he added. "She's going to be all right."

Another switch—him comforting her with hollow words of reassurance; usually it was the other way around. He felt like giving her a hug, but Fiona's body language made it clear that would not be welcome.

The awkwardness between them was defused by three quick raps on the back door. Relieved, Lee opened it to find Stan Paloggia standing on the stoop with a potted orchid and a grin as wide as the Jersey Turnpike.

Stan hovered around Fiona like an eager beagle. Actually, he was a lot like beagles Lee had known—short and stocky, with a voracious appetite, thick around the middle. His voice, too, was a kind of a bray, like the hoarse baying of a hound on the hunt.

"Hiya," he said, craning his neck to see around Lee. "Is the lady of the house in?"

"She's right here," said Lee, opening the door. "How are you, Stan?"

"Oh, can't complain," he said, and Lee waited for the inevitable continuation: *If I did, no one would listen anyway.* But Stan had fixed his eyes on Fiona, neglecting the rest of his usual litany.

"Hello, Stan," she said, wiping her hands on her apron. "Is that for me?"

"Yep," he said, handing her the flower. "Dug it out of my greenhouse today. Thought you might like it." Stan was a prolific gardener. He had built his own greenhouse in back of his home, and his collection of orchids was breathtaking.

"It's lovely," Fiona said. "What is it?"

"*Phalaenopsis fuscata*," Stan said proudly.

The flower was beautiful in the unreal, absurdly perfect way of orchids—so flawless, it looked artificial. The petals were spread out like the blades of a windmill, yellow-tipped, with a scarlet blush on their base. It was sexual and rather obscene. Looking at the flower's five petals, Lee saw the legs, arms and head of the NYPD's latest young victim. *One head, two legs, two arms . . . minus a finger. Why?*

"What're you starin' at, buddy?" Stan asked. "It's just a flower. You look like you seen a ghost."

"Sorry," said Lee. "I was just thinking."

"I tried that once—ended up in bed for a week," said Stan, chuckling. Stan always laughed at his own jokes.

"Yeah, right," Lee said.

His mother threw a suspicious glance at him. "I'll just go put this in my room," she declared, marching off with the orchid.

Stan clapped a hand onto Lee's shoulder.

"What do you say we go into the parlor? I think your mom can manage okay without us. I just love that this house has a 'parlor.' People were a lot smaller when this place was built, weren't they?" he remarked as Lee stooped to clear the low doorway into the dining room.

"Yeah, they were."

Stan himself couldn't be more than about five foot five, Lee figured, though he was built like a brick oven—"solid muscle, bone and gristle," as he liked to describe himself.

They went through the narrow dining room into the tiny parlor. All the rooms in the house were small by modern standards, with thick stone walls, low ceilings and creaking wood floors. It was built around 1740, which was old even for this part of the Delaware Valley, and Fiona loved the place.

"What's up with your mom?" said Stan. "She's got that kinda glowering look today."

"She'll get over it."

Stan settled himself comfortably on the horsehair sofa along the far wall, leaning against a red velvet pillow.

"She always does. I call her the Bouncer, on account of her bouncing back from everything so fast."

Lee laughed. "I'll bet she loves that nickname."

Stan grinned. "Not so much." He leaned back, hands locked behind his head, and studied Lee. "How 'bout you, Slim? You look a little spooked. Somethin' wrong?"

"No," he said, sinking into an overstuffed armchair by the fireplace that Kylie called "The Comfy Chair," after an old Monty Python sketch. "Just working a case."

Stan shook his head. "I swear, I don't know how you do that stuff. Doesn't it drive you nuts? I mean, you must have trouble sleeping."

"Someone's got to do it."

"Yeah, but it must be rough sometimes."

"It is."

"How's that good-lookin' girlfriend of yours—what's her name?"

"Kathy."

"She's a cutie—love that curly black hair."

"We broke up."

"Oops. Fiona's right—I do put my foot in my mouth too much."

"It's not your fault. You didn't know."

"It's odd that your mom didn't mention it to me."

"That's because I haven't told her."

"Why not?"

How to respond? He had learned that dealing with the fallout from a breakup was frequently more draining than the event itself.

"Guess I just didn't feel like talking about it."

Stan raised his hands in sympathy. "I get that, believe me—when Rita and I were divorced, I got so sick of people askin' me if I was okay. I thought I was gonna puke if one more person gave me that sympathetic routine, y'know?" He leaned in toward Lee. "So if that's not what your mom's upset about, what is it? Something's the matter—I know it."

"Fiona's always been moody, Stan."

"Naw, it's more than that. I can tell. I can read her like a book." Stan had a roster of clichés he rotated the way other people rotated their tires.

"She's worried about Kylie."

"Yeah? Anything in particular?"

"Just a grandmother's worry, I think." Lee didn't want to lie to Stan, but he couldn't betray Fiona's confidence. Trying to walk the thin line between those poles was tricky.

"I'm gonna ask her what's up."

"I wouldn't, Stan."

"Why not?"

"Trust me on this one. Don't."

Stan raised his hands in surrender. "All right. I hear you. I'll make like a clam and shut up."

Just then Fiona entered the room with a tray of drinks. Rye and soda for Stan, a glass of single malt for Lee and red wine for her.

Stan raised his glass. "Cheers. Here's to the holidays."

"Cheers," Fiona said, with a glance at Lee.

"To the holidays," Lee said, raising his glass.

Outside, the feeble December sun slipped behind the old willow tree growing along the underground spring. Ninety miles away, a killer sharpened his knives in preparation for the hunt.

# CHAPTER TWENTY-SIX

Edmund looked out the bus window and sighed with contentment at the sight of rain-splattered streets. It was going to turn to snow later, they said—it was already snowing in the suburbs—but for now he could enjoy the rain. There was nothing better than a rainy night in the city. Fewer people on the streets, and even in the midst of a crowd, you could have the feeling you were alone. He loved darkened movie theaters and amusement park rides through blackened caverns and canals, the only light coming from dim bulbs that pulsed gently, casting a dim reflection on the surrounding walls. *Seeing but unseen*—that's how he liked it.

The bus rumbled up to a stop, the engine sputtering as the driver shifted the transmission into Park. A lone wheelchair rider huddled on the pavement in front of Bellevue Hospital, rain dripping from his baseball cap onto his rubber poncho. The windowpane Edmund gazed out of dissected him neatly in half, the image blurry in the increasingly thick downpour. The driver lumbered to the back of the bus and pressed the switch to the automatic lift attached to the rear door. The bus shuddered as the lift's machinery whirred, gears churning. The wheelchair occupant slid into the corner reserved for him, locking the wheels of his chair into place with swift, practiced movements.

The other passengers averted their gazes, obviously trying not to stare, but Edmund, having been stared at all his life, didn't give a damn what a cripple thought of him. He looked directly at the man, taking in every detail. Hispanic, middle-aged, well put together, the muscular shoulders visible even beneath the heavy rain gear. He wore padded leather biking gloves, which covered his palms but left the fingers exposed. His hands were thick and powerful-looking. Edmund guessed the man had been a gimp for a while, maybe even all his life. He imagined crippled legs under the poncho: white, spindly as a chicken's legs, the muscles atrophied from years of inactivity. He turned away, disgusted, and looked back out the window at the night.

Catching the flow of the streetlight, the raindrops glistened like jewels as they slid down the glass windowpane. He was transfixed by their beauty and purity. In that moment he saw the secret revealed to him in the reflection of a street lamp on a rain-soaked bus window. He must live his life in search of purity and perfection. Fleeting as it was, it was the only thing really worth living for. Everything else was ugliness, as deformed as the useless legs of a cripple.

# CHAPTER TWENTY-SEVEN

Kylie didn't have much time to spare between arriving home from school, dressing for the concert and getting back in time for a pre-concert brushup rehearsal. She wolfed down some dinner and dashed upstairs to change. She had a ride with her friend Meredith, whose father was playing piano for the concert. She behaved normally enough during dinner, though that didn't surprise Lee. With him and Stan around, she was bound to be on her best behavior—at least for now.

Kylie attended Stockton Elementary, the same public school Lee and Laura had gone to at her age. It was on the little town's Main Street, just down from the Stockton Inn. The classes were tiny—only ten or so students per grade—and the L-shaped nineteenth-century stone and clapboard building was more than big enough to house grades K through six.

The entire school participated in the annual Christmas concert, and it looked as though half the town had turned up to attend. People bundled in winter coats and mittens flowed through the gate to the school's side yard, their breath coming in thick white shafts of steam. A winter storm watch was on for all of Hunterdon

County, and a few flakes fluttered from the sky as they lined up to go inside. Lee looked at his mother, hatless as usual—she liked to flaunt her hardy Scottish constitution—but he noticed she had wrapped her tartan scarf tightly around her neck. He recognized the red and gray pattern of the Clan Campbell. Lee found it odd that she still sported the clan colors of the man who had betrayed and deserted her. Stan stood stalwartly at her side, one hand resting lightly on her elbow in a proprietary way. Lee was a little surprised she put up with it. But Fiona was nothing if not surprising.

As he followed the crowd of people up the steps to the tiny auditorium in the rear of the building, Lee inhaled the familiar musty smell of damp wood and flagstone. His and Laura's days at Stockton Elementary had been happy ones. Their parents were still together, their family unit intact, cozy and secure. The future had stretched out before them, promising and lazy as the waters of the Delaware that flowed under the narrow bridge to Pennsylvania.

But that had all changed the night their father left, never to return, and their family shrank from four to three. That got Lee to thinking about the Alleyway Strangler and his family. What was the arithmatic of his family, and what had it done to him? Had killing become a kind of mathematical puzzle for him? *One is the loneliest number. One missing digit.* But *why*? And even if he knew why, would it help him find the Strangler?

"Excuse *me*." A middle-aged woman in a red wool coat and matching hat glared at him, and he realized he had stepped on her toes.

"Sorry," he mumbled, taking a step backward. That caused him to bump into Stan, who gave him a playful nudge.

"Quite a crowd tonight, huh?"

"Yeah," Lee said, preoccupied with why someone would remove just one finger from a victim. What was the significance of that? And what was the meaning of the elaborate pattern he had punctured into her torso? Or was the killer just toying with them all? The whole thing could be an elaborate red herring to throw them off.

They all managed to shuffle into the auditorium at last, and the concert got under way fifteen minutes late. It was clear the school hadn't anticipated such a large turnout. But cultural events in the area were thin compared to New York, and everyone looked pleased to be there.

The program was a mix of Christmas carols and Hanukah songs, as well as a few more challenging pieces, including selections from Benjamin Britten's *A Ceremony of Carols*. Kylie sang with the altos, who acquitted themselves with honor in the difficult "As Dewe in Aprille." Looking at her eager, shiny face, Lee tried to imagine the dark thoughts and feelings his niece must be grappling with. But he knew from his own struggle with depression that it could come and go. One minute the sun was shining, and the next you were submerged in a flood of anxiety and darkness. He hoped he would be able to help her, though he realized each person's experience was different.

Fiona sat stiff and upright in her chair, as always, her clear blue eyes focused on the stage, a proud little smile working the corners of her mouth. He knew she loved her granddaughter, but he could see why Kylie might feel uncomfortable talking with her about deep and troubling feelings. He only hoped his niece would be able to talk to him.

After the concert they joined the surge of bodies headed backstage. Families crowded around their happy and excited children—the younger ones hopped and squirmed and dashed in and out of the clusters of people, until they were stopped by teachers or parents and given the age-old caution of "No running!"

Looking at the happy faces around him, Lee was saddened to think of the Adlers sitting primly in their immaculate Westchester living room, no daughter to share the holidays with ever again. They might not be the most appealing people he had ever met, but their tragedy could not be denied.

Kylie was standing with a group of friends, and when she saw him, the expression that crossed her face took his breath away. It was a mixture of relief, regret, apprehension and joy. He held his distance and waved, but she ran over to him and flung herself into his arms. She was tall for her age and solidly built. He staggered backward, then lifted her in a bear hug.

"Uncle Lee, thank you so much for coming!"

He hugged her back, inhaling the honeysuckle scent of her yellow hair. Laura's hair had smelled exactly the same. Kylie looked more like her mother every day, he thought—the same firm chin, thin nose and deep-set blue eyes.

"You were great. I'm so proud of you."

She looked over her shoulder, then whispered to him. "Our choir director says I'm the anchor of the third-grade altos."

"Good for you! You have to have a really good ear to sing alto."

"Fiona says I got it from you."

He laughed. Musicality was not among Fiona's many talents—this ability seemed to have come from Duncan Campbell. Lee could still remember his clear tenor ringing out over the others in the church choir in their little Presbyterian church. He hated all the good memories of his father—they just confused him and made him angrier.

"Your grandmother has a theory for everything," he said.

Kylie shot him a quizzical look, then wrested herself from his arms and ran back to rejoin her friends.

It was a happy, buzzing crowd that exited the little school yard that night—children safe in the embrace of their families, looking forward to the delights of the coming holidays. Gingerbread and Christmas cookies, the piney smell of decorated trees, presents and stockings and houses full of visitors. Lee stepped with them into the frosty air and watched the thick, fat snowflakes falling faster and faster from the sky. A thin sheet of white already covered the ground under their feet.

Here everything felt peaceful and secure, but somewhere ninety miles to the east, a predator was likely planning his next move.

# Chapter Twenty-eight

As predicted, the winter storm blew in from the west throughout the night. The weatherman had estimated twelve to twenty-four inches overnight, and by ten o'clock the snow was coming thick and fast, with three inches already on the ground. Lying in bed shortly before midnight, Lee heard the rattle of snowplows heaving up and down the street, their metal blades clanking harshly on the pockmarked pavement.

The snow murmured as it fluttered from the sky. Thick, wet flakes clung to the windowpanes, enclosing the inhabitants of the house. The wind whipped and whistled in the eaves, rustling and nestling against the stone walls, tapping at the windows and whining like a dog wanting to come in. It was hard to resist the pull of sleep, but he managed to stay awake, listening to the storm. He did some of his best thinking late at night.

He thought about the notes the Alleyway Strangler had written. Some of the hints about his identity could be false—but which ones? The man could be playing with them, leaving red herrings along with real clues. Of course, it was possible that every clue contained in the letters was false, but Lee didn't think so. This

UNSUB was too arrogant for that. He was enjoying the challenge of tossing out real clues about his identity—and he was also a sadist, toying with them intellectually.

A fierce gust of wind rattled the nearly three-hundred-year-old shutters. Lee sat up in bed and switched on the light in the antique sconce next to the headboard. Outside, the snow clung to the windowpanes like cold white hands, the pattern of flakes resembling long, thin fingers clutching at the glass. *One little piggy went to market . . .* He remembered his father reciting that nursery rhyme to him as he wiggled Lee's toes one by one, starting with the big toe and working down to the little toe. *One little piggy stayed home . . .* If only his father had stayed home, instead of walking out of the house on a night very much like this one. *What kind of man does that to his family?* He felt the anger rising up his neck like steam in a pipe.

What kind of monster did this UNSUB have for a father? Surely worse than Duncan Campbell—who, though far from ideal, had graced them with his glamorous presence for a time. His love might have been somewhat distant, but at least it was there—for a while. But this killer . . . he was made, not born, Lee thought. He didn't believe the Bad Seed theory of criminal psychology. He'd read of a few well-documented cases of brain damage or genetic mutation being responsible for criminal pathologies, but for every one of those there were thousands of cases of abusive and neglectful parents spawning killers. Psychopaths were more often than not the sad result of hopelessly dysfunctional families and brutal environments—and those, coupled with certain physical or mental vulnerabilities, could produce a perfect storm of psychopathology.

He felt a draft of air on his left cheek and turned to see a few flakes slipping through a space between the two ancient windows where the wood had warped and left a small gap. The wind had shifted, and a thin stream of air whooshed through the opening. He pulled the covers up higher and made a mental note to mention it to Stan in the morning. Stan liked to keep everything shipshape, perhaps hoping Fiona would learn to love him for his skill as a handyman and gardener.

But that's not how it worked. It was sad, really—Stan Paloggia was so *worthy*. If only people could fall in love with worthy mates, he thought, the world would be a better place. But love wasn't necessarily given to the deserving or the wise. Lee suspected if she had it to do all over again, Fiona would have still chosen the dashing, edgy Duncan Campbell, with his brooding black eyes, restless intellect and fine tenor voice.

The sound of his mother's snoring rose from the room below. She had always been a sound sleeper. Even during a crisis, she could sleep through the night. But Lee had always been a finicky, light sleeper—a trait inherited from his despised father. He hoped Duncan Campbell was dead, because if he was alive and Lee chanced to meet him, the first thing he would do was take a swing at him. And he feared it wouldn't stop there. It was odd that he chased murderers, with his murderous thoughts toward his own father.

Or, as Dr. Williams would say, maybe that's exactly *why* he hunted killers. She was right, of course, but it was still irritating. He made a mental note to call her—

it had been a few weeks since their last appointment. It was exasperating, the relentless logic of the unconscious mind. He sometimes wished he were a cocktail pianist playing in some smoky dive in Jersey City, instead of a forensic psychologist. Even that would be about his father on some level, though—Duncan Campbell had taught both his children to play.

As the snow danced and fluttered outside his window, he finally fell into a restless sleep populated by unquiet dreams of young women fleeing from an unknown assailant. He awoke around three in the morning with the impression that the faceless pursuer was his father, his dark eyes full of malice. He pulled the covers up to his chin and waited for the pale, reassuring light of dawn.

# CHAPTER TWENTY-NINE

"No, please—*please,*" she begged, her eyes wide with terror.

Edmund smiled and inhaled the musky scent of fear. They all had it, and it intoxicated him. He shook his whole body, as a dog might shake water from its coat, as the sweet sensation trickled through his veins, his nerve endings tingling with pleasure.

"Are you frightened of me?" he whispered, bending lower over his captive, until his torso formed a right angle with the wall.

"Yes, yes—I'm frightened," the girl replied, her eyes scanning his face to see if that was the correct response.

But there was no correct response. No magic words to undo the spell, no incantations to save her from him. He liked them to think there was, of course, but there wasn't. He enjoyed the begging, leaving the door to freedom open just a slit so they could see the light through it—just enough to keep alive that tiny spark of hope that they might escape, that he might have mercy on them and not kill them after all. If they just did what he wanted, said what he required, it could all be all right.

Except that it couldn't. No one he took would ever get away. The last thing they would see would be his face—his scarred, hideous face. Hope was his to give and his to take away, just as their lives were his to give and take away.

He looked down at this one. She wasn't as pretty as the last one—her features were coarser, and her skin didn't have quite the same sheen—but she would do. Yes, she would do quite nicely.

He turned and selected one of his instruments from the assortment laid out on the table. Behind him, she whimpered.

"Please—*please* let me go."

"Shhh," he murmured. "It'll all be over soon—you'll see."

He turned back to her. The steel gleamed briefly in the light from the bare overhead bulb, and he was drowned in the sound of her screams.

# Chapter Thirty

The storm turned out to be even more severe than expected. Lee came down the next morning to learn that trees had fallen all over the county, their branches weighed down by the heavy cascade of snow. It was warm enough that the snow had fallen wet and thick—"a packing snow," as Fiona would say—good for snowballs and forts but not sledding. Phone lines were down too, and half of Hunterdon County had no electricity. Motorists were being cautioned to stay off the roads at least until the afternoon.

Unfortunately, the town of Stockton was in the grid where the power had gone out. That meant that Lee's cell phone, which was dead, and its charger were useless, at least for the time being. The gas worked, though, and his mother insisted on making him breakfast on her gas stove.

After choking down a few bites of bacon and scrambled eggs, Lee gulped the rest of his coffee and rose from the table.

"I'm going to cross the bridge and see what's happening in Pennsylvania."

His mother raised an eyebrow. "Do you think it's a good idea to go out? They said—"

"I need to get to a phone."

She put her hands up in surrender. "You heard what they said about the roads."

"I'll drive carefully," he said, kissing her on the cheek.

"Take my car—I have snow tires," she said, handing him the keys. "Kylie will be sorry she missed you." His niece was still in bed—like all the Campbell women, she was a sound sleeper.

"I'll be back."

He stepped out onto the porch and into a brilliant sunny day, the light intensified by the coating of white everywhere. The winter sun reflected hard and bright in his face, and he held up a hand to shield his eyes from the glare. The snow on the front walk was knee-high, and his feet sank deeply into it with each step. He was glad he had worn his Santana snow boots, though he could already feel the damp seeping in through the tops.

The snow was piled high on top of everything—the stone bench by the springhouse wore a perfect rectangle of white. The sounds of the outdoors were muffled by the drifts and snow underfoot, his feet making a soft crunching noise with each step. Stan Paloggia had already plowed Fiona's driveway, so getting off the property would be easy. He imagined Stan, up at daybreak, chugging happily down the driveway in his yellow John Deere with the snowplow attachment. Stan loved being useful; he seemed happiest when doing favors for people, especially Fiona.

The question was whether the county plows had made it as far as her road yet. Lee brushed the snow from his mother's big black Ford—she drove a Crown Victoria, just like the ones New York cops used. It started up on the first try; he backed it up and rolled slowly down the driveway. Luckily, Fiona's road had been cleared, the snow piled high along one side of the narrow country lane.

He passed people bundled in down parkas shoveling snow from their driveways as he drove toward Stockton's tiny main street, but he didn't see another car on the road until he reached the bridge to Pennsylvania. An old blue station wagon rattled across the steel bridge, its rear wheels fishtailing as it hit the metal grate. The Delaware flowed sluggishly beneath him, the gray water curling in currents and eddies under the bridge. Lee crept across the short span to Pennsylvania, driving northwest on the River Road.

The beauty of River Road was startling. Tree branches bowed gracefully under a coating of soft snow as thick and creamy as the icing on a cake. Lemony rays of morning sun rippled and dipped into the hollows of the drifts in the deep woods on either side of the road, glinting on the windshield as the road wound and twisted along the banks of the Delaware. Out on the river, ice floes drifted lazily downstream; from time to time wisps of snow blew down from the trees overhanging the two-lane road. It was a scene of such captivating loveliness that Lee's mood began to lift as he followed the curves in the road.

Lumberville was the closest town, about three miles along River Road, and he swung into the parking lot of the General Store, a stone and clapboard building snuggled just a few feet off the road. The sign in front proclaimed the building's construction date to be 1803; Lee imagined horses and wagons rattling up to its door in a time when River Road was little more than a mud rut.

The General Store was open for business, which was booming, judging by the number of cars squeezed into its tiny parking lot. A popular place for locals to gather for coffee, news and gossip, it seemed to be doing a brisk business. A couple of snowplows sat at the entrance to the lot, their engines still steaming.

The storm door slapped against its metal frame as he entered, stomping the snow from his boots. The great round walnut table in the front of the store was occupied by half a dozen men in lumberjack shirts, wool caps and knee-high Wellingtons—the snowplow crews. They were men with rough, callused hands and sunburned faces and crosshatched maps of lines under their eyes from years of squinting into all kinds of weather. A couple of them nodded at Lee when he entered before turning back to their conversation over thick white mugs of steaming coffee. A plate piled high with doughnuts sat in the middle of the table. The steam radiator in the corner hissed, mixing with the clatter of coffee cups and silverware and the hum of conversation.

"What can I get you?" asked the pixyish girl behind the counter. Her dark bangs came to a perfect point in the center of her forehead, and a pair of silver lip rings adorned the left side of her mouth. Her eyes were dark and heavily kohl-lined, and she wore a multicolored wool vest, obviously hand-knitted. He guessed she was a Solebury student, probably a senior art major.

"Coffee, please," he said, inhaling the deep, rich aroma of an African roast. His mother was a fine cook, but she'd never quite gotten the hang of making good coffee. Spotting a pay phone on the back wall, Lee took his coffee to a small corner table and dug a handful of coins from his pocket. First he dialed Butts's cell phone and reached his voice mail. He left a message telling the detective that he would drive back to the city as soon as the roads were cleared.

Then he dialed the voice mail to his own cell phone. When the recording told him he had two messages, he entered the four-digit code and waited. He heard the crackling sound of bad reception, then Brian O'Reilly's voice.

"I didn't hear the *(crackle)* . . . this thing recording?"

He covered his other ear and listened intently. The connection was bad—not on the pay phone but between O'Reilly and his cell phone. The detective's voice came in and out, so that what he heard was: ". . . thought of something . . . might be . . . sister . . . if you get this . . . I'll be here."

The message ended in the sputtering of a bad connection; then a recording came on, ordering him to put more money into the pay phone.

"Damn," he muttered, his hand trembling as he fumbled for more coins. He slid a couple of quarters into the slot and listened to the next message. It was from Kathy. This time the reception was better.

"It's me," she said, sounding both forlorn and irritated. "Look, I—I just want to say that I'm sorry if I'm being a jerk about this. I'm just not *sure*, okay? About anything, I guess. I just . . . oh, I don't know. I suddenly wanted to hear your voice. But you're not there, so—guess I'll catch you later."

He deleted the message; he didn't need to deal with her right now. He wanted to know what Brian O'Reilly had said. He pressed the button to repeat the message again, but he caught even less the second time. A burst of laughter from the table of plow drivers obscured O'Reilly's words. He put his finger into his other ear again and played it a third time, with no improvement. There was no way to tell when O'Reilly had called; cell phones were notoriously slippery about giving the time messages were recorded.

Behind him, one of the drivers, a short, black-haired man with tobacco-stained fingers, was waiting to use the pay phone, so he pressed the button to save the message and turned the phone over to the plow driver.

He returned to his table, where his neglected coffee sat cooling. He took a sip. It was good, but he had lost his interest in coffee. What he wanted more than anything was to know what Brian O'Reilly had said. His hand closed around his useless cell phone in his pocket. O'Reilly's number would be on it, but that did him no good unless the phone was charged. His number was unlisted, and Lee didn't want to hit up his source in the NYPD for the number a second time. He cursed himself for neglecting to bring the charger with him to the store.

Gulping down the rest of his coffee, he headed for

the exit—maybe the electricity was back on at his mother's house. A blast of cold air hit him in the face as he opened the door to the outside. Inside, another burst of laughter was cut abruptly short as the storm door slammed behind him.

# Chapter Thirty-one

Driving back on River Road, Lee felt a sense of urgency and tried to compensate by driving more carefully. The sun had melted the top layer of snow into a surface of slick ice, and he coached himself to slow down, but a gnawing in his stomach and a tightening in his right temple urged him on. *Too much damn coffee*, he told himself, but it was more than that. He needed to be back in the city, and with miles of snow-packed roads between him and his goal, his impatience grew with every passing minute.

The snow was beginning to topple from the branches now, as the heat of the sun made it wetter and heavier. The wind had picked up too, blowing great clouds of white mist across the road, obscuring it from view.

"Christ," he muttered, shifting into low gear as he crept around a curve in the road. His cell phone let out an abrupt beep, and he swerved, startled by the sound. The rear tires lost their traction, sliding on the smooth surface of the road, and suddenly the car was traveling sideways.

Dimly recalled driving advice darted through his head: *pump the brakes, and turn in the direction of the skid.* But what did that mean? Should he pull the wheel toward the direction the rear tires were headed in? Pumping the brakes, he wrested the wheel toward the center of the road, to avoid having the car swing in a full circle. It worked—to some extent. The rear of the car swung back in the other direction, but now the car was headed toward the opposite guardrail. He steeled himself for the impact, keeping his hands firmly on the wheel. He was grateful there were no oncoming cars as he braced his body for the impact.

The sound was louder than he expected. It rang like the report of a rifle through the wintry air, startling the stillness of the postcard landscape. His body was protected by the shoulder harness, but his head rapped sharply against the steering wheel with a *thunk.* Dazed, he sat staring at the snow cascading down from the tree branches overhead. He felt the ripple of adrenaline, thin and cold, as it drained from his veins. It was followed by a welcome sensation of relief that turned his limbs to lead and made him suddenly sleepy. He could see the Delaware through the thin layer of trees, the slate gray water sluggish, pockmarked with swirling currents and eddies. His anxiety melted like the top layer of snow in the afternoon sun, and peace settled over him like a blanket. He wanted nothing more than to stay there, in the warm car, staring at the river.

Just then he realized the car was sprawled over one lane of the road—anyone taking the curve too fast would surely hit him. He reached for the gear shift, his hand shaking. He put it into Reverse and pressed tentatively on the gas pedal; the rear drive wheel spun a little before gaining traction. The big car backed obediently into the road, the eight-cylinder engine humming quietly. He straightened up and pulled over to the side as much as possible, given the drifts of plowed snow along the road. He put on the emergency flashers and stepped out to view the damage.

When the frosty air hit his face, he was seized by a wave of dizziness, and he leaned on the door handle until it passed. To his relief, there wasn't much damage to the car. There was a dent in the front bumper, and a deeper one in the metal guardrail, but other than that, the car looked sound enough. He sighed a prayer of relief for his mother's old-fashioned ways; the Ford's sturdy bumper barely showed any damage at all. She was right when she said they didn't make cars like they used to. As he slid into the driver's seat, it occurred to him that maybe the same thing was true of mothers. For better or worse, Fiona would always be Fiona.

He looked behind him to see if there was any oncoming traffic; not a single car had passed since his collision. Just as he was about to pull back onto the road, his cell phone chirped again. He snatched it from the dashboard and looked at it, wondering why it had suddenly come to life. The metal was warm to the touch. It had been sitting in the sun for some time now, the heat intensified by the effect of the car's windshield. The battery must have revived a little, he thought as he flipped it open.

There was a new text message from Butts: CALL ASAP.

He tossed the phone onto the passenger seat and considered whether he should go back to Lumberville or continue on to his mother's and hope her power had been restored. He decided to continue on. He swung the big car back onto the road, the packed snow crunching under its heavy tires. Gritting his teeth, he peered at the road ahead, forcing himself to crawl along at twenty miles per hour.

He maintained that speed all the way to his mother's house. When he arrived, he saw Fiona, in a bright red parka, shoveling the front walk. He pulled into the parking spot and sprang from the car. Another wave of dizziness swept over him, and he almost fell, but he caught himself by leaning on the hood of the car.

"Mom!" he called to her. "Why don't you leave that for Stan or me?"

"Don't be silly," she puffed, heaving a shovelful of snow over her shoulder. "It's good exercise, and you have enough to do. Besides," she said, with a sweep of her gloved hand, "Stan already cleared the path. I just want to make it wider."

He started to argue but realized it was no use; at the same moment he was hit by a wave of nausea. He took two steps, sank to his knees and vomited. Dazed, he stared at the steam rising from the coffee-colored contents of his stomach splattered over the pristine white snow.

He looked up to see his mother standing over him, her cheeks blazing from the cold and exertion. She looked worried.

"What on earth happened to you?" she asked, reaching down to touch his forehead.

He drew back, his skin tender to the touch, and raised his own hand to feel the egg-shaped lump rising from his head.

"Shit," he said.

He was so concentrated on trying to reach Detective Butts that he had forgotten hitting his head on the steering wheel. Two things were immediately clear to him:

(1) He had a concussion.

(2) He wouldn't let it slow him down.

He looked up at his mother. She was leaning on her snow shovel, her breath coming in thin white gusts. He paused; he wanted to make sure whatever lie he formulated was a good one before speaking.

But she was too quick for him.

"You have a concussion, don't you?" It was an accusation, not an expression of sympathy.

"Don't be silly," he said. "I just drank too much coffee, and it upset my stomach."

"And this?" she demanded, pointing to the bump on his head.

That was going to be harder to explain, he thought as he rose unsteadily to his feet. But he was determined to get back to the city as soon as possible, even if it meant taking the bus. Whether he had a concussion or not, Butts needed him.

# Chapter Thirty-two

His mother followed him into the house, clucking and scolding, shaking her head when he asked to use the phone.

"You know, one of these days you're going to just—" she began.

"*Please,*" he said. "It's important."

"Of course you can use the phone, if it's working. But you'd better lie down and rest before you faint dead away."

"I will," he lied. "I just need to make a couple of calls."

She went into the kitchen and returned with a package of frozen peas wrapped in a towel.

"Put this on your head," she said. "It'll help with the swelling."

There was no point in arguing. He went to the phone extension in the living room and picked up the receiver. To his relief, the phone line was working, though it sounded scratchy. He called Butts, got a busy signal, then dialed Brian O'Reilly's number. A woman picked up on the second ring.

"Oh, I'm sorry," Lee said. "I must have the wrong number."

"Are you trying to reach Brian O'Reilly?" Her voice was low and thick, as if she had been crying.

"Uh, yes. I—"

"Brian is dead."

The news hit him like a body blow. He took a step backward and sank into the armchair next to the couch.

"*What?* What happened?"

"I don't know yet."

"Well, what—"

"Are you a friend of Brian's?"

"My name is Lee Campbell. I'm—"

"I know who you are. I'm very sorry about your sister. Brian wanted more than anything to find out what happened to her."

"I know. I—I saw him just a couple of days ago."

"Then tell me something. Did he seem suicidal to you?"

"Well, no—depressed, maybe, but not—"

"The police say it was suicide."

Just then Kylie wandered into the room, carrying Fiona's big, ill-tempered tabby, Groucho. The cat was growling and trying to break free, but Kylie had him in a half nelson.

"Who are you talking to?" she demanded, with the tactless directness of a child. She was still wearing her pink flannel pajamas, and her uncombed blond hair shot out in all directions in wispy cowlicks. Lee was surprised his mother was allowing this, but maybe she was treating her granddaughter delicately, hoping to stop her self-destructive behavior.

Lee covered the mouthpiece with his hand. "I'm on a business call, sweetie," he said.

"Why are you wearing peas on your head?"

His hand went up to the package of peas, which he had placed on top of his head when he sat down. He had completely forgotten about them.

"This is to help with the bump on my head. Do you mind playing with Groucho in the other room?"

Kylie shrugged. "Okay. I think he wants to watch cartoons. Do you, Groucho?" she asked, nestling her face close to his. The cat responded by throwing a left hook in the direction of her cheek, but she was quick, pulling away in time to avoid the flying claws. She tightened her hold on him and padded into the parlor.

"I'm sorry," Lee said into the phone when Kylie had gone. "That was my niece."

The woman sighed, or shuddered, or maybe it was a sob; he couldn't tell.

He lowered his voice. "I need to . . . are you Brian's—"

"I'm his sister."

"Oh. I didn't know he had a—I really didn't know very much about him."

"Nobody did. That's the way he wanted it."

"Can we—can I see you when I get back to the city?"

"Sure."

"Thanks—I'll call you."

"Good. I have to go—I have a lot of calls to make."

"Can I just—what's your name?"

"Gemma."

"Thanks, Gemma."

He was about to hang up when he heard the beep of

call waiting. He clicked the receiver once and answered it.

"Hello?"

Detective Butts's growl of a baritone came ringing through the phone line, as clearly as if he was standing next to Lee.

"Oh, man, I'm glad I got you. Your cell phone is bouncin' straight to voice mail."

"I know. The storm—"

"Sorry to track you down at your mom's, but we got another body."

"Oh, God. Where was she—"

There was a buzzing sound, a series of clicks, and the line went dead again.

"Damn," he muttered, slinging the receiver back into place. "Goddamn it!"

His mother appeared in the doorway, her arms folded. "Please don't swear in front of your niece," she said icily.

He stood up, swayed a little and caught himself on the back of the chair.

She scowled at him. "Am I going to have to tie you down to prevent you from doing something foolish?"

He started to explain, but the room took his head for a little spin, and he had to sit down again. His head was beginning to pound.

"I'm going," he muttered. "Even if I take the bus, I'm going back to the city, *now*."

"Suit yourself," she said airily as she left the room—but he knew he would have hell to pay later.

Lately, it seemed, there was a lot of hell to go around.

# Chapter Thirty-three

The Hunterdon County buses were running on a cut-back schedule, but there was one leaving at four o'clock that afternoon for New York. Fiona gave up trying to make him stay and agreed to return his rental car in Somerville, the nearest large town, where there was an Enterprise office. Of course, Stan Paloggia was only too delighted to help. He had come and gone twice already since Lee had returned from Lumberville—once to deliver mail from Fiona's mailbox at the end of the long driveway, and the other to bring coffee and Danish from Errico's Market, which was giving out hot coffee to everyone who had lost electricity in the storm. Fiona's house had power, but any excuse for a visit would do for Stan. Afterward, he chugged off in his John Deere to find someone else in need, humming tunelessly to himself, his nose red and dripping from the cold. Lee had never seen him happier.

Kylie spent the afternoon sledding with her friends Meredith and Angelica before going over to Angelica's house for hot chocolate and video games. Lee stood at the kitchen window listening to the shrieks of glee from the girls as they piled on top of one another on his old Flexible Flyer, wobbling unsteadily down the hill leading to the springhouse until one of them fell off, amid more squeals and giggling. He swallowed a couple of ibuprofen to control the drumming in his head and gulped down a couple of glasses of water. For some reason, he was very thirsty.

Listening to the girls, he found it hard to believe his niece was struggling with the kind of issues that lead to self-mutilation. To his eyes, she looked like a normal, happy little girl. Before she left for Angelica's house, she wrapped her arms around him in a bear hug and planted a kiss on his cheek.

"Thank you for coming to my concert, Uncle Lee."

He nestled in the warm scent of her hair, inhaling the fresh smell of the woods.

"I really enjoyed it. I'm so glad you're enjoying music; it's something we share."

She pulled away and looked at him searchingly for a moment. "Fiona says my mom liked music too."

"She did, honey. She had a wonderful singing voice." Lee noticed they were both using the past tense to talk about her. He wished he had more time to spend with his niece, but the case was pressing on him. He couldn't resist lifting the phone receiver every ten minutes or so to see if the line was back on, but it was still dead.

When Lee came downstairs with his overnight bag a little after three, his mother stood in the doorway to the parlor, arms crossed, a frown on her face.

"May I have a word with you?"

"Sure," he said, following her into the living room.

He thought she was going to try to talk him out of going again, but apparently she had given up on that.

"Look, I know you're really busy right now, but . . .

I was wondering if you could make some time to spend with Kylie—just talk to her, you know. I know she really looks up to you."

The pounding in his head increased, and his mother's face was beginning to blur. He blinked his eyes in an attempt to focus.

"Well, I—"

"I really feel like I can't handle this on my own."

"What about George?"

She gave a dismissive wave of her hand. "Oh, you know George—he's a big, sweet baby. God knows what Laura saw in him." She clapped a hand over her mouth. "I'm sorry, I didn't really mean that. It's just that he's—well, he's very kind, but—"

"Kind of clueless."

"I'm afraid so. Big and sweet and clueless. Like a teddy bear."

He pressed his fingers to his right temple and blinked again.

She peered at him, frowning. "What is it? Your head bothering you?"

"No, no," he lied. "Look, I'd really like to help with Kylie, so why don't we make a plan for her to visit me in a week or so? Do you mind sending her on the bus?"

"That's fine—she likes the bus."

"I'll see if I can talk to her then. Meanwhile, keep me posted, okay?"

She sighed and looked down at her long hands, with their elegantly tapered fingers. "You sure you have to go back today?"

"I'm sorry, but they just found another girl."

"Oh, God," she said, looking out at the Currier and Ives landscape of eighteenth-century stone buildings surrounded by soft, billowy snow. "Brigadoon"—that's what his mother called her property—had been featured on the cover of *New Jersey Life*, and *Elegant Homes* had done a spread on it a few years ago. In addition to the main house, there was a stable with its own walled paddock, a carriage house and a springhouse. Under Fiona's stewardship, Brigadoon was a fusion of comfort, taste and elegance. Now, though, his mother's face reflected the despair he knew she must be feeling. Her only daughter was gone, probably dead, and now her only grandchild seemed to be spiraling into a lonely place where she might soon be out of reach. Fiona Campbell was a relentless optimist, but even she seemed to be bending under such burdens.

"Why do they do it, Lee?" she said softly, almost to herself. "What makes people do wicked things like that?"

"Nobody really knows for sure," he replied. "But it's my job to try to stop them."

She took a deep, shuddering breath and turned to him. Her face was a mask of pain, but her eyes were dry.

"Then you go do it," she said. "You go do your job."

# Chapter Thirty-four

Lee went straight from the Port Authority to the Thirteenth Precinct, where the other members of the task force were already gathered. The station house was deserted except for a desk sergeant and a sleepy-looking civilian clerk. He nodded at the sergeant and went through to Butts's office, where he found the others seated around a bulletin board covered with crime scene photos.

He took a seat next to Jimmy Chen, who was dressed in a blue turtleneck and soggy hiking boots instead of his usual Italian suit. Everyone in the room looked damp and bedraggled, except for Krieger, who was crisp and immaculate as usual in a white cable-knit sweater, ski pants and black thigh-high boots. In the corner underneath the window, the room's only radiator sputtered and hissed.

"Where did they find her?" Lee asked.

"MacDougal Alley, behind a row of garbage cans," Butts said. "She had been dead for over twenty-four hours, so he put her there before the storm."

"Who found her?"

"Guy walkin' his dog," said Butts. "The dog started

digging in the snow, wouldn't give up, so the guy goes over to see what's up and finds her."

"That's not a very secluded spot," said Lee. "Why didn't someone didn't see her sooner?"

"He put a tarp over her this time," said Butts. "The lab is checkin' it for trace evidence."

"Same MO otherwise?" Lee asked.

"Ligature strangulation, yeah," said Butts. "But there seems to be a change in what you would call his signature."

"How so?" asked Detective Krieger, cocking her head to one side. "Didn't he take a finger this time?"

"He did," Butts said, holding up a photo of the girl's left hand, missing the pinky finger. "Exact same one as before, in fact. But this is different." He held up a photo of the young woman's nude torso. As before, there were minute, evenly spaced puncture wounds, but this time the pattern was immediately apparent: it was a pentagram.

"More of that—what did you call it?" said Butts.

"Piquerism," said Lee.

"Yeah."

"What, is he into witchcraft now?" Jimmy Chen asked.

They all looked at Lee. He blinked his eyes to eliminate the blurred edges around everything; a couple of trolls with sledgehammers had now taken up residence inside his head.

"I don't think we should jump to conclusions," he said. "We have to look at everything in context. What do we know about the victim?"

"Name's Mandy Pritchard. She's a part-time student at Columbia."

"So he has a thing for college students," Jimmy mused aloud.

"Could be a coincidence," said Krieger.

"Maybe," said Lee. "But I think we have to consider someone who moves comfortably in the world of academia, someone who would fit in on a college campus."

"Another student?" suggested Butts.

Lee shook his head. "I don't think so. This guy is likely to be older—maybe even much older. He's as pure an example of an organized killer as I've ever seen. And he calls himself The Professor."

Krieger frowned. "So are we talking about a real professor?"

"Not necessarily. There are a lot of people who come and go on a college campus."

"But the notes," Jimmy said. "Don't they indicate a high level of education?"

"Did he leave one this time?" Lee asked Krieger.

"No, he didn't—or at least we haven't found it yet," she replied.

"Interesting . . . I wonder why he didn't leave one this time."

"Maybe he was in a hurry," Jimmy suggested.

"Except that he's completely organized and plans every detail carefully," said Lee.

"Could he be losin' it?" Butts asked. "Starting to fall apart from the stress?"

"That would be great, but I don't think so. Everything else points to just as much control as before."

"The lab is looking for DNA, prints, trace evidence—anything they can find," said Butts, listlessly fingering a chocolate doughnut. It took a lot to put the detective off his food, and Lee didn't envy Butts being in charge of this case.

"Maybe this time we'll get lucky," Jimmy suggested.

"Yeah, right," said Butts, but no one believed it.

"I was hoping for a handwritten note, but he's too smart for that," Krieger commented.

"So what's with the pentagram?" asked Butts. "Looks like some kinda devil worship to me."

Lee studied the photo. The tiny puncture marks were evenly spaced, even more precise than the last time, and made up a perfect pentagram.

"No," he said slowly. "He's not falling apart. If anything, he's getting more confident."

In the corner, the ancient radiator hissed and clanked, the metallic rattling keeping time with the pounding in Lee's temples. Looking at his colleagues' grim faces, he wished he could take his words back, but it was too late. It was too late for a lot of things; the question was whether it was too late to stop this killer before he struck again.

# CHAPTER THIRTY-FIVE

The meeting ended around nine, all of them bleary-eyed and exhausted, leaving to make their way home through the snowy streets. Butts left to grab a bus out to Jersey—he had wisely declined to drive in, given the weather. Lee was the most fortunate, living less than a mile from the precinct house. He had brought only a backpack to his mother's, so he slung it over his shoulder and decided to head home on foot. The pounding in his temples was lessening, but he still felt fuzzy and unfocused, and he figured the walk might clear his head.

He took copies of the crime scene photos, slid them carefully into his backpack and stepped out into the night. . . .

Across town, Edmund sat at the piano, hunched over the keyboard, concentrating on the manuscript in front of him, his fingers pressing hard upon the ivory keys. The notes wove and danced on the page before his eyes, and he could feel the tiny felt hammers striking the strings—he loved the fact that the piano was a percussion instrument. The glorious harmonies of Bach's Prelude XXI echoed from the baby grand's sounding board, filling the air with the mathematical purity of his music.

He finished the piece and shivered with pleasure. This, truly, was happiness—to be the conduit for the genius of Bach, to live in this moment, more than three hundred years after his death, in this Greenwich Village apartment. . . .

Lee turned the key in the lock on the front door of his apartment and for a moment had the feeling someone else was there. He flicked on the light, stepped inside and locked the door behind him, listening carefully. He heard nothing except the sound of people in the street outside, their voices muted by the thick layer of snow blanketing the city. He took a few steps in and looked around. Nothing looked out of place—the throw quilt lay on the couch where he had tossed it after his last nap, the last pair of shoes he'd worn were exactly where he'd left them, and the leftover coffee grounds were still in the Krups filter in the kitchen. Yet he couldn't escape the feeling that something was different—that someone had been there while he was away, leaving an energy trail behind them.

Then he remembered: Chuck was staying with him. There was no sign of him, though—his bedroom was a model of military neatness, the bed made with hospital corners, his shoes neatly arranged on the floor of the closet. Lee wondered where he had gone; he hadn't left a note. But then, he had originally planned to spend another night in New Jersey, so Chuck probably wasn't expecting him back yet.

He went back out to the living room, where the piano beckoned silently, light from the street lamps shining darkly on its polished wood. He slid onto the bench, lifting the lid to the keyboard, and took out his dog-eared copy of *The Well-Tempered Clavier*. Peeling away a dried-out piece of Scotch tape holding it together, he placed it carefully on the music rack. Bach was eternal, universal, elemental. No matter how bad things got, there was always Bach.

He turned to the D Minor Prelude and began, concentrating on precision and technique. There were so many roads into music, so many different ways of playing, so many elements to focus on. One day you could work on legato line and phrasing, the next on dynamics, and so on. . . .

Across town, Edmund turned to the tempestuous C Minor Prelude. Normally he wouldn't play it so early in a session, but there was nothing better than playing something stormy to calm the soul. He gave himself over to the Prelude's restless symmetry and felt his shoulders relaxing as his fingers moved faster, flying over the keys as the music grew more furious. . . .

Lee played on, lost in the music. It still amazed him that, through black ink markings on a page, he could communicate directly with the greatest creative geniuses the music world had ever known: Beethoven, Brahms, Chopin, Debussy, Saint-Saens, Mendelssohn—and the greatest of them all, Johann Sebastian Bach. There was a longing inside him that only the music of Bach would fill. He dove into the next Prelude and felt the tingle of pleasure the opening bars always brought him, a prickling on his skin, endorphins flooding his brain.

Just as the final chord was dying away, the phone rang. His head full of Bach, he picked it up without checking caller ID. He regretted it immediately.

"Hello, sugar." The voice was as smooth as ever, but

there was an undertone of panic even she couldn't hide.

"Hello, Susan."

"Is he there?"

"You mean Chuck?"

She laughed softly. "No, Genghis Khan, silly. Well—is he?" She sounded impatient.

"No, he's not."

"But he is staying with you, right?"

He had an impulse to lie, just to confound her, but knew she would only make him regret it later. But at least he could torment her a little.

"He didn't tell you where he was going?"

"I guess I neglected to read that part of the memo, sugar." Her voice was playful, but he knew that the steel underneath it could rip a man's heart to shreds.

"He's staying with me, at least for now."

"What do you mean, 'for now'?"

*Aha*. He had the upper hand, if only for a moment.

"Nothing," he said, trying to give the impression he was hiding something.

"Well, can you tell him I called?" He could tell she was curious but wasn't going to take the bait. Her self-control had always been impressive.

"Okay."

"I didn't do it, you know," she said, her voice tight. The mask dropped for a moment, and he sensed the pain that drove her compulsive behavior.

She sounded so pathetic, he almost believed her—almost.

"Do what?" he said.

"He *must* have told you," she said, annoyed.

"Chuck doesn't tell me everything," he said, wanting to hear her version of events before he showed his hand.

"He thinks I stepped out on him."

*Stepped out on him.* Who did she think she was, Blanche DuBois?

"Well, did you?"

"I just said I didn't."

"Why should I believe you?"

There was a pause, and he could feel the chill descend.

"Just tell him I called," she snapped, and the line went dead.

He stood cradling the phone in his hand, staring out the window at the Ukrainian church across the street. It was cold and still in the weak northern light. He shivered and hung up the phone. He had no idea where Chuck was. His best friend's personal life might be falling apart, but he had to put that aside. He looked longingly back at the piano, then sat in the red leather armchair by the window and picked up his case notes. Lives were at stake, and that knowledge lay heavily on his shoulders.

He pulled out the photos of the two victims and studied them side by side. The pattern on Mandy Pritchard was obviously a pentagram, though what it meant, he couldn't say. The one on the first victim, Lisa Adler, was more ambiguous. It was a kind of spiral, like the shell of an ancient sea creature. . . . As he sat staring at the photos, his eyelids became too heavy to hold open. The room was warm, the chair was comfortable, and he was unable to fight the lure of sleep.

The bump on his head throbbed, but his fatigue was stronger than the pain. His head fell forward as he succumbed to exhaustion and fell into a deep slumber.

His dreams were filled with dark figures prowling downtown alleyways. His legs wouldn't move fast enough to run, and he was unable to call for help; no sound came from his mouth as the killer closed in on the young woman lying helplessly in the shadowed doorway.

Then his dream shifted, and he was floating in a warm green sea, with tentacles instead of arms. He felt peaceful and free, hovering in the oceanic currents, his soft body gently pulsating with each wave of salt water. The radiator in the corner of the room suddenly clanked, and he awoke with a start. The photo was still in his lap, and he realized at that moment what the pattern on Lisa's torso reminded him of: it resembled the curve of a chambered nautilus. He didn't know what the significance of that was—maybe none—but the feeling of his dream was still strong in his mind as he got up, stretched and went off to bed.

# CHAPTER THIRTY-SIX

Sunday morning Lee got up early and went to the gym. Chuck's bedroom door was closed, so he figured his friend had come in late the night before. After a strenuous workout with the punching bag, he felt better, though there was still a tightness behind his temples. He showered at the gym and took the train to the Bronx to meet Brian O'Reilly's sister. He had arranged to meet her at her brother's apartment, where she was going through his things and preparing for the wake.

Gemma O'Reilly's resemblance to her brother was startling. She had the same heavy-lidded eyes, full, upturned lips, and square chin. He couldn't help noticing her striking green eyes, lined with long sandy lashes. It was a good face, with strong, generous features, which Lee's mother always claimed indicated character. It was one of her odder notions—she thought someone with a weak chin possessed a weak will.

"Please, come in," Gemma said, holding the door open. She wore a black turtleneck sweater over forest green stretch pants that brought out the emerald flecks in her eyes. Whereas Brian was burly and bloated from alcohol, she was tall and slim and wiry. She looked at least fifteen years younger than her brother.

"Thank you for coming," she said, closing the door behind him. She led him into the kitchen. It was clear that this was where the family did most of their living. "Please, sit down."

He pulled a chair up to the table. It was odd to be there again. The kitchen felt strangely still, with the familiar aftermath of death. Lee had experienced it many times, but he had never gotten used to it. It wasn't emptiness—it was *absence*. The presence of the two of them only seemed to heighten the awareness that Brian was missing, with his booming voice and larger-than-life personality.

"You want some coffee?" Gemma asked. "Or something stronger?" she added, waving a hand toward the assortment of bottles on the counter. "My brother left behind quite a collection."

"Coffee's fine."

"My brother was quite the whiskey drinker," she said, handing him a mug of cinnamon-scented coffee. "He took the whole Irish heritage thing to heart. Did he drink with you when you came over?"

"Yeah, he did."

She took a seat across from him and smiled sadly. "Silly question—of course he did. He'd drink with anyone who would drink with him." She flushed, frowning. "I didn't mean that the way it came out."

"It's okay—I know what you mean. I have some personal experience with heavy drinkers."

"You do?" She sounded relieved.

*Misery loves company*, he thought.

"Yeah. I'm Scottish. Or, at least, my family is."

"I see. Say no more," she said in an exaggerated Cockney accent.

"Nudge, nudge, wink, wink," he murmured, taking a sip of coffee. It was good—strong and rich, though he could have done without the cinnamon.

"You a Monty Python fan too?" she said.

"Isn't everyone?"

"Brian and I used to watch them when we were kids. We memorized all their sketches. Used to drive our parents crazy on car trips—we'd run their routines over and over, until they ordered us to stop."

The corners of her mouth trembled and wavered, but she took a deep breath and let it out slowly. "I promised myself I wasn't going to go to pieces until after the funeral," she said firmly.

He couldn't help admiring that—his family put such stock in stoicism. *Old habits die hard*, he thought, reflecting on his own tendency to bottle up his grief and rage.

"Anyway, let me tell you why I wanted to see you," she said.

"Please."

She leaned forward, her voice low, as though someone might overhear her.

"I don't believe my brother killed himself. I think he was murdered."

# CHAPTER THIRTY-SEVEN

It took a moment for her words to sink in. It was a sentence he had heard uttered dozens of times in movies and on television but never in real life—until now. It occurred to him that she might be testing him, or attempting to lighten the mood with dark humor.

But one look at her face, and he knew she wasn't kidding.

"What makes you say that?" he asked.

"Brian was a Catholic. He hated God sometimes, and he was depressed, but he believed it was a mortal sin to take your own life. And as a cop, he'd seen what suicides did to families. He never would have done that to me."

Looking into her green eyes with their tawny lashes, he could believe that. How could a man desert a woman like her, even if she was only his sister?

"Look, Ms. O'Reilly—"

"It's Mrs. Hancock, actually, but call me Gemma."

His stomach did a little flip-flop of disappointment at hearing her married name.

"Uh—Gemma, what evidence do you have that he didn't die by his own hand?"

She extracted an eight-by-ten glossy from a manila envelope and slid it across the table. It was a photograph of her brother's body lying on the living room floor. His head had nearly been blown away, and a semiautomatic lay at his side. It was a Glock 26, a standard-issue off-duty gun for a member of the NYPD. He looked at her to see if her face registered grief or disgust, but all he saw was determination. Her square chin was set, her mouth firm. No trembling of those perfect lips now—she looked like she wanted to slug someone.

"How did you get this?"

"I'm a journalist—and a cop's sister. I have more friends at the precinct than I do in my book club."

*My book club.* He knew she was married, but he couldn't resist sizing her up as a potential mate. There was just something about her.

"Okay," he said. "What is it about this picture—"

"Just look at it."

"But I'm not a detective. Why not go to one of his friends on the force?"

She leaned her long arms on the table, pressing her breasts together. He tried not to look at the shape they made under the black sweater.

"Look at the picture."

He did. Brian O'Reilly lay on his back, what was left of his head surrounded by a pool of dark blood. The gun lay next to the body, on the right side. The shell casing was a few feet away.

"Where was the point of entry?" he asked.

"His right temple."

"That's a little odd. Most people would—"

"Yeah—most people would put the gun in their mouth. But not always."

"Then I don't see the—"

"My brother was left-handed," she said. "Whoever killed him didn't know that."

"This is how you found him?"

"I didn't touch anything, if that's what you're asking."

"Did you tell the investigating officers?"

She looked away. "No."

"Why not?"

"Because I don't know who I can trust."

"What do you mean?"

She got up and poured them both more coffee, the green pants clinging to her hips as she moved. He leaned back to admire the view. She sank back down into the chair and slid his mug to him.

"What did my brother tell you?"

"Not much. We did a lot of drinking."

"That was Brian, especially in the last few years. He always liked his booze, but after Des's death . . . he kind of fell apart."

"Who was Des?"

"His partner for twenty years. They worked hundreds of cases together. He didn't mention Des Maguire?"

"Des? Nope."

"Short for Desmond."

"How did he die?"

"His house burned down with him in it."

"Arson?"

"They never found any evidence of it. But I always thought there was something fishy about it. Brian wouldn't talk about it, but I think he did too."

"Jesus. Who—?"

"Des was dirty, taking bribes and drug money—you name it, Desmond Maguire did it."

"And Brian knew?"

"He always suspected. And then when Des was killed, there wasn't much doubt."

"So the crime was never solved?"

She shook her head. "They didn't try very hard."

"Why not?"

"Either because Des was a dirty cop and they didn't much care—or because someone on the force was responsible for his death. Brian knew that, and it's one of the things that kept him on the bottle."

"So you think all of this hindered the investigation into my sister's disappearance?"

"It didn't help."

"Why are you telling me all this?"

"Because I want your help in solving my brother's death."

"I don't know—"

"My mother's a good Catholic. If she hears Brian committed suicide, she'll—"

"Where is your mom?"

"Ireland. She moved back years ago, during the economic boom there, and now she's too old to do much traveling."

"Does she know yet?"

Gemma looked down at her nails, which showed evidence of recent chewing. "I haven't called her yet. Isn't that terrible? I just can't tell her Brian killed himself, when I know he didn't."

"How are you going to prove it?"

"I'm an investigative journalist. It's what I *do.* And

it might bring us closer to finding out what happened to your sister."

Lee looked out the window at the soft light filtering through the white curtains. These waters were deeper than he'd imagined. He looked at the woman across from him with the hazel eyes and green stretch pants.

"Okay," he said. "I'll help you."

# Chapter Thirty-eight

Edmund had realized early in life that no one really cared about him. Even as a child, he'd known this was wrong—everyone should have someone who loved them, and yet he didn't. He was alone and abandoned, drifting in the soup of humanity, uncared for and uncaring. He knew his father blamed him for his mother's desertion. Even worse was the fact that his mother had found it so easy to leave. Edmund's loneliness was an abyss waiting to swallow him. He had two choices: to feel sad or very, very angry. But the sadness was unbearable, with its groaning heaviness. Anger was easier.

He discovered that if he could make another creature suffer, to feel something of his own gnawing emptiness, he didn't feel so helpless. At first it was neighborhood cats and dogs—whatever he could get his hands on—but after a while that wasn't enough. One day while wandering down the country lane they lived on, Edmund found a neighbor's child playing out in front of their cottage. He had an idea. He would kidnap the boy, take him home and keep him in the toolshed, where his father kept him for punishment. *He would become like his father!*

For days he watched the boy and his family, memorizing their routine, following their movements. He learned that the family liked to go to the local pub on Saturdays and church every Sunday. The wife took her aerobics class on Monday and Wednesday afternoons, and her feckless younger sister came to look after the child. The husband's drive from work was about twenty minutes, so the sister would be alone with the boy for almost two hours.

He decided that that was when he would do it. The sister lived in the next town and was less likely to recognize him—and since she was younger and less experienced, she would be more prone to panic and waste time when she saw that the boy was missing. It was just a question of how and when—of being ready when the time was right.

That time came on a windy Monday afternoon in late March. The trees were just beginning to bud, and the light was softening—spring was in the air. He was only ten, but he was big and strong for his age, and the neighbor's child, whose name was Sam, was only six. Sam was in front of the house, riding his tricycle up and down the sloping driveway leading to the carport. It wasn't much of a hill, but Sam would ride to the top and coast down to the garage, over and over.

Edmund crept out of his house and hid behind an azalea bush. The sister was inside; he could see through the picture window in the kitchen that she was at the stove. The phone inside the house rang, and he watched her pick up the receiver. He waited until she turned her back; then he darted across the street toward Sam, who had just finished riding up the small hill.

The sudden rush of movement must have startled him, because Sam let out a yelp before Edmund could get his hands on the boy. The sound alerted the sister, who was out of the house in seconds, the door banging behind her.

"What is it, Sam?" she yelled, her face tight. "Is that boy bothering you?"

Sam didn't answer; fat tears spurted from his eyes, and his lower lip trembled. Edmund turned away in disgust; the boy was nothing but a crybaby.

"Didn't your parents teach you not to bully children half your age?" the sister hissed, but Edmund ignored her. He walked away without answering, disappointed with himself for crafting such a clumsy plan.

He vowed that the next time he would be more careful. He would be prepared.

# Chapter Thirty-nine

Gemma O'Reilly Hancock drained the last of her coffee and set the mug on the table.

"I'm starving. Do you mind if we get something to eat?"

"Sure."

"Irish bar food okay? I'm buying."

"You don't have to—"

"It's the least I can do, after you came all the way up here to see me. And if you don't mind my saying so, you look like you could use some stodgy Irish food."

"Okay, thanks." She was a handful, this one—willful and determined, and now she wanted to buy him lunch. He wasn't sure how he felt about that, but so far he liked her.

Hanahan's was a local joint with a steam table, like the Hell's Kitchen places in the old days. Wizened Irishmen with whiskey beards and shoe-leather breath sat hunched over pints of Killian's Red, their fingers as gnarled as a leprechaun's walking stick. Presiding over the scene was a bartender straight out of *Butch Cassidy*—muttonchop whiskers, crisply starched shirt with red and white stripes. He looked like a baritone from a barbershop quartet. Lee half expected him to break out into a chorus of "Goodnight, Irene." He nodded and smiled when he saw Gemma.

"You're a regular here?" said Lee.

"My brother is—was," she replied. "I can't remember the number of times I trudged over here to find him and take him home." She looked at the steam table and rubbed her hands. "I hope you don't think it's insensitive of me to have an appetite when I just lost my brother."

"Why would I think that?" he said as they settled into a red leatherette booth with cracked upholstery.

"Some people would prefer me to be pining away, refusing all food and drink, like a Gothic heroine in mourning."

"Well, I wouldn't be one of those people."

"But I never lose my appetite—almost never, anyway."

"Yeah?" He wanted to ask what did make her lose it.

"It's embarrassing, but I am who I am. Come on—the corned beef here is really good."

She was right. They piled it onto thick dinner rolls smeared with mustard and ate like stevedores. Her appetite was contagious—he joined her in a second helping, washed down with pints of Killian's Red.

"That's better," she said, wiping a spot of mustard from her sweater, yellow on black.

"So what do you know about my sister's case?"

"Mostly what I heard from my brother. And sometimes at the station I overheard things. At one point I actually started keeping notes."

"Why were you so interested?"

"Something just didn't smell right. I had a weird feeling about it—and then I kept overhearing things."

"What kind of things?"

"Arguments, whispered comments—that kind of thing. Sometimes when Brian was on the phone and I'd come into the room, he'd hang up or pretend to be ordering Chinese food."

"How could you tell?"

She smiled. "I'm a journalist. I have built-in bullshit radar. I know when someone is trying to hide something."

"That must be hard on your husband."

She blushed and looked away. "We, uh—we're not together right now."

"Join the club."

"You too? Separated or divorced?"

"I'm not married. Let's just say that we've hit some rocks."

"You'll work it out."

"I'm not so sure about that."

She looked at him with those Emerald Isle eyes of hers, and that was when he knew that at some point they were going to end up in bed together.

He ran his index finger idly over the condensation on the beat-up wooden table and asked the question both of them had been avoiding.

"Do you think your brother's death is somehow related to my sister's disappearance?"

Gemma glanced around the bar, but the only customers within hearing distance were a couple of middle-aged barflies flirting over a game of darts. The woman giggled every time she made a throw, and the man eyed her spandex-clad rear end hungrily as she wobbled up to the board to retrieve her darts.

"It does seem like a strange coincidence if they're not connected, doesn't it?" Gemma said.

"But what are we talking about here? Conspiracy theories?"

"I only know that there was something fishy about the investigation of your sister's disappearance, and there's definitely something odd about my brother's death."

"Was there a suicide note?"

"Yes—but it was typed. Who types a suicide note? And it doesn't even sound like him, for Christ's sake."

"Can you get a copy of it?"

"Sure—why?"

"I'm working with a forensic linguist on a case. If you can get me a copy of the note along with a sample of your brother's writing, I can show them both to her."

"You'd do that for me?"

*That and a lot more,* he thought, but he just nodded. "Sure."

"The funeral is tomorrow night, if you want to come, at St. Barnabas Church. It's on East 241st Street."

"I'll be there. Was that your brother's church?"

"When he was still attending church. Our parents went there. We're actually related to the first pastor, Reverend Michael Reilly. His family dropped the *O* when they came over because they thought it sounded less Irish."

"But your family kept it."

She gave a wry smile. "We've always been stubborn. It made my father angry that people could be made to feel ashamed of their heritage."

"Good for him. Hey," he said, "doesn't the Catholic Church deny funerals to people who commit suicide?"

"Not anymore. Those old buzzards in the Vatican have actually loosened up some of their restrictions."

"Is it too personal to ask if you're—"

"A believer? No, I'm not, and no, it's not too personal," she added with a smile.

"Then why—?"

"I'm doing it out of respect for my parents and the people in the old neighborhood—most of them still believe." She took a last swallow of beer and leaned back against the wooden booth. He tried not to gaze at her breasts, but the sweater made it a challenge. "You're working the Alleyway Strangler, aren't you?"

"How did you—"

"Brian mentioned it before he . . ." She looked down, tightening her grip on her empty beer mug.

"I'm part of the team, yes."

She shook her head. "That's a whole other kind of weird. Do you think your sister was taken by that kind of . . . person?"

"I used to think so, but now I'm not so sure."

He looked out the window of the bar at the wind-whipped pedestrians tilting their way home through another blast of winter, and it occurred to him that right then he wasn't sure of much of anything.

# Chapter Forty

When Lee arrived at his apartment that evening, Chuck was sprawled on the couch watching television. He looked as though he hadn't slept at all. His eyes were glassy, his skin pasty, and he wore a wrinkled rugby shirt over sweatpants. That wasn't like Chuck—the only time Lee had seen him lolling around in sweatpants in their Princeton days was when he had the flu.

"Heya," he said, tossing his keys into the basket by the front door.

"Hey," Chuck answered without looking up.

"I didn't hear you come in last night."

"I didn't want to wake you."

"You okay?"

"Yeah, fine," Chuck said, still not taking his eyes off the screen.

"Where'd you go last night?"

"I went for a run."

"For four hours?"

"What are you, my mother?"

"Hey, I'm just concerned."

"I stopped by a bar," Chuck said. "Want to check my blood alcohol level?"

"You're a big boy—it's none of my business, all right?" he replied, peeved at his friend's rudeness.

Lee went to the kitchen and poured a glass of water, drinking it slowly. He needed time to think—Chuck's behavior was so unlike him, it was unsettling. He came back into the room.

"Whatcha watching?"

"Football."

"You don't like football."

"Jesus Christ!" Chuck exploded. "Can't a guy just watch a little TV without getting the third degree?"

"Okay," Lee said. "Message received."

He went to his room, changed into sweats and went out for a long run. After a quick shower upon returning, he grabbed the case file from the living room, went back to his bedroom and closed the door. A couple of minutes later there was a soft knock on the door. He opened it. Chuck stood there, looking miserable.

"Christ, I'm acting like a real shit," Chuck said. "I don't know what's wrong with me."

Lee put a hand on his shoulder. "It's called depression—welcome to the club."

Chuck smiled grimly. "Yeah? Am I going to be checking into the hospital too?"

"I hope not. The Bronx Major Case Unit isn't going to run itself."

"You got that right." He ran a hand through his blond crew cut, which was as shaggy as Lee had ever seen it. "You have dinner yet?"

"Nope."

"What do you feel like? My treat."

"You can never go wrong with Indian."

"Done—get your coat."

The tabla player at the Raj Mahal was in rare form. He and the sitar player sat cross-legged on the tiny stage in front of the window, so that passersby could see and hear them. Lee had walked by the place a few years back—lured in by the music, he had returned again and again for the live classical Indian music as well as the creamy, almond-scented chicken kurma and spicy lamb vindaloo. The Raj's tabla player was especially gifted—when he saw Lee, he smiled and launched into an inspired riff. Lee always tipped the musicians generously. In college he had played cocktail piano in a swanky restaurant to help pay for textbooks, and he knew what it was like to count on customer tips.

"So," Lee said after they ordered, "Susan called last night."

"Yeah?" Chuck plucked a piece of papadum from the basket on the table and popped it into his mouth. He was trying too hard to look uninterested. "What did she say?"

"Oh, you know Susan—wanted to know where you were."

"What'd you tell her?"

"The truth—that I didn't know."

"Serve her right, to be worried about me for a change." He broke off another piece of papadum. "What else?"

"She said she didn't do it."

Chuck grunted. "Yeah—right. I've been dealing with criminals for too many years not to know a lie when I hear one."

"Maybe she didn't." Lee couldn't believe he was defending Susan Morton, but he knew Chuck still loved her. And they had a son and a daughter, so there were the kids to think about.

"I can't believe you're saying that."

"What if those phone calls have another explanation? Maybe she was looking into getting cosmetic dentistry and didn't want you to know."

"You're stretching it, Campbell—you know it, and I know it."

"Still, I think you should—"

"Is it getting on your nerves, having me around?"

"That's not what I'm saying. I just don't want you to throw it all away without—"

"Funny. I got the impression you don't much like her."

"That has nothing to do with it. I just—"

"You don't like her, do you?"

"It doesn't matter what I think."

"You dumped her, after all. Though I never could understand why." He shook his head. "Sometimes I feel like we're living in different universes."

"Well, you know what they say: one man's meat . . ."

"Yeah, right." Chuck smiled, but in that smile Lee saw the truth: he was still hopelessly, shamelessly in love with Susan Beaumont Morton. At that moment their food arrived, and talk of love and betrayal took a backseat to chicken kurma with basmati rice.

# CHAPTER FORTY-ONE

Mandy Pritchard's parents were the Wasp equivalent of the Adlers—refined, educated, well-spoken and utterly grief-stricken. Mrs. Pritchard was a striking woman with long black hair and pale skin; her husband was tall and professorial, with misty blue eyes behind square glasses and a thin, patrician nose. He was an architect, and she was a lawyer.

They stood behind the glass partition in the city morgue, unable to take their eyes off the form on the table on the other side of the glass. A crisp white sheet covered their daughter's body; at a nod from Detective Butts, the attendant would oh-so-discreetly pull down the sheet to reveal the earthly remains of their only child, the little girl they had carried and coddled and caressed, their promise of immortality wiped away by the brutal hand of a psychopath.

Lee often wondered what it must be like, this final moment, the last time they would ever lay eyes on their beloved child. The Pritchards definitely didn't look like open-casket people. Would they carry this sad image with them forever, seared into their brains, or would it gradually be replaced by happier memories of their daughter's first bicycle, first puppy, first prom dress?

Mrs. Pritchard was working her mouth, compressing her lips tightly, hands clasped, knuckles locked in a kind of hopeless prayer position. Her husband had gone as pale as the sheet covering poor Mandy; his handsome face wore a stony expression of stoic grief. They were both delaying the terrible moment, as if by postponing it they could somehow prevent it. Lee knew all the tricks, all the mind games you played with yourself to get through grief and loss and its aftermath—they didn't work, of course, but they were all you had, and desperate people often acted irrationally.

Finally Mrs. Pritchard took a deep breath and nodded to Butts, who in turn signaled the morgue attendant. When the sheet was lifted, she gave a low, throaty moan and crumpled into her husband's arms. He didn't appear very steady himself—if he hadn't been forced to support his wife, Mr. Pritchard looked as if he, too, might collapse.

What the Pritchards didn't see was the stippling on their daughter's torso. They didn't see the missing finger, either—but the ligature marks on her neck were all too evident. Purple and thick and ugly, they were a reminder of how she had died. Mrs. Pritchard buried her head in her husband's chest and waved at Butts.

"No more, please," she gasped.

Butts signaled the attendant, who dutifully covered Mandy's face.

"All right," said Mr. Pritchard. "What's next?"

His attempt at being businesslike was touching. His wife was too far gone to put up any kind of front. She stood leaning against him, making no attempt to wipe her tear-smeared face.

"Well," said Butts, "if you think you're up to it, we'd like to talk to you about your daughter."

Mrs. Pritchard's mouth moved, but no sound came out. Her husband squeezed her hand and turned to Butts. "We're up to it," he said. "Whatever will help you catch the monster who did this."

They accompanied the Pritchards back to the precinct, offered them coffee and did what they could to offer comfort. Jimmy was out interviewing Mandy's classmates, so it was just Butts and Lee back at the station house. They didn't get anything unexpected from the interview. Mandy was a good girl, a straight-A student working on a degree in biology at Columbia; she was working while taking classes part-time.

"We could afford to pay for her education, but she didn't want everything handed to her, so we all agreed she would work her first two years at school," Mr. Pritchard said apologetically.

"Where did she work?" asked Lee, handing him a cup of coffee.

"For a veterinarian on the Upper East Side. She was hoping to go to grad school to become a vet."

"Oh, God," his wife said. "Do you suppose whoever—did this—met her there? If we had only insisted on paying for school—"

"Now, Mrs. Pritchard," Butts responded, "you can't start thinkin' like that. Nobody did anything wrong—not you, not your daughter. There's some creep out there who does terrible, evil things, and it's our job to catch him."

"I just keep wondering what we could have done," she said, her eyes pleading.

"Nothing. You can't protect your child from creeps like this, and you can't spend the rest of your life thinkin' you shoulda done something different."

The door opened, and Elena Krieger entered the room. Immediately the atmosphere became more charged. The air seemed to crackle, as though electric ions had swarmed in through the door with her.

"I'm sorry," she said, seeing the Pritchards. "I didn't realize—"

"That's because you didn't bother to knock," Butts retorted.

Krieger stiffened. "I had some information that I thought might interest you."

Butts glanced at the Pritchards, who looked intimidated by Krieger. "This is Detective Krieger," he said. "She's helping us with the case."

"Pleased to meet you," said Krieger formally.

"Why don't you wait outside?" Butts told her. "We're almost done here."

"No, wait," Mrs. Pritchard piped in. "I—I'd like to hear what she was going to say."

"I'm sorry, ma'am," Butts said. "We don't release every detail of our cases to the public."

Mr. Pritchard's face reddened. "Is that what we are—the public?"

Lee stepped in. "What Detective Butts is trying to say is that in every investigation there are details only known to the investigators. It's important in order to help solve the case and bring your daughter's killer to justice."

"I see," said Mrs. Pritchard softly. "Whatever will help you find this—this animal."

Butts looked grateful for Lee's intervention—sometimes he forgot to smooth feathers and feelings, especially when civilians were involved.

"Thanks for understanding," he said. "We'll be in touch if there are any developments."

Mrs. Pritchard clasped his hand and held it. "Thank you, Detective. Thank you for bringing our daughter's killer to justice."

Butts looked extremely uncomfortable, but he just squeezed her hand and nodded. "We'll do whatever we can—I promise you that."

"I know," she said, her eyes brimming over. "I know you will."

"Come on, Anne, let's let the detectives do their job," Mr. Pritchard said, taking his wife gently by the shoulders and ushering her out.

When they had gone, Butts turned to Krieger. "Okay, what is it that couldn't wait?"

She regarded him coldly. "Perhaps you aren't so interested. I can come back another time."

His jowly face reddened. "Oh, cut the crap, and just tell me what it is!"

Krieger gave a triumphant smile. "I have the killer's note."

Butts's mouth flew open in astonishment. "He *did* write one?"

"Yes."

"How did you find it?"

"He mailed it to me."

# CHAPTER FORTY-TWO

The statement left Lee and Butts temporarily speechless.

Then the detective ran a hand through his thinning hair. "Christ, he's a devious bastard." He held out his hand. "Let's see it."

Krieger produced a single sheet of paper encased in a plastic evidence bag.

"Did you log it in yet?"

"Yes. Of course I made a copy, but I want us all to study the original first, in case we see anything useful."

The note was typed, as before, with the same font, and looked to be from the same printer.

> Dear Detective Krieger,
>
> I thought it would be fun to keep you in the loop, so to speak, by sending this straight to you—after all, you're the linguistics expert, right?
>
> And a very luscious creature you are too, I must say. I do hope you're enjoying our little game; otherwise, what's the point? Get it? The point! As a German, I'm sure you enjoy puns.

So I hope you like the little "twist" in my design. I must say, it did take a while, and as you can imagine, my subject wasn't very cooperative, but I'm a patient man. (Oh, yes, I'm a man, but you knew that already, didn't you?)

Bye for now,
The Professor

"He thinks he's so clever," Butts muttered. "Just wait until I get hold of him."

"So, any new observations?" Lee asked Krieger.

"The obvious things we already know are that he's educated, literate, worldly—"

"And resourceful," Lee added. "Isn't your address unlisted?"

"Yes, but my teenage nephew could get around that," she scoffed.

Lee tried to imagine Elena Krieger as an aunt but couldn't quite manage it.

"He's a smug son of a bitch," Butts remarked.

"Yes," Krieger agreed.

"What's he talking about with the 'twist' in his design—the pattern on the girl?" asked Lee.

"I'd have to say so," said Krieger. "He even mentions her reaction, to rub it in that he did it while she was alive, in case we had any doubt."

"He's gloating," said Lee.

"He who gloats last . . ." Butts murmured.

"Those designs obviously have a meaning, but what is it?" said Lee.

"Some connection to his identity?" said Krieger.

"Right. Like he's taunting us with a puzzle of some kind."

Krieger studied them. "They're very precise. Maybe he's an architect."

"Or a biologist. Maybe a marine biologist." Lee reminded them that he'd discerned a chambered nautilus design in Lisa Adler's puncture wounds.

"What about the notes?" Butts asked. "Find any connection to the designs in them?"

Krieger held up the first one. "No, but I've been pondering his comment that 'one is the loneliest *number*.' "

"You think he might have a connection to numbers?" Lee asked.

"Could be," said Krieger. "But it's such an ambiguous statement—it could mean so many things."

They worked for another hour, then headed their separate ways, agreeing to be in touch first thing in the morning. Lee took the subway to the Bronx, just in time to catch Brian O'Reilly's funeral.

St. Barnabas Catholic Church was a clunky Italianate building looming over the intersection of Martha Avenue and 241st Street, in the same Bronx neighborhood of Woodlawn where Brian O'Reilly had lived. It looked more like a courthouse than a church, with its imposing granite walls, severe columns and triangular Romanesque façade. No cozy Baroque fussiness, warm wooden carvings or welcoming garden here—the sinner who entered its stern arch doors could be assured he would be judged and found wanting. Lee could hear the mournful strains coming from the vast pipe organ as he ascended the wide front staircase.

The interior was just as forbidding—the stained-glass windows lining the side walls did little to dispel the feeling of being inside a large box. The ceilings were oddly low, with none of the sweeping grandeur of other Catholic churches. The musky aroma of incense was overpowering. He slipped into the last pew just as the priest stepped up to the altar, where a graphically lurid carving of the Crucifixion was bordered by statues of Joseph and the Virgin Mary holding the Baby Jesus.

He was struck by the similarity to pagan altars he had seen. The high marble table with its ornate carved figurines could double for a Druid or Aztec altar, where human sacrifices were delivered to appease pagan gods. A large corkboard holding photographs of Brian was surrounded by bouquets of lilies and roses and sat to one side of the altar. To the right of the altar was a large white casket.

The church was nearly full. Lee noticed several solid blocks of attendees in dress blues—the NYPD was well represented. The priest lifted his arms as the organ music died away. Tall and bespectacled and balding, he wore a long robe and purple vestments—the very icon of a parish priest.

"Bless us, O Lord, as we commend the spirit of our brother Brian O'Reilly into your care. 'Seek not death in the error of your life, neither procure ye destruction by the works of your hands. For God made not death, neither hath He pleasure in the destruction of the living.' "

As the priest droned on, Lee craned his neck, looking for Gemma. The dense phalanx of bodies in front of him prevented him from seeing much of anything, so he leaned back in the wooden pew and gazed at the mourners near him, wondering if Brian's killer was among them.

". . . 'We shall all indeed rise again: but we shall not all be changed. In a moment, in the twinkling of an eye, at the last trumpet,' " the priest intoned solemnly. " 'For the trumpet shall sound, and the dead shall rise again incorruptible.' "

A whiff of sandalwood incense wafted down the aisle, choking Lee's airway. He was unable to stifle a hacking cough; a few people in front of him turned around to glare at him. A dark-haired woman with the sharp nose and beady eyes of a crow cleared her throat loudly in disapproval.

The ceremony was a formal, old-fashioned Catholic rite, with none of the modern indulgences of get-up-and-say-whatever-you-feel memorials he had attended in Manhattan. There were hymns and readings and biblical passages; the priest himself delivered the eulogy. Lee didn't know who had written it, but he suspected Gemma was the author—it was full of fond personal reminiscences and memories.

". . . 'Death is swallowed up in victory,' " the priest declared. " 'O death, where is thy victory? O death, where is thy sting?' "

Lee had some choice responses to that one, but he just shifted in his seat and looked around some more. He wasn't sure what he hoped to find, other than Brian's killer, but part of him thought that he (or she) would have to be pretty stupid to turn up here. On the other hand, what if his killer was someone who knew him well, and *not* showing up would look more suspicious? Both possibilities were equally viable, depending on the identity of the murderer.

" 'Now the sting of death is sin: and the power of sin is the law,' " the priest proclaimed. He was clearly enjoying himself. *Actors, lawyers, clergy*, Lee mused—all cut from the same cloth. They enjoyed performing in front of people, mesmerized by the sound of their own voices. He watched the congregation drink in his words—the crow-beaked woman in front of him nodded somberly. *He has an attentive audience, at any rate.*

The priest appeared to be lurching into the homestretch. "But thanks be to God, who hath given us the victory through our Lord Jesus Christ. Therefore, my beloved brethren, be ye steadfast and unmovable: always abiding in the work of the Lord, knowing that your labor is not in vain in the Lord. Amen."

"Amen," murmured the congregation. The crow-nosed woman crossed herself piously and shot a glance at Lee. He smiled at her; she scowled and looked away.

He waited around for Gemma to extract herself from the throng of well-wishers who had attached themselves to her as if she were coated in Velcro. He stood watching, waiting for some behavioral clue on anyone's part that indicated guilt or evasion of some kind. The crow-faced woman glanced around in a way that could be interpreted as nervous, but she struck him as a busybody who just wanted to keep an eye on what everyone else was doing.

Lee was beginning to tire of waiting—Gemma was still surrounded by people delivering condolences and sympathy. He had a long subway ride to his therapist's office, so he pulled on his coat and was about to leave the church when he noticed a thin man in a camel hair overcoat. The man's worn face was troubled, and he was fidgeting with his gloves; he seemed to be struggling with a decision of some kind. He stood just outside the circle of well-wishers and glanced furtively at Lee from time to time, as if trying catch his eye.

Lee stopped putting on his coat and gazed directly at the man. A thin, cold thread of anticipation shot through his stomach when the man held his gaze, then nodded toward the other side of the altar, near the organ keyboard. He nodded back and strolled in the direction of the organ, studying the stained-glass windows along the way, as if he was just idly wandering around the church. When he reached the other side of the organ, a hand clamped down on his elbow, and he turned to see the man in the camel hair coat clutching his arm. Without a word, he pulled Lee toward the back of the church, glancing nervously around him as he went, as if he was afraid of being followed.

He opened a door behind the altar and pulled Lee through it. Lee started to speak, but the man put a finger to his lips. Closing the door behind them, he took Lee down a set of stairs to a basement that clearly served as a combination rehearsal space and classroom. There were desks and a chalkboard and a piano in one corner. The man ducked inside the restroom, then came back out immediately.

"All right," he said at last. "We're alone. Dr. Campbell, is it?"

"Yes," said Lee. "Who are y—"

"We don't have much time," the man said, his lined face showing intense worry. He had thick black hair with a single swath of gray in the front, and dark, deep-set eyes rimmed with pouches, as if he had missed many a night of sleep. It was impossible to guess his age—he was probably younger than he appeared. His voice was scratchy, and he cleared his throat constantly. "They'll notice I'm gone and come looking for me," he said.

"Who?" Lee asked.

The man waved off the question impatiently. "How much do you know?"

"About what?"

"Don't waste time! I'm talking about Brian O'Reilly."

"Well, I'm not sure," Lee said—he had no idea if he could trust this guy.

His companion looked as if he were about to explode. "Brian O'Reilly did not kill himself," he hissed. "He was murdered."

"How do you know?"

The man cleared his throat nervously. "O'Reilly's partner, Desmond Maguire, was also murdered—but they did a better job covering that one up. O'Reilly was about to stumble onto that fact, so they had to kill him."

"Who are 'they'?"

Just then they heard heavy footsteps clunking down the basement stairs. The man clamped a finger to his lips, and Lee held his breath.

"Is anyone down here?" said a man's voice. Lee recognized it as belonging to the priest.

"Just using the bathroom, Father," he called out.

The priest appeared at the bottom of the stairs, still wearing his robe and purple vestments.

"I am so sorry to rush you," he said. "But we have

another service after this one—happily, a wedding this time."

"Of course, Father," Lee's companion said, clearing his throat again. "We were just leaving."

"Thank you," said the pastor, ascending the stairs. "Again, my apologies."

"Go—I'll follow you," the man whispered.

Lee climbed back up the narrow staircase, emerging into the main chapel, where the crowd had thinned out considerably. Most of the guests had left, and a couple of altar boys were preparing the room for the wedding, bringing in fresh flowers for the altar. There was no sign of Gemma. Thinking he heard footsteps behind him on the stairs, Lee turned around to say something to the man in the camel hair coat, but he had vanished. Lee peered back down the staircase, but there was no sign of him. Was there another exit? Perhaps he had left through the basement somehow.

Lee hurried up the aisle and out the front door of the church. Outside, the last of the cars in the funeral procession was just pulling out to follow the cavalcade of vehicles heading for the cemetery. He ducked around to the rear of the building to see if he could spot his mysterious companion, but there was no sign of him. He looked at his watch—he was due at his therapist's office in half an hour. Even if he left now, he was sure to be late.

He made one more circuit around the church, but there was still no sign of the strange man. He wanted to call Gemma but realized the only number he had was Brian's landline. That was too risky—he couldn't know who might be listening in. He wrapped his scarf around his neck and pulled his collar up as a stiff wind whipped around the side of the building. Shoving his hands into his pockets, he jogged in the direction of the A train.

# CHAPTER FORTY-THREE

As he predicted, Lee arrived late. Dr. Williams had squeezed him in right after her last regular patient—he slid into the office just as the Con Edison clock tower in Union Square chimed the quarter hour.

"So what's going on?" asked Dr. Williams, closing the door behind him. "You missed your session last week. And you're late this week—that's not like you."

"Sorry about that," said Lee, sitting on the couch opposite her. "I did call and tell you."

She smiled. "I wasn't complaining. I'm just wondering what's happening."

He looked around the office, with its familiar, African-inspired décor. Dr. Williams sat in her usual spot, the leather swivel chair, her ubiquitous iced tea in the tall blue thermos at her side. Today she wore a knit wool skirt and a lemon yellow blouse that showed off her milk chocolate skin.

"I got called in on a case," he said.

"A tough one?"

"As bad as it gets. Have you read the work of Robert Keppel and Richard Walter?"

"I've heard of them, but crime isn't my specialty."

"They've created a way of classifying sex offenders and murderers."

"That sounds useful."

"Basically, they divide them into four types. This guy is a Type Four, the worst of the worst—a real sadist."

"You're working on the Alleyway Strangler."

"Yeah."

She shuddered. "I live not far from where the first girl was found. It's all my neighbors can talk about."

"It's pretty horrendous."

"No wonder you look so stressed. That's a huge responsibility."

"He's smart too. Full of wit and playful humor . . . he's really enjoying this."

"Unlike you."

"It's still a mystery to me why some people become so twisted that they're compelled to do these things."

She looked at the bookcase with its volumes on psychology and human behavior, tomes of wisdom and experience and learning—none of which sufficiently explained the evolution of a ritualistic serial killer.

"Why do some people have horrendous childhoods and go on to lead productive lives, and others are turned into these . . . killing machines?" he said.

"There are so many elements in a person's life, so many factors, that it's impossible to trace and explain all of them."

"I want to kill this guy with my bare hands."

She took a sip of tea. "How's your boxing going?"

"It's a good way to release my anger."

"Better than feeling depressed."

"Much better."

"But you're still angry."

"Yeah."

"At life's unfairness, your sister's disappearance, your father's betrayal. Which you still can't talk about."

"All in good time, my pretty, all in good time," he said, doing a passable imitation of Margaret Hamilton as the Wicked Witch of the West.

She smiled. "Do you wish you could have as much fun as this killer you're chasing?"

"Of course. And there's been a . . . development in my sister's case."

She sat up straighter. "Oh? What is it?"

He told her about Brian O'Reilly's death, Gemma, and the strange man in the church.

"That is mysterious. I wonder if this is something you shouldn't be involved in. Maybe you should report it to—"

"To who? From what this guy says, the cops themselves may be involved—at least in that precinct. And I don't know enough to report to anybody yet."

"I'm afraid you may be in danger."

"I'm more worried about Gemma."

She cocked her head and smiled, the way she did when she was prying. "I get the feeling there's something more going on there than you're telling me."

He felt himself reddening. *Damn Celtic complexion.* "There's nothing much to tell. She's Brian O'Reilly's sister."

"Attractive?"

"Yeah, I guess." *Liar, liar, pants on fire.*

Dr. Williams took another sip of tea. "Okay, whatever you say."

That night Lee tossed and turned in bed. He knew he should try to sleep, but he couldn't help thinking about his conversation with Dr. Williams. He realized that, for all that separated them, he and the killer were more alike than he wanted to admit. There were times when hate filled him, a rancor as bitter as dandelion greens, an evil vine wrapping itself around his heart, choking the breath from his body. He struggled with the clinging tendrils clutching at him, but when he was in this state, Lee knew he was closest to feeling what *he* felt—the man he had begun to think of as more than just his prey, the hunted, but also his doppelgänger.

The killer was like a reverse image of himself, a mirror negative, a darker brother. He struggled with his lack of faith in any meaningful concept of God; this man served a cruel and exacting god. He fought every day to hold back the tide of his own rage and disappointment; this man gave in to these feelings, embracing them like old friends.

He finally drifted off around three o'clock, to a night of restless dreams and murky, fleeting images. He awoke to the sound of Chuck shaving. For a split second he imagined he was back in their old rooms in Princeton. Those were sweet times, with youth and innocence and the bright future of an Ivy League graduate ahead of them. Life was rugby, classes, girls and eating clubs. Even at the time, he knew enough to savor those days, realizing they would never return. He listened to Chuck puttering around in the bathroom, heard him turn the shower on. He watched the steam seeping through the crack in his bedroom wall, made a note to talk to the super about it, then hauled himself out of bed, hoping Chuck didn't use up all the hot water.

# CHAPTER FORTY-FOUR

The evidence room at One Police Plaza was climate controlled and antiseptic, but Lee could taste the dust in the air as he followed the clerk down the endless aisles of boxes.

"Here you go," said the clerk, a sleepy, dusky-skinned Latina with gold bangles in her ears that jingled when she walked. She pulled out a cardboard file box labeled in block letters with a black Magic Marker: CAMPBELL, LAURA. There was something surreal about seeing his sister's name so objectively rendered by an unknown hand on the side of a featureless cardboard box, jammed in with thousands of others just like it. Sweat sprang onto Lee's forehead as he signed the release form on the clipboard the clerk held out to him.

"Follow me," she said, handing him the box.

He trailed after her, lugging the box, reminded of all the clips he had seen of criminals hauling their case files to court. There was something demeaning about the whole criminal justice system, necessary though it was.

The clerk led him to a locked room in the Records section. It was empty except for a couple of long tables and a water cooler. She unlocked the glass door and held it open for him.

"Just knock on the glass when you're done," she said, "and I'll come let you out."

"Thanks," he said, heaving the box onto the table. Tiny granules of dust floated into the air and settled onto the heavy wooden table.

She left, locking the door behind her, and padded back to her station around the corner. He lifted the lid from the box and, for the first time since his sister's disappearance, looked at the case files.

There wasn't much. Copies of witness statements, the original Missing Persons report he and his mother had filed. He remembered the day they went to the station house together, his mother stern and anxious and full of questions. She couldn't seem to believe that the desk sergeant they spoke with didn't immediately produce her daughter as soon as they reported her missing. It was as though she expected Laura to be hiding in a closet somewhere in the building and that she would jump out yelling "Surprise!" with that big, toothy grin of hers. Laura had been living in the city less than a year when she disappeared. Kylie—thank God—was with her father that weekend.

The initial police response had been lukewarm, to say the least. In the scheme of things, a missing adult female didn't seem to interest them much. Forms were duly filled out, records made and copied, and Lee and his mother were promised that someone would be assigned to the case if Laura didn't turn up soon. The sergeant reassured them that in most cases the person did surface, usually in a short amount of time.

But from the minute he was assigned to the case,

Detective Brian O'Reilly took it very seriously indeed. He reported it at once with the FBI National Crime Information Center (NCIC), as well as the NYPD, and he called Lee several times a week with updates.

And now he was dead—murdered. At first he had thought Brian might simply be a suicide his sister, Gemma, just couldn't accept. Lee had seen it before—family members never want to believe a loved one could take their own life, but they could and did every day. The position of the gun wasn't that conclusive—he had seen guns end up in odd places in crime scene photos. But the man in the camel's hair coat was pretty convincing; Lee now believed Gemma's conclusion about her brother's death.

He dug through the pile of papers, reports, phone records, e-mails and departmental forms. One thing he had learned since coming to work for the NYPD was that paperwork was the bane of all cops' existence. It was endless, inescapable and tedious—but if you didn't do it, there was hell to pay. Brian O'Reilly might have been a drunk, but he was thorough. Every step of the investigation into Laura's disappearance was documented: phone calls made, interviews conducted, leads followed.

Lee was startled by the ringing of his cell phone, which he had forgotten to turn off. He grabbed it. The caller ID said *Chuck*, so he answered it.

He immediately regretted it. The call was from Chuck's home phone in New Jersey, not his cell phone, and the caller was Susan Morton.

"Hello, sugar," she said. Her voice was coated with the usual layer of syrup, but something was off.

"Hello, Susan," he said, his voice flat, uninflected.

"Long time, no see," she purred. She was trying too hard, pushing for effect.

"What can I do for you?"

She laughed her trademark laugh, like the tinkling of tiny bells, but it sounded forced. She was scared. Trying not to seem like it, but she was frightened.

"Why must you always be so businesslike?" she said. "Can't we just chat for a moment? What have you been up to, sugar?"

"Are you looking for Chuck?"

She sighed, and in that sound he heard anger and frustration as well as resignation.

"Maybe I'm just calling to talk to you."

"I'm sorry, Susan, but I was just heading out the door," he lied. Cowardly, perhaps, but he had forced out all the coldness he could afford already and had no wish for a confrontation.

"Oh," she said. "Okay." She sounded so forlorn, he almost felt sorry for her.

"I'll tell him you called," he said, his voice softening.

"Oh, that's all right," she said. "He knows I'm trying to reach him. I must have left a dozen messages on his cell phone. Never mind. Guess I'll just have to stay in the doghouse for a while."

"I'll tell him anyway."

"Oh, you're a sweetheart, really," she said.

There was a knock on the glass partition of the door, and he looked up to the see the clerk standing there.

She pointed at his phone. "I'm sorry, sir, but you can't use your cell phone down here."

"I gotta go," he said to Susan, and he slipped the phone back into his pocket.

The clerk unlocked the door and poked her head inside. "I gotta leave in about fifteen minutes. You want to stay much longer?"

"No, I'll be right out—thanks," he said. There wasn't much he hadn't already seen here and nothing he was unaware of.

He picked up the papers on the table and put them back into the box. As he did, a slip of paper slid out and onto the floor. He bent to pick it up. On it, scribbled in Laura's handwriting, was a name and a phone number: *Thomas—202-555-1852.* He recognized the area code as belonging to Washington, D.C. He had no idea who Thomas might be. Presumably Detective O'Reilly had followed up on the lead, but he was dead now.

Lee copied down the phone number, then put the lid back on the box and called for the attendant. When he got home, he was going to give Thomas in Washington, D.C., a call.

# Chapter Forty-five

Wednesday was the first day of Hanukah, so Butts was spending the day with his wife's family. "I think religion's a bunch of bunk," he'd said the night before, "but being Jewish has its perks. We may not get such cool presents, but we get a lot more days off."

Lee knew perfectly well that Butts would find time during the festivities to sneak off and work on the case, but he'd just smiled and nodded.

The first thing Lee did that morning was to dial the phone number of the mysterious Thomas. A man picked up on the second ring.

"Hello?" He sounded middle-aged, wary.

"Is Thomas there, please?"

The pause that followed told Lee the man knew something he didn't want to divulge—for whatever reason.

"Who's calling?"

He had the lie ready just in case.

"I'm his cousin. He asked me to look him up if I ever—"

"He moved to Philly."

"Oh, do you have a number for him?"

"No."

Lee could tell the man was getting ready to hang up. He made a stab at one last bit of information.

"Is he still working as a—"

To his relief, the man took the bait. "No—he's in construction now."

"Oh, right."

"Look, I gotta go."

"Thanks so much for your help."

After he hung up, his initial feeling of triumph wore off quickly. He had a first name, city and a profession—now all he had to do was find a man named Thomas working construction in Philadelphia. *Piece of cake,* he thought grimly as he looked across the street at a crowd of people gathering in front of the Ukrainian church. Dressed in bulky winter coats and ski hats, they huddled together on the steps, their breath visible as white wisps in the frigid air. A young man distributed sheet music, and soon the sound of Christmas carols floated across the street.

*God rest ye merry, Gentlemen,*
*Let nothing you dismay,*
*Remember, Christ our Saviour*
*Was born on Christmas day,*
*To save us all from Satan's power . . .*

*If only it were that easy,* Lee thought as he dialed Brian O'Reilly's home number. Gemma picked up on the second ring.

"Hello?"

"Hi," he said, unexpectedly warmed by the sound of her voice. "Can we get together?"

"I was going to call you—I have a copy of the note."

"Great. I have something to tell you too."

They arranged to meet at Jackson Hole, on the Upper East Side, in an hour. Lee slipped on his coat and headed downstairs. The carolers across the street were just hitting their stride, their voices clear and sweet in the thin stillness of winter.

*Hark! The herald angels sing,*
*"Glory to the newborn King,*
*Peace on earth, and mercy mild*
*God and sinners reconciled!"*

Alas, some sinners were not so easily reconciled with God—or man, for that matter, Lee thought as he slid out into the frosty air. The door closed behind him, the dead bolt clicking into place with the hollow sound of finality.

# CHAPTER FORTY-SIX

"Sorry I'm late—I couldn't find a damn cab!"

Lee looked up to see Gemma's shiny, flushed face. It was as if all the stale air in the room had been pushed aside the moment she entered the Lexington Avenue restaurant. He felt the rush of blood to his own cheeks as she sat down opposite him. She wore a powder blue angora sweater, a little black skirt wrapped tightly around her trim hips. A shiver of pleasure ran up his spine at the sight of her.

"Are you all right?" she said, peering at him. "You're not getting sick, are you?"

"No, no, I'm fine," he said. "It's just a little cold in here."

She looked around the spotless restaurant. "Uh-oh—Mommy and Daddy will be starting a lawsuit to make sure their precious children don't catch cold and hurt their chances of getting into Barnard."

"You live around here, right?"

"Farther uptown—Yorkville, which isn't quite so chichi."

Lee looked around. "I was beginning to wonder if

the smell of money was going to my head. I mean," he said, lowering his voice, "these girls are loaded, right?"

"Oh, please!" She pointed to a tiny chocolate brown backpack hanging on a chair behind a pretty brunette. The girl's head was lowered as she gossiped with her friends, her shiny hair hiding her face. "You see that chic little leather backpack? What she paid for it could cover my monthly rent and utilities, even with the Con Ed rate hike."

"That's what I thought, but I wasn't sure."

Gemma smiled and unfolded her napkin. "Men never know the price of luxury items or shoes. Quick, what would a hammer cost in a hardware store?"

"You could get a decent one for about ten dollars. Anything less wouldn't be worth buying."

"See what I mean? You know the price of hammers but not Versace backpacks."

"I didn't even know who Versace was until he was killed."

Gemma laughed—a low, throaty chortle. "Don't get me wrong—I'm not exactly a fashion maven."

"I wouldn't know the difference between Gucci and Kmart. I don't know what the purpose of all this high fashion stuff is."

"What's the 'purpose' of a geranium? It doesn't seek a higher goal or a justification for its existence. It simply *is*."

"But geraniums were made by Nature."

"And people make Gucci bags. We're part of Nature."

Lee shook his head. "I'm amazed by how some people spend their time and money."

"Well, I'm going to spend my time and money having the biggest burger on the menu," she said. "What are you having, Big Guy?"

"*Big* Guy?"

"I was thinking you need a nickname."

"Why?"

"Doesn't everyone need a nickname?"

"It seems wrong for me—too bulky."

"Okay, how about Thin Man? I could call you that."

"I'm not *that* thin, am I?"

"You're pretty skinny. I'll bet everyone in your family is."

"Yeah, my mother always was—still is, actually."

"And your father?"

Lee pretended to study the menu, his eyes burning into the entrées section.

"Not much to say, really. He was there for a while, and then he wasn't. Oldest story in the book—here one day, gone the next."

"But everyone's story is different."

"Maybe. I just don't have anything to add."

When he thought about his father, he felt a cold, hard lump in the center of his soul, protected by many years of scar tissue. He had no desire to go in and dig around, opening old wounds, afraid it might unleash a tidal wave of rage so powerful, it would drown him and anyone close to him.

"Thanks for coming to the funeral," she said. "Who was that man you were talking to?"

"I was hoping you might know," he said, and he told her the whole thing.

When he finished, she said, "Wow. Did he seem like a kook to you?"

"Not at all. But he did seem really frightened. I was hoping he might have contacted you."

"I don't think so. But there are a few messages on Brian's voice mail I haven't listened to yet. I'm not sure why. Maybe I'm afraid I won't hear anything that helps solve his death—and equally afraid I will. Does that sound completely mental?"

He winced. *Mental* was what some of the beat cops called Lee behind his back. Word of his struggle with depression had gotten around pretty fast, and some members of the force were less than sympathetic about working with him.

"No," he said. "It doesn't sound mental—it sounds human."

She put a hand on his. Electricity shot up his arm at her touch.

"Thanks for being so supportive."

After they ordered, Gemma leaned down to fish something out of her bag. He could smell her shampoo, something fruity and tart, like lemons.

"Here's a copy of the suicide note," she said, handing him a sheet of paper. "And here's a copy of an e-mail he wrote to me a few days before his death."

"I'll give it to our forensic linguist and see what she says."

"Thanks."

"What will you do if it's not a suicide?" he asked.

"I don't know. It could be pretty dangerous trying to find out what really happened. I hate to say it, but not all the bad guys are outside the police force."

"Yeah," he agreed. "That's what our mystery man seems to think."

"Well, corruption is nothing new under the sun.

What's interesting is that we have a sense of fairness and justice at all."

"You know, no matter how close I get to the center of all this stuff—studying these psychopaths, trying to get inside their heads—there's always something elusive about it, a central mystery that's always just beyond my grasp. It's like an itch I can't ever scratch—a goal that's always receding."

He looked at the pretty waitress stepping over a knapsack on the floor. She looked annoyed, her pert mouth pinched, her eyes narrowed in exasperation. Something about her face reminded him of Susan Morton. *Hell hath no fury . . .*

"Do you think if you ever got to the heart of things and really understood one of these guys completely, you might lose interest?" Gemma asked. "The Loch Ness syndrome?"

"What's that?"

"Have you ever thought about what it would be like if we ever found out exactly what is living in that lake?"

"I see what you mean," he said. "It would be kind of a letdown, in a way."

"Sometimes it's the elusiveness of a goal that makes it so seductive."

"So maybe we're happier in a constant state of longing?" he said.

"Once you have something, it loses its appeal."

"Well, *some* of its appeal."

She smiled, a wry twisting of the corners of her mouth. Their conversation had become a form of foreplay, a delicate dance in which they tested the level of each other's desire.

"There are so many mysteries in life," she said. "Like why we're attracted to some people instead of others."

Just then their food arrived, and life's grand questions had to wait for a couple of rare hamburgers dripping with caramelized onions.

Just as he was about to take a bite, Lee's cell phone rang. He dug it out of his pocket and looked at the caller ID—it was Kathy. Guilt twisted in his stomach; his first impulse was to ignore it, but he turned to Gemma.

"Will you excuse me a moment?"

"Sure."

He slipped out into the street and flipped open the phone.

"Hello?"

"It's me," she said, her voice hesitant and insecure. "I—I just don't like where we left off last time, and I was wondering if we could meet again. I know you're busy, but I—"

He looked back into the restaurant, where Gemma sat, studying some papers. He felt the pull of her, even from there.

"Sure," he said. "I'll call you later."

He snapped his phone closed and went back inside.

# CHAPTER FORTY-SEVEN

Edmund's lips curled in a smile as he stared at the Asian woman across from him in the diner. She bent over her menu, trying to ignore him, her smooth black hair sliding over her face, following the delicate angle of her neck.

He leaned back in the booth and picked up his own menu. He was patient—sooner or later she would have to look up again. He was an ugly man addicted to beautiful women. The irony wasn't lost on him; he understood how he must appear to them, and yet he also saw the fascination in their eyes, as they caved before his charisma and charm.

The Asian woman's hair was shiny and black, sleek as a seal. He continued to stare, knowing it made her uncomfortable but not caring. In fact, he liked it—her discomfort was part of the foreplay, a little dance he did with his victims. And even if he wasn't going to take her, he thought, he would still enjoy the dance.

He thought about where he would leave her. An alley, of course—but which one? He had discovered a few new ones in his late-night rambles around the city, some really nice ones, with tidy little dwellings on either side. *Mews*, they called the nice ones. The not-so-nice ones they just called alleys. The shed where his father had locked him up—where he had dragged him on that terrible night—hadn't been so nice. It had smelled of motor oil and hay and rusty pitchforks. He had lain on the dusty floor of the shed for a long time, his cheek throbbing, his tears stinging the burned flesh. He'd wanted so much for his mother to come, scoop him into her arms and tell him everything was going to be all right. But his mother never came—she was already gone, leaving him and his sister alone with his father. He hated her cowardice, just as he hated his father's violence.

For years that hate had nowhere to go. It lived inside him, a burning furnace in his soul, until it twisted into a shape unlike that of other, normal human beings. Then, finally, he found a place for it, an expression of his darkness that was his alone.

He smiled at the waitress as she approached his table. He was hungry.

# CHAPTER FORTY-EIGHT

"You really think this creep's gonna turn up?" asked Butts the next day as they approached the Tenth Avenue campus of John Jay College.

"I think it's likely," Lee replied. "This is the kind of offender who likes to insert himself into every phase of the investigation."

Lee was about to give his lecture at John Jay, and Butts was attending it to see if the Alleyway Strangler showed up.

"Why not just hold a press conference and see if he comes to that?" the detective said as they ascended the broad staircase to the entrance.

"We can do that too, but I think there's a good chance he'll come to my lecture."

"So if you take a drink of water and tap the bottle twice on the lectern, that's my signal."

"Right," Lee said, showing his ID to the young woman at the security desk.

"But how do you indicate which guy it is?" Butts asked, fumbling for his badge.

"By looking at him."

"Okay," Butts said, flashing the girl his detective

shield. "There's not a lot we can do unless he makes trouble."

They made their way through the turnstile and started up the stairs to the second floor.

"Wouldn't it be helpful to have a look at his face, assuming he shows up?" said Lee.

"Yeah—frustrating, though. If it is him, I'll wanna slap his ass in jail."

"Well, you can't do that, but you can get a good look at him."

Butts grunted and trudged up the steps behind him.

Half an hour later, Lee looked out over the audience in the lecture hall. He hadn't expected quite such a large turnout. The room was crowded with future cops, criminologists, psychologists and even a few firemen. Maybe Lucille Geffers was right when she told him that he had acquired some cachet around campus. He cleared his throat and began.

"As most of you are probably aware, the majority of homicides are situational, and in most cases the victim knows his or her killer. And yet there seems to be a public fascination with criminals who fall outside the normal spectrum of murderers. Among these are the repeat offenders we now refer to as serial killers.

"The term 'serial killer' has been thrown around a lot lately in the media. Appealing to our more sensationalist appetites, journalists like to splash these stories across the front page. After all, it sells papers. Some people claim statistics show there's been an increase in the number of serial offenders operating at any given time in this country.

"They may be right, though a more likely explanation is that methods of detection and record keeping have improved. Contrary to popular opinion, it's not a recent phenomenon. There are well-recorded examples of serial offenders going back to the Middle Ages. I would guess they have always been with us, even when they managed to escape detection."

A thin young woman in the front row shifted in her seat and bit her lip.

"Nonetheless, there is cause for concern. As law enforcement becomes more sophisticated, so do the criminals. We have to use every means at our disposal to make sure they don't gain the edge. One of those means is what has come to be known as criminal profiling—working up a psychological fingerprint of the offender. Just as the so-called 'hard sciences' of forensics have advanced, so has our understanding of criminal psychology.

"Ideas about these criminals have evolved since the early groundbreakers at the FBI first began collecting and examining data in the 1970s. Some terms are still with us—like *organized* and *disorganized*, for example. But we now have a more nuanced idea of how these offenders operate—what drives them, what we can expect if they continue and, most important, how to stop them."

A few people in the audience leaned forward in anticipation; others scribbled energetically in notebooks. Still others typed into their laptops, netbooks or tablets. In the back row, Butts pulled out a stick of licorice and began chewing on it.

"Robert Keppel and Richard Walter have come up with four classifications of murderers," Lee continued. "Today I want to talk about the most dangerous of all, the sadistic sexual offender."

A tall, thin man in the back row leaned back in his seat and licked his lips. His body language displayed arrogance, contempt and, above all, pleasure. Everyone else in the audience looked interested and apprehensive—and the waifish girl in the front row actually looked frightened. Lee took a drink of water and tapped the bottle on the lectern. Butts's head immediately shot up, his body instantly alert. Once he had the detective's attention, Lee glanced at the tall man in the back row. Butts followed his gaze, nodded, then went back to his licorice.

The whole thing took only a few seconds, but in that brief moment Butts knew who their suspect was, and the thin man knew equally well that he had been fingered. His sly smile let them know that it didn't bother him a bit. He settled back in his seat, locking his hands behind his head in an insolent gesture.

That was when Lee knew he was either very arrogant or very, very smart. Either way, it was bad news. Taking a drink from his water bottle, he continued.

"The term Keppel and Walters use for this offender is an 'anger-excitation' murderer. There are several reasons this type is the most dangerous of all. They tend to plan their crimes carefully and are classic 'organized' offenders. They often have a knowledge of forensics and are better at eluding capture. They blend in with society, often having good jobs, a stable marriage, and may even have children. They may even be active and well respected in their community. A prime example would be Dennis Rader, the so-called BTK killer, who had a wife, children and a stable job and was active in the local Lutheran church."

The man in the back row took out a notebook and

began to write in it. Butts, too, noticed this—Lee could see he was keeping an eye on the guy. To do any more at this point would be a mistake. The last thing they wanted to do was cause him to leave, especially if he was their mark. He cleared his throat and went on.

"Because these killers are psychopaths or sociopaths and feel no empathy, they are masterful at compartmentalizing. They often live two completely separate lives."

The man in the back row tilted his head to one side and licked his lips. Several seats down from him, Butts shifted in his chair and chewed more vigorously on his licorice stick.

A young Asian man in the third row raised his hand. "What do you mean, they feel no empathy?"

"They seem to lack the ability to experience any fellow feeling for other people. Research indicates this may be physiological—hardwired in their brain."

The young man frowned. "Why are they like this?"

"No one really knows. Genetic factors may play a part, but continued and severe childhood abuse is often present."

The man in the back row frowned and crossed his legs.

"Whatever the cause," Lee continued, "they lack that essential aspect of being human the rest of us have, so they learn to fake it to blend in. What most people would think of as their 'normal' life is for them just a set of surface behaviors, allowing them to engage in their 'real' life, acting out fantasies they have had for years, usually since childhood."

Lee glanced at his notes, though he didn't need them.

"These fantasies are violent, sexual and sadistic.

While other sexually motivated killers are seeking power, revenge or even reassurance, the payoff for the anger-excitation offender is *the suffering of his victim.* That is the element he finds most exciting, and another reason he is so dangerous."

The young woman in the front row squirmed, and several audience members winced, chewed on their pencils or frowned. The man in the back row leaned forward, fingertips pressed together, his expression calm but interested.

"This type of killer can be highly intelligent, charming and charismatic. Ted Bundy is a classic example. This makes it easier for him to find high-risk victims, who may also be intelligent, educated and attractive. However, this offender has a weakness: he enjoys attention. One of the ways Dennis Rader was finally caught was that he couldn't resist communicating with the police."

A hand shot up in the front row. It was the nervous blond girl.

"Yes?" Lee said.

"Do you believe that's how you'll catch the Alleyway Strangler?"

He paused before replying; it was important to choose his words carefully.

"I believe that the killer you are referring to will make a mistake as a result of his arrogance and ego, yes."

A serious-looking young black man with a buzz cut raised his hand.

"Has the Alley Strangler been in touch with you?"

"I'm sorry, but there are certain details that haven't been released to the public at this time."

"What can you say about him?"

"We're pursuing all possible leads."

"Do you think you'll catch him?" the man in the back row asked in a thin, dry voice that crackled like dead leaves.

"Oh, yes," Lee said. "In the end, we'll get him."

# Chapter Forty-nine

Detective Leonard Butts was irritated. Sitting at the back of the lecture hall, he was only half listening to Campbell's lecture; most of his attention was focused on the tall, thin man a few seats away. He couldn't look at the guy directly, but he could sense the man's presence. Butts was only there in case the UNSUB turned up, and Campbell had given Butts the signal that this could be their perp. He longed to jump from his seat, collar the guy and drag him down to interrogation. But all he could do was sit tight and wait.

Butts fidgeted and scratched himself, sighed and shifted in his seat, until he thought he would go nuts. He kept an eye out in case the thin man bolted from the lecture hall, but his mark showed no evidence of any desire to leave.

The room was too hot, his shirt collar was itchy, and his feet were beginning to swell. He longed to pull off his leather oxfords and rub his toes. He wished the thin man would leave so he could dash after him. Not that he could do anything, really—the man had committed no crimes they were aware of, and you couldn't arrest a guy for acting suspicious. Too bad, Butts thought. If this was the UNSUB, it would be frustrating to just watch him walk out.

Finally the lecture was over. Butts gathered up his coat and hat, trying to act like just another spectator. But he kept an eye on the thin man, who was also putting on his coat. The man didn't look his way once, which was good—Butts was doing his best to remain anonymous. He was closer to the exit door, so he shuffled behind the line of people into the hallway. The thin man was right behind him.

Once outside, Butts turned around to see the man smiling at him as he buttoned his coat.

"Hello, Detective Butts. I thought that was a very interesting lecture, didn't you?"

Leonard Butts was not usually at a loss for words, but all he could do was stare at the tall specter of a man who stood before him. In the lecture hall, he had only caught glimpses of him from the side, and now for the first time he had a really good look. The man's height and excessive leanness were arresting enough, but there was something terrible and mesmerizing about the thin, jagged scar across his face. It was like the mark of Cain, physical evidence of the evil in his soul. It seemed to pulsate with an angry red heat. He couldn't take his eyes off it.

"You know, I was taught it's rude to stare," the man said. Butts wasn't good with accents, but this guy's seemed vaguely British.

"Yeah?" said Butts. "You wanna take a slug at me? Go ahead."

A couple of students leaving the lecture room glanced

at Butts as he spoke. A young Latina woman whispered something to her companion, and both girls giggled.

The thin man brushed some lint from the sleeve of his elegant wool coat. "Fisticuffs are so vulgar. And, speaking of vulgarity, don't you find that name a bit overwrought—the 'Alleyway Strangler'? I mean, talk about Gothic!"

Butts narrowed his eyes, hands on his hips. "You got a better one?"

The man leaned back on his heels and crossed his long arms as he watched the rest of the stragglers leaving the lecture hall. "Nice try, Detective. But if I were to suggest a name to you, it might just match a communication you may have received from a person claiming to be the killer. Notice I say, *claiming* to be. Who knows if he or she really is?"

"How do you know we've received somethin'?"

"I said, *may* have received. If you have, allow me to congratulate you."

"Why's that?"

"This killer is obviously clever. You'll need all the clues you can get."

"I don't think he's that smart. In fact, I think he's pretty stupid."

"Oh, really?"

"He thinks he's a lot smarter than he is. Where I come from, that's called arrogance. And anyone that arrogant is pretty stupid."

The man attempted to smile, but the result was a grimace, as though the muscles of his face didn't work properly. "What if he's as smart as he thinks he is?"

"I got news for you. No perp is as smart as he thinks he is."

The man's grimace broadened. The effect was grotesque, like a death mask. "There's always a first time, Detective."

Butts suddenly had the idea of snapping a picture of him with his cell phone. But the man must have read his mind—by the time Butts dug the phone out of his jacket, he had slipped around the corner. Butts nodded to McKinney, the plainclothes officer who had been leaning against the wall pretending to be absorbed in a conversation on his cell phone.

McKinney nodded back and followed The Professor.

# CHAPTER FIFTY

"Where the hell have you been?" Butts barked at Lee when he emerged from the lecture hall.

"Trying to escape the usual well-wishers and hangers-on. I did my best to dodge them, but Lucille Geffers came over and wanted to chat. I got away as soon as I could. So," he said, looking around, "did you get anything from him?"

"He's our guy."

Butts proceeded to recap the conversation, speaking in a low voice in case anyone might be eavesdropping. But the hall traffic had thinned out to the occasional backpack-toting student preoccupied with the approaching Christmas holidays, and no one was paying attention to them.

"If you do another lecture, you think he'll come to that?" he asked Lee.

"He might. It would be a risk, but he enjoys risk."

"I put a tail on him," Butts said.

"I suspect he'll be very good at shaking anyone following him."

"McKinney's a good man."

"It's worth a try."

Butts shook his head. "I actually tried to get him to take a swing at me, for Christ's sake, so I could arrest him for assaulting an officer."

"He's too smart to fall for that."

"No kiddin', Doc. Look, I'm gonna go down and book an appointment with a sketch artist, get this guy's mug on paper, at least. Then we can circulate it within the department so our guys can be on the lookout for him."

"That's a good idea."

"Did you get a good look at his face?" Butts asked as they took the stairs down to the first floor.

"I'm a little nearsighted, and the back row was kind of far away."

"That's some scary looking scar he's got," Butts remarked as they joined the throng of students and professors headed for the exit.

"A scar, huh? That should help identify him. Unless . . ."

"What?"

"There's a chance the scar is actually part of a disguise."

A couple of students turned around to look at them. Lee put a finger to his mouth and exchanged a glance with the detective.

"You mean he might have faked it, to mislead us?" Butts whispered.

Lee didn't answer until they were out of the building, surrounded by the ambient noise of Tenth Avenue. A swath of yellow taxis rattled uptown, their suspensions clattering over the potholes, the sound blending with the chatter of pedestrians and the click of leather heels on concrete. Lee pulled Butts over to the side of the building.

"It's such an obvious identifying feature. Why would he engage in a long conversation with you and let you get a good look at him, unless what you were seeing was really an illusion?"

"So I'll have every cop out there lookin' for a guy with a scar—"

"And he could slip through the net because he hasn't got one."

Butts gazed at the pocket park across the avenue, where a man was selling Christmas trees. They were lined up in front of the park's chain-link fence, a miniature forest of evergreen. "Christ. I don't know what to tell the sketch artist now."

"Why don't you start by describing him as well as you can? You can add the scar later. It might be real, you know—he certainly is scarred psychologically."

"So it could be real."

"It might be. He is deeply damaged, and it could be physical as well as emotional. Sorry I can't be more definite."

"Whaddya gonna do, Doc? We all got our cross to bear," Butts said, thrusting his arm out to snare a taxi. "That's what the wife says, though I gotta say, I think some crosses are a hell of a lot heavier than others."

"You can say that again," Lee agreed as a cab screeched to a halt in front of them, brakes squealing.

"What's goin' on with that forensic anthropologist of yours?" Butts asked after giving the driver the address for the precinct. "Haven't seen her for a while. What's her name—Kathy?"

"Right, Kathy Azarian. We're kind of . . . taking some time off." Lee looked out the window of the cab as it sped past an Italian restaurant. The facade had been painted pumpkin orange. *Peter, Peter, Pumpkin Eater.* He wondered what she was doing with him. The thought stung like acid.

"That's too bad," said Butts. "I like her."

"Yeah, I don't know if we're really right for each other," Lee said.

"Why don't you make a list?" Butts suggested, fishing a sandwich out of his pocket. Lee was dismayed to see that it appeared to be egg salad.

"A list?" he said.

"Pros and cons—good things and bad things about each of 'em."

"That sounds kind of . . . clinical."

Butts settled back in his seat and unwrapped the sandwich. "It worked for me. When I met my Muriel, I was datin' another girl, see? I liked 'em both, but I knew I had to make up my mind. So I made a list. I put what I liked about them each on one side and what I didn't on the other."

"What happened?"

"I broke up with the other girl." He took a large bite of his sandwich. " 'Course, I got in trouble later."

"You did?"

"Yeah. Muriel found the list, and she wasn't too thrilled. I tried to explain that she won, so she should be happy about it, but that didn't help much."

"But she married you."

Butts grinned. "How 'bout that? I got lucky in the end."

"Did you manage to convince her that the list was a good thing?"

"Hell, no. Listen, when you see Kathy, whatever you do, don't mention that damn list, okay?"

"I won't."

"Promise?" he said, wiping off a stray chunk of egg salad from his mouth.

"Cross my heart, hope to—"

"Don't say that. I don't like people sayin' that."

"I forgot you were superstitious."

"Nothin' to do with superstition—I just don't like hearin' people say that, okay?"

"All right."

*Cross my heart, hope to die.*

# Chapter Fifty-one

Fiona sent Kylie into the city as promised on Friday, and Lee took her to her favorite restaurant, the Gothic-themed Jekyll & Hyde Club on Sixth Avenue. An actor dressed as a mad scientist escorted them past the gargoyles and skeletons to a table in a corner next to some French tourists.

The air was tight between them. Kylie seemed indifferent to everything, with none of her usual excitement when they visited Jekyll & Hyde. Instead of watching the waiters dressed as macabre characters prowling among the tables, she twisted a strand of blond hair idly between her fingers, a bored expression on her face. She then picked up her fork and swirled her vegetables into a whirlpool on the plate, concentric circles of green and red. *Like Christmas lights.*

It was Christmas almost six years ago that her mother disappeared; Lee wondered if Kylie knew that. He wasn't sure how much Fiona or George had told her. Distressing information was guarded closely in his family. The avoidance of conflict made it that much more unsettling when something bad did happen. In spite of his training and knowledge, he had reacted to

Laura's disappearance by plunging into a deep well of despair.

He looked at his niece. Kylie dangled her fork between thumb and forefinger, idly gazing at the patterns she was making on her plate. Lee took a deep breath and placed a hand on her arm. She looked up at him with a surprised expression that quickly hardened into indifference. It tore his heart to think what that emotional control cost her. She was learning at the hand of the master, and he felt it was his job to make sure she knew there were other options. Fiona Campbell had lived her life skimming across emotional surfaces like a dragonfly on a pond, avoiding the anguish of loss through sheer willpower.

"Kylie," he said, "is everything okay with you?"

She stared back down at her plate. "Sure." It was clear she wasn't trying to convince him.

"Is there anything bothering you?"

Her eyes still on the plate, she said, "Why do you ask?"

"I just thought you might want someone to talk to," he said lamely.

"What has she told you?" Kylie asked, her mouth sullen. The expression was so like Laura, he was caught off guard.

"Who—Fiona?"

She rolled her eyes. "*Duh.*"

"Nothing," he lied.

"Get real," she shot back. "She told you, didn't she?"

"She mentioned—"

"That I've been cutting." Her voice was hard, flat.

"Yeah," he said. "So have you?"

"What do you think?"

"I think you have."

"I tried it once," she said. "I saw one of the older kids at school doing it."

"But why?"

She shrugged. "I don't know. Because it looked cool. Because she said it made her feel better. Because I wanted to see what it felt like."

"And what did it feel like?"

The line between her eyebrows deepened, and she bit her lip. "It made me feel better."

"God, Kylie."

"Are you angry at me?" Her defensive manner softened, and she sounded like a little girl again.

"No, I'm not angry. I'm just puzzled—and sad."

"I won't do it again."

"That's not the point. The question is why you did it in the first place."

"I *told* you," she said, on the verge of tears. "Because I wanted—"

"Because you wanted to feel better."

He looked across the room at a table of children giggling and pointing at a talking skeleton. The statue's bones clattered as its jaw rattled on, the grinning mouth seeming to mock the living from beyond the grave. He couldn't hear what it was saying, but he supposed there was an actor in a control room somewhere doing the voice. The talking heads of creatures and portraits on the walls often made personal remarks about the customers, so there were probably closed-circuit cameras everywhere.

The thought sent a shiver through him—being spied upon was too much like his experience with his mysterious caller. He was being stalked by a twisted voyeur, and in a way these children were too—except they were enjoying it. They were about Kylie's age and were celebrating a birthday. A beleaguered and exhausted-looking young woman—their chaperone?—stared off into space, an empty piña colada in front of her. He looked back at Kylie, who was gazing up at him with a hungry expression. Hungry for what, he wondered—understanding, knowledge, comfort?

"Kylie," he said, "I want you to know something."

"What?" she asked, her lower lip beginning to tremble.

"Your mom may not be coming back."

"I know." Her voice was soft.

"You do?"

"Grandmother likes to pretend she's coming back, and I pretend to believe her. It makes her feel better."

"But—"

"I know it's not true. She loved me, and if she were alive, she would have come back by now. I know that. So she must be dead."

He tried to think of something comforting to say, but all he could say was, "God, Kylie."

"It's okay, Uncle Lee. Grandmother thinks I believe she's still alive. Don't tell her I told you."

This was so *wrong*, the child taking care of the adult, he thought. No wonder she was cutting herself. He had never suspected that Kylie felt as he did—that Laura was never coming back. His heart ached for the child, for the delicate deception she had spun out for her grandmother's sake. How long had she suspected the truth?

"Is that—is that why you're cutting yourself?" he stammered.

"I don't know. All I know is that it did make me feel better."

"Look, Kylie, if you ever need to talk to someone, I mean, about the truth—"

"I know, Uncle Lee—I can talk to you," she said, but he sensed she was just humoring him. He felt her receding from him, traveling down the same dark tunnel he had been desperately trying to claw his way out of. But the tunnels were not connected; they as were separate as if they existed in different universes. Like him and Kathy Azarian . . . Right now, the only person he really felt connected to was the Alleyway Strangler. But was it enough to find him before someone else died?

# Chapter Fifty-two

If there was one thing Victoria Hwang hated, it was being late. She stood on the subway platform grinding her teeth and picking at the cuticle of her left thumb, impatience creeping up her spine like kudzu.

She forced herself to take deep breaths, pulling the musty, subterranean air in through her nostrils. It smelled like mildewed gym lockers and stale urine. She exhaled slowly through her mouth, just as she had learned to do in yoga class. *In, out, in, out. Nothing you can do about it, so you might as well relax.*

"Easier said than done," she muttered through clenched teeth as she paced the platform of the 110th Street station. She was supposed to meet her parents in Chinatown at seven, and it was already after six thirty. She dug her cell phone out of her coat pocket and glanced hopefully at the screen, but there was no reception underground, with layers of dirt and rock and steel between her and the nearest cell tower.

"Damn," she murmured and shoved the phone back into her pocket. A middle-aged woman frowned at her from one of the wooden benches lining the platform wall, then quickly looked back down at her magazine.

The woman was tall and reedy, with a green tweed skirt and matching hat. Her sturdy-looking calves protruded from the sensible wool skirt, culminating in thick ankle boots perfect for striding over moors and fens. She brought to mind a British headmistress, ruddy-cheeked and hale from years of hearty lamb stew and brisk exercise in good English air. She had a horsey face, with a long nose and prominent cheekbones, and her big-boned hands clutched a green brocade handbag. Victoria barely noticed the tall man at the other end of the platform, who appeared to be engaged in reading the *New York Times*.

Victoria paced the platform, cursing herself for not getting an earlier start. She knew New York subways could not be counted on, especially on weekends. She saw a young couple in blue jeans and matching black T-shirts gazing longingly down the platform, as if that would cause the train to magically appear. She smiled and turned away, squelching an impulse to do the same. She felt a tap on her shoulder and spun around, her heart throbbing wildly in her chest. Her breath came in shallow gasps, and sweat spurted from her forehead as she turned to see the English schoolmarm, a startled look in her mild gray eyes.

"Sorry to disturb you," the woman said. Her accent did sound vaguely British, but it had a touch of something else Victoria couldn't quite place. "I was just wondering if you had the time."

"Oh, yes—sorry," Kathy answered, digging out her cell phone. "It's, uh—six thirty-three."

"Thanks very much," the woman replied, smiling to show broad, uneven teeth. Kathy watched as she trundled back to the bench, tottering awkwardly on her sensible shoes. Her gait suggested that the shoes were new, or too small—she didn't look comfortable in them.

Victoria turned away and forced herself to take deep breaths. *Damn panic attacks*, she thought, blinking to dispel the black dots dancing before her eyes. Lately, anything could set off a panic attack—the tap of a stranger's hand on her shoulder, the sound of rapid footsteps behind her, the sight of a lone figure lurking in a darkened alley. Ever since being mugged a year ago, Victoria double-locked her doors at night and slept with a baseball bat next to her bed. She'd had an expensive alarm system installed in her apartment, with a state-of-the-art call center that was manned twenty-four hours a day.

She fished around in her bag for the magazine she always carried—and that, it seemed, was just the cue the train was waiting for. It glided into the station, the rows of shiny new silver cars almost entirely empty. At the far end of the platform, the tall, thin man slipped into the last car.

Victoria got into the same car as the sturdy English schoolmarm. The woman plopped her stringy body into one of the seats and immediately immersed herself in her magazine. Kathy tried to read her own magazine, but it was a trade publication in her field, architecture, and she didn't find it very absorbing right now. She was too disturbed by her panic attack. Forcing herself to take deep breaths, she closed her eyes and allowed herself to be lulled by the forward motion of the train. She almost missed her stop at Canal Street.

She and the tweed-clad woman were the only two people left in their car as the door opened and the conductor on the loudspeaker blared the name of the stop.

"Canal Street. Change here for the—"

Victoria leaped from her seat and was already halfway out the door before he finished his announcement. She stood on the platform for a moment, trying to remember which exit stairs to use, when she saw the schoolmistress trundling along the platform toward the nearest turnstile. She followed her toward the exit.

She scarcely noticed the tall man behind her taking the stairs up to the street two at a time until he was just a few steps behind her. When she reached the top, she shuddered nervously and headed toward her parents' apartment.

She forcibly shook off her bout of nerves as the man followed her through the shadows of the buildings lining Canal Street. He was, she was sure, simply going in the same direction as she and would soon be lost in the endless parade of pedestrians on Chinatown's busiest thoroughfare.

# Chapter Fifty-Three

Lee rented a car and drove Kylie back to Stockton the next day. After dropping her off, he headed for Philadelphia to meet Kathy. He wanted to make another stab at working things out with her, but he also felt pulled there by the presence of the mysterious Thomas. It was totally irrational to think he could ever hunt him down, but he knew rationality wasn't always his strong suit.

He hugged the river and crossed into Pennsylvania around Trenton. A shroud of mist blanketed the Philadelphia skyline as Lee drove over the Ben Franklin Bridge. The constant stream of traffic had turned the snow on the ground into slush, hissing under his tires as he turned onto the Race Street exit. Still hugging the river, he headed south toward the Old City, past the beer pubs and cheesesteak joints on Third Street. Driving past the graceful steeple of Christ Church, he was amazed, as always, to think that when it was built, it was the tallest building in North America.

Anxiety began to gnaw the pit of his stomach, so he switched on the radio to distract himself. He turned the dial until he reached the local NPR station, WHYY, where Terry Gross was interviewing a scientist about global warming. Looking out the window, he found it hard to imagine the landscape around him ever being warm again. A wicked winter wind whipped the bare trees lining the sidewalks, and even the buildings looked cold.

A lot of the cops he worked with probably didn't listen to public radio, with its leftist slant and liberal attitudes. He wondered what Butts listened to at home. There was so much about the pudgy detective he didn't know. Hell, there was so much about Kathy he didn't know, when it came to that. And how could you ever really know another person? But he suspected that most people longed to be known, to be *seen* and fully understood. Perhaps it was that, and not sex, that drove people to mate and procreate and live together in hope of forging something deeper and wider than the sum of its parts.

*The sum of its parts* . . . The phrase rattled around in his head, like a light aircraft looking for a place to land. He was sifting through the meaning of it when he remembered that Krieger had also suggested that the killer might have a connection to numbers.

*The sum of its parts.* Were the strange designs of punctures on the victims a mathematical puzzle of some kind? he wondered as he turned east onto Chestnut Street. He parked at a meter and walked to the restaurant, with its brick-colored walls and black-on-gold painted columns, the colors of the Belgian flag. He didn't see Kathy downstairs, so he squeezed past the regulars hunched over the bar, sucking on pints of Belgian wheat beer and porter, and climbed the steep steps to the second floor. It was happy hour, and the bar was crowded; the sound of loud laughter and clinking glasses followed him up the stairs.

The place had become a favorite of theirs early on—it boasted over three hundred imported and local brews. The menu included the beer's country of origin as well as its alcohol content, and the mussels and fries were second to none. There was even a beer called Delirium Tremens (alcohol by volume 8.5 percent.)

On the second-floor landing, a skeleton lay grinning in his transparent coffin—one of the many tongue-in-cheek images of death sprinkled throughout the place. In honor of the season, the skeleton wore a bright red Christmas bow around its neck. Lee liked all the jaunty references to death. There was something unaccountably comforting about eating dinner in a room with a full skeleton in a corner.

He didn't feel much like food now, though, and the sight of Kathy in the back of the long, narrow room didn't help. She looked up when he entered, a tight smile on her face.

"Hi," she said, as he slid into the chair across from her at the long table. The seating was European style, and you might share a table with up to eight other people on any given night. Today all the action was downstairs, though, and they had the upstairs to themselves. Kathy wore a fuzzy red turtleneck sweater that showed off her black hair. She looked fantastic. He wished she didn't. He decided not to tell her how great she looked.

He thought about ordering a Delirium Tremens but instead selected an equally potent draft ale, Old Curmudgeon. It's what he felt like lately, so he figured he might as well drink it.

"How's the case going?" she asked when the waitress had gone.

"Not so good. We're kind of stuck right now. How about you?"

"My dad's away at a conference, so I'm staying at his place to look after Bacchus. I don't know why he doesn't get rid of that musty old cat—he's terribly allergic to him."

"He probably loves Bacchus."

Her look said, *Don't go there*, so he didn't.

She took a long swallow of beer. "It's a myth, you know."

"What is?"

"This whole notion that you meet someone, fall in love and live happily ever after. The idea that anyone can fulfill all your needs or desires or fantasies."

"But does that mean you can't be happy with someone?"

"Expectations are too high. We want perfection, when what we're stuck with is human nature."

"Well, sure . . ."

She frowned, which deepened the little dimple in her chin. "See, I hate it when you do that."

"Do what?"

"Say 'sure' when I make a point."

"I was just agreeing with you."

"No, you weren't. You were implying that you'd thought of it already, and what I'm saying is obvious."

"I didn't mean—"

"It sounds arrogant."

"You think I'm arrogant?"

"Sometimes."

"Is Peter arrogant?"

She put her beer mug down with a thump and glared at him. "Oh, come on, Lee—really."

"Sorry, it's just that—"

"I know this is hard for you. It's hard for me too."

"Maybe I shouldn't have come," he said, hoping she'd disagree. But she didn't.

"Yeah," she said. "Maybe not."

Silence lay between them like a puddle of unhappiness. He felt soggy, sodden, miserable.

His cell phone rang, and he seized it, grateful for the interruption. It was Butts.

"What's up?"

"Where are you?"

"Philly."

"How fast can you get back?"

"What's wrong?"

"We got another body."

"I'm on my way." He pocketed the phone, relief flooding his veins with equal parts shame. Someone was dead, and yet he was glad for the chance to be rescued from this desultory conversation. He would have to wait for another time to hunt down the mysterious Thomas, but that could wait.

He looked at Kathy, struck once again by the graceful symmetry of her face.

"I have to go."

Maybe it was his imagination, but he thought she, too, looked relieved.

"Go," she said, and he went.

# Chapter Fifty-four

Traffic was light. Lee reached lower Manhattan in two hours flat, coming in through the Holland Tunnel. He headed straight for Cortlandt Alley, a narrow lane in Chinatown between Canal and White Streets. He found a meter on White, parked the car and showed his credentials to the sergeant guarding the area. Ducking under the yellow crime scene banner, he walked past the graffiti-covered metal grates, deserted loading docks and looming fire escapes to where Detective Butts stood, surrounded by a cadre of crime scene technicians.

The detective grunted when he saw Lee. "'t'Bout time. What the hell were you doing in Philly?"

"Long story," Lee said, looking at Elena Krieger, crouched over the body. "Who's the victim?"

"Name's Victoria Hwang. She lives uptown, but her parents live down here. We sent a uniform to their place to tell them a little while ago."

"Is there a note?"

"Uh, yeah." Butts looked away. "There's something I should tell you about that."

"What?"

"It's addressed to you." He handed Lee a pair of white latex gloves. "Give Detective Krieger another coupla minutes, and then we'll have a look."

"Where's Jimmy?" Lee asked as he pulled on the gloves.

"Chen? Over there," Butts said, pointing. "Interviewing potential witnesses."

Jimmy was surrounded by a group of middle-aged Chinese men, who were smoking and talking with animated gestures. Jimmy towered over them. Butts pointed to a faded red sign tacked over one of the rusted doorways. The top of the sign was in Chinese. The bottom read: NY TTF

"TTF?" said Lee.

"Table Tennis Federation," Butts replied. "It's a big deal down here, apparently.

"His knowledge of Mandarin should come in handy," Lee said, looking at his friend. A stocky Chinese man with thick shoulders and eyeglasses was explaining something to Jimmy as his companions watched, nodding. Jimmy's face was serious, as he bent his long back down to lessen the distance between them—he had at least half a foot on the other man.

"Chen says this place is a big deal," said Butts. "All kinds of people train here, even Olympic athletes."

Peering down the narrow stairs leading to the basement room, Lee could hear the rhythmic plunk of a dozen Ping-Pong balls and the occasional shout of victory or defeat. Apparently the presence of a murder victim a few yards away wasn't enough to dim the enthusiasm of the table tennis community.

He turned his attention back to the alley, the pavement glistening damply in the gray afternoon light. The warm snap had melted most of the snow in the city, but this narrow passageway saw little sunlight, and the street was still wet. Lights glowed softly in some of the apartment windows facing the alley. The whole scene was disconcertingly beautiful.

Elena Krieger straightened up and brushed the dirt from the knees of her tight-fitting navy ski pants.

"Well," she said, joining them, "there's a new twist."

"What's that?" asked Lee.

"He took two fingers this time," Butts said.

Krieger glared at him. "I was about to say that this girl is Asian."

"You think that's why he left her in Chinatown?" Butts asked Lee.

"It could be significant, but it's hard to say. It could also be because there are more alleys downtown."

"Or maybe he attacked her here," suggested Krieger.

Lee shook his head. "Even if he did, he probably transported her somewhere else to—"

"To do what he does," Butts finished for him.

"Right. He has to complete the ritual somewhere private, where he won't be disturbed."

"His place?" Butts suggested.

"I think we should keep our minds open about that."

"Why'd he take two fingers this time?" asked Butts. "Does that mean his signature is—whaddya call it—evolving?"

"I'm not sure what it means," said Lee.

"Oh, my God," said Krieger.

"What is it?" Butts said.

"*One is the loneliest number.* Do you think he was referring to—to the fingers?"

"Could be," said Lee. "But still, why would he take *two* this time?"

Just then Jimmy Chen finished with the Ping-Pong players and walked over to join his colleagues. The Chinese men stood for a moment smoking and talking in low voices. Then, taking a final drag on their cigarettes, they filed back down the stairs to the table tennis club.

Jimmy glanced back over his shoulder at them. "I told them to keep their damn cigarette butts away from our crime scene. If I see one butt in this alley, there's going to be hell to pay."

"Learn anything?" asked Butts.

"None of them saw anything. The guy who discovered the body said there was no one else in the alley when he found her. Communicating was a bit of a challenge, though—some of those guys speak Cantonese."

"You mean you couldn't understand them?" said Butts. "I thought Chinese was Chinese."

Jimmy regarded him coolly. "There are fourteen separate language groups in mainland China. The Han Chinese alone speak eight mutually unintelligible languages."

Krieger crossed her arms. "In Germany we have regional dialects, but we can all understand one another."

"China is an ancient culture," Jimmy said. "In fact—"

"Okay, knock it off," said Butts. "I'm sure it's all fascinatin', but we got work to do here."

"Detective Butts said the note was addressed to me this time," Lee said to Krieger.

"Yes," she said, looking uncomfortable. "I haven't had a chance to study it properly yet. After it's been processed at the lab for fingerprints and trace evidence, I'll analyze it. Do you mind waiting a while to read it?"

"All right," he said, though he did mind.

"Right," said Butts. "And once they're done with Miss, uh, Hwang at the ME's, we'll have a chance to look at her—"

"To see what he did to her this time," Jimmy added grimly.

"Yeah," said Butts. "So until then, let's try and canvass the area for any more potential eyewitnesses, huh?" He squinted up at an apartment window, where a couple of people were peering down into the alley. "You take this building," he said to Jimmy, "and I'll send a coupla sergeants to cover the one across the street."

Because they were shorthanded, Krieger agreed to accompany one of the sergeants on interviews, leaving Lee and Butts standing alone in the gathering dusk. They could hear the bustle of Canal Street, the constant stream of pedestrians and traffic on one of Manhattan's busiest thoroughfares. The occasional squeal of brakes and impatient honking punctuated the rumble of trucks as they clattered over Canal Street's numerous potholes.

"You wanna have a look at her before they take her away?" Butts asked as the ME's black van backed down the alley.

"Yeah," said Lee. He trudged over to where Victoria Hwang lay. She was the center of all the action, as the crime scene techs scurried about, collected evidence, dusted for prints—but in a way she looked neglected, lying unattended in the same spot where the killer had dumped her.

He gazed down at her. She was young, though not especially pretty; she was fully dressed in a red wool coat, and her shiny black hair looked as if it had been combed and carefully arranged. She lay on her back in the same pose as the others, her hands clasped over her stomach. The index and pinky fingers of her left hand had been neatly severed.

A tech from the ME's office approached him, a slight young man with pale eyes and freckles. " 'Scuse me, but mind if we move her now?"

"Sure, go ahead," Lee said, stepping aside, relieved. He made a silent vow that she would be the last victim of this killer he would ever have to look at. He just hoped it was a vow he could keep.

# CHAPTER FIFTY-FIVE

Alone in Butts's office the next morning, Elena Krieger looked at the letter in her hands, irritated that her palms were sweating. Her fingers trembled—not from fear but from anger—as she read it again for what felt like the thousandth time. The typed text was neat as always, free of obvious grammatical errors or misspellings, a clear indication of the author's intelligence and education.

Dear Dr. Campbell,

I know, it's so frustrating, isn't it? You want your suspects—or UNSUBs, as you so touchingly call them—to fit into neat little categories, and when they don't, it's so disappointing. What do you have on me thus far? What kind of killer am I? Power-assertive? Really, am I the kind of man you would see lifting weights at a gym? Hardly—I think I'll leave that particular activity to you. Anger-retaliatory? I shouldn't think so. My dear old mum gave me no cause to hate women . . . so just exactly what am I? I guess that's for me to know and you to find out, hmm? At any rate, I'm sure I've left plenty of lovely clues in this missive for that sexy linguist friend of yours to decipher. I'd love to perform some cunning linguistics on her—who wouldn't? You two should really think about getting together, you know, and creating your own master race. (Oh, you're thinking now, is he a neo-Nazi of some kind?) Happy hunting!

The Professor

Krieger's face heated when she read the dirty pun. He thought he was so smart! She vowed he would be brought to justice if it was the last thing she did. And the snide comment about procreating with Campbell—disgusting. Not that she would mind—he was a very attractive man, though too thin for her taste—she preferred more robust specimens. But Elena Krieger made it a rule never to get involved with colleagues. That could only lead to trouble, and she had enough trouble just being Elena Krieger.

This UNSUB clearly knew who she was; his last letter had even been addressed to her. Of course, it would be easy enough for someone like him to find out she was working the case, and she tried not to dwell on the sensation that she was being watched. Nevertheless, she knew that on some level, her job put her in peril. It was also part of its appeal to her. She thrived on adrenaline—there was no kick quite like danger.

She put the letter down on Butts's desk and looked at her Rolex. She was early—the others would arrive soon. She leaned on the desk and stared out the window at East Twenty-first Street. A couple of uniformed cops leaned against a blue and white patrol car, smoking. A thin whiff of smoke snaked its way through the closed windows, and she wrinkled her nose in disgust. *Revolting habit.* Though she had occasionally indulged back in her German cabaret days, it now struck her as repulsive—though perhaps not as repulsive as Leonard Butts, with his pudgy, untidy body and messy ways.

She looked at his cluttered desk and shuddered. How on earth she had been saddled working another case with him she couldn't understand. He didn't like her any more than she liked him, and yet here they were, together again. It reminded her of that old American television show, *The Odd Couple.* Felix and Oscar—Butts was exactly like Oscar, but she didn't see herself as the fussy, prissy Felix. She did admire his passion for order, though—order was the closest thing Elena Krieger had to a religion, and she was convinced that this commitment to organization had led to her rapid advancement within the NYPD.

She gazed out the window at the logo on the side of the patrol car.

**COURTESY**
**PROFESSIONALISM**
**RESPECT**

*Right,* she thought. Elena had been around the NYPD long enough to see the cracks in that façade. There were good, decent people on the force, but there were also corruption, racism, and egos. God, the egos! Of course, she was aware that hers was one of them—Elena Krieger liked to think she had no illusions about herself. She was equal to the machismo and posturing within the force, but the sheer amount of it could be wearing. She was tired of having to prove herself; both her gender and her identity as a foreigner marked her as an outsider. These days, anyone with an accent was suspect, no matter what country it came from.

Still, she thought as she looked down at the pair of lumpy uniformed officers lounging against their patrol car, she had an advantage over most of her colleagues. She was hardworking, smart and ambitious. But what really set her apart was her discipline. She knew it was a stereotype about Germans, but if she fit the stereotype, so what? She was convinced that her dedication and capacity for hard work would pay off in the long run.

She glanced at her Rolex again, her one personal luxury, running her fingertips lightly over its diamond-encrusted face. She had to hand it to the Swiss—they knew how to make watches. She didn't wear it because it was a status symbol; she wore it because it was a finely crafted piece of machinery. Elena Krieger liked things that *worked*. She couldn't stand having anything broken or damaged around—chairs with missing slats, cracked or chipped dishes, ripped upholstery.

Her personal rule was either mend it within a week or throw it out. It didn't matter whether or not the object had sentimental value—if it was broken, it had lost its usefulness. Period—no exceptions. She had once discarded a cuckoo clock that had belonged to her grandfather because it couldn't be mended. Her father had been upset when he found out, but that was just too bad, she thought. He should have taken better care of it.

Elena Krieger was deeply threatened by entropy.

Her entire life was a struggle against chaos, decay and entropy. She had a horror of disease, aging and impairment of any kind. She had long ago made a pact with herself that if she were ever permanently incapacitated, she would take her own life. She had the drugs stowed safely away in the back of her underwear drawer, and her lawyer had a copy of her living will, which stated that she was not to be kept alive if through injury or disease she were to enter "a persistent vegetative state."

She stepped away from the window. Her colleagues' meeting with the NYPD top brass should be over by now. She was glad she hadn't been asked to join Campbell and Butts to explain why another girl had turned up dead. Well, maybe she was a little peeved at being left out, but she was more relieved than not.

She looked at her watch again. They were fifteen minutes late. Probably that fat little detective had stopped somewhere to eat. It was disgusting the way he was always shoveling food into his mouth. She could hardly bear to look at him.

The phone on his desk rang, and without thinking, she snatched it up.

"Elena Krieger here."

At first there was silence, then a soft whimpering in the background, and what sounded like a girl's voice pleading. Elena strained to hear what she was saying—it sounded like "No, please—don't."

"Who is this?" she barked into the phone, fighting the wave of nausea and panic sweeping over her. "Who's calling?"

The whimpering stopped. There was the sound of heavy breathing, and a man's voice said, "Tag, you're it."

Then the line went dead.

Elena Krieger stood with the receiver in her hand, staring at the phone. The sound of that voice would stay with her for some time.

*Tag, you're it.*

# CHAPTER FIFTY-SIX

When Butts and Lee arrived at the precinct, they found a very shaken Elena Krieger. Even her Germanic stoicism couldn't hide the fact that she was upset; worry lines creased her elegant forehead, and her hand trembled as she handed the note she held to Lee.

"It was addressed to you, so I thought you should—"

"Thanks," he said, taking it from her.

It was a copy of the original note found on Victoria Hwang, which was still being processed in the lab for possible prints, DNA and trace evidence, though no one in the room expected any good news about that.

"Before you read it, I—I think he called here," she said.

"What?" Butts exclaimed. "Are you shittin' me? What did he say? How do you know it was him?"

She regarded him coolly. "To answer your questions in order, no, I am not 'shitting you,' and what a lovely expression that is, by the way."

Butts snorted impatiently. "Just tell us what happened."

She went on to recount the phone call, the girl in the

background, and the creepy comment the caller made before hanging up.

"What did his voice sound like?" asked Lee.

"Educated, definitely British."

"And the girl?" said Butts. "Someone could just be pullin' your leg. There's a lot of crazies out there who like to home in on investigations."

"Yes, I know," she said. "I thought of that. And it might have been someone just playacting—but if it was, she was very convincing."

"This town is full of out-of-work actors," Butts remarked. "And they all need money. I can see some sicko paying one of 'em to do this."

"Could the girl's voice have been a recording?" Lee asked.

"It was pretty faint, way in the background," she said. "Yes, it could have been a recording."

"You're thinking he recorded Victoria or another one of his victims?" said Butts.

"Maybe," Lee answered. "But why didn't the call go through the switchboard?"

"He musta had my direct line," said Butts. "That's not so hard to get hold of." He looked at Lee and nodded at the note. "So, what's he got to say there?"

"There's a lot of posturing—he alternates between taunting us and showing off how much he knows." He handed the note to Butts and turned to Krieger. "But you're the linguistics expert. What can you tell us?"

She bit her lip. "Based on vocabulary and word usage, I'd say it's definitely written by the same person as the other two. Highly educated, articulate, obviously, as we said before. The phrase 'my dear old mum' suggests once again that his origins are the British Isles."

"Why do you think he addressed it to you?" Butts asked Lee.

"He wants to be in the middle of the investigation—to follow it and insert himself every step of the way. He sees me as someone who is trying to 'figure him out,' so the note is an attempt to make a connection."

The door was flung open, and Jimmy Chen entered, out of breath.

"I was just at the morgue," he said.

"Yeah? What did you learn?" asked Butts.

Jimmy held out a manila envelope. "We're dealing with one sick bastard."

"We knew that already," Krieger said. "Let's see the photos."

Jimmy spread the pictures out on the desk. Victoria Hwang's body, like the others, had been disfigured by tiny pricks in her torso. This pattern was different yet again—it was circular, a series of overlapping swirls, sort of like the center of a sunflower.

"What the hell?" said Butts. "What is this?"

Jimmy looked at the others. "He would probably say, that's for him to know and us to find out."

# Chapter Fifty-seven

It was evening by the time their meeting broke up. Butts left to catch a bus to Jersey, and Jimmy had some more witness interviews to do before heading to his parents' place to look after his brother for a few hours. He took copies of the case photos with him, and Lee agreed to join him downtown later.

As Elena Krieger was putting on her coat to leave, Lee approached her.

"Can I ask you something?"

"I suppose so. What can I do for you?"

"I have a letter I'd like you to look at, if you have a couple of minutes."

She crossed her long arms. "What kind of letter?"

"It's a suicide note."

"What do you want to know?"

"Whether it's real or not."

She looked intrigued. "You have reason to believe it's fake?"

"Yes," he said, taking out the note and the sample of Brian O'Reilly's writing Gemma had given him. "Here's some of his writing for comparison."

She raised one plucked eyebrow. "You have a sample of the dead man's writing?"

"I know his sister." He knew he was being evasive, but he didn't want to explain any further—he hoped Krieger wouldn't connect it with Laura's disappearance. "It's for another case I'm working on."

"I see," she said, sounding unconvinced. "Let me have a look." She laid the notes side by side on the desk and studied them, bending low over the papers. He tried not to stare at the dark line where her breasts touched. She bent lower, squinting, and he realized Elena Krieger was nearsighted—but apparently too vain to wear glasses. He didn't care so long as she helped him get to the bottom of Brian O'Reilly's death.

She straightened up and handed him the papers.

"These are the writings of two different people," she stated.

"So the suicide note is a fake?"

"I don't know the circumstances of this alleged suicide," she replied briskly. "It is extremely unusual to find a typed suicide note, though not unheard of. But I can tell you, these are not the writing of one man. Here," she said, snatching the papers back from him. "Look at the consistent misuse of the apostrophe in *it's* here in the unquestioned document. There is no such punctuation error in the purported suicide note."

"You're right!" Lee agreed. "What else?"

"Well, there are so many things. The vocabulary in the suicide note is more sophisticated, the sentence construction more elegant—to be honest, they don't resemble each other in any way."

"Thank you," Lee said. "Thank you very much."

She regarded him with undisguised curiosity. "So this is another case you're working on?"

"Thanks so much," he said again instead of answering her question. "I owe you one." He put on his coat quickly and opened the door. "See you tomorrow!" he said, slipping out into the hall. He could feel her disapproval trailing him all the way to the lobby.

At home, he called Gemma O'Reilly, got her voice mail, and left her a message to call him back. Then he changed into running shoes and sweats and went for a jog along the East River.

The warm weather that had followed the storm had continued—the air was unseasonably balmy as he headed east through the streets of the East Village. He inhaled the salt air along with the faint aroma of fish bones as seagulls wheeled above, their faint, shrill voices carrying out to sea on an offshore wind.

His breathing synchronized with the rhythm of his feet on the pavement, snatches of phrases running through his head. *Anger-excitation, an-ger-ex-ci-ta-tion, an-ger-ex-ci-ta-tion.* He ran faster, harder, hoping to make the words go away, but they stayed, circling his brain like the seagulls overhead. *AN-ger-ex-ci-TA-tion, an-GER-ex-CI-ta-tion . . .*

He sprinted past the tennis courts to the old tugboat dock at the bottom of the park. It used to be open farther south along the water, but now the esplanade stopped at the northern end of the soccer fields, where a small brick house stood alone at the edge of the water. Years ago a park ranger had told him it was built as a tugboat dock and shelter for their pilots. The building looked lonely and abandoned—vines crept up its ancient walls and twisted around its cracked windowpanes, the interior cold and dark.

He stopped to stretch, and for a moment he had the feeling something inside the house moved. He peered at the nearest window, but an iron fence encircled the building, and he couldn't get closer than a few yards away. He decided it was his imagination and turned around to go back. As he turned around, he had the feeling that he was being followed. He craned his neck around behind him, but there was no one in sight.

He ran hard all the way back to his place, unable to shake the uncanny sensation of being trailed by . . . what? Or whom? He told himself it was ridiculous, but he was glad when he turned the lock on his front door, double bolting and sliding on the security chain. There was no sign of Chuck. He wondered if his friend had softened and gone to Jersey to be with his wife, but his things were still neatly arranged in the spare bedroom.

He showered and changed, then went back out, heading south toward Chinatown to meet Jimmy. As he crossed Houston, his cell phone rang. He dug it out of his pocket; the screen said *Fiona.*

"Hi, Mom," he said, thinking it was odd she was calling. Fiona Campbell hated cell phones.

"I tried calling your apartment, but your voice mail picked up," she said, sounding irritated.

"Well, you've got me now," he said, stepping aside to avoid a deliveryman riding his bicycle on the sidewalk. Piles of slush on the avenues made cycling on the roads hazardous. He watched the man weave around pedestrians, balancing two large plastic bags of food on either handlebar.

"So what do you think?" Fiona said.

"About what—Kylie?"

"Of *course* Kylie," she said, sounding even more irritated.

"She's clearly struggling with some issues."

"Well, obviously. But what do you think we should do about it?"

"I don't think you're going to like my answer."

"Try me."

"I think she needs professional help."

"I knew you were going to say that."

"I also think that we need to stay out of her hair. Right now she just feels pressured by us; even our concern for her is another source of stress.

"But we're her *family*!"

"Sometimes the people closest to you are the ones who can help you the least. I'm pretty sure she sees us as part of the problem right now," he added, shaking his head at an Italian maître d' gesturing energetically to him outside his Little Italy restaurant.

The temperature was falling, but the man stood in the street wearing nothing but a black three-piece suit, smiling and beckoning people to come inside. The only two Manhattan neighborhoods where Lee saw much of the hard sell were Little Italy and the Indian places on East Sixth Street. They weren't even owned by Indians—most of them were actually Bangladeshi—but the scene was similar to Little Italy. Owners and managers stood in the street in formal dress in all weather, smiling and cajoling potential customers.

"So I'm just part of the problem now," Fiona said petulantly.

Lee smiled at the underdressed maître d' and shook his head again. The man's face fell a little, but he gave a friendly wave as Lee walked away.

"Not you in particular, Mom—all of us. That's just the way it is sometimes. We all need to back off a little—but get her someone she can feel safe talking to."

"She can't feel safe with me?"

"She feels *obligated* to you, Mom—to all of us. She needs to talk to someone who's neutral, who doesn't expect anything of her."

"Well, if that's how you really see it," Fiona said huffily, "then we'll get her a therapist."

"Good," Lee said. "I can talk to George about it if you want. I can probably get some recommendations for good therapists in your area."

"No, that's quite all right," she said. "George and I are responsible for her; we'll find her a therapist."

"Okay, Mom. I have to go—I'm on the way to meet Jimmy Chen."

"Jimmy Chen?" Her voice softened. "How *is* Jimmy these days?"

"He's good, Mom—he sends you his love."

"Such a nice young man," Fiona sighed. "So polite."

Lee smiled. Jimmy was a lot of things, but polite wasn't one of them. In fact, he had admitted that some of his behavior was to dispel the stereotype of the polite Asian. Lee didn't have the heart to tell him that he didn't find the denizens of Chinatown especially polite.

"I'll tell Jimmy you said hi," he said. "Let me know what happens with Kylie, okay?"

"All right," she said.

He swung west on Grand Street, past the loud fishmongers in dirty white aprons smeared with fish blood, past the rows of ducks hanging on metal hooks in windows, past the bins of inscrutable Chinese vegetables looking like the spawn of alien life-forms, some huge and green and hairy, others brown and mysteriously dimpled. He turned south on Mott, striding past strolling tourists sipping from plastic cups of bubble tea, past the jumble of restaurants with names like Double Happiness and Golden Pavilion, past the shacks of hard-faced women selling cheap plastic jewelry and papier-mâché dragons. He inhaled the aroma of garlic sauce, soy and vinegar, of sizzling platters of crabs and bubbling cauldrons of sweet-and-sour soup, taking in the fascinating, bustling chaos of Chinatown.

He arrived at Jimmy's a little after eight. His friend opened the door and beckoned him inside.

"Want some ramen, Angus?"

"Sure."

"Barry loves ramen," Jimmy said, closing the door behind him.

"Isn't that a Japanese dish?"

"Hey, we invented noodles! Even Fettuccine Alfredo wouldn't exist if it weren't for us," Jimmy said, carrying three steaming bowls of soup on a tray.

"And Marco Polo."

"Whatever. Barry!" he called. "Your ramen is ready!"

Barry appeared at the door to his room in his pajamas, clutching a stuffed panda. He looked like an overgrown child.

"Hi," said Lee. "Remember me?"

"Remember me," Barry echoed. "I'm Barry, short for Barrington."

"He knows," said Jimmy. "You remember his name? He's Lee."

"Leeleeleelee," Barry sang, sitting down at the low table in front of the rattan couch.

They ate in silence for a while, Barry slurping loudly as he sucked the noodles into his mouth.

"This is good," said Lee.

"Goody-goody good good," Barry said, gulping down the rest of his soup.

"Okay, now we're going to work for a while, Barry," said Jimmy. "So do you have some math problems to do in your room?"

Barry hugged his panda and looked at his brother.

"What is it, Barry?" Jimmy asked.

Barry squirmed. "The supersonic wolves. I think they're there."

Jimmy turned to Lee. "He thinks there are supersonic wolves living under his bed."

"I can hear them," Barry said.

"Okay," said Jimmy. "Do you want me to come in?"

"Can I stay here?"

Jimmy looked at Lee.

"I'm okay with it, if you don't think the photos will be too disturbing," Lee said.

"Okay," Jimmy said to his brother, "but you have to be quiet."

"I have to be quiet," Barry replied, settling on the sofa with his stuffed panda.

"Very quiet," said Jimmy.

"In *fact*, very quiet," Barry echoed.

They cleared the table and spread out the pictures of the victims in the order in which they were killed.

"I'm trying to figure if there's a meaning to his progression," said Lee. "First he takes the little finger. He does that twice. Then, with the third victim, he takes two fingers. Why?"

"He's escalating."

"But not in the usual sense. His MO is the same; there's no increase in violence, and the placement of the bodies is the same, except for this one detail. What does it *mean*?"

"Maybe it doesn't mean anything."

"I don't buy that. He's extremely methodical and precise. If you combine it with the—graphics—it has to mean *something*. "

"Okay," said Jimmy, looking at the photos. "First he cuts off one, one again, then two—"

"And then there are the designs he makes on them. They keep changing. What's that about? It has to mean something, but what?"

Barry's voice came from behind them, with its peculiar flat tone. "The Fibonacci sequence."

"What did you say?" asked Lee.

"The Fibonacci sequence. Each succeeding number is arrived at by adding the two previous numbers. One, one, two, three, five, eight—"

"Wait a minute—start over, would you?"

"One, one, two, three, five, eight . . . the golden mean."

"The golden what?" said Jimmy.

"The golden ratio," Barry said in a singsong voice. "The higher you go in the Fibonacci sequence, the more closely the ratio between two successive numbers in the sequence approximates phi."

"What's phi?" asked Jimmy.

Barry rocked gently, staring into space as he recited. "Phi is an important mathematical constant known as the golden mean. Specifically it is approximately

1.61803." He pointed to the pictures of the designs on the girls' torsos. "In fact, these are Fibonacci designs seen in Nature."

"Oh, my god," said Lee. "What if that's *it*?" He looked up at Barry, still clutching his stuffed panda, his face expressionless. "Barry, you're a genius!"

"No hugging," said Barry.

Lee looked at Jimmy, who said, "He's afraid you're going to hug him. He doesn't like to be touched."

"Barry, I promise I will never, *ever* hug you," said Lee. "But I could kiss you!"

Barry frowned. "No kissing."

Jimmy and Lee looked at each other and burst out laughing. As he watched them, Barry's face broke into an awkward smile. His muscles appeared unaccustomed to the expression—his smile was like cracks appearing in a concrete floor.

He hugged his stuffed panda. "I'm a genius."

"You sure are, Barry," said Lee. "You're a goddamn genius."

"Goddamn genius," said Barry, with a little giggle. "I'm a goddamn genius."

"So if Barry's right," Jimmy said, "then next time the UNSUB will—"

"He'll cut off three fingers," Lee said.

He stared out the window. Somewhere, out beyond the friendly bustle of pedestrians, street vendors and the traffic of Chinatown, a killer lurked, calmly calculating the mathematics of death.

# CHAPTER FIFTY-EIGHT

Edmund listened carefully for the sound of his father's deep, heavy breathing before slipping out of his bed and tiptoeing downstairs. He headed for his hiding place, where he kept his treasures—in the cubby under the basement stairs. He didn't dare keep them in his room; his father would be sure to find them there. But the cubbyhole was his secret: he had carved a slat out of the side panel of the hollow steps, working at night and on days when his father was out on his rounds, selling whatever the latest product was. He had been a failure as a sheep farmer, but as a salesman, he excelled.

He sold anything and everything, and he was good at it; he could really turn on the charm for lonely housewives. He had even let Edmund come along with him a few times, until the women seemed to be paying more attention to the boy than to him. After that, he went alone, leaving Edmund and his sister at home alone.

Flashlight in hand, Edmund crept down the steps to his special place and carefully pulled out the wood flap he had carved out of the stair. When it was pushed back into place, you could barely see where he had sawed the wood. He reached in and pulled out his treasures: tattered copies of *Playboy, Penthouse,* and a Marks & Spencer clothing catalogue for good measure. Sometimes seeing the girls in dresses was just as good as seeing them without any clothes. He turned around to find the corner of the basement where he usually sat with his magazines and flashlight, but he stubbed his toe on something, and the pain caused him to drop his flashlight. It clattered to the floor with a terrible sound and rolled under the stairs.

Everything after that seemed to take place in slow motion, like one of those dreams where you can't move or make any sound. He bent down to fetch his flashlight, but he heard his father's bare feet thundering down the steps from the upstairs bedrooms, and in a flash he was at the top of the basement stairs, the light shining behind him, the bulb bare and harsh, so that Edmund couldn't make out his face, only his scraggly hair sticking up in all directions.

He didn't need to see his father's face, though: he knew what it looked like, contorted by rage and meanness and evil intent. He had seen it enough times; there was no need to look now. There was no need to try to explain or beg for mercy or escape either; he submitted to his fate dumbly, passive as a cow going to slaughter.

His father might have said something; later he couldn't remember. All he could remember was the feeling of those rough fingers as his father grabbed him by the scruff of the neck, pulling him out to the branding shed as if he were one of the sheep. He remembered the smell of his own burning flesh, and the sound of it: a hissing, as if his father had planted a snake on his cheek. He didn't remember feeling any pain. He supposed it hurt, or maybe he was in the kind of fugue state that his father's violence sometimes caused, where he detached from his body, surrendering to a welcome numbness.

He remembered what his father said afterward. "Now we'll see how you do with the girls, you randy little bugger! How does it feel to be a *monster*?"

Later that night, he saw his father at the bonfire, piling on the magazines one by one, the flames licking and shooting into the night sky, his face as fierce as if he were guarding the gates of hell itself.

# Chapter Fifty-nine

Morris Epstein was an absentminded professor straight out of central casting. A nervous little mole of a man with tobacco-stained fingers, he trailed a cloud of stale cigarette smoke behind him. His teeth were as gray as the wisps of hair growing around his ears, and his bald pate was as shiny as a polished apple. His prominent brown eyes appeared even larger and rounder behind a pair of black bifocals mended at the corner with duct tape. They perched lopsidedly on his short nose, which didn't look up to the task of supporting such thick lenses. He was constantly pushing them back into place, after which he emitted a sniffling sound, as though the effort had triggered an allergic reaction.

They had interviewed a steady stream of faculty members of various colleges around town, including Yeshiva, where one of the victims was a student, but Morris Epstein was their first Columbia professor.

He sat in the chair Lee offered him and gazed around the room, gnawing on already well-chewed nails. Butts entered moments later, rumpled as usual, a packet of potato chips protruding from his jacket pocket.

"Good afternoon. I'm Detective Leonard Butts, and this is my colleague, Dr. Lee Campbell."

"Is this about that terrible strangler?" Epstein asked. "The one who's been killing college girls?"

"Yes, but there's no need—" Butts began.

"Am I a suspect?" Epstein blurted out, giving his glasses a push with his index finger.

"Not at this time," the detective replied. "We'd just like to ask you a few questions."

*Not at this time.* Why had Butts given such a qualified answer? It was a good way to scare potential suspects, but Lee couldn't think why the detective would want to frighten this inoffensive little man.

"Very well," Epstein said, "as long as I make it to my three o'clock lecture."

"I'll be sure to keep that in mind," said Butts.

Lee noted the detective was keeping control of the interview by withholding whether or not he'd grant Epstein's request.

"Now, then, Mr. Epstein," Butts began.

"Actually, it's *Dr.* Epstein," the professor corrected him.

"*Dr.* Epstein. You're in the math department at Columbia, right?"

"Yes. I teach undergraduate courses in trigonometry and calculus. And a graduate course in the history of mathematics. Did you know that calculus was invented by Sir Isaac Newton?"

"No, I didn't," said Butts. "Now—"

"A lot of people know that the Egyptians came up with the system of numbers we now use, but you'd be surprised—"

"I'm sure I would," Butts interrupted. "If I could just ask you a few questions—"

"I'm sorry—was I rambling?" he said, repeating the glasses-pushing ritual. "I tend to do that when I'm nervous. That's what my wife tells me, at any rate. Are you married, Detective?"

"Yeah. Now, if you—"

"Wonderful creatures, women. Of course, they're utterly beyond comprehension, but that's what makes them so appealing, don't you think?"

Lee was impressed. He had seen suspects try to out-macho Butts, which never worked, out-maneuver him, which rarely did, and even try to soften him with humor and charm (he was as impervious to that as he was to Elena Krieger's charms). But he had never seen an interviewee simply do an end run around him. It was hard not to admire Morris Epstein, even if all his chatter was the result of nerves, as he claimed.

"Look, Mr.—uh, Dr. Epstein," Butts said, running a hand over his brow, "you got a three o'clock lecture, right?"

"That's right."

"And I got a case with a hole in it the size of the Lincoln Tunnel. So if you don't mind, I'd like to ask you a few things, and then you can go teach your class."

"I'm ready when you are."

"We have reason to believe the person we're looking for might be a math teacher."

"How intriguing. May I ask why?"

"I'm sorry, but I can't divulge the particulars of this case."

Lee noticed that the detective's vocabulary had taken

an upswing. One effective technique of interviewing a suspect was to mirror their body language. Maybe Butts was doing the verbal equivalent, adjusting his language to fit the way the professor spoke. The stubby detective's unsophisticated appearance and crude manners masked a keen investigative mind.

"Why not a student?" Epstein said.

"What?" said Butts.

"Why couldn't your killer be a math student? Did you consider that?"

"We did, yeah."

"And?"

Butts looked at Lee.

"We felt the UN—uh, the suspect—would be older," Lee answered.

"I was wondering when you were going to speak," Epstein said to Lee, stabbing at his glasses again. "You were about to say *UNSUB*, weren't you? I know what that is. It's short for *Unknown Subject*."

Butts and Lee exchanged a glance, and Epstein smiled. "Come, now—everyone who watches television knows that term."

"I'm glad you know your police terminology," said Butts. "Now, then—"

"You're that profiler, aren't you?" Epstein said to Lee. "The one whose sister disappeared."

"Yes."

"Any leads on what happened to her? Why aren't you working on that case?"

"That investigation is at a dead end," Lee said.

"That's terrible."

Lee glanced at Butts, whose face was a deep shade of purple.

"All right, *Dr.* Epstein," the detective said, "if you ask *one more question*, I will personally see to it that you miss your lecture."

The professor shook his head ruefully. "I am so sorry," he said meekly. "I'm doing it again—chattering because I'm nervous."

"Okay, then," said Butts. "What we'd like to know is if there are any members of the math department who you would consider . . . odd."

Epstein laughed. "My dear detective, we're talking about *mathematicians*. We're *all* odd."

Butts bit his lip. Lee had never seen him so frustrated in an interview.

"Let me put that another way," he said. "Is there anyone in your department who you might—"

"Whom I might suspect of being a serial killer?" Epstein said.

Butts rolled his eyes.

"Well, that's what you're asking, isn't it?" Epstein asked.

"Okay," said Butts. "Is there anyone in your department—"

"As a matter of fact, there is," Epstein answered in the conspiratorial tone of a parlor room gossip.

"And do you want to tell me who that might be?"

"Will I get to my lecture on time?"

"Yes, you will."

"First, may I have a cup of coffee?"

Butts stared at him.

"My wife said she heard that police precinct coffee was horrible, and I want to see for myself. I've never been in a police station, you see. She'll never forgive me if I don't try the coffee."

Butts sighed heavily but opened the door to go get the coffee.

Epstein called after him. "Milk and sugar, please."

Butts left the interrogation room and returned in less than a minute. He handed Epstein a paper cup of black coffee.

In response to his frown, Butts said, "We're all out of cream."

Epstein took a sip and shuddered. "She was right—it's wretched. Not as bad as the coffee in the math department, mind you, but dreadful."

Lee suspected that the coffee contained a fair amount of Butts's DNA, in the form of saliva.

"Now, then," the detective said, sitting across from the professor, "you were saying?"

"Ah, yes—the serial killer. It's terrible, really, what he does to those young girls."

"So this colleague of yours," Butts prompted. "What's odd about him?"

Epstein sipped his coffee thoughtfully. "He's—*different* from the rest of us."

"How so?"

"Well, Detective, I imagine there are certain types of people who become police officers. I mean, there's bound to be a range of personality types, but they would tend to have certain traits in common, right?"

"Such as?"

"Men of action who like authority and power, who are courageous, maybe athletic, decisive—that kind of thing."

"Okay—go on."

"It's the same in a math department of a large university. We all tend to be bookish, rather *un*athletic, highly intelligent, somewhat socially challenged and so on. In other words, classic nerds. Of course, there's some variation—Paul Dumont, who also teaches physics, is a rock climber. Physicists tend to be more athletic, for some reason. But he's still a nerd."

"So this guy you're thinkin' of—"

"He's odd in a different way. He's . . . how to say it?"

Butts leaned back in his chair and crossed his arms. "Take your time, Doc."

"Well, the rest of us have a kind of *innocence*, if you will. Our IQs might be in the stratosphere, but there's a curious naïveté about us, if you get my drift?"

"I know what you mean," Lee said, thinking of Jimmy Chen's brother, Barry.

"Well," said Epstein. "This colleague of mine . . . I hate to say it, but he's—sadistic."

"How so?" asked Butts.

Epstein shook himself as a dog might shake water from its coat. "There was—an incident. It happened quite a while ago, but I've never forgotten it."

"What's his name?" said Butts.

Professor Epstein looked at Lee beseechingly. "I feel somewhat uncomfortable about being placed in this position. What if I'm wrong, and you arrest him?"

"I understand your concerns, Dr. Epstein," Lee reassured him. "At this time we're simply looking for potential suspects. We would never arrest someone without sufficient evidence pointing to his guilt."

Epstein sighed and nibbled on his index finger. "All right. His name is Moran—Professor Edmund Moran."

Butts scribbled down the name. "So this incident you mentioned—when was it?"

"It was maybe five years ago."

"What happened?"

Epstein gave his glasses a mighty shove. "It was about this time of year—around the holidays, you know. Several members of the math faculty were up for tenure—including Professor Moran."

"And yourself?" said Butts.

"I already had tenure," he replied, without attempting to hide the satisfaction in his voice.

"Go on," said Lee.

"Well, one of the other professors up for tenure has a withered leg—polio as a child, you know, just before the vaccine was widely available."

"What's his name?"

"Nathan Dryansky. His parents were Holocaust survivors."

Lee glanced at Butts. Though the detective rarely spoke of it, he knew that Butts had lost family members in the camps.

"Go on," Butts said evenly.

"Well, I happened to be on my way to a class on the second floor just as Professors Dryansky and Moran were coming down the stairs. They're marble and quite slippery, you know," he said, looking at Lee, who nodded.

"Dr. Moran was behind Professor Dryansky, and as I passed them, I heard Dryansky cry out. I turned around to see him tumble down half a flight of stairs. Moran was closer to him than I was, and I expected him to run down and help Dryansky to his feet, but he just stood there grinning. So I dashed down and helped him get up. He wasn't badly injured, but he was quite bruised and terribly embarrassed. All the while, Dr. Moran just stood there with the strangest smile on his face. It was quite horrible, really. Not only that, but I had the impression . . . well, it's only speculation, of course—" He looked at the other two imploringly.

"Go ahead," Butts said.

Epstein gave his glasses a halfhearted push and stared at his hands. "I had the feeling Dr. Moran might have pushed him."

Lee and Butts exchanged a glance.

"Thank you, Dr. Epstein," Butts said.

"Did Moran get tenure?" Lee asked.

"Not that year. He did the next, however. He wrote a rather influential paper on the Fibonacci sequence in nature as seen in the chambered nautilus."

"Did you say the Fibonacci sequence?" Butts asked, his voice tight with excitement.

"Yes. You know of it?"

"We know something about it," Lee replied.

"I must say, I'm impressed," Epstein said. "Uh, am I free to go?"

"One more thing," Butts said. "This Professor Moran—what does he look like?"

Morris Epstein flinched. "He's tall and thin, with a dreadful scar on his left cheek."

Butts and Lee exchanged a look.

"Okay, thanks," said Butts. "We appreciate your time."

Epstein held up the coffee. "May I take this with me?"

Butts stared at him.

"Go ahead," Lee said. "It's all yours."

# Chapter Sixty

After Epstein had gone, Butts and Lee headed for the detective's office.

"It's a good thing Dr. Epstein didn't know his rights," Lee remarked dryly, closing the door behind them. "He could have gotten up and left at any time."

"Most people are intimidated by the badge," Butts answered with no hint of contrition. "We haven't got a lot goin' for us, but at least we got that." He threw himself into the swivel chair behind his desk and grabbed his phone.

"Who are you calling?" Lee asked.

"I'm gonna have Moran's place tossed."

"What makes you think a judge will give you a search warrant?"

"It's him—Moran is our guy."

"We don't have any evidence yet. I think we should call him in for an interview."

There was a quick rap at the door.

"Yeah?" said Butts.

The desk sergeant poked his head in the door. He was big and young and blond, with baby fat, like a pudgy golden retriever.

"Sorry to disturb you, Detective, but I have a Mr. and Mrs. Hwang here to see you."

"Christ," Butts muttered, replacing the phone. "Okay," he said to the sergeant. "Show 'em in."

The sergeant ushered a middle-aged Asian couple into the room. Mr. Hwang was a slight man with worried eyes, his thick black hair graying at the temples. He wore a pressed white shirt, buttoned at the collar, simple black pants and a smudged gray parka. His wife had a pretty, delicate face creased with grief. She wore a red wool coat and clutched an enormous pocketbook in her gloved hands.

"Please, have a seat," said Butts, pulling up chairs for them. "I'm Detective Leonard Butts—I'm in charge of the investigation into your daughter's death. This is my colleague, Dr. Lee Campbell."

The couple nodded and seated themselves, Mrs. Hwang tightening her grip on her purse.

"Pleased to meet you," he said. "I'm so sorry for your loss."

"Thank you for seeing us," Mr. Hwang said. His accent was thick, and he pronounced the words carefully, enunciating each one slowly, as if speaking them was a sacred ritual.

"First let me just say that we're doing everything we can to—" Butts began, but Mr. Hwang held his hand up.

"Excuse me, please," he said. "I do not want to take up your time. I know you work very hard, very busy, and we"—he indicated his wife, who nodded and attempted a smile—"have very much gratitude."

"It's our job," Butts said, "and like I said, we're doing—"

Again, Mr. Hwang held up his hand. Politely but

firmly he said, "No need to explain. We just come to say we offer reward," he continued, with another glance at his wife, who nodded. "We offer reward to anyone who help catch this terrible person."

This seemed to be Mrs. Hwang's cue—she began digging energetically in the depths of her massive purse.

"We cannot offer lot of money," her husband continued in his laborious, painstaking manner. "But we give what we can."

Mrs. Hwang produced a crisp white envelope and waved it in the air.

"We bring cash reward," Mr. Hwang said, "so you can give—"

This time Butts interrupted.

"Look, Mr. Hwang, Mrs. Hwang," he said, "I really appreciate that—I do. But please, keep your money. If we catch this guy, no one's going to need a reward. And I don't think any amount of money is going to help—we're going to get this creep, and we'll do it with or without the public's help. Okay?"

The Hwangs were evidently unprepared for this response. They looked at each other, then at Lee, and finally back at Butts.

For the first time, Mrs. Hwang spoke. Her voice was high and light and more singsong than her husband's, but her accent wasn't as thick.

"Detective," she said firmly, "in China, family take care of each person. Son, daughter, father, mother—we consider *responsibility*." She said the word slowly, carefully, as if it was important to get the idea across. "We have duty to our daughter. We fail to protect—okay, we understand no parent can always protect child. But now we do what we can for justice, you see? For justice for our daughter. We just want do something. We feel better, we do something—anything. You see?"

Butts looked at her without saying anything, then held out his hand. "Sure," he said. "I'll keep it safe for you."

"You give to anyone who help you find this man," said Mr. Hwang.

"Sure," Butts said, taking the envelope. "I promise."

"Thank you, Detective," said Mr. Hwang. "Thank you," he repeated to Lee.

"Thank you," said Mrs. Hwang.

"You're welcome," said Butts. "Thanks for coming by. We're doing everything we can, I promise."

"We know," said Mr. Hwang. "We believe in justice system."

Taking his wife's arm, he escorted her gently out of the room.

When they were gone, Butts sank back into his chair. His bulldog face sagged, and he looked as if he was about to cry. He closed his eyes and put his head in his hands.

"The justice system," he said. "Jesus Christ. For God's sake, Lee, let's get this creep."

# CHAPTER SIXTY-ONE

In the end, Butts agreed with Lee that they should call Columbia University the next day to see if Edmund Moran would come in for an interview. When Lee got home that night, Chuck was sitting on the living room couch doing paperwork.

"Hey," Lee said, closing the door behind him.

"Hey," Chuck replied without looking up. "Chinese food in the fridge."

Lee went to the kitchen, microwaved a couple of spareribs and noodles, and came back out into the living room with a plate of ribs and lo mein.

"How's it going?"

"Fine," Chuck said. "You?"

"Okay."

Lee perched on the arm of the couch and chewed for a while. Then he said, "Sure you're okay?"

Chuck stopped what he was doing. "Sorry, but I have a lot of paperwork to do. I can take it into my room if you want."

"No, that's okay. I'll go for a run."

"You sure?"

"It's fine, really." He finished the rest of the food in

the kitchen, then went through to his bedroom to change. When he emerged dressed in running gear, Chuck was still on the couch, head in his hands.

"Hey," Lee said. "What's going on?"

"I'm fine," he said, but his voice was ragged and thick.

"No," said Lee. "You're not. Stop playing goddamn games with me and tell me what's going on."

Chuck raised his head, his face tragic. "Susan had a spot on her mammogram."

"Okay," Lee said. "You know that most of the time those anomalies turn out to be nothing."

"That's not the *point*!" Chuck replied, his pale skin reddening. "I wasn't there to give her support!"

Lee sat down opposite him in the red leather armchair.

"Look, Chuck, there's always going to be something. No one's life is trouble free, and if it's not this, it'll be something else. If you go running back to her at every bump in the road—"

Chuck stared at him. "It could be breast cancer, for Christ's sake!"

"You don't know that yet. Why don't you wait until she—"

"Why don't I just wait until she's *dead*? Then I can be done with her once and for all! How about *that*?"

Chuck got up and began to pace the room. Lee had never seen him like this—agitated, hostile, frightened. He wondered if his friend was on something.

"Okay," Lee said, trying to keep his voice calm. "Do you have any friends in Jersey you can call on to help out? Maybe she can go for her follow-up with a girlfriend."

Chuck snorted. “You know as well as I do that Susan doesn’t have ‘girlfriends.’ She has admirers and acquaintances and plenty of ‘frenemies,’ but—”

“What about neighbors? Aren’t you friendly with that older couple next door?”

“You mean the Gogolicks?”

“Yeah.”

“Charlie is nice enough, but Jean is a space cadet. I can’t see relying on her in a crisis.”

“What about—” Lee began, but he was interrupted by the ringing of his landline. The caller ID showed *Gemma*.

“Who is it?” Chuck asked.

“Brian O’Reilly’s sister. I can call her back.”

“No, no—take it,” Chuck said. “It’s okay.”

“I can call her back—”

“*Take* it.”

Lee picked up the phone. “Hello?”

“Hi, it’s me—uh, Gemma.”

“Hi.”

“You have a minute?”

“Uh, sure.” He watched as Chuck put on his coat and hat. Lee waved at him, trying to signal him to stay, but Chuck ignored him. He unlatched the door and slipped out of the apartment. Lee had an impulse to toss the phone down and go after him.

“You there?” said Gemma.

“Yeah,” he said. “I’m here.”

“Sorry I didn’t call earlier—I’ve been slammed with work.”

“I showed the notes to our forensic linguist.”

“And?” Her voice was tight with anticipation.

"Brian did not write the suicide note."

"I *knew* it!" she said triumphantly.

"You realize what this means?" he said. "Your brother's killer is still at large."

"Yeah, I know. We'll both have to be careful from now on."

But as she spoke the words, he realized that *careful* might not be good enough.

# Chapter Sixty-two

Murtis Pullman slid her feather duster into its slot on her cleaning cart and took a bottle of Coke from her lunch bag. She plopped down into the chair by the door in the office, lifted her legs up onto another chair, leaned back and took a long swig of soda, savoring the acidic bite on her tongue as the liquid slid down her throat. She only liked Coke in glass bottles—none of this canned stuff the kids drank nowadays; she could taste the metal on her tongue. There was a bodega in her Washington Heights neighborhood that sold Coke in the old-fashioned bottles, and she stocked up every week, bringing them to work with her.

Murtis had been on the cleaning staff at Columbia University for thirty-three of her sixty-seven years on God's green earth. She had seen department chairs come and go, generations of students pass through the halls and rooms she dusted and swept, and she had seen professors receive or be denied tenure. Some of them shared bits of their lives with her—the good news and the bad—and the really nice ones even brought her gifts on the holidays.

Murtis Jefferson Pullman was a lady of great and

generous girth; her skin, brown as a coconut, was as clear and firm as that of a woman half her age. She felt that Columbia belonged as much to her as to the generations of fey, waifish students who wandered through the hallowed halls with their oversized backpacks and thirst for knowledge. She looked upon them with a mixture of motherly affection and disdain. Murtis had all the knowledge that anybody really needed: she had the love of her Savior in her heart. Since she had found Jesus, her outer life mattered not a whit. The sweetness she carried inside made up for her lowly position in life, her humble occupation of cleaning up after other people far more privileged and respected than herself.

She took another swig of Coke and looked around the tidy office. He was a neat-freak, this one—everything stacked so perfectly on his shelves, the book bindings lined up so that they all were on the same plane. His desk was immaculate and nearly bare, with only a clock and a phone on it. No family pictures in clunky homemade frames, no sentimental keepsakes; the office was as orderly and impersonal as a hotel room. She wondered if he had any family—there was something heartbreaking and disturbing about the obsessive neatness.

She barely saw him—once or twice darting out of the office as she arrived to clean it—and he nodded curtly to her, ducking out of sight to avoid further contact. Murtis was used to odd behavior—they were a strange lot, these university professors, with their rumpled suits, bow ties and stringy hair. And none were more peculiar than the math and science professors.

Murtis swallowed the rest of her Coke and glanced at her watch. She could afford a few more minutes' rest before getting back to her chores. She felt a song coming on. She leaned back, closed her eyes and let it wash over her. Songs often popped into her head, gifts from her sweet Savior. They were always about Jesus, and they came complete with words and melody. She sang them softly to herself as she worked, and sometimes she would sing them to her nephew, Jeffrey, who lived with her, and he would play them on the piano, putting chords to her melodies. Jeffrey encouraged her to take them to Pastor Jackson, but Murtis had no such ambition; she was happy enough to have these songs in her heart, and the knowledge that they were a special gift from her Lord.

*You are my only Savior, sweet and good and true.*
*My life was emptiness and pain before I knew you.*
*I lived in a world of suffering and sin*
*Before I opened my heart to let you in.*

She smiled to herself as the lyrics floated through her head—if Jeffrey was there when she got home, she would sing them to him. She took a deep breath and heaved her bulky body from the chair, wincing at the sharp twinge in her left knee. No doubt about it, the pain was getting worse. She should probably think about taking that nice young doctor's advice about losing weight. Murtis sighed—she loved her honey buns from the local bodega, smeared in cinnamon and sugar. . . .

As she reached for her feather duster, she thought she heard a sound coming from—where? Murtis froze, listening intently. There it was again—coming from beneath the floor, of all places. It was a kind of squeaking noise, like something a small animal might make. The office was on the first floor, and she wasn't aware of a basement underneath the building, but she supposed there must be one. And if there was a basement, no doubt there were mice—or, worse, rats.

In her years at Columbia there had of course been occasional infestations of vermin from time to time, but she had never heard this sound. There it was again, louder this time—*eee-eeek, eee-eeek.* She shuddered. Yes, it must be coming from the basement, and it was probably a rodent of some kind. It sounded trapped, poor thing—she reminded herself that God loved even the humblest of his creatures. Still, it was her duty to report it to the chief of the maintenance staff. God might love rodents, but universities did not. Murtis made a mental note to tell her boss about it as soon as she finished her rounds.

She took up her feather duster again and began humming her new melody as she cleaned. She was happy that the good Lord had given her the gift of a song. It was a good day, Murtis thought, one she would remember.

Later, she would reflect that she remembered that day, but not for the reasons she had thought.

# Chapter Sixty-three

"You had a long day," Muriel said as Leonard Butts closed the kitchen door behind him and wiped his feet on the rubber mat. No one except door-to-door salesmen and Jehovah's Witnesses ever knocked on the front door—family and friends came and went through the side door leading into the cheery kitchen where Mrs. Butts now stood, her hands covered in flour. A red-checked apron covered her fleshy body, and her sleeves were rolled up to the elbow, exposing her plump white forearms.

"Smells good," Butts said, hanging his coat on the rack by the door. He lowered his stocky form into the nearest chair and rubbed his forehead wearily. The smell of meat sautéing in olive oil reached his nostrils, and he heard the comforting sound of sputtering fat in the broad iron skillet on the gas stove.

"I'm making your favorite, breaded pork chops," his wife replied, kissing him on the forehead before returning to her work.

"That's not on my new diet."

"I know. I thought you could use something nice this week."

"You're too good to me," he said, reaching for her.

"I'm covered with flour," she protested, but he wrapped his arms around her and pulled her close, burying his head in her comforting bosom. Here with her in their warm and cozy kitchen, he could feel his body releasing the stress of the past few days.

"What is it, Buttons?" she asked when he released her.

He knew his face was damp with tears, but he made no attempt to wipe them off. He looked at the signs of domesticity all around him—his little wife in her cheery apron, the pictures of their son, Joey, smiling at him from the refrigerator, the hand-sewn sampler over the sink his mother had spent so many hours on when he was a boy, with its ornate stitching and brocade borders: GOD BLESS OUR HOME.

He took in a deep breath and let it out slowly, thinking of Mr. and Mrs. Hwang in their kitchen. Would they take the pictures of their daughter off the refrigerator, because they were too painful to look at, or leave them to remind them of happier times?

"What's wrong?" Muriel repeated, wiping at a tear with a floury finger.

"Another family lost their little girl," he said. "And they tried to pay me to find her killer. They didn't have the money, but they tried to give it to me anyway."

"Oh, Buttons," she said, cradling him in her arms.

"We know who the guy is—or probably is—but we haven't got a lick of solid evidence yet."

"You'll get him," Muriel said. "I know you will."

"I hope you're right," he said. "God, I hope you're right."

Later that night, Leonard Butts crept down the hall

and pushed open the door to his son's room. A thin shaft of light from the hall lamp fell across the boy's bed. Joey lay on his back, one arm flung over his head, the other clutching a baseball mitt. Pennants for all the major-league teams were carefully arranged on the wall above the bed—Butts remembered the rainy Saturday he helped Joey put them up.

A baseball signed by Derek Jeter sat in a glass case on the bookshelf. Joey's dirt-encrusted cleats lay in the center of the room, where he had left them—no amount of scolding from his mother had so far affected his boyish untidiness. *The carelessness of youth,* Butts thought—and, he hoped, the freedom from care as well. He longed to keep his boy as far from the troubles of the adult world as he could.

Looking at Joey, his blond hair the same shade as his own at that age, his face so much like Muriel's, with the same upturned nose and pointed chin, Butts felt a tugging in his heart that reached to the center of his being. Parenthood was so many things—all the clichés and all the pratfalls, the corny Hallmark sentiments and the frustrations. And there was a dark side too—sometimes Butts feared that Muriel loved Joey more than she loved him, and other times he was threatened by the boy's promise, by the fear he would eclipse his father in all things.

But now, looking at his son sleeping so sweetly, surrounded by his beloved baseball mementos, Butts felt only tenderness—a swelling, all-enveloping love so fierce, it frightened him. If anything happened to Joey—if anyone were to hurt him, Butts thought—he would instantly slip from the ranks of law enforcers and turn into a single-minded beast bent on vengeance.

Not justice—vengeance. In that way he was able to identify with the criminals he pursued, to understand their rage and fury. It wasn't hard for him to imagine circumstances where he would feel exactly the same as the monster he now pursued.

These weren't thoughts he shared with anyone—not his wife, not Lee Campbell, no one. It was as if saying these things out loud might release the demons of fate and start events tumbling down a disastrous path he was powerless to stop. He liked to think of himself as rational, but perhaps his Polish fatalism ran deeper than reason. You didn't tempt fate, and you kept your head down so that the dark forces of evil didn't find their way to your doorstep.

He took one last look, closed the door to his son's room, and tiptoed down the hall to his bedroom, where his wife was waiting to welcome him with her plump, warm body.

# Chapter Sixty-four

The bleating of his bedside phone shook Lee out of a deep slumber. Thrashing around to throw off the covers, he knocked the receiver to the floor.

"Damn!" he muttered, leaning down and fishing around under the bed. Retrieving it, he put it to his ear and sat upright against the carved Victorian headboard. "Who is it?" he barked, glancing at the clock, which read 7:05 A.M.

"Sorry to disturb you, sir." The accent was British, distinctly working class, and he recognized it at once.

"What can I do for you, Sergeant Ruggles?"

Ruggles was Chuck Morton's desk sergeant at the Bronx Major Case Squad. Efficient, devoted and helpful, he was the kind of right-hand man most station commanders could only dream of.

Ruggles cleared his throat. "Well, sir, I was wondering if you had heard from Captain Morton. I just spoke with his wife, and she says he hasn't been home for several days."

"Wait a minute," Lee said, rubbing his forehead to clear the cobwebs from his brain. "Are you telling me that Chu—uh, Captain Morton—hasn't been at the station house?"

"He didn't turn up yesterday, sir," Ruggles said. "When I called his cell phone, it bounced straight to voice mail. When I finally got through to his wife, she said she hadn't seen him either. And he's usually here by this time in the morning, but there's been no word from him. That's why I'm calling you, sir, seeing as you're his best friend and all."

"Christ," Lee muttered, throwing off the covers. "I'll call you back, Sergeant, okay?"

"Right you are, sir—thank you, sir."

Lee slung the receiver back into place, threw his legs over the side of the bed and heaved himself to his feet, swearing. He was not a morning person.

He marched into the hall and threw open the door to Chuck's room. His friend lay in bed, curled in a fetal position. He wasn't asleep, though—his eyes stared blankly at the opposite wall.

"Hey," Lee said. "What gives?"

Chuck didn't look up.

"What's going on?" Lee demanded, alarmed.

"I don't feel well," Chuck said, his voice shaky.

"Are you sick?"

"Not like that," Chuck said, trembling all over. "I've never felt this way before."

"How's that?" Lee asked, but he already had a good idea about the answer.

"Like the walls are closing in. Like I don't want to get out of bed or do anything. And scared. Really, really frightened."

"Of what?"

"Nothing. Just frightened."

"Shit," Lee said, sitting on the side of the bed.

"What is it? What's wrong with me?"

"You're depressed."

Chuck looked stricken. "You mean *this* is what it's like? It's—it's unbearable. I just want to fall asleep and never wake up. Good God, Lee, why didn't you *tell* me?"

"You can't really make another person understand," Lee said. "If you haven't been through it, you can't really know."

"Goddamn it," Chuck said. "I feel like I can't face anyone. I just want to go back to sleep."

Lee stood up. "Okay, first thing is to deal with the anxiety." He went to the bathroom cabinet, pulled out a bottle of pills and shook one into his palm. He went back into the bedroom and handed it to Chuck. "Here, take one of these."

"What is it?"

"Xanax. You don't have any drug allergies, right?"

"No. What'll it do?"

"Calm you down, take away the anxiety."

"Cheers," Chuck mumbled, popping it into his mouth.

"Now, you could go back to sleep, but why don't you come to the gym with me?"

Chuck stared at him as if he had lost his mind. "What?"

"Build up some endorphins—maybe get you through the day at work, if you're up to it. Get out some of that anger and aggression you're turning in on yourself."

"I can't—" Chuck began, but Lee grabbed the sleeve of his pajamas and pulled.

"Yes, you can. Trust me—I've been there. You *can* get out of bed."

"Goddamn it, Lee," Chuck protested, but Lee refused to give up. He pushed and prodded until his friend made the few stumbling steps toward the bathroom. He waited in the hall until he heard the sound of water running.

"I don't have a meeting until ten," he said when Chuck came out. "If we go now, we can both get to work by then."

"I'm not going anywhere," Chuck muttered.

"Yes, you are," Lee replied, tossing him a sweatshirt and gym shorts. "Don't think about what you feel like—just put one foot in front of the other." He shoved a change of clothes for them both into a gym bag. "Come on, let's go."

The Xanax kicked in pretty fast, and Chuck followed him meekly up First Avenue to the gym on Twenty-third Street. Lee signed him in as a guest, then escorted him to the punching bag. He found a couple of pairs of boxing gloves and put one on Chuck.

"I haven't done this since college," Chuck protested.

"You were pretty good back then," said Lee. "Just hit that damn bag with everything you've got. *Do it!*" he commanded when his friend hesitated.

Chuck began slowly, then got faster and faster, until finally he was whaling away at the bag, punching furiously, his breath coming in short gasps.

"Sometimes it helps if you swear," Lee suggested.

"Goddamn—fucking—*crap*!" Chuck bellowed, his face crimson. "*Goddamn fuck me!*"

Finally he stepped back, sweating, his blue eyes clearer.

"How do you feel?" Lee asked.

"Better. Not great, but better."

Lee got on the other side of the bag and slammed his own fists into it while Chuck took a break. They traded back and forth like that until their shoulders ached and the sweat poured down from them, landing in fat droplets on the floor. A couple of beefy weight lifters making the rounds of the Nautilus machines stared at Chuck from time to time as he whaled away, muttering curses under his breath. Finally he stepped away and wiped the sweat from his forehead with a towel.

"Want to spar?" Lee asked.

"Really?"

"Sure, why not?"

"Okay."

"You want headgear?"

"Nah, I'm okay."

They faced off in a corner of the room, gloves up, eyes locked. They danced around each other for a while, until Chuck threw a tentative left hook.

"Come on," Lee muttered. "Do it like you mean it."

Chuck responded with a hefty uppercut followed by a series of quick jabs. The last punch landed in Lee's ribs, throwing him off balance.

"Nice," he said, coming back with a combination he'd been working on: three jabs, a right hook, left uppercut. The uppercut landed on Chuck's chin.

Chuck smiled. "Oh, you wanna play rough?"

He came in like a hurricane, throwing punches left and right in such quick succession, Lee had trouble parrying them. All the fury of the last few weeks of his life seemed to gather into Chuck's upper body, sending him into a frenzy of blows. Lee took a hard punch to the stomach, followed by a left hook to his head that sent him reeling. He sank to his knees, his head spinning.

"Oh, shit! Sorry," Chuck said, bending down to help him up.

"Hey, it was my idea," Lee said. "I have only myself to blame."

"You might have a shiner," Chuck said, examining his right eye.

"Serves me right. So how do you feel?"

"Better, thanks."

"Had enough, or shall I give you another licking?"

"Can't wait to see what Elena Krieger says about your black eye."

Lee rolled his eyes. "Just as long as she says it in German."

Chuck grinned. "Be still, my beating heart. That woman is trouble. Sexy but trouble."

*So is your wife,* Lee thought. They showered and changed into the clothes Lee had brought. Looking at his face in the locker room mirror, Lee didn't see much of a bruise around his eye, though he was feeling a little dizzy. He didn't mention the car accident and concussion to Chuck—it would only make him feel guilty.

"Thanks," Chuck said as they stood on the windswept plaza in front of the gym. "I won't forget this."

"I'm glad you feel better," Lee said. "This could be a single episode, but just be aware it might return."

"I'll remember that," Chuck said, his voice husky.

"Thanks." He reached out as if to shake Lee's hand, then grabbed him in an awkward bear hug.

When they stepped apart, neither of them made eye contact.

"Okay, I'm going to catch the train to the Bronx," said Chuck.

"Oh, shit! I forgot to call Ruggles back."

"I'll call him on my cell," Chuck said. "Thanks again."

"Sure—anytime."

He watched his friend stride away in the direction of First Avenue, energy and bounce back in his step. He hoped Chuck would never again have to experience the deadening pain of clinical depression, but part of him—the part that knew too well how misery loves company—didn't want his friend to get off quite so easily.

Lee had been doing pretty well lately, but it wasn't so long ago that he was frozen, immobile, on his couch, unable to move, surrounded by an eternity of pain, jittery and exhausted all at once. When he was having a bad episode, he had no memory of what life had been or might be without depression. There was no past and no future, only the gray haze of psychic pain and the unbearable burden of consciousness.

He chided himself for wishing that kind of suffering on his friend as he crossed Twenty-third Street, heading toward the Thirteenth Precinct. He was early for the meeting and had just enough time to grab a bagel for himself and Butts at Ess-a-Bagel. He was curious to see if Butts had managed to get hold of their main suspect. Interviewing Edmund Moran would be interesting, to say the least, he thought as he headed south on First Avenue, the sun glinting on the damp pavement. There was a smell of expectation in the air, and he increased his pace as he loped past the rows of Christmas trees for sale, anticipation tight in his throat.

# CHAPTER SIXTY-FIVE

Edmund was excited. Tonight was the night. He would take her, ripping her away from everything and everyone she held dear, and make her his. He could hardly contain himself, humming as he went about his preparations in his spotless kitchen. It was important to be thorough, careful—he owed his success to his attention to detail.

That and his superior IQ, of course. He remembered when he was in sixth form, when his teacher, Mrs. Fontaine, had told him it was "off the charts." She had said he had a responsibility to use a gift like that. He smiled as he packed the long piece of rope into his kit. He was using it, all right—he wondered what soft little Mrs. Fontaine, with her lopsided wig and crooked teeth, would say if she saw precisely how he was using it.

He prepared his tea with a dollop of cream—not a glug or a swirl or a slurp but a dollop—and watched the swirling pattern as it mixed with the hot liquid. He drank it slowly, savoring the moment of preparation for his next outing. He looked at the roses in the vase on the kitchen table, the white petals at their decadent peak—full, fragrant and pliant. He could detect the smell of decay lurking just beneath the sweetness. The transience of all things tugged at his heart, and a single tear slid down his cheek. He wiped it away angrily. Loathsome emotion, sadness. That was one reason he loved Bach—the cold clarity and restrained emotion gave him room to breathe. Emotion was messy, unpredictable, *uncontrolled.*

Finishing his tea, he wound the rope carefully before placing it into the duffel bag. He bought a new length of rope for each of them, pristine and white and untouched—just like the girls. Of course, he knew they had been touched, pawed by grimy adolescent boys who didn't deserve them. But they had never been touched the way *he* would touch them—he was certain of that. He alone deserved them; he alone knew what they really needed. They just didn't know it yet.

He folded the silk blindfold with care, placing it next to the rope. He put the knife in last, fondling the blade for a moment before zipping the duffel closed. The logo on the front said *Gold's Gym.* The bag had belonged to his first victim. He liked that little detail—it struck him as amusing. He slung the bag over his shoulder, turned off the kitchen light and stepped out into the night.

# Chapter Sixty-six

"I can't believe we got him!" Butts said the moment Lee entered the office. "He's coming in for the interview in just a few minutes."

"You mean—?"

"Professor Edmund Moran. I can't believe how easy it was—I just called Columbia, they put me through to his office, and he said yes right away."

"Interesting, he agreed so quickly," Lee said. "He probably knows we have no real evidence pointing to him."

"But he's the guy, all right," Butts insisted. "That voice—I'd never forget that voice."

"We have to be very careful. Did you call Detectives Chen or Krieger?"

"Nope. Just you and me, Doc—we'll crack this son of a bitch," said Butts, his eyes burning with eagerness.

"I admire your confidence," Lee said. "But I should remind you, this man is the worst kind of sociopath. He has no conscience, no remorse, and he has a genius-level IQ."

Butts frowned. "Are you sayin' we can't handle him?"

"I'm just saying, watch your step. Techniques that work on most people won't work with him."

"So what's your idea?" said Butts.

"To start with, we get into the interrogation room first, establish it as our space. When he enters, he'll feel less comfortable."

"You know, a lot of times if you leave a perp alone in the room for a while, they get nervous, and by the time you come in, they're ready to confess."

Lee put a hand to his forehead, which was beginning to throb. "That won't work with him. He doesn't experience stress and anxiety like a normal person."

"So we go in first, then let the sergeant bring Moran in?"

"Right. We don't want to give him the impression we think he's anything special. Just a run-of-the-mill suspect we're not especially interested in."

"How are we gonna pull that off?" asked Butts.

"Just let me take the lead, okay?"

"Sure, Doc, whatever you say. Hey, you okay?" Butts asked, studying him. "You look a little green."

"You have any aspirin?"

"I think so," Butts said. Fishing around in his desk drawer, he produced a bottle of pills. "Here you go."

"Thanks." Lee popped two of them and gave the bottle back to Butts, who tossed it into the drawer. Then they walked down the hall to the interrogation room.

Lee noticed that Butts immediately began pacing the cramped room like a matador about to enter the bullring. It occurred to him that a bullring might be a safer place to be right now.

The desk sergeant poked his head into the room. “Guy here to see you—says his name is Moran.”

“Fine,” Butts said. “Bring him on back.”

Lee’s breath quickened, and white spots danced in front of his eyes. He sucked in a lungful of air, held it, then released it slowly.

The door opened, and Edmund Moran entered the interrogation room.

He was not what Lee had expected. The scar on his face was not as pronounced as Butts’s description had led him to believe, and even with the scar, the face was not ugly; in the right light, Lee imagined it could be rather handsome. The features were regular, well-formed, if severe, with high cheekbones and a long, straight nose. Lee realized with a shock that there was enough resemblance between him and Moran that they could be brothers. He was also taken aback by the physical poise of the man. Instead of evincing the nerdy shuffle of a classic math geek, he moved with athletic fluidity and grace.

“Dr. Campbell, how nice to meet you. I quite enjoyed your lecture the other day,” Moran said, extending his hand. Lee had no choice but to shake it. There was nothing to be gained by starting off in a confrontational mode. Moran’s voice was cultivated and faintly British, just as Butts had reported. It was raspy around the edges, as though he had sustained an injury to his vocal cords.

Phrases from the interrogation handbook floated through his head. *Put him at ease; make him think you’re on his side*. Edmund Moran was too intelligent to be fooled into thinking they were his allies, but it was too early to ruffle his feathers.

"Please, have a seat," Lee said, pulling over a chair. Butts remained in a corner, arms crossed, perhaps in case Moran might try to shake his hand. Their visitor carefully folded his coat over the chair Lee offered, then sat in it as if he were perfectly at home in his own living room. He was the picture of ease.

He twisted around to look at Butts. "It's good to see you again, Detective," he said, removing a pair of expensive-looking kid gloves. He leaned back in his chair, regarding his interrogators through half-closed eyes. He reminded Lee of a sleeping crocodile. *Subject appears calm. Attempting to establish and maintain control—classic psychopathic personality behavior.*

Edmund flicked an imaginary piece of lint from his shoulder. "So, am I under arrest?"

"Why?" Butts asked. "Are you guilty of somethin'?"

Moran smiled. "Isn't that rather your job to find out?"

"You can go anytime you want," said Lee. "Do you want to leave?"

"By no means. I'd like to help you with your investigation in any way I can." He spoke earnestly, but the undertone of mockery was unmistakable.

"Great," Lee said. *Subject inserting himself into investigation, even to the point of being exposed. Ego-driven, arrogant, attention-seeking.* "Would you like a cup of coffee?"

"I don't think so. It wouldn't do to leave traces of my DNA behind, would it?"

Butts slapped a fistful of crime scene photos onto the table—the Alleyway Strangler's victims, all young, all dead, photographed from various angles, their faces ashen, lips tinged with blue, their bodies a canvas for the depravity of a madman. Butts peered at Edmund.

"So," he said, "you know any of these girls?"

Moran regarded the pictures with detachment, as one might study a mildly interesting math puzzle.

"Can't say I do. But then, I suppose people look different dead, eh?"

"Not all that different," Butts shot back.

Edmund looked at Lee and smiled but continued to address Butts. "Detective, your esteemed colleague here has no doubt told you that psychopaths don't have the same physiological responses as 'normal' people. And the person who did this is clearly a psychopath. So if I did recognize these girls, you wouldn't expect me to break into a sweat, now, would you?"

Lee met his gaze. "Sometimes the lack of reaction is more telling than an emotional response."

"Oh, tut-tut, Dr. Campbell. No matter what my response is, you could regard it as suspicious. I'm damned if I do and damned if I don't—isn't that so?"

"Why do you sign your notes the way you do?" Lee asked. "Isn't that taking a risk?"

"Well, now," said the professor. "Since that information hasn't been released to the public, the only person who knows what the signature is must be the killer. Isn't that right, Detective Butts?"

Butts looked at Lee, and Moran laughed.

"Dear me—is that the best you've got?"

"What about the wound designs on the girls?" Lee said. "We're pretty sure we know what they mean. Care to tell us if we're right?"

"Are you profiling me, Dr. Campbell?" Moran crossed

his arms and leaned back in the chair. "How's it going?"

"Disappointing, actually."

"I'm sorry to hear that."

"I'm afraid you're more predictable than I thought."

Moran's eyes narrowed. "Oh, really?"

"I was hoping for a few surprises, but on the whole you've been rather dull so far."

Lee turned away but could feel the man's gaze burning into his back. He took a deep breath and told himself to relax. His palms were sweating, and he felt another wave of dizziness sweep over him. He couldn't let Moran see any vulnerability. Lee had the advantage now, playing on the man's ego, his vanity—he knew what buttons to push. He just had to maintain control over himself, keep the outward appearance of calm. . . .

"You know, you're looking a bit peaked, Dr. Campbell," Moran said. "How's the investigation into your sister's death going?"

Lee had anticipated that and fought against the mounting rage in his gut. He turned to face his foe.

"Now I *am* disappointed in you—playing that card so early in the game. You must have a very weak hand."

Butts looked as if he were about to explode. His face reddened, and he clenched his fists. Lee shot him a glance with a clear meaning: *Don't interfere.*

The moment wasn't lost on Moran. "I'm afraid your colleague doesn't have your patience, Dr. Campbell—the poor fellow looks as if he's about to burst."

"You'll be laughing out the other side of your mouth when I get a search warrant to toss your place," Butts muttered.

"And how will you convince a judge to order a

search warrant, Detective? What exactly do you have that constitutes probable cause?"

He was right, of course—all they had were their suspicions, and judges were finicky about issuing search warrants just because a suspect's behavior was attracting attention. He seemed to know as well as they did that there was no hard evidence against him. It was time to shift gears. Flattery often worked on sociopaths, even if they knew you were using it as a technique.

"Detective Butts isn't used to dealing with people of your intellectual gifts," Lee remarked. As he expected, this did not sit well with Butts, who exhaled a puff of air, scowling.

Moran laughed. "Dear me, Dr. Campbell—I don't see how insulting the poor detective will gain you any ground."

Lee shrugged. "Who says I'm insulting him? It's unusual to find someone like yourself operating in our world."

"Like myself, and 'our world,' is it? Are you deliberately avoiding using the word *suspect*? I can't imagine why—I *am* a suspect, aren't I?"

"Let's just say you're a person of interest," Lee replied.

Moran threw his head back and gave a loud guffaw, showing even, pointed incisors. " 'Person of interest!' Oh, I like that. I do—it sounds like the title of some truly dreadful Movie of the Week."

"We have other suspects we're developing," Lee said.

"Do you indeed?" Moran looked at Butts. "Is that true, Detective?"

"Yeah," Butts said tightly. "Several of them."

"Oh, I am glad to hear it. I was afraid you had run out of people to chase. Because that's where the fun is, isn't it—in the *chase*? The thrill of the hunt—you know what I'm talking about, don't you? I'm surprised you didn't talk about it more in your lecture, actually."

He directed this remark to Lee, who placed his hands on the table and leaned in toward him. In spite of the aspirin, a hammer had taken up residence in his head. He tried not to let it show, to keep his gaze steady as he looked into Moran's eyes, which were so dark, they looked black.

"Why don't you tell me about it?"

"Touché, Dr. Campbell, and nice try—and how endearing, leaning in like that. 'Invade the subject's space, put him off guard.' Though I'm not so easy to put off guard, as you know. Look, I'll tell you what," he said when Lee didn't move. "I'll show you mine if you'll show me yours."

Butts looked startled, which made Moran laugh. "Good heavens, Detective, you didn't think I meant—" He broke off and regarded Lee with a gaze so suggestive and insolent that Lee felt the blood rush to his cheeks. "No doubt he's a handsome fellow, but I'm afraid I don't swing that way. Not yet, at least," he added, with a glance at Butts, who was clenching his fists so hard, Lee imagined his nails must be biting into the flesh of his palms.

"That's too bad," Butts muttered. "Because where you're going, you're gonna be getting a lot of action. Might as well enjoy it."

Anger flashed across Moran's face, brief as a summer thunderstorm, then vanished as quickly.

"Do you really think you can scare me with *threats*,

Detective?" He turned back to Lee. "You really need to put a leash on your bulldog here, or he'll ruin your whole plan. You *do* have a plan for interrogating me, don't you?"

Lee sat down in the chair opposite him. "Not really. I'm just enjoying hobnobbing with such a superior intellect." He noted that the professor couldn't suppress an expression of pleasure at the compliment. The way to a psychopath's heart was through his ego—they couldn't help themselves. "What exactly did you mean when you said, 'Show me yours, and I'll show you mine,' by the way?"

"Curiosity killed the cat, Dr. Campbell. But since you're so eager to know, what I meant was that we might share experiences of the hunt, as it were. You know—war stories. You're invited to play too, Detective," he said to Butts. "I'll bet you have some nice, juicy tales to tell."

"Thanks, I'll pass," said Butts.

"Pity," he said, turning back to Lee. "So what do you say? Shall we share a few tales of pursuit and capture? You go first."

"You start. It was your idea."

"Which is exactly why you should go first. My game, my rules."

"Okay," said Lee. "What do you want to know?"

Moran's eyes gleamed. "What it's like when you close in on your prey. What do you feel, how intense is it, how long does it last?"

"Well," said Lee, "there's a moment right before you have them, where it's all anticipation—the uncertainty and tension is nearly unbearable. . . ." He stood and walked around behind Moran as he spoke.

"Yes? Go on," the professor said, trying to appear indifferent, but his voice betrayed his excitement.

"You're afraid they might escape, and there's that moment right before—"

"Yes?"

"And then you *pounce*!" he said, clamping both hands onto Moran's shoulders.

Throwing off his grip, the professor leaped from his seat with lightning speed and cocked a fist as if he was going to slug Lee. Arresting his attack midway through, he sat back down again, panting. The long scar on his cheek pulsed purple as his entire face colored with rage. He wiped the sweat from his upper lip and managed a smile.

"Oh, very good—you almost had me there. If I had retaliated, you could have arrested me for assaulting a police officer."

"Actually, he's not a cop," Butts said. "He's a civilian advisor."

"And I could have you hauled in for police brutality," Moran snarled.

His face returned almost immediately to an expression of calm indifference. It was like watching a painter throw a wash over a canvas—deliberate, studied, artful. The man manipulated his emotional responses the way a sculptor molded clay. The only moment where he had lost control was when Lee caught him off guard. It was just a moment, but it was a window into the depth of his rage, his malevolence.

"Well," Moran said, standing up, "this has been fun—or, rather, would have been fun if you weren't so pathetically desperate to get a reaction from me," he said to Lee as he pulled on his expensive kid gloves.

"Not going to 'show me yours'? Well, then, just one more question," Lee said. "How did you get your scar?"

Moran turned to him, and he could feel the man's malice like a hot wind in his face. "We're done here," he said.

And then he was gone. The air in the room felt fouled and the lights dimmer than before he had entered.

"Wow," Butts said. "That guy is pure ice. It's like tryin' to cut through a glacier with a penknife."

"Yeah," Lee said. "We're going to need a bigger boat."

# Chapter Sixty-seven

Butts put a 24/7 watch on the professor, but Lee imagined that Moran wouldn't have much trouble shaking any tail they put on him. They also agreed to put Detective Chen in charge of a background investigation. Just as Lee was leaving the precinct, Gemma called, and he agreed to meet her at the boathouse café in Central Park.

"I have to get out and get some air," she said apologetically. "I've been inside working on a story all day."

"That's fine," he said. "I'll take the subway up."

She was sitting in the corner by the big fieldstone fireplace when he arrived, hunched over a laptop, a cup of hot chocolate in front of her. The room was filled with tourists and red-cheeked children toting sleds and toboggans, their laughter bouncing off the stone walls, creating a cheerful background din. The sharp smell of grilled onions and New England clam chowder hung in the air.

"Hi," she said, closing her laptop when she saw him. "Thank you so much for looking into my brother's death." She wore a white parka with fur trim on the hood, formfitting ski pants and knee-high tan boots. She looked like a magazine ad for the outdoor life.

"Now what?" he asked. "We have a fake suicide note and a mysterious stranger at Brian's funeral, and you don't trust the cops your brother worked with. What's our next step?"

She bit her lip. "I think Brian's death reaches into something deeper within the NYPD, and I'm afraid to find out what it is. I won't lie to you—I'm scared. It's funny," she said, "but I was actually hoping I was wrong and that it was a suicide after all. How sick is that?"

"It's not sick at all," he said as a couple of young children in snowsuits pushed past their table, almost spilling Gemma's hot chocolate.

She grabbed it and scowled at them. "Watch where you're going, kids."

The boy shot her a nervous look before dashing off to join his sister.

She shook her head. "If my dad had caught us running around like that in public, we'd have had hell to pay."

"You know, you don't have to pursue this any further," Lee said. "You can let it drop."

"I'm a *journalist*, for Christ's sake! And it's my brother we're talking about." She took a sip of chocolate. "I wonder who your Deep Throat is."

"You didn't recognize him at all?"

"No, but I haven't been around cops much since Brian retired."

"Do you have any idea about what Des Maguire might have done that got him killed?"

She intertwined her fingers as if in prayer, putting her hands to her mouth. He had seen the gesture before; it was something she did when she was thinking hard about something.

"I remember overhearing part of a conversation with Des once," she said, "when they thought I was upstairs. Des was saying something like 'The boys in Ulster are counting on us,' and Brian was trying to talk him out of something."

Lee frowned. " 'The boys in Ulster?' I don't think they were talking about upstate New York."

"That's what I was thinking."

"Did Brian have ties to the IRA?"

"Not that I ever knew about. He always claimed he disapproved of terrorism for any reason."

"What about Des?"

"He was very outspoken about his opposition to what he called the British occupation of Northern Ireland."

"Could he have been gunrunning?"

She swept a hand over her forehead, displacing a lock of auburn hair. "You think that's what it was?"

"It's the best guess I have so far."

She took a gulp of chocolate and wiped her mouth. "I can bring it to my editor and see if—oh, damn!" she cried as another group of kids darted by, jostling her arm. Chocolate cascaded onto her ski parka—brown splashed on white, the color of dried blood. "I *told* you to calm down!" she shouted at the children, then collapsed in tears.

Lee laid a hand on her wrist. "You know," he said, "I think we should talk about something else for a while."

"S-so what about your case?" Gemma said, blowing her nose loudly. "Any progress?"

"I can't really talk about it, except to say we all keep hoping he'll make a mistake before—"

"Before he takes another victim?"

"Yeah. You know," he said, "I meant we should talk about something—"

"Lighter?" she said, drying her nose.

"Yeah," he said. Their eyes met, and they burst into convulsive, uncontrolled laughter. Several of the mothers at the next table looked at them anxiously. That made them laugh harder. It wasn't really laughter; it was release of tension, and they were powerless to stop it. Their diaphragms convulsed so hard, it hurt, and tears spurted into their eyes.

After a few minutes, it slowed down, and Gemma said, "Where were we?"—which made it start all over again. People nearby looked at them quizzically, the way people do in public when others seem to be having more fun than they ought to be having.

Finally they were played out and sat for a moment catching their breath.

"Wow," she said, drying her eyes, "that was intense."

"Yeah. Feel better?"

"Yes, I do." She finished what was left of her chocolate and shoved her laptop into a case at her feet. Without looking at him, she said, "Want to come to my place?"

The question took him off guard, but there was only one answer.

"Yes," he said. "Yes, I do."

# Chapter Sixty-eight

Debbie Collins finished her lunch of vegan lentil soup in the campus dining hall and adjusted the straps on her backpack before heading off to meet with her math professor. She was nervous because she hadn't been doing well in class lately, and she had arranged to meet with him privately to discuss how she might do better. Math had never been her strong suit—she was a philosophy major, with a minor in Russian literature. Completely useless choice, her mother had told her, but her father supported her decision to study whatever she wanted.

She had always been Daddy's girl, she thought as she stepped out of John Jay Hall and headed across the quadrangle. He understood her love of learning for its own sake. There would be time later to think about earning money, he said—college was the time for exploration and intellectual curiosity. *There's nothing like this in Iowa*, she thought as she passed Butler Library, with the names of great philosophers emblazoned on its marble façade: Sophocles, Plato, Aristotle. The sight of its perfectly symmetrical classical columns always made her breathe easier.

But the butterflies in her stomach fluttered harder as she entered the Mathematics Building. Her shoes clicked too loudly as she walked down the hall leading to her professor's office, echoing down the corridor. *Why am I so anxious?* Her fingers crept up to twist a stray strand of hair around her ear, a nervous habit. It wasn't as if her professor was unkind or rude; he was actually quite gracious, even to undergrads. His manners were impeccable—courtly, even. Yes, that was it—he was *courtly*. That word fit him perfectly. And he was strangely compelling—attractive, even, in an offbeat way. Debbie had always gone for the oddballs and loners and, like a lot of impressionable girls from the Midwest, arrived at Columbia already primed to have a crush on a professor.

Still, he made her uneasy. He was so tall and thin, and that scar on his face . . . it was hard not to look at it and wonder how he'd gotten it. Sometimes she found herself imagining what had happened to him—a duel with a Romanian count, or a scuffle with a Hungarian duke. Her scenarios were always romantic and rather overwrought, a product of being nineteen and fresh from a farm in Iowa. Her imagination had always been what her mother called "overactive," but her father said it just meant she was smarter than most people.

Smart or not, Debbie found that her hand shook as she raised it to knock on her professor's door. To her surprise, before she could rap the door with her knuckles, it opened abruptly. There, standing before her, was her professor, with that quizzical half tilt of his head she often noticed in class.

"Right on time, Miss Collins," he said. "Won't you come in?"

He stepped aside and made a courtly gesture for her to enter. *Yes, he is courtly,* she thought as she entered the office. But it didn't quiet the pounding of her heart or the sinking feeling in the pit of her stomach. When the door closed behind her, it rang in her ears like the slamming of the door to a crypt.

# Chapter Sixty-nine

Maybe going home with Gemma O'Reilly Hancock wasn't the wisest thing to do under the circumstances, but Lee was drawn toward her like a moon caught in the gravitational field of its mother planet. There was just something about her.

They started on the couch and ended up in the bedroom in a tangle of blankets and pillows—she was a self-confessed "pillow freak."

Sex with Gemma was like diving into a dark, warm pool of water. His body tingled, twinged and tightened, and his breathing became deeper. His stomach unloosened its knots; even his forehead released its tension. He wanted to know every inch of her, inside and out. He feasted on her subtle flavors and scents, the faint aroma of raspberries behind her left ear (but curiously, not the right ear, which smelled more of lemons). Her kiss was spicy, like cloves or cinnamon, and as for her other lips . . . he could lose himself there, sinking into the pleasure of tasting her center.

Gemma was a fierce, hungry lover whose boyish athleticism inevitably brought up thoughts of Kathy—but he pushed them away by reminding himself that, after all, she had broken up with him. He couldn't sit around pining away for her, for God's sake—not when someone like Gemma practically threw herself at him.

Afterward, she brought him tea, and they watched her new kitten play around the bedroom. The animal's youth and innocence felt so foreign to him. For the kitten, everything was a mystery, potential danger or possible plaything. A cubbyhole in the desk was a tower from which to spy and pounce on anything that moved below; the laundry basket was a secret hiding place, the dust ruffle on the bed a constant source of amusement.

Gemma laughed her dry, throaty chortle as the cat poked her head all the way inside one of her slippers.

"Wouldn't it be great to live as a kitten for just one day—to have that kind of one-track enjoyment of the moment?" she said as the kitten struggled to free itself of the slipper.

"But we wouldn't be able to appreciate it, because we'd have the mind of a cat."

The kitten pulled its head out of the slipper and sat on its haunches in the middle of the carpet, looking confused. They both laughed.

"I guess you're right," she said. "Do we ever really appreciate what we have?"

He gave her a squeeze. "I do right now, that's for sure."

"Mmm," she said, snuggling against him, her cinnamon-scented hair tickling his neck. "What are you driven by in your line of work? The need to confront evil where it lives? Fascination with it?"

"I suppose. And the question of why some people turn out to be psychopaths and others don't."

"Their ability to dehumanize other people always stuns me," she said, twisting a lock of his hair around her fingers.

"You might be surprised how many people have really disturbing fantasies. But for the serial offender, it's that crucial moment when he *acts* on them. That's when he leaves the human race behind and sinks into the seventh circle of hell."

"We all take refuge in illusion sometimes, don't we?" Gemma said. "I mean, women lie about their weight, men lie about their height, and everyone lies about their age."

"That's true. And we convince ourselves our illusions are true."

"I think some illusion is necessary. I like science fiction, for God's sake!"

"Not many people can take reality twenty-four hours a day," Lee said. "But most of us don't create an entire fantasy world of our own."

"Right."

"Well, for this guy the real world isn't as real to him as the fantasies in his head. He lives more fully inside his fantasies than he does in reality."

"Sounds like any number of science fiction geeks I've known."

"Except that *they* generally know the difference between fantasy and reality—and, in any case, their fantasies don't usually center on rape and murder."

She bit his ear. "Do you feel guilty because you're normal?"

He smiled. "You flatter me."

"What do you mean?"

He raised himself up on one elbow. "How normal do you really think I am?"

"Well, you're not a psychopath."

"No."

She cocked her head to one side, studying his face. "So?"

"Life is unfair," he replied, setting his teacup on the bedside table. The kitten immediately attempted to leap onto the table—failing, it tumbled onto its back.

Gemma laughed and lifted the kitten onto the bed. "Does anyone really change? Or are we all pretty much formed by the time we're adolescents?"

He finished the last sip of cold tea. "I think people can change, but it's a long, painful process. Not this guy, though—he's a full-fledged psychopath."

"That's too bad—for him and his victims," she said, stroking the kitten.

"Yeah," he said. "It is."

The kitten sunk its tiny sharp claws into her hand, biting it.

"Ow!" she said, pulling her hand away.

"See?" he said. "Nature's a bitch."

"Come kiss it and make it better," she said.

She didn't have to ask twice.

# Chapter Seventy

When Lee arrived at the station house the next day, the others were already there. Their faces were grim, and they avoided looking at him. He wondered briefly if they knew where he had spent the night, or if he had violated some unspoken rule. Jimmy handed him a cup of takeout coffee but avoided eye contact. Without any preamble, Butts handed him a letter wrapped in a clear evidence bag.

Dear Dr. Campbell,

I'm afraid one of the things you're forgetting is that we are playing what is referred to in game theory as a zero-sum game. To put it bluntly, only one of us can win. Here's a nifty little chain of logic I thought I'd share with you. (I've made a small substitution, which I'm sure you'll appreciate.)

1. All men are mortal.
2. ~~Socrates~~ Lee Campbell is a man.
3. Therefore, ~~Socrates~~ Lee Campbell is mortal.

Bye for now,
The Professor

Lee handed the letter back to Detective Butts. His hand shook a little, though whether from lack of sleep or fear, he wasn't sure.

"It arrived this morning—by regular post?"

Butts held up a postmarked envelope, addressed with a laser printer.

Dr. Lee Campbell
c/o Detective Leonard Butts, NYPD
Thirteenth Precinct, NYC

"It was in with my mail," said Butts.

"And addressed to Lee," said Elena Krieger. She looked luscious as usual, in a short tailored jacket over navy blue slacks.

"But why send it here?" asked Jimmy. "From what you say, this guy is clever enough to get your address, even if your number is unlisted. He'd enjoy flaunting that he knew where you lived, right?"

"Maybe he wanted to make sure we all saw it," Lee suggested.

"That doesn't make sense," Butts said. "He knew you'd bring it in the minute you got it."

Lee had to agree he was right. He wasn't thinking very clearly today, and his headache had returned. Maybe spending the night with Gemma had been a mistake. Saying no to her would have taken more willpower than he had, but maybe that was a flaw in his character. He took a gulp of lukewarm coffee, bitter and harsh.

"Same author as before?" he asked Krieger.

"Oh, yes," she said. "The same person who wrote the others wrote this one."

"He's threatening you," Butts said. "We can haul him in here for that, can't we?"

Krieger crossed her arms and frowned, a single line appearing on her smooth forehead. "I don't think this constitutes a legal threat. The language is too vague. To say someone is mortal isn't to suggest you're going to kill that person."

"Oh, come *on*!" said Jimmy. "He's obviously trying to scare Lee."

"Oh, he's trying to scare him, all right—but that's not necessarily enough to convince a judge to issue a warrant for his arrest."

"Crap," said Butts. "You serious?"

"He's carefully crafted this to avoid making an outright threat," Krieger said. "Not only that, but do we have any concrete evidence that Dr. Moran wrote this letter? You suspect he's the author of all the letters, but unless you come up with physical evidence . . ."

"Yeah, I know," Butts growled. "I doubt there are any prints or anything on this one, but I'm sending it to the lab anyway."

"Wouldn't the combination of this letter and your interview with him constitute probable cause?" asked Jimmy.

"I don't see how," said Lee. "He admitted nothing in the interview."

"He just sat there gloating," Butts muttered.

"So what's next?" Jimmy said. "We just sit and wait for him to go after someone else?"

"I've got a tail on him," Butts replied. "You're welcome to volunteer for a shift."

"Count me in," said Jimmy. "What about you, Angus—you in?"

"Yeah," Lee said. "I'll join you."

"Okay," Butts said. "Why don't you take the next shift? That starts at—"

The phone on his desk rang, and he grabbed it.

"Butts here. You're kiddin' me!" he said after a moment. "Goddamn it, McKinney, what the hell! Okay, never mind, just . . . oh, I don't know, just keep tryin' to find him, huh?"

He slammed the phone down and ran a hand through his wispy blond hair. "Goddamn bastard managed to lose McKinney on the Columbia campus."

"Should we go up there?" Jimmy asked.

"Hell, yeah," said Butts. "Meanwhile, I'll send a couple of uniforms to help McKinney. Christ, he could be anywhere. . . ."

They all completed the thought in their own heads: *and doing anything.*

# Chapter Seventy-one

Debbie fought her way through the blackness, dragging her reluctant body back to consciousness. She opened her eyes to a dim yellow light shining from the ceiling above her. *Where was she?* It looked like a cave or a grotto of some kind, with crumbling plaster walls and low ceilings. She moaned and instinctively tried to stretch her arms above her head.

That was when she felt the ropes around her wrists. Unable to budge her arms from their restraints, she tried moving her legs, but they, too, were bound. Panic flooded her veins as she jerked against her bonds, arching her spine and snaking her torso back and forth. But she only succeeded in getting rope burns, as the cords cut deeper into her flesh.

Worse, she attracted his attention. She smelled him before she saw him—a cool, green smell with a hint of musk, like rainwater on a midsummer lawn. Her brain was so foggy . . . she had trouble focusing on his face as he bent over her. When she did, a shiver of fear rippled through her body as everything came rushing back. How she had gone to his office, how he had opened the door even before she knocked and beckoned her in with his usual courtly manner. That's when the memory stopped, though, as though someone had drawn a curtain between the past and the present. It was clear she had been drugged, though. She wasn't much of a party girl, but she knew a drug hangover when she felt one—the heaviness in her limbs, her hazy thinking, the pounding headache. It must have been in the tea he gave her.

"How are you feeling, my dear?" he asked, his eyes brimming with concern, the irises so dark, they appeared black. His body cast a long, thin shadow, blocking out the light, his bony, raked shoulders hunched over her like those of a great bird of prey. He reminded her of the turkey vultures who huddled at the edges of her father's farm fields when one of the cows was sick or dying. Her father always said those birds could smell death before it came. She shuddered. She hated turkey vultures, with their wrinkled crimson heads, hooked beaks and beady black eyes.

"W-water, please," she said, her tongue thick.

"Why, certainly," he replied, moving away. She twisted her head to look at what she was lying on and saw that it was a metal hospital gurney. "Here we are," he said, holding up a bottle of Evian water.

"I w-want to see you open it," she rasped, suddenly suspicious. He had drugged her once—he could easily have put something into the water bottle too.

"Afraid it's been spiked?" he asked, smiling. "Good for you—you're learning. Though it's too bad caution came too late," he added, twisting the cap on the bottle. She was relieved to hear the familiar snap of the plastic seal breaking. "See?" he said. "Nothing to worry about."

He held it to her lips. She sucked at the bottle greedily, pulling the clear liquid into her body, swallowing it in great gulps, even as she fought her panic and dread. *Too late . . .* The phrase darted through her mind like an evil drumbeat. She knew it was a bad sign, that her situation was desperate and that he did not plan for her to survive. She also knew the fact that he was giving her water meant he wasn't in any hurry and that he was going to take his time doing whatever it was he planned to do to her. That thought brought her so close to the edge of despair that she had to draw on everything inside her—everything dear and close and meaningful—to keep from losing her mind.

She thought of her little sister, Clara, riding her broad-backed roan pony across the fields of her father's farm as Debbie followed on her swaybacked chestnut, Old Nathan. She thought about Clara's untidy blond braids bouncing as they trotted over ditches and creeks, through birch forests and dirt lanes bordered by poplar trees. She imagined Nathan loping along under her, with his sideways gait and lopsided canter, her knees tight against his warm flanks.

She imagined the smell of alfalfa in the spring and summer clover and a barn full of fall hay and field corn, the kernels deep yellow and as hard as the pellets of her brother's shotgun. She thought of the smell of her mother's canned peaches simmering in syrup, of the jars of her dill pickles lined up like sentinels in the pantry, of the rough, cracked flesh of her father's hands as he pulled on his tractor cap to go out and harvest the winter wheat. She thought of the hoarse braying of her beagle pup, Charlie, when her brother rode his bike into the driveway, the loose gravel crunching under the tires setting the dog to howling.

The strength she took from these memories allowed her to push down the scream forming in her throat. She swallowed it along with her panic, determined to keep up the appearance of calm. Debbie Collins knew little about sadistic serial killers or sociopaths, but some survival instinct deep inside her told her it was her fear he needed to see, her humiliation and desperation. And she resolved that she wouldn't give it to him. He could do what he liked, but he would not see fear in her eyes. She steeled herself to look at him, to study his face for what it might betray in the way of weakness or hesitation, uncertainty or doubt—anything she could use to gain an advantage, to stall for time, to play on his emotions in any way she could.

But looking at him was like gazing into a void. There was no life in those empty eyes; it was like looking into the face of a wraith. The warmth of human kindness had long ago evaporated from the shriveled, blackened remnant of what had once been his soul. Looking at him, Debbie felt hope wither and fade away, and in its place a despair descended such as she had never known before.

# Chapter Seventy-two

The NYPD trip to the Columbia University campus accomplished little except to annoy and alienate the administration, to say nothing of the other professors, who were irritated at being summoned out of their classes and tutorials for interviews. A search of the grounds turned up nothing; the last time Professor Moran had been seen by anyone around campus was the day before. The fall term was almost over; with Christmas only a week away, most of the classes had already ended in preparation for finals and the winter break. The address on East Seventy-fourth Street in the university's file for Moran had turned out to be fake—Jimmy reckoned that the numbering put it somewhere in the East River.

"Beats me why the idiots in personnel couldn't figure that one out," Butts muttered as he trudged toward the next fruitless interview.

Lee returned home late that evening, exhausted and discouraged, to find Chuck's suitcase sitting in the foyer. He found his friend putting clean sheets onto the guest bed.

"I washed all the bath towels too," Chuck said, tucking in a corner of the sheets, military-style. Chuck was the most regimented person Lee had ever known; it was a wonder they were such good friends.

"What's up?" Lee said.

Chuck busied himself putting on the blankets. "Oh, didn't you get my message?" He was clearly trying to sound casual, as though it was no big deal, but Lee wasn't buying.

"I just got off the damn subway," he said. "What's going on?"

"I've decided to give it another try with Susan," Chuck replied, fluffing the pillows before plopping them onto the bed.

"Did something happen?"

"I just felt so miserable knowing I wasn't there for her during her cancer scare, and I couldn't stand it. I couldn't concentrate at work; I was losing sleep, having trouble eating." He straightened up and patted his flat stomach. "I've lost five pounds since I left. I can't live like this."

"You're depressed," said Lee. "It's not forever—it passes."

"Well, if I'm this depressed being away from her, then I guess I'm meant to be with her."

"It's not that simple," Lee insisted. "You're depressed because you're at a difficult crossroad in your life. It doesn't necessarily mean you're supposed to—"

"I've made up my *mind*!" Chuck yelled, his neck reddening. "Can we just *leave* it at that? If I want your advice, I'll ask for it, okay?"

Lee retreated a step. "I get the message." He turned

around and started to leave the room, then turned back. "Oh, what were the results of the ultrasound? Did she have a biopsy? Does she have cancer?"

Chuck didn't look at him. "No," he muttered. "It was an adenoma—a benign cyst."

"Well, good. I'm glad to hear it," Lee said, and he left the room, closing the door behind him.

Later, he heard the sounds of Chuck leaving, the door opening and closing, his key turning in the lock; then all was quiet. A lethargic, heavy snow had begun to fall outside. He lay down on the bed and drifted off to sleep listening to the slow patter of wet flakes on the air conditioner outside the bedroom window.

He dreamed that he and Laura were in the street outside her Greenwich Village apartment at twilight hailing a cab. As they stood in the dimming evening, the concrete turned into mud, and they sank in up to their knees. The more they tried to extricate themselves, the deeper they were pulled into the muck. Panicked, he tried to call for help, but they suddenly seemed to be the only ones on the street. Greenwich Village had turned into a desolate country road—gone were the buildings, stores, people and vehicles. They were alone at dusk on a road stretching into an endless horizon, slowly sinking down, the earth itself sucking them into an embrace of death.

Their eyes met, and the look on her face was sad but knowing—knowing *what*?—but neither of them could speak. They could only gaze at each other, sharing their last moments of life as the earth closed in around them. . . .

He stirred and opened his eyes. Every detail of the dream was seared into his brain. There wasn't much mystery about the meaning; he had long imagined that his sister was buried deep in the earth somewhere, possibly in the countryside surrounding the city. Ever since 9/11 his dreams had taken on a more tragic tone. The look he and Laura had exchanged reminded him of last, frantic messages typed or phoned to loved ones from people whose lives had ended in that smoldering pile of rubble.

He shivered, glad to be out of the world of his dream, and lay listening to the faint street sounds outside. His bedroom was in the back of the building, with no windows looking out on East Seventh Street, the quietest room in the apartment.

The smell of cigarette smoke assailed his nose—someone must be smoking out on the street. He hated it when the odor drifted into his apartment, but it was unusual for it to waft all the way to his bedroom. Then he smelled it even more strongly and realized with a start that the smoke wasn't coming from the street at all—it was coming from somewhere inside his apartment.

Disjointed thoughts crowded his head as he climbed out of bed and pulled his robe from the closet. *Had Chuck returned?* But Chuck didn't smoke—not since Princeton, when the two of them had shared packs of Marlboro cigarettes at rugby parties; smoking and tapping beer kegs were among the postgame rituals. And Chuck would never smoke inside his apartment, no matter what had passed between them—or would he?

Lee figured he must have changed his mind and come back—the fact that he was smoking showed just how stressed out he was. Still, that was no excuse for lighting up inside the apartment. Angry, he threw on his robe and opened the bedroom door, prepared to give Chuck a tongue-lashing. He stumbled into the living room and turned on the standing lamp by the piano.

Sitting in the red leather armchair, his feet resting on the footstool, was Professor Edmund Moran. He held a cigarette between the index and middle fingers of his left hand. In his right hand was a revolver. When he saw Lee, his lean face broke into a smile. The long, thin scar on his cheek twisted it so that the right side of his face was smiling, while the left side was more of a grimace.

"Good evening," he said pleasantly. "Would you like a cigarette?"

# CHAPTER SEVENTY-THREE

"There's no smoking in here," Lee said.

"Oh, but there *is*," Moran replied, "by definition, because *I'm* smoking. What you meant is that you'd *prefer* I didn't smoke. I wish people would be more precise in their speech and avoid these illogical syllogisms."

"I'd prefer you didn't smoke."

"Very well—why didn't you just say that in the first place?"

He rose from the chair and stubbed the cigarette out in the spider plant on the windowsill. Lee tensed and readied himself to spring out of the way of a bullet, but Moran sat down again calmly.

"Oh, don't worry," he said. "The gun is just to ensure I have the upper hand, in case you had a mind to do something tedious, like attack me. Or call the police," he added, seeing Lee's eyes linger on the telephone next to the couch. "I wouldn't advise it. I may not look athletic, but I'm quite agile, I assure you. I can be down the stairs and halfway to Third Avenue before your groggy neighbors manage to dial 911. And I *will* shoot to kill," he said, pointing the muzzle at Lee's chest.

"What do you want?" Lee asked.

"Please, sit down. There's no need to be uncivil. After all, you and I are engaged in much the same kind of pursuit. We have so much to talk about. I did ask you to sit down," he said when Lee didn't move. "Please—I insist." Lee perched on the arm of the sofa, but Moran shook his head. "On the sofa, if you would be so kind. You're making me quite nervous. I should think you don't want a man with a gun trained on you to be feeling jumpy."

Lee sat slowly on the couch, without taking his eyes off Moran, who leaned back in the chair, still pointing the revolver directly at his chest. Lee noticed that the muzzle had been fitted with a silencer. *Organization, planning, follow-through.* Moran was as pure an example of an organized killer as he had ever seen. His job was to find a weakness—if there was one.

Moran wagged the gun at him. "You're no doubt wondering how I managed to get in?"

"Not really."

"Oh, come along, of course you are! Don't be so coy. I am a skilled pickpocket, among other things," Moran announced, holding up the key Lee had given to Chuck. "I'm afraid your friend was so preoccupied, he wasn't much of a challenge," he added with a sigh, tossing the key to Lee. "Oh, take it, by all means," he said in response to Lee's surprised look. "I'm quite done with it. I wouldn't risk coming here again. I just wanted to have a quiet little chat in private, and this seemed like the best place for it. At the station house there were so many other people around—that horrid little detective friend of yours, for one. Does he ever stop eating? A strictly Freudian interpretation would be that he has an oral fixation, but I prefer to think he's just gluttonous." He crossed his legs and smiled. "What do you think? You're the professional psychologist. Or is it psychiatrist? You have a Ph.D., not an M.D., if I recall correctly."

"So you know everything about me."

"I know what's relevant—the fact that your sister disappeared six years ago, and your father ran off when you were just a boy. Oh, yes," he said, in response to Lee's tightening jaw, "I know that. But that's common knowledge, isn't it?"

"What do you want?"

"I already told you—just a little chat, *mano a mano*. Which, by the way, actually means *hand to hand*, not *man to man*, as some people think. It was originally used in bullfights to describe two matadors competing for the admiration of the crowd."

Lee crossed his arms and leaned back, hoping to create the impression of being relaxed. "I've got all night," he said with a glance at the gun. "Shoot."

Edmund gave a little laugh, which twisted the left side of his face grotesquely. "Oh, I do like a man who preserves his wit in the face of danger. One thinks it's only in the movies, but I'm so glad to see that that's not true. So here's what I propose, Dr. Campbell," he said, leaning forward. "You call off your colleagues in this little chase, and I'll let the girl live a little longer."

Lee couldn't help the expression of alarm that came over his face. He hoped Moran was bluffing but feared he wasn't.

"Oh, yes, did I neglect to mention I have another . . .

victim?" the professor said. "Quite a lovely girl, actually, with that corn-fed Midwestern naïveté you can't fake. I like that in a woman, don't you? Oh, that's right—you prefer more assertive types. That journalist is quite a looker, by the way. Don't worry," he said, as Lee clenched his fists and bit his lip. "She's not my type. At least not at the moment, though I suppose my tastes could change. . . . So, what do you think? Do we have a deal?"

"What deal?"

"You may continue in your pursuit of me, but *alone*—call off your friends, or the girl dies right now."

"Why me?"

"I like you. Do I need another reason? You're Ivy League–educated, like me—a man of the world, so to speak. You, too, enjoy the finer things in life—Bach, for example. You have *class*. Oh, don't blush—you know it's true."

Lee wasn't blushing, but he could feel his face reddening out of anger and frustration. *How did Moran know that Lee liked Bach? Had he been rooting around in the apartment before Lee awoke?* He felt violated, sullied by the man's presence.

"I don't have the authority—" he began.

"Call them off or she dies *now*," Moran repeated.

"All right," he said slowly, "it's a deal."

"You sure now?" Moran said. "Don't try to double-cross me. You'll regret it. I don't like people who go back on their word."

"I won't. I promise."

"You'll have to convince your colleagues that it's for the best. That may take some doing."

"I'll handle it."

"Very well."

"Do you—can you give me any kind of clue as to where she—"

Moran held up a hand, the fingers long and thin and tapered—the hands of an artist, some people might say.

"Please," the professor said. "Don't embarrass yourself by begging. It will leave a bad taste in my mouth, and I have so enjoyed our little chat. We have so much in common. It's too bad you don't know more about mathematics," he added with a sigh, "but nobody's perfect."

"I wouldn't want to disappoint you."

Moran smiled again, the scar distorting his face, showing long, yellow teeth on the left side of his mouth. "It's amazing what you can learn if you apply yourself. For instance, did you know that irrational mathematical constants go on forever? I quite like that, don't you? In a sense, you might say they're immortal."

"Unlike us."

Moran frowned. "I never took you for the glass-half-empty type, Dr. Campbell. Of course, there *is* your ongoing struggle with depression. I suppose that can put a damper on even the brightest of spirits, eh?"

Again Lee felt the heat rising to his face. He longed to lunge at the man sitting opposite him and beat him to a pulp.

Perhaps sensing his rage, Moran dangled the gun in his direction. "Now, now—mind you control that hotheaded Scottish temper of yours, or I shall be forced to defend myself. In any case, I must be going," he said, unfolding his long body from the chair. "My lovely captive awaits me." He sauntered to the front door and opened it, then turned back to Lee. "Oh, and if you try to follow me, I'll shoot you."

He slipped through the door, and Lee could hear his quick footsteps descending the stairs. He sprang from the sofa and charged down the steps, yanking open the front door to the building, but there was no sign of Moran. The street was empty except for a sleepy-looking man in striped flannel pajamas and an overcoat walking a minuscule white pom-pom of a dog. The dog sniffed energetically at the row of trash cans in front of McSorley's, then lifted its tiny leg and let forth a thin stream of liquid. The urine melted into a puddle of steamy slush as the dog gave a couple of satisfied kicks with its hind legs and trotted triumphantly back to its owner.

Lee went back upstairs and climbed into bed, where he lay staring at the ceiling until a pale and weary dawn crept underneath his curtains.

# CHAPTER SEVENTY-FOUR

"You gotta be *kiddin'* me," Butts said later that morning when Lee told him of Moran's visit. "Who does this bozo think he is, Zorro?"

"So what do you think of his proposal?" Lee asked.

The detective tossed his half-eaten bagel into the trash. "It's out of the question—you're not even a *cop*, for Christ's sake! I never heard of anything more—"

The phone on his desk rang, and he seized the receiver.

"Detective Butts." He sank down into his chair and listened. "What's her name?" he said. "Yeah, fax me anything you have on her, would you? Thanks." He hung up and looked at Lee. "Well, one thing's for sure—he wasn't bluffing. Another college girl has gone missing. Her name's Deborah Collins, and she was reported missing this morning by her roommate."

Lee's cell phone rang. The caller ID read *Fiona*, and he considered not answering it, but it could be an emergency. He flipped open the phone.

"Hi, Mom—has something happened?"

"No, I just wanted to—"

"So there's no emergency?

"No, but—"

"I'm sorry, but I really can't talk right now."

"Your niece—"

"We have another missing girl—I really have to go."

"But I just want—"

"I'll call you later—*I have to go*," he practically shouted. He closed the phone and slid it into his pocket, knowing he would have apologies to make later.

"So how will this pervert even know if we have other people lookin' for him?" Butts said.

"I don't know, but he seems to know a lot of things already."

"He's bluffing. And are you tellin' me that he's not gonna kill this poor girl anyway?"

"No, but there's a chance he will keep her alive longer if he thinks—"

"The answer is still no!" Butts roared as Elena Krieger entered the office.

"The answer to what?" she asked, removing her matching gray beret and wool cape. As usual, she looked as if she had stepped out of a high-end catalogue.

Butts told her the whole thing, and she cocked her head to one side.

"What do you think?" she asked Lee.

"I think it's worth a try. I can be in constant phone communication with a backup team, so long as they don't come too close to me."

"Where are you going to go?" Butts asked as the fax machine behind him hummed. He turned and plucked two pages from the document feed. "You don't know where to find him."

"I'll go back to the Columbia campus. I think there's a chance I'll turn up something there."

"Well, here's who we're lookin' for," Butts said, pinning two pictures of Debbie Collins up on the bulletin board above the photos of the other victims. She was a sweet-faced strawberry blonde with freckles and cornflower blue eyes. "I think we should send a SWAT team to his goddamn office," Butts said, staring at the photo.

"No!" said Lee. "It might push him to kill her—even if it means getting caught himself."

"I agree," Krieger said.

"We don't even know where he's holding her," said Butts. "After that stunt he pulled, comin' to see you last night, I can get a judge to write a search warrant to toss his joint. Maybe we'll find something there."

"But if you do that, he might kill the girl," Krieger pointed out.

"Well, I'm not going to just sit around!" Butts bellowed.

His desk phone rang again, and he grabbed it.

"Yeah? Chen, where the hell are you?" He listened for a moment, then frowned. "Okay, you can talk to him." He handed the phone to Lee.

"Yeah, Jimmy?"

"Hi, Angus—what am I missing?"

"I'll tell you later. What's going on?"

"I had to take my brother to the hospital. He had an accident, had to get a few stitches. He'll be okay. I just have to drop him off at home, and then I'll be right over."

"Get your ass over here!" Butts yelled into the phone from across the room.

"Hear that?" Lee asked.

"Yeah. I'll have to bring Barry with me. He can sit in the lobby—he has a book of math puzzles."

"Okay."

"I'm at the hospital—I'll be there in a few minutes."

When Jimmy arrived, they caught him up on what was going on. He listened, wide-eyed, to Lee's story of his encounter with Edmund Moran.

"Jesus," he said. "This guy is cold. What are you going to do?"

There was a timid knock on the office door.

"What now?" Butts muttered, opening it. Barry Chen stood in the hall, clutching a paperback book of Sudoku logic puzzles. His left forearm was swathed in bandages, and a stain of yellow hospital disinfectant seeped out from the edges of the gauze. He carried a knapsack over one shoulder.

Jimmy stepped forward. "What is it, Barry?"

"I've finished," Barry said, rocking gently back and forth, his eyes focused straight ahead. He didn't seem to notice there were other people in the room.

"The whole book?" Jimmy said. "I just gave it to you!"

"I've finished the whole book," Barry repeated. "In *fact*, you just gave it to me, and I've finished the whole book."

"This your brother?" Butts asked.

"Yeah," said Jimmy. "Sorry about that."

Barry's gaze fell on to the computer on Butts's desk. "Can I use the computer?"

"That's not mine," Jimmy said.

"If I let him, will he screw it up?" Butts asked Jimmy.

"He'd be more likely to fix anything that's wrong with it. He fixes all the computers of the people in our building."

"He can use it," Butts growled, "if it'll shut him up."

"Will you sit there quietly?" Jimmy asked Barry.

Still rocking, his brother nodded. "In *fact*, I will sit there quietly. No talking, only sitting quietly."

"Okay, go ahead," said Butts.

"Sitting quietly," Barry whispered. "*Quiet.*"

He sat down at the computer without making eye contact with anyone in the room, including Jimmy. Krieger stared at him with fascination. Hunched over the machine, he typed methodically, seemingly unaware that everyone was watching him.

"Okay," Butts said, "let's get back to work."

"Just give me twenty-four hours," Lee said. "If I can't turn up anything, then you can search his apartment, his office—everything."

Butts bit his lip. "Where the hell is he keepin' them?"

"Wherever it is," Lee said, "he feels very secure there."

"You think it's around Columbia somewhere?" Jimmy asked.

"I wouldn't be surprised, since Debbie Collins was last seen by her roommate on campus," Lee replied.

"But it's by no means certain," Krieger interjected.

"That's it," Butts declared, seizing the phone. "I'm havin' his place tossed."

Lee grasped his wrist, and Butts glared at him like he was about to throw a punch at Lee.

"*Twenty-four hours,*" Lee said. "*Please*. Her life may depend on it."

"What the hell you gonna do, Captain America?"

Butts said. "You find the guy, and then what? We know he's armed. Will you karate-kick your way to the girl?"

"Give me a gun," said Lee.

Butts shook his head. "Out of the question. It's against regulation, not to mention common sense."

"I'll go with you," said Jimmy.

"He specifically stipulated I go alone."

"I'll go undercover—I'll dress like a student."

Krieger smiled, and Butts snorted. "You—a student?"

"I could pass for a grad student," Jimmy insisted. "I'll wear a backpack and sneakers."

"That just might work," said Krieger.

"Come on," said Jimmy. "You can't just let Angus go out there and get killed by this maniac."

"Get . . . killed . . . maniac," Barry hummed behind them, still typing. Lee realized they had all forgotten about him.

Butts glowered at him, then turned back to Jimmy. "That still doesn't solve the problem of where he's hiding the girls."

"You should start with the campus," Krieger said.

Butts ran a hand through his meager blond hair, making it stand up in pointed spears, like the crown on the Statue of Liberty. "Where the hell do you hide a kidnap victim on a college campus?"

"Especially one as populated as Columbia University," Krieger added.

"The tunnels," Barry said, without taking his eyes off the computer screen.

"I thought you said he was going to be quiet!" Butts bellowed. "For Christ's sake, Chen—"

"Wait a second," said Lee. "What did he just say?"

"What did you say, Barry?" asked Jimmy.

Barry stopped typing. "The tunnels," he said without looking up. "Columbia University has a series of subterranean tunnels connecting many of the buildings on campus. The oldest of the tunnels was originally built when the site was home to a mental institution in the nineteenth century." His tone was flat, as though he was reciting memorized knowledge.

Butts stared at him. "What the—"

"Barry has a photographic memory," Jimmy explained. "He must have read that somewhere."

"What else can you tell us, Barry?" Krieger asked, her eyes gleaming.

"There are rumors of a tunnel between the Butler and Low Libraries," Barry continued, "but no such tunnel has ever been found."

"Barry," Lee said. "Is there an entrance to the tunnels in the math building?"

"There is an entrance on the basement level of the Mathematics Building, which was taken over by radical students during the riots of 1968."

Butts looked at Barry, then back at Jimmy.

"I'll have a SWAT team on standby. Go!" he said. "And take him with you!"

They didn't stick around long enough for him to change his mind.

# CHAPTER SEVENTY-FIVE

Jimmy Chen's Crown Victoria was parked in front of the precinct. The three of them piled into the car, Barry in the backseat, Lee in the front. Jimmy threw the big Ford into Reverse, backed it out into the street, and peeled off down Twenty-first Street, heading west. He rolled down the driver's side window, reached out and stuck a flashing light onto the roof of the car. In the backseat, Barry made a little moaning sound.

"He doesn't like the flashing light," Jimmy said to Lee. "He can't handle a lot of sensory input. Cover your eyes," he called back to Barry.

Lee glanced back at Barry, who was rocking and moaning, his hands over his eyes. The white bandage on his left arm had begun to unravel.

"Here, let me fix that," Lee said, reaching back, but Barry shrank from his touch and moaned louder.

"He doesn't like to be touched," Jimmy said, turning right on Third Avenue. "We had quite a time at getting that arm stitched up. We ended up using a heart monitor as a distraction. He loved watching the pulse monitor jump up and down. He likes anything rhythmic and repetitive—don't you, Barry?"

"I like rhythm and repetition," Barry said, continuing to rock. "I like mathematical constants."

"Hey, Barry, why don't you show Lee how far you can recite the decimals of pi?" Jimmy said, weaving in and out of traffic. Lee closed his eyes as Jimmy nearly sideswiped a delivery guy on a bike.

"Yeah, Barry," Lee said. "I'd like to hear that."

Barry stopped rocking. "Pi is three point one, four, one, five, nine, two, six—"

Jimmy swerved around an H & H Bagels truck, causing Barry to lose his balance and tip over on the seat. He sat up straight again and continued.

"Five, three, five, eight, nine—"

"Shit!" Jimmy muttered as a young girl with a ratty white terrier on a leash took a step into the intersection. He hit the horn hard, and the girl jumped back. "Watch where you're going—you wanna get killed?"

"Why not use the siren?" Lee asked, even though Jimmy's driving was beginning to make him nauseated, his head throbbing in sync with the flashing light.

"Barry couldn't take that," Jimmy said. "He'd start howling. I mean howling—like a wolf, you know."

"Supersonic wolves," Barry said. "Seven, nine, three, two, three. Eight, four, six, two, six . . ."

"That's amazing, Barry," Lee said. "You really are a genius."

"I'm a genius," Barry echoed. "Four, three, three, eight, two . . ."

Jimmy took Madison Avenue north from Madison Square Park, past the shops and restaurants of Murray Hill. He jerked to a stop in front of a bookstore north of Thirty-second Street.

"Be right back!" he called out as he dashed inside. He came out a few moments later with a thick book of math puzzles, tossing it onto the seat next to him. "For later," he told Lee as he buckled himself in and started the engine. He continued up Madison, heading toward Central Park when he reached the fifties. Barry kept up his recitation the entire way. Lee lost track of how many numbers he had gone through but figured it must be well over a hundred by the time Jimmy headed north on Park Drive. The traffic in the park was light, and they zoomed past joggers with strollers, inline skaters and speed racers on bikes, emerging at the northern exit on 110th Street.

The Mathematics Building was on the far western side of the campus bordered by Broadway. Jimmy slid into a metered parking place half a block away, slammed the gearshift into Park and turned around to face his brother.

"Barry, give me your backpack, okay?"

Barry clutched the pack to his chest. "Six, two, six, eight, three . . ."

"I need it for a very important job," Jimmy pleaded. "Please?"

Barry shook his head. "Eight, eight, two, three, five . . ."

"Enough with the numbers!" Jimmy yelled. "Give me the damn backpack!"

Barry clutched it harder. "Three, seven, eight, seven, five . . ."

"You don't need it," said Lee. "Just leave on your tie and scuff yourself up a little. You can pass as a professor."

"Yeah, or a math geek like him," Jimmy replied, mussing up his smooth black hair.

"Math geek like me," Barry said. "Nine, three, seven, five, one . . ."

"Is he going to be okay here?" Lee said.

"He has his computer. I'll lock the car."

"But he can still get out, right?"

"This car has a setting that I can use to lock him in. Barry, I'm going to lock the car, okay?" Jimmy said. "If there's an emergency, just use the police band radio."

"Nine, five, seven, seven, eight . . ." said Barry.

Jimmy checked in with Detective Butts on the car radio.

"I've got uniforms guarding every entrance," Butts told them. "And I'm alerting campus security. We've got a SWAT team on standby."

"If we need more backup, we'll call for it," said Jimmy.

"Don't be a goddamn hero," Butts growled, his voice scratchy from electronic interference on the line.

"Oh, come on—you know me better than that," Jimmy said. "Over and out." He turned to Lee. "Let's go. Barry, if you get to the end of your sequence, you can start it over, okay?" He held up the math puzzle book. "And I got this for you. That should keep you busy for a while."

Barry snatched the book and opened it. "Keep me busy for a while. One, eight, five, seven, seven . . ."

"How does he keep track of where he is?" Lee asked.

"I dunno," said Jimmy as they climbed out of the car, locking the doors behind them. They loped toward the main entrance to the campus on 116th Street, heading through the majestic wrought-iron gate and up the steps to the campus. Mathematics Hall was a four-story brick and fieldstone building just to the north of the entrance. The campus looked deserted—most of the students and faculty had already left for the holiday break. The lights on the tall fir in front of Low Library glowed coldly in the bitter winter wind.

As they walked up the steps to the Mathematics Building, Lee's cell phone rang. It was Gemma. He switched the phone onto vibrate and shoved it back into his pocket. They entered the Mathematics Building and headed down the spiral staircase from the lobby toward the basement level. Seeing no one on that floor, they poked around until they found a metal door with an emergency alarm bar on it. The door appeared to be ajar, the alarm deactivated. Lee gave it a gentle push, and it swung open. No bells or sirens went off. He looked at Jimmy and took a deep breath.

"Here goes."

A set of narrow steel steps led down to the sub-basement level, and as the door closed behind them, Lee felt as if they were entering Hades itself.

The tunnel was dusty and close and airless, lit by overhead fluorescent bulbs pulsating with a sickly green glow. A cold sweat broke out on Lee's forehead as they threaded their way down the passageway. His headache, never quite gone, had returned full force. The walls were dank and damp, made of crudely mortared river stone. Insulated pipes and wires lined both sides of the passageway, and the floor was littered with a wide variety of detritus—discarded bits of wiring and wood, cigarette butts, paper, and condoms.

Jimmy glanced at the condoms and shuddered.

"Gross. Can't imagine wanting to do it in here. Which direction should we head in?"

"Let's try this corridor," Lee said, turning left. The tunnel was silent except for the hum of machinery and electrical wiring. They could hear the distant sound of dripping and an occasional rapid scurrying within the walls.

"I hate rats," Jimmy whispered as he followed Lee, his gun drawn.

Lee resisted the urge to cough as the dust in the air clogged his windpipe. A thin trickle of sweat slid down the side of his face; the hand he wiped it away with already felt gritty. The thick stone walls were scribbled with algebraic equations, geometric shapes and formulas, as well as more mundane forms of graffiti. Someone named Benoit had left his signature everywhere. There were also Latin phrases, biblical quotes, cartoons and witticisms, including some obscene puns.

Jimmy tapped on Lee's shoulder, and Lee felt a cold stream of adrenaline flood his system. "My cell phone's useless down here. How about yours?"

Lee looked at his own phone. The screen read, SEARCHING FOR SERVICE.

"Nope," he said. "Nothing."

"So much for backup," Jimmy sighed as they continued on.

They crept along—listening, watching, waiting. The whole thing could be a wild goose chase, but Lee could feel his heart thumping against his rib cage as they continued down the stuffy, claustrophobic corridor. There was plenty of room to stand up in, but they both crouched instinctively, the low ceilings making them feel as if they had to duck to avoid hitting their heads on the overhead pipes and electrical wires.

"Wow," said Jimmy from behind him. "No wonder the administration doesn't want the students down he—"

Lee spun around as Jimmy was interrupted mid-sentence by a muffled *thwack*, followed by the sound of a body dropping, deadweight, to the floor. He saw an inert Jimmy lying on the ground. Above him stood Edmund Moran, a metal pipe in his hand.

"Why, hello," he said as he retrieved the gun from Jimmy's holster. "Fancy meeting you here."

# Chapter Seventy-six

A surge of adrenaline shot up Lee's spine as he realized the hopelessness of his situation.

"How does it feel to be face-to-face with your nemesis once again?" Edmund asked. "Except that this time, I have *all* the cards."

"Aren't you overstating the case a little?" Lee said, fighting to remain calm.

"You really think so? I have two guns now, and you have—oh, that's right; that would be none."

"Where is Debbie Collins?" Lee said.

"Well, now, if you had come by yourself as I requested, I might just show you. But you didn't take me seriously, did you?"

"What have you done with her?"

"This is really so tedious," Edmund said. "Like a broken record. Here," he said, thrusting a piece of rope at Lee, "help me tie up your friend before he regains consciousness." He trained Jimmy's gun on Lee. "I assume this is loaded. But if not, I have another one," he added, lifting his jacket to display the pistol tucked into his belt. "An embarrassment of riches, you might say.

Hurry up," he snapped as Lee bent down to tie the rope around Jimmy's wrists.

Lee tried to think of a way to make the bonds easy to escape, but Moran was watching him closely. He instructed Lee to tie his friend to one of the pipes in a corner of the corridor, then inspected the knots.

"You're no sailor," he said with a smirk, "but it will do." He produced a pair of handcuffs and snapped them around Jimmy's left wrist, fastening the other end to the pipe. "Insurance," he said. "Unless you prefer I kill him now, of course."

Fearing Jimmy might already be dead, Lee bent down to check on him but was sent sprawling by a vicious blow to the temple. He hit the ground hard, his head spinning, the taste of dust thick in his mouth.

"Careful," Moran said. "Doing anything without my permission can be hazardous to your health. Come on, get up," he said, waving the gun at Lee.

Lee tried to stand, but his legs gave way, and he fell back onto his side.

"Good Lord," Moran said. "That was just one little tap. You have a lot more ahead of you, so you'd better suck it up."

Lee managed to get unsteadily to his feet and felt the cold steel of a gun muzzle on the back of his neck.

"This way," Moran said, indicating a turn in the passageway ahead.

Lee walked on, Moran a step behind him. His head was throbbing, and his knees felt weak as he ran scenarios through his head. What if he turned and rushed Moran? Could he move fast enough to disarm him?

A hundred yards or so along the corridor the tunnel emptied into a large room with vaulted ceilings. Furniture was scattered around the room, much of it from an earlier era. Some of the chairs looked to be from the sixties, but a heavy oak desk looked even older. Notebooks and papers were scattered over it, all covered in a thick layer of dust.

On one wall gleaming metal pipes were labeled **STEAM** in bold lettering. On the wall opposite someone had written *Abandon Hope, All Ye Who Enter Here*. Next to it was a cylinder labeled **DANGER: CAUSTIC**. Behind that was a large, sinister-looking cabinet with dials and a sign that read **DANGER: 4160 VOLTS.**

Moran smiled. "Welcome to hell."

# Chapter Seventy-seven

"Interesting, isn't it?" Moran said as Lee looked around the room. "They worked on the Manhattan Project down here. There's even a cyclotron on the first floor of Pupin Hall. But that's not what we've come here for."

He ducked behind one of the brick columns and reappeared wheeling an old-fashioned metal gurney. On it was Debbie Collins, whom Lee recognized from the photos in Butts's office, dressed in a hospital gown. Her arms and legs were tied to the gurney with a combination of ropes and handcuffs, and she appeared to be unconscious.

Moran pushed a strand of strawberry blond hair from her face. "I haven't begun my work on her yet. I was thinking you might like to watch, but you know, I have a better idea. As a profiler, it's your job to experience what the criminal does, correct?"

Lee just looked at him. He couldn't get his eyes to focus. He wasn't about to tell Moran, but everything was blurry around the edges.

Moran raised the gun. *"Correct?"*

"Yes."

"So I'm going to offer you an unprecedented opportunity. I will allow you to feel *exactly* what I do—isn't that exciting?"

"What do you mean?" Lee said, but he had a sinking feeling he knew the answer. His head pounded in sync with the humming machinery around him. *Ker-thump, ker-thump.*

Moran rifled through a tool kit on one of the chairs and produced a stylus, the kind artists used. Its metal tip gleamed in the greenish fluorescent glow.

"I'm going to let you be the artist this time," he said. "I have a design all ready for you. You're perhaps wondering where I got this charming gurney? I didn't know it until fairly recently, but this campus was the site of a mental institution in the nineteenth century. Isn't that fascinating?" he said, producing a piece of paper with a design in charcoal that looked like the branches of a fir tree.

"Here you are," he said, holding it out to Lee. "My—our—next creation. Or should we do the fingers first? The next number in the Fibonacci sequence is three, by the way. Did you figure that out? Of course you did," he added, searching Lee's face for his reaction. "It's elegant, isn't it? Anyway, your choice—fingers or torso. I have a nice scalpel for the fingers here somewhere," he said, turning to look in the tool kit.

*It's now or never,* Lee thought, and he lunged at Moran. He succeeded in knocking him to the floor along with the tool kit, scattering its contents across the concrete floor. Chen's gun went flying across the room. Moran reached for the one in his belt just as Lee threw himself onto the professor, landing a roundhouse punch on the left side of his face. He could feel the rough, raised skin of the scar crinkle under his knuckles, and he raised his hand to deliver another blow.

Moran was quick, though, and had an unexpected wiry strength. Writhing like an eel, he delivered a vicious kick to Lee's stomach, knocking the breath out of his body. Lee gulped in as much air as he could and staggered to his feet. He felt a red-hot burning in his left thigh and only afterward heard the report of a gunshot. He sank to his knees and closed his eyes, bracing himself for the next shot, certain it would be to his head.

But nothing happened. He opened his eyes. Standing at the edge of the room, in the entrance to the tunnel, pale but alive, was Jimmy Chen. In his hand was his backup revolver, which was pointed directly at Edmund Moran's head.

"Drop the gun," Jimmy said. "You have two seconds before I shoot."

Moran turned to face him, hands raised.

"Dear me," he said. "I should have killed you when I had the chance. Always follow your first instinct—it's usually the best."

"Drop it," said Jimmy. "*Now.*"

Moran flung the gun at him and took off at a dead run toward the exit on the other side of the room. Jimmy fired a warning shot, then took off after him. The professor made it as far as the sinister cabinet with the voltage warning when his foot slipped on one of the stray pieces of paper scattered about the floor. Arms flailing, he skidded on the paper and slid into the side of the electrical housing.

What happened next was hard to tell exactly, because his screams, combined with the buzzing sound from the high-voltage wires, were distracting. Sparks flew into the air, fireworks of yellow and white, like a demonic Fourth of July sparkler, with Moran's body as the point of origin. Lee and Jimmy watched as his body went rigid, then collapsed to the floor. Neither of them moved for a moment; then Jimmy limped painfully toward the fallen man.

Nearby, Debbie Collins stirred on her gurney. Lee dragged himself over to it and took her hand.

"We're here," he said. "The police are here. It's going to be okay. We're going to get you out of here."

Jimmy knelt to check Moran's pulse.

"Is he—?" Lee said, but Jimmy shook his head.

"Nope. Bastard's still alive, though not by much." Jimmy glared at Lee, shaking his head.. "You idiot. You goddamn stupid *idiot*."

"It's nice to be appreciated," Lee muttered through clenched teeth.

"Jesus! What were you *thinking*? You been watching too many crimes shows on TV?"

"Can I get a little help here?" Lee said, clutching his leg to stanch the flow of blood. He felt no pain yet—his mind was preternaturally calm. He supposed he was in shock. He looked down at the thick red liquid burbling from the hole in his thigh. There was something mesmerizing about it, this tiny crimson fountain in his flesh, and he stared at it, fascinated. He heard a ripping sound and looked up—Jimmy had removed his own shirt and was tearing it into long strips of cloth, still muttering.

"Who *does* that? Nobody, that's who! Only *idiots* or dumb-ass actors on television!" he said as he knelt to wrap the strips tightly around Lee's leg. Goose bumps formed on the smooth skin of his back and shoulders, and he shivered as he tied off the tourniquet. Then he wrapped the remaining strips around the wound itself, tucking them inside one another with swift, practiced hands.

"Hey, you're good at this," Lee said. He, too, was beginning to shiver. Suddenly it felt cold in there, and he shook so hard, his teeth rattled.

"Oh, great," Jimmy moaned. "That's all we need now—you're going into shock."

"Th-that's w-what I th-thought," Lee said, trying unsuccessfully to control the spasms in his jaw muscles.

"Terrific," Jimmy said. "Just terrific." He picked up his jacket from the ground and placed it over Lee's shoulders.

"Wh-what about you?" said Lee. "W-won't you b-b-be cold?"

Jimmy glared at him. "Don't be an ass. Oh, that's right—you already *are* one. Trying to get yourself goddamn killed. *Idiot.*"

"I was just trying—"

"Save it. Now the question is how the hell we're going to get out of here. Any ideas, Einstein?"

"The way we came," I guess.

"Oh, crap, that's, like, half a mile," Jimmy groaned.

But just then they heard voices. Lee looked up to see Detective Leonard Butts standing in the doorway. Behind him were half a dozen men dressed in bulletproof vests and SWAT jackets.

"What took you so long?" Lee said, and then he fainted.

# Chapter Seventy-eight

"So what was with the Houdini routine?" Lee asked Jimmy as the EMTs closed the ambulance doors. Butts insisted on sending them both to Columbia Presbyterian, which wasn't far away, though Jimmy protested he wasn't badly hurt.

"Look, Chen," Butts growled. "Just go along with Doc to make sure he leaves the nurses alone, okay?"

Jimmy agreed on the condition that Butts take his brother back to the station house until he could come get Barry. Debbie Collins was already on her way to the hospital in another ambulance.

Lee lay on the stretcher, attended by a pretty paramedic, while Jimmy sat next to him, holding a disposable ice bag to the back of his neck.

"Seriously," Lee said. "How the hell did you get free?"

Jimmy moved the ice bag a little and smiled down at Lee. "There's a lot you don't know about me, Angus. I misspent my teens training to become a magician. Did gigs at the local senior centers in Chinatown, a few bar mitzvahs in Queens. I wasn't very good at it—my patter was lousy. But I was very good at getting out of ropes—and picking handcuffs is the easiest trick in the book, once you get the hang of it."

"What did you use?" Lee said.

"That floor was littered with discarded hardware and stuff. I just used a bent nail—easy as pie."

"Lucky for me," Lee said, smiling at the paramedic as she adjusted the IV bag hanging over him. She was very young, with lustrous hair and dark eyes—Indian, perhaps, or Pakistani. Her black hair reminded him of Kathy, and he realized with a pang that he wished she were here with him. Then he remembered the missed call from Gemma.

"Can you hand me my jacket?" he asked Jimmy. "I need to make a call."

The pretty paramedic frowned. "Just be lying still, sir, please."

"But this is important," Lee protested.

She wagged a finger at him. "You must not be exerting yourself, sir."

Jimmy smiled and dangled the jacket over Lee. He fished the phone out and held it up. "Is this what you're looking for?"

The paramedic snatched it from him. "When you are at the hospital and your condition is stabilized, you may ask about phone calls. Until then, please remain calm."

The ride to the hospital was brief, and Lee was rushed past the other people in the emergency room to a private room in the back, beyond the nurses' station. Jimmy followed him, still holding the ice pack to the back of his head.

The serious young doctor who attended them both pronounced Lee's wound a "through and through."

"You were lucky—the bullet didn't hit any bone," he said, holding the X-rays up to the light. He was tall and thin, with pale blue eyes and such fair skin, it appeared translucent. His bony wrists protruded from his white coat, which looked several sizes too small.

"So that's good, right?" Jimmy asked.

He nodded. "A few stitches and some antibiotics, and he should be fine. What about you?" he said to Jimmy.

"Nothing much—just a whack on the head," Jimmy said.

The doctor frowned. "Head injuries can be dangerous. We should take an X-ray just to be sure."

Jimmy submitted reluctantly, grumbling all the way. Lee had seen this kind of macho stoicism in other cops, as well as on the rugby field at school. It was as if there was something shameful about accepting medical attention, even when it was obviously required.

"Can I use my phone in here?" he asked as the doctor prepared to have Jimmy wheeled to the X-ray lab.

"No cell phone use is allowed back here," the doctor replied. "You'll have to wait until you leave the ER."

After they had bandaged Lee's leg and given him a prescription for antibiotics, he and Jimmy took the elevator to the floor where Debbie Collins was being held for observation. The hospital offered Lee a wheelchair, but he elected to use crutches.

"You might as well get used to those, Angus," Jimmy said as he hobbled along next to his friend. "Looks like you'll be using them for a while."

When they arrived at Debbie's room, a doctor was seated next to her bed, listening intently, making notes in her chart, which he held fastened to a clipboard on his lap. He was a solidly built African American with a thick head of steel gray hair. A pair of rectangular spectacles with wide wire frames perched on his nose, giving him a professorial air. *The Professor* . . . So many unanswered questions there, Lee thought. Debbie was very pale, her freckles prominent under the hospital lighting. Her blond hair with its red highlights had been combed and pulled back from her face, making it appear even rounder.

The doctor rose from the chair when they entered and extended his hand.

"I'm Lee Campbell, and this is Detective Chen," Lee said, shaking the doctor's hand. His palm was dry, with strong fingers, the handshake warm and assertive.

"Dr. Kendra," he said, "resident psychiatrist. It's a pleasure to meet you. Ms. Collins was just telling me how you rescued her."

Debbie looked up at them from her hospital bed and managed something resembling a smile. Lee guessed from her flat affect and dazed expression that she was still under the influence of whatever sedatives Moran had given her. He was glad for her—later, when the drugs wore off, the nightmares would begin.

"How's she doing?" Jimmy asked.

"Very well," Dr. Kendra replied, but without much conviction. Lee knew that even if she had escaped physical injury, the wounds to her psyche were likely to be deep and lasting.

"I was almost done with the examination," Dr. Kendra said. "I'll check on you later, okay?" he told Debbie. "And your parents there are on their way in from Newark Airport right now."

She nodded—she seemed to be only vaguely aware

of her surroundings. Lee hobbled out to the hall on his crutches with Dr. Kendra while Jimmy stayed with Debbie.

"How is she doing, really?" Lee asked.

Kendra frowned and pushed his glasses up higher on his nose. "It's hard to say, really. She's still fairly heavily sedated."

"What did he give her?"

"I'm thinking something fairly standard—one of the benzodiazepines, like Librium, Valium, Xanax. We'll know more when we get the blood work back."

"Is it okay if we talk to her?"

"She's still in a state of shock, but it might help her to talk to the men who rescued her. Just don't stay too long."

"We won't—thanks, Doctor."

"I'm just glad you found her in time," Kendra said, shaking hands again.

His words made Lee wince. *Was it in time, really?* He had seen the effects of emotional trauma enough to know how devastating they could be.

Lee returned to the room and lowered himself awkwardly into the spare chair next to Debbie's bed. One of the crutches clattered to the floor. They were going to take some getting used to.

"I was just telling her how I saved your ass," Jimmy said.

"Yeah, right," Lee, smiling at her. "Did he tell you how he used to be a magician?"

"Really?" she said, her blue eyes as wide as the meadows of the Midwest. "Is that how you found me, using magic?"

"Yeah," Jimmy said. "That's how we found you."

She tried to smile, but something went wrong, and her face crumpled in on itself. When the sobs came, they shook her whole body, tears spilling from her eyes in thick droplets, sliding onto her blue hospital gown.

Lee and Jimmy looked at each other; then each of them took one of her hands.

"It's going to be okay. You're safe now," Lee said, but he feared Debbie Collins would never feel safe again.

# Chapter Seventy-nine

By the time he and Jimmy left the hospital, it was dark. They shared a cab downtown, after the doctor cautioned Jimmy against driving for a few days. The two of them sat silently in the backseat of the cab, lost in their own thoughts; the frenetic action of the past few hours had left them a bit stunned. Lee gazed out at the buildings whizzing by as the cab rattled down Fifth Avenue, all decked out in holiday splendor. The Cartier Building was encircled by a huge red bow, like an oversized Christmas package. Tourists in front of Saks and Lord & Taylor waited patiently in long lines to look at the animated window displays. They huddled close together in the icy wind, bulky in their down parkas and winter coats, in front of warmly lit Christmas scenes.

Lee looked down at the cell phone in his hand. He needed to call Gemma, but suddenly he wanted desperately to talk to Kathy, to tell her he was all right, to hear the concern in her voice. He hesitated before dialing Gemma's number. Her voice mail picked up, so he left a brief message and hung up without mentioning the events of the past few hours.

He looked over at Jimmy. His friend's eyelids were heavy, as though he were half-asleep. Lee's thigh was throbbing, so he fished around in his jacket for the painkillers they had given him at the hospital, swallowed a couple and leaned back in the seat. They had left the hospital without finding out the fate of Edmund Moran, whether he had lived or died. Lee gazed out into the darkness. Something told him Moran had survived his injuries; a man that evil was too hard to kill.

He was right. When they arrived at the station house, Butts informed him it looked at though the professor would survive his injuries. Apparently the amount of voltage he had received wasn't enough to kill him, though there was a chance of permanent brain injury. He was in a coma, though there was brain activity. Lee couldn't decide how he felt about that. On the one hand, he wanted the man brought to justice, but on the other, he knew that as long as the professor was alive, he could harm other people. A jail cell wasn't secure enough for someone like Edmund Moran.

Elena Krieger was just leaving when they arrived. To his surprise, she grabbed Lee by the shoulders and studied his face.

"You are all right," she said finally. It was a statement, not a question.

"Yes, I am."

She let go of his shoulders. "You were both far too reckless."

He smiled. "That's a good one, coming from you."

She frowned at Jimmy. "You see what I have to put up with?"

Jimmy took a step back and waved her off. "Oh, no, don't try to get me into the middle of this."

Krieger shook her head one last time before striding out of the station house.

Jimmy watched her go. "Oh, man, if I were straight—"

Lee snorted. "She'd make mincemeat out of you."

Barry Chen could hardly be pried off Butts's computer when Jimmy announced he had come to take him home.

"In *fact*," Barry said, "I am still doing math problems."

"You can do them at home," Jimmy said. "Come on, Barry—it's been a long day."

"In *fact*," Barry replied without taking his eyes off the screen, "it is the shortest day of the year."

"Really?" said Butts.

"Today is the winter solstice," Barry said. "By definition, that is the shortest day of the year."

"Okay, that's it," said Jimmy, closing the laptop. "Come on, we're going."

Lee expected that Barry would react with anger, but he simply sat back in the chair, blinked twice and got up.

"Come on, we're going," he echoed, slinging his backpack over his shoulder.

"Hey, thanks for your help," Butts said. "We couldn't have done it without you."

"You are welcome," Barry said, staring at a spot somewhere over the detective's left shoulder. "Couldn't have done it without me, in fact."

Lee felt like giving him a hug but put his hand out instead. "Thanks, Barry."

Barry looked down at the extended hand, then grasped it in both of his. His grip was surprisingly firm. He gave a single shake, then released Lee's hand and gave a little bow. He turned on his heel and marched out the door in his peculiar stiff gait, bent forward at the waist, as though charging into a strong wind.

Jimmy gave Lee a half-rueful, half-taunting grin. "See you later, Angus. Try not to fall off those crutches."

"Yeah," Lee said, and they hugged awkwardly, the crutches complicating things further.

Jimmy turned to go.

"Hey, Chen," Butts called after him.

"Yeah?"

"You're not a total loser after all."

"Velly nice of you to say so, Boss," Jimmy said in an offensively exaggerated Chinese accent.

He was out the door before Butts could react. The detective's phone rang, and he snatched up the receiver.

"Butts here." He cradled the phone on his shoulder while he fished a chocolate bar from his desk drawer and unwrapped it. "Yeah, he's right here." He handed the phone to Lee. "Captain Morton for you," he said, taking a bite of chocolate.

Lee took the receiver. "Hello?"

"I hear you got your man." Chuck sounded nervous, though he was trying to cover it.

"Yeah. He almost got us."

"I hear you got banged up a little."

"A little bit. No more boxing for a while."

"Too bad. I was looking forward to a rematch."

"Yeah? You didn't learn your lesson the last time?"

Butts sat at his desk and put his feet up on it, chewing contentedly, a smile on his face, though whether it was from the chocolate or the conversation, Lee couldn't tell.

"Listen," Chuck said. "I just wanted to say . . . thanks. For everything."

"Sure. Everything okay out there?"

"Yeah, fine." Lee heard a woman's voice in the background. "Susan sends her love," Chuck added, obviously in response to prompting.

"Thanks," Lee said. *I'll bet she does.* He heard the beep of call waiting. "We've got another call coming in—sorry."

"No problem. See you later."

"Yeah—see you," he said, clicking the receiver and handing it to Butts.

"Detective Butts, Homicide," he said, taking it. "Yeah?" he said, tossing the candy wrapper into the trash. As he listened, his expression changed, and he rubbed his eyes wearily. "I see. Right, yeah. Okay, thanks for lettin' me know."

He hung up and looked at Lee.

"Looks like Edmund Moran will be standing trial after all. He just came out of his coma."

# Chapter Eighty

As he walked home, Lee remembered what the professor had said to him that night in his apartment. *Irrational mathematical constants go on forever. In a sense, you might say they're immortal.* He didn't believe in gods or spirits or the afterlife, but if he had ever known a man who had made a pact with the devil, it was Edmund Moran. Of course, he knew black magic was the fantasy of the naïve and superstitious, but the professor's words haunted him as he climbed the front steps to his building.

Alone in his apartment, Lee called Gemma. This time she picked up on the second ring.

"Hi, it's me," he said, lowering himself into the red leather armchair by the window.

"Are you okay? I just heard on the news—"

"I'm fine. How about you?"

"I'm all right. I just called to say that my mom has had a stroke."

"Oh, no—I'm sorry to hear it."

"I'm about to get on a plane to go see her."

"In Ireland?"

"Yeah."

"Oh. She knows about Brian?"

"I think that's what caused her stroke."

"Does she know how he died?"

"I couldn't stop her from finding out. With the Internet and everything these days, you can't really . . ."

"Hide things from people?"

"To put it bluntly, yeah." She paused for a moment. "I hate to say it, but I'm relieved to be going away for a while."

*I'm not so happy about it,* he thought, but all he said was, "Really?"

"I'm scared, Lee. I want to find out what happened to Brian, but I—I don't want to end up like that."

"I don't want you to either."

"Hey, I was thinking," she said. "Maybe we could—oh, damn, that's my taxi! I'm sorry—I have to go."

"Have a safe trip."

"I'll miss you."

"Yeah, me too."

He hung up, her words echoing in his ears. *Maybe we could . . . what?* What was she about to say?

He reached for his crutches, knocked one of them to the ground and leaned forward to pick it up. His head began to swirl as he straightened up in the chair. He suddenly realized that he was bone tired.

But he still had one more call to make before dragging himself off to bed. He lifted the receiver and dialed the familiar number in New Jersey. His mother picked up in one ring. Had she been waiting by the phone?

"Are you all right?" she said, cutting to the chase.

"I'm fine."

"Thank God."

He gave her a brief summary of the chase and capture of Edmund Moran, then took a deep breath.

"How's Kylie?"

"Oh, you know—struggling."

"Look, Mom, I—"

"You're busy, I know."

"Not anymore. I know Christmas isn't for a few days, but I'll drive out tomorrow if you want."

Normally her response to such news would be brisk, dismissive, matter-of-fact, but he could hear the relief in her voice.

"Good," she said. "We need you." Not *Kylie needs you* but *We need you.* Was his mother softening at long last?

"Okay," he said. "See you then."

"Lee?"

"Yeah?"

"Pick up some Cornish pasties from Peter Myers's place, will you?"

He smiled. He'd thought she was about to use the *l* word but was oddly relieved when she didn't. Some things in life should remain constant, he thought as he hung up—the surliness of the waiters as McSorley's, Peter Myers's Cornish pasties, and Fiona Campbell. *Let Fiona be Fiona*. It was curiously comforting, reaffirming his belief in human nature.

He hoisted himself up from the chair, unsteady on the new crutches, and hobbled toward the bedroom.

When he reached the door, his phone rang again. He continued into the bedroom but changed his mind when he heard the voice on his answering machine.

"Hi, it's me—uh, Kathy. I just wanted to find out—"

He threw the crutches to the ground and lunged for the phone. Grabbing it, he sank back into the chair.

"Kathy?"

"Oh, hi—I didn't think you were—"

"I'm here."

"I heard on the news—"

"Yeah. We got him."

"Good. I'm glad. You're okay? I heard someone was shot."

"It was me, but I'm okay."

"Where did you—"

"My leg. I'm all right."

"Oh, thank God."

"That's just what my mother said."

"Great minds think alike."

"Yeah, right."

"I miss you," she said.

"Do you?"

"What are you doing over the holidays?"

"I'm heading out to Jersey tomorrow."

"How would you feel about stopping by Philly on the way back?"

"Okay, I guess."

"Good. I—well, thanks."

"I'll call you from my mom's."

"Merry Christmas."

"Same to you."

After they hung up, he went to the piano and opened *The Well-Tempered Clavier*. Bed could wait. Sometimes music was more important than sleep. And at times like this, only Bach would do.

As he began to play, he heard the church choir across the street, their voices faint and brave in the gathering darkness. He stopped to listen. The Ukrainian choirmaster shared his taste in music, he thought as the choir sang the opening bars of "Jesu, Joy of Man's Desiring."

*Jesu, joy of man's desiring,*
*Holy wisdom, love most bright;*
*Drawn by Thee, our souls aspiring*
*Soar to uncreated light.*

Lee looked out the window, where a soft snow had begun to fall. It was the longest night of the year, as Barry had said. But even darkness had its place, he thought as he watched the flakes whirling and spinning in the glow of the street lamps. Darkness and light, doing their eternal dance, as they had ever since the universe began, until the last star burned out, its brilliance and glory only a memory in the cold and sightless void. *Sometimes we embrace the darkness,* he thought, *becoming one with it, and sometimes we gather in churches and sing to one another, meeting the night with the sound of our combined voices.* Why this was he might never know, but that it was part of the greater Mystery, he was certain.

Across the street, Bach's brilliance rang out into the

stillness of the night as the snowflakes danced in the halo of the street lamps. Lee sat at the window and listened until he fell asleep, dreaming of created and uncreated light.

## ACKNOWLEDGMENTS

Once again, thanks first and foremost to my editor, Michaela Hamilton, a true polymath—musician, cheerleader, athlete and role model. Thanks to my friend and colleague Marvin Kaye for introducing me to her, and for his continued support in all my literary endeavors.

Special thanks to my dear friend Gisela Rose for her superb editing skills and invaluable perspective, and to my awesome niece Kylie Isaack for her work as "resident math genius"—you rock! Thanks also to my agent, Paige Wheeler for her professional advice, good cheer and support, and to Liza Dawson for always being there when I need a friendly ear.

Thanks to Andrea Simmons, my Web Sensei, Promotional Maven, and all-around supporter, and to Gary Aumiller for all his advice and help. Thanks to Wes Ostertag for his very helpful input and suggestions in the area of mathematics, and to Melissa Tien for her keen eye and editorial advice. Thanks too to my good friend Ahmad Ali, whose support and good energy has always lifted my spirits.

Special thanks once again to Robert ("Beaubear") Murphy and the folks at the Long Eddy Hotel, Sullivan County's best kept secret. Thanks to Anthony Moore for helping me with computer health and safety, and to my sisters Katie and Suzie, and to cousin Carey for being in my life.

Thanks to my mother, Margaret Simmons, for her continued support and editorial advice, and to all the brave men and women who risk their lives every day to catch the bad guys. I just write about this stuff—you are the real thing.